THE PRIDE OF MONTE CRISTO

J D HOWARD

To our Dear
Friends Barbara + Rusty
Best!
JD 3/30/19

This is a work of fiction. Apart from the known persons, events, and locales that are a part of the narrative, other names, characters, places, incidents, and conversations are the product of the author's imagination and used fictitiously. Many events, incidents and locations are based around historical happenings while others are fabricated entirely by the author.

Editing: Skyler Cuthill
Illustrated by Deborah A. Fox
Cover: Matthew Morse
Rear cover photo courtesy of the Granite Falls Historical Society

prideofmontecristo@gmail.com

Son Earth Publishing

ISBN-13: 978-1-7336043-0-7
ISBN-10: 1-7336043-0-8

For Skyler & Cassidy – My Heroes

"A mine is a hole in the ground owned by a liar."

— *Mark Twain*

COLUMBIA PEAK

(Preface)

In Fredrick Jackson Turner's thesis, *The Significance of the Frontier in American History*, he states, "The unequal rate of advance compels us to distinguish the frontier into the trader's frontier, the rancher's frontier, or the miner's frontier. The early pioneer was an individualist and a seeker after the undiscovered; but he did not understand the richness and complexity of the life as a whole; he did not fully realize his opportunities of individualism and discovery. He stood in his somber forest as the traveler sometimes stands in a village in the Alps when the mist has shrouded everything, and only the squalid hut, the stony field, the muddy pathway are in view. But then suddenly a wind sweeps the fog away. Vast fields of radiant snow and sparkling ice lie before him; profound abysses open at his feet; and as he lifts his eyes the unimaginable peak of the Matterhorn cleaves the thin air, far, far above. A new and unsuspected world is revealed all about him."

The overarching theme of Turner's frontier thesis was that through the conquest, expansion, and extraction of resources in the new west, any man could get rich. So, when prospector and seeker Joseph Pearsall (1855-1916) stood at the top of an unnamed pass high in the Cascade Mountains above the mining camps of Galena and Mineral City on the Fourth of July in 1889, a great discovery lay before him. Near the tree line in the saddle of a ridge near Columbia Peak (7172') Pearsall gazed at the rugged unnamed craggy peaks, steep valleys, and glaciers around him. Amazed at the grandeur, Pearsall lifted his field glasses to his eyes and scanned the peaks across the divide to the north before him. A bright reflection of sunshine reflected off the side of a granite face, it was the glimmering evidence of valuable ore deposits! This new and rich discovery, 2,000 feet above the North Fork of the Skykomish River, was a shining example of why Turner published his thesis in 1893.

In his search, for the headwaters of the Sultan River, Joe Pearsall, a newcomer to Washington Territory and a former school teacher, stood and gazed upon a miner's dream come true. Bands of red streaked granite that he believed to be gossan, a sulphide ore which marks an area for the possible hidden wealth of gold, showed clear and glistening in the afternoon sun. Next he scanned a nearby ledge and saw a red gleaming glitter; his heart jumped into his throat, it was galena, the ore of lead, and he knew in this region that that meant silver. Pearsall immediately began to scramble down into the valley he'd found.

After hours of hard, difficult hiking he located the red streaked granite site and chipped away at the exposed vein with his small pickaxe until he had enough samples. Pearsall spent the night in the valley, then loaded his canvas backpack with the ore and returned to Mineral City where he met up with his prospector friend Frank

Peabody (1854-1930). That evening he revealed in confidence his discovery and showed the ore samples to Peabody. In the morning Peabody broke camp and headed to Seattle with the samples to have them assayed for their metallic content.

Shortly thereafter in Seattle, Peabody met former acquaintance John "Mac" Wilmans (1858-1916), who at 31 had already made and lost a number of fortunes in mining. He happened to be on his way to Arizona to investigate the purchase of a cattle ranch, but when Peabody revealed a piece of the ore to Wilmans he was impressed, so impressed that they took a sample to be assayed, the results were gratifying. Wilmans quickly decided to put his cattle ranch plans on a temporary hold and accompany Peabody to Mineral City and the discovery site.

The two men traveled by steamboat to the supply center of Snohomish City, where they purchased horses and set out on the Cady Trail. Along the way they met up with Pearsall and continued on horseback. At the mining outpost, Galena, roughly 10 miles upstream from present day Index, the men tethered their mounts, since there was no horse trail up the mountain, and backpacked farther up Silver Creek to Mineral City and beyond. Along the way Mac Wilmans began to feel the early stages of a cold coming on. By the time they reached the top of the pass that Pearsall had been at days before Wilmans was exhausted but able to view the golden-red vein across the divide that ran from the bottom to the top of the mountain. He allegedly exclaimed, "Boys, the world is ours!"

That night the men camped on the ridge, built a roaring fire and spoke of their future mining possibilities. In the morning Wilmans was suffering from a severe cold and could not continue to the site. Peabody stayed on the ridge with Wilmans while Pearsall scrambled down to collect more samples. By the time Pearsall returned Wilmans' cold had intensified to a high fever and the trio decided to head back, but before they left Mac Wilmans suggested that the ridge where they'd spent the night should be named Wilmans Pass.

They spent three nights in Galena so Wilmans could regain some strength, then traveled by horseback down the Skykomish River and back to Snohomish City, where they boarded their horses and were able to catch a riverboat to Everett, and from there a steamer to Seattle. Once there they had the new samples assayed to favorable reports. Wilmans knew that any news of the strike could cause a major gold rush and swore the two men to absolute secrecy. That done, he decided to give Pearsall and Peabody a $150 grubstake to supply the two men and receive a share in any claims made. Wilmans instructed the men to return to their still unnamed and unmapped valley to gather more samples, stake as many claims as they could, and return to Seattle with a report. But first a formal partnership was formed: it was decided that because Wilmans would be funding the operation he would own three-quarters of whatever the claims earned while Pearsall and Peabody would each receive a one-eighth interest. Pearsall and Peabody had their shares bonded for the sum of $7,500 to be assured of receiving the same amount in return for their work.

In August of 1889, Pearsall and Peabody returned to the ore location and staked claims with wooden pegs at each corner of each claim for Mac Wilmans. Since it was discovered on July 4th the first claim was named the Independence of '76, but then shortened to the '76. This name was also given to the valley and small creek that ran through it. The next claim was staked and marked on their map the following day. It was decided to title this claim and the basin and large creek that flowed down its middle, Glacier. The two miners then returned to Mineral City to spend the night, and the following day they traveled to Snohomish City to record the claims with the county auditor.

Meanwhile Mac Wilmans had approached two Seattle friends of his, Tom Ewing and George Grayson, to invest in the new mining venture, which they agreed to. Wilmans then set out to Arizona to pursue his cattle ranch and was in Park City, Utah, visiting his two brothers, Fred and Steven, when he got the news that Pearsall and Peabody had staked and recorded the two claims. Wilmans realized he'd need other substantial capital from more investors in order to develop the claims properly. He confided the discovery to his brothers and the potential wealth in the Cascade Mountains. The three brothers made a change of plans, they decided to abandon Mac's Arizona cattle ranch and instead all three would purchase a sheep ranch in California at a much lower cost, thereby freeing up valuable dollars to put towards the new mining interest. Fred Wilmans was quickly dispatched to Seattle and the Cascade Mountains to inspect the new endeavor.

With fresh grubstake funds, Pearsall and Peabody outfitted themselves while they waited in Seattle for Fred Wilmans before they all headed to Mineral City and the '76 and Glacier claims. Once Fred landed at Seattle in late August of 1889 he found Pearsall and Peabody and together they headed for Snohomish City to gather their horses and strike out.

Fred Wilmans was stunned by the beauty of the Cascade Mountains and thunderstruck when, from the top of Wilmans Pass, he viewed the red-gold band of color on the side on the mountain his brother had described to him. The blood in his veins raced as they climbed down into the valley and began to stake even more claims.

Well above the '76 Claim the Ranger Claim was staked. When that was done Pearsall saw what appeared to be another pass just above him. He climbed the pitch and discovered an accessible glacier which he walked out onto. Joe Pearsall looked down into a bowl-shaped cirque that was ringed by jagged peaks, at the northwestern end of which there was a timbered ridge that rose five-hundred feet from the valley floor and divided the basin into two bowl-like gulches. Pearsall gazed downward and spied the same red-gold glittering streaks on the opposite side of the '76 Claim. He was shocked and astounded; the vein ran completely through the mountain!

Emboldened, the men staked more claims: The Pride of the Mountains, Pride of the Woods, the '89, the Baltic, and the Mystery Claims, most of them high on the sides of mountains or on the edge of cliffs. As they toiled at their task they began to name the surrounding peaks and streams. Over the following days they staked more and more claims until they were satisfied with a total of twelve. At that point the two prospectors decided to follow the headwaters of the river that drained the two basins while Wilmans headed back to Seattle over newly named Wilmans Pass.

Thinking they were following the Sultan River, since their compass heading had the river headed in a westerly direction, they probably felt confident they'd eventually circle around to the small settlement of Sultan and hike the Cady Trail, and back to Mineral City. But when the stream turned north, Pearsall and Peabody soon discovered that they were not tracking the Sultan, but were instead traveling along an unknown waterway. The going was extremely rough and they were running low on food. Soon both were starving, exhausted, and desperate until eight days later they finally came upon an outpost on the south side of a wide, deep river. They were at Sauk City, near what is known today as Rockport, where the Sauk and the Skagit Rivers come together. Pearsall and Peabody reexamined their situation and decided that since they were so far from Mineral City they'd continue to Seattle via Indian canoe on the Skagit to Mt. Vernon, then trek to La Conner and board a steamer.

In April of 1890 the Wilmans brothers amassed a crew of workers and headed for their site to establish a mining camp and begin the construction of a log cabin, which was eventually titled the '76 Cabin. Slowly ascending Silver Creek, they improved and widened the trail to accommodate the eventual use of horses. While most of the men built the trail, other workers packed in supplies to the camp location. The Wilmans brothers concluded that if they were to ever get the wealth out of their extremely remote location they would need a concentrator at the site to crush and process the ore for shipping and a railroad to transport the ore to a smelter for processing, which would take serious investment on a bold scale. To convince investors to buy into the project they decided they needed a grand name, a name that could conjure spectacular wealth even among the stingiest of capitalists.

Every evening the men would gather round the campfire at '76 Cabin for friendly conversation as plates of beans and biscuits were devoured. One night the conversation circled around to what the new claim site should be called. Fred Wilmans pulled a thick, heavy text from his backpack, held it up in the fire light and suggested the camp should be titled Monte Cristo after the book, *The Count of Monte Cristo* by Alexander Dumas. A number of the men had read it, the rest had heard about it, and they all concluded that the images of fortune and mystery the book evoked made a perfect fit for the mines that they hoped would fill their personal treasure troves.

Two months later the horse trail was completed and items such as, mining tools, black powder, and food stuffs; salted pork and meat, beef jerky, sugar, bacon, flour, and plenty of coffee could all now be transported to the camp on horseback. More log cabins were built and the daily work turned to staking still more claims, thirteen more, and actual mining commenced. Blasting holes were bored into the sheer rock by hand-held steel shaker drill bits hit by sledge hammers. The work was slow and tiresome, the men were lucky if they could blast and dig 3 feet a week into a vein. Machinery was needed: air compressors, air drills, and steam engines. But without a railroad, or a wagon road at the least, for heavy hauling, the men had to settle for hand work in the time being.

That summer the existence of the mining camp got out. A new group of miners hiked in using the horse trail from Silver Creek and began to stake claims. Soon more prospectors began to show up and by August of 1890 the *Weekly Sun* newspaper in Snohomish City ran an article stating that the mining possibilities in Monte Cristo would far exceed the prosperous mining districts in California and Nevada. Gold fever was just beginning to build, but not for Joe Pearsall.

With other mining claims back over in the Silver Creek district and in Idaho, Pearsall decided to sell his one-eighth interest in Monte Cristo to Mac Wilmans for $40,000 ($1,000,000 today). Pearsall saw himself as more of a prospector and discoverer than one to be tied down as a daily miner.

In 1892 Charles Colby, John D. Rockefeller and a group of eastern capitalists formed a syndicate and began to invest in Monte Cristo, purchasing nearly all of the Wilmans claims and others in an effort to gain control of the potential mining wealth. Soon thereafter the Rockefeller group built a three blast-furnace smelter in Everett and titled it the Puget Sound Reduction Company. They also built a railroad from Everett to Monte Cristo and constructed over-head tramways from the mines to haul the heavy ore in buckets down to a concentrator.

By the mid-1890s the smelter had produced 3,000 ounces of gold, 60,000 ounces of silver and 500,000 pounds of lead from the Monte Cristo area mines. The population of the camp and mines had grown to over 1,000 people during the summer months; there were hotels, boarding houses, saloons, a mercantile, school, telegraph office, and planked streets. Over three-dozen mines employed men that worked for wages of $3.00 a day ($63 today). Most of the miners lived up at the mines in bunkhouses or in boarding houses down in what everyone was now calling Monte, Washington's most heralded gold rush boom town.

The Pride of Monte Cristo

I

CASCADE COLOR

There were so many things to take-in and experience in this unfamiliar world — right smack dab in the middle of the northern pioneer boom. And at such a place too, this untamed frontier town of unpainted structures and mud rutted streets called Everett; it seemed to be exploding right up out of the wilderness.

Walking down a street called Pacific there was a survey crew across the way working on a freshly cleared block of land, they were hanging flags and pounding corner stakes into the ground. Beyond them a team of horses pulled a Fresno scraper grading the newly up-earthed soil and in the distance a logging crew was cutting downed timber into lengths and hauling them away with oxen. Everywhere else smoldering stump piles spewed black smoke straight up into the sky; where the trees still stood they were taller and wider than any I'd ever seen.

To the east a massive sweep of forested hills and mountains lay before me. Country lowlands grow into jagged peaks in the distance, some with a dusting of snow; one looking like a pyramid carved by the giant swath of a heavenly spatula and another far to the north, a bulging volcano covered in white. The range ran along the eastern horizon like a narrative of natural wonder, it seemed to speak to me — a granite expanse of geological perfection, each ridgeline and peak flexing their upward majesty. I found myself exhilarated by this wild territory framed by mountains and ringed by a wide slow-moving river in front of me that gleamed in the morning sun.

Stopping, I inhaled a deep breath of fresh air and took measure. This land was wide open and at the beginning of its life, and in a way we were similar — here was a new community on a quest of incorporation while I was at the starting point of a self-discovering journey. There was no way of knowing what would find me on this adventure, but I was savoring its beginning. I started walking again with a smile as wide as the river before me and as bright as the sky above.

Up ahead was a telegraph office, I stepped inside the narrow building and set my easel down then took off my over-loaded pannier. The smell of burning tobacco filled my senses at first but then the piercing, continual *dits* of the telegrapher hitting the key machine filled the air. Once the man was finished he stood up from his desk and walked to the front of the room.

"Mornin' young fella. How can I help ya'?" Was the operator's greeting as he set his smoldering cigar in an ashtray on the counter. He had a long full white beard, a green visor hat, and wore a black vest over a white buttoned shirt, a well-worn pencil was behind his ear.

"Morning sir, I'd like to send a telegram," I said.

"Well, we're the 3S office for the track line but we just strung a new wire up to Erskine's office over on Bayside, so you're in luck son, I can do work for the public now. But there's no need to call me sir. The name's Ivan, Ivan Pottinger."

"Okay, Ivan," I replied. "Good to meet you."

"So! Standard rate local is five cents a word and if'n yer' sending out of the territory then its ten cents a word, both 'er a ten word minimum. I know it's a lot more than the price of a red stamp but it sure is a whole heck of a lot quicker!" he said with a grin.

"That sounds a bit much," I said, thinking it over. "But then I've never sent one before, I guess it's worth it so everyone back home knows all is well, ten words for out of the territory should work fine."

"Yep well. I'll tell ya' this, when they hung the first line from coast to coast in '61 it was a dollar a word, by-golly," Ivan said. "The cost of modern communication ain't cheap, but lemme say this: the words you write down there will get anywhere faster than if God's own angels carried 'em, so it stands to reason it will cost a little bit more."

He handed me the pencil from behind his ear and a form to fill out with the to and from, name and address lines on it. I thought about what I could say with so few words for a moment, and quickly filled it out with the name and address then finished with, '*At Everett. Taking train to Jacob's. Will write. Love, Oliver.*'

I handed the form back, Ivan glanced at it.

"San Francisco?" he asked. "What're ya' doin' all the way up here?"

"Headed to my Uncle's hotel up in the mountains at a mining camp called Monte Cristo. I'm going to live with him and my Aunt for a while, and paint," I replied as I handed over a dollar.

"Paint? Like houses and such?" Ivan asked, picking up his cigar.

"I'm an artist and do paintings. Landscapes, mostly. But sometimes portraits."

"Well, good luck in Monte, son. And if ya' need to send any more telegrams find Ed Baker's office. I went up into the mountains two weekends ago, the scenery's beautiful."

"Perfect. That's why I'm here. Thank you Ivan."

He stepped back over to his desk with the cigar in his mouth, set the form down next to his key machine and began to send a series of *dits*. Seeing him make a start I flung my pannier over my back, picked up the easel and headed for the depot.

Looking up Chestnut Street to the north there were people carrying suitcases, parents with children, and men in work clothes headed to the station across the way, a horse and wagon were coming up the muddy street. I crossed over to a news stand and then stepped over a series of railroad tracks and walked into the depot, it was alive with the talk of excited travelers. I glanced around and saw the ticket booth at the side of the room.

"Good morning," I offered to the attendant.

"Howdy, a fine morning isn't it? Headed east today?" he asked through a dark handlebar mustache.

"Yes, all the way to Monte Cristo, but I wanted to check on a trunk of belongings I sent here on steamship from California."

"Okay, what's the name?"

"Oliver Cohen."

"Alright, let me check on that," he replied, picking up a clipboard. He leafed through a few pages and found my name.

"Looks like it got here yesterday. We've still got room on the freight car if you'd like it loaded."

"Yes, that'd be fine. How much for a one-way ticket?"

"It's $1.25 per person, plus the trunk's a dollar."

"Sounds good, how long's it take?"

"About four hours. It departs in ten-minutes with an arrival time in Monte around 2:30 PM as long as there's no delays."

"That's not bad. Can I bring my pannier in the coach?"

The ticket man looked at my large back pack and easel, then said, "Wednesday's a good day to travel, not many tourists. So that's fine."

I paid the fee, picked up my load and walked out onto the platform, hot steam poured from the deep brown locomotive's stack behind the large headlamp. The letters 'E. & M. C. Ry' were painted in gold on its side. I wandered over to the wharf that looked out over the river.

Out on the water two Indians were paddling by in a canoe and upriver, a man was on the other side starting to chop down a fir tree on the bank. Through the other trees I could still see the mountains in the distance and the sun was beginning to warm the air. Just then the train whistle blew loud and long, the bell sounded, and I could hear the conductor call out, "All aboard!"

Turning on my boot heel I walked over to the train while passengers came out of the depot. Friends and relatives said their goodbyes and hugged and stepped aboard a railroad car. The women wore long dresses and hats, some had suitcases, and others carried parasols and cloth purses. Almost every woman had a child at their side and stood beside men in work clothes who looked like they were miners headed to jobs. The bulk of the passengers were getting on the first two coach cars so I walked past them carrying the easel to the third, took off my pannier, and climbed aboard.

Inside, I went to the back near a coal heater in the corner and took a seat two rows in front of it on the river side. The interior and benches were a pleasing quarter-sawn oak and it had a finished fir floor. In the raised curved veneer ceiling there were small horizontal windows on each side running the length of the coach. A moment later two women with children came aboard but took seats near the front then, a few workmen entered with thick British accents, full of consonants tripping over each man's tongue, as if neither of them had ever seen or heard the letter H in their life. I grinned and gazed out the window. I thought about Uncle Jacob and Aunt Eva and wondered what their hotel was like when the train jerked forward.

The coach car rumbled and moaned as we pulled away from Everett. The *ka-klack, ka-klack,* from the steel wheels rolling over the tracks increased as we picked up speed; a young girl came down the aisle. She latched onto each bench seat backrest as she came down the corridor so as not to fall. Her long brown hair was in pigtails with red ribbons tied on the ends, she noticed my pannier and made a funny, inquisitive face.

"That's sure a big boxy suitcase, mister."

I smiled, "Yes, it is. It's called a pannier, and I carry it on my back."

She nodded and said, "I'm Alison and I'm seven and a half. How old are you?"

"Me? I'm 23."

"Where's your family?"

"Back in California, but I have an Aunt and Uncle in Monte Cristo."

"California, that's a long ways away," she said and skipped back up the aisle. As I watched her she reminded me of being young and care free; my thoughts changed and turned to my Father, who was gone now, his soul liberated from his body. I missed him dearly and thanked him silently for giving me a life but I still felt the emptiness of his sudden loss inside of me. I took a deep breath and looked out the window.

The coach door opened quickly and the conductor walked in. He wore a blue suit and had a hat with the letters 'EMCRR' on it and stepped over to the first group of passengers. He asked for their tickets, so I reached into my pocket.

Out on the river a sternwheeler was coming downstream, it was white with two levels and had a pilothouse on top. A couple of men were standing on the hurricane deck and the lower level freight door was open. As it churned past I marveled at the paddlewheels turning, pushing it downriver.

Up ahead, not too far away, I could see a low truss bridge. The air brakes sounded below the car and we began to slow down. Part of the bridge was slightly swung open but as we got closer I could see it was slowly closing. There was a man running along it back to our side of the river who I guessed was a railroad worker. A moment later we picked up speed and the tracks began to turn out over the bridge. Once the car made the turn I could see upriver a depot with a sign that read 'Lowell' and a number of homes were on a hill to the west above a large grouping of brick buildings with smokestacks and a water tower, the charred remains of a saw mill was up river from it all.

Once across the bridge there was a homestead to the south at a bend in the river. As we traveled past I could see a large three-level barn, a home and a few outbuildings where chickens scurried about. Then we were surrounded by a field of tall beautiful corn. I opened my window to breathe in the crisp morning air and could smell the fresh crops. Quickly we were back in a sparse forest and soon enough we crossed over another bridge that spanned a waterway. I looked to the right and there was the river again with a small island in the middle of it. In no time at all we began to roll by a few more home-steads with gardens and small fields of crops until we came into view of a few more homes. I could see the river again on the right and a few buildings up ahead. Just then the coach door opened.

"Snohomish City!" the conductor cried into the car. He closed the door and the air brakes blasted. From my seat it looked like the main part of town was blocks away, down closer to the river. Two and three story Victorian styled homes with covered porches and gingerbread gables doted the neighborhood. As we rolled to a stop I could see people waiting on the depot platform, families with baggage and men in work clothes.

New passengers began to climb aboard while others stayed seated. Most of the new riders boarded the two front cars but a few entered the car I was in, they were all excited and very talkative.

"First ting' I is going to da' mercantile when I get to Monte," one man said with a Norwegian accent to his friend.

"Yeah, well, that's fine by me. But if the boss ain't around I'm headin' straight to the saloon!" the other exclaimed. By the way they talked I thought they might be miners, but if they were one was dressed like no miner I'd ever seen. He wore a brown bowler hat, blue silk vest with silver pinstripes and black pleated trousers, all of it dirt covered. They both had muddy brogan boots and over stuffed gunny sacks full of who knows what and a week's growth of stubble on their faces. The other wore a black engineer's type hat, and had a thick heavy coat and canvas trousers.

There was a well-dressed family that got on board, a man and a wife and their two young twin girls, each wearing the same store-bought green dresses. The man wore a black suit and a stove pipe hat. His wife had a feathered hat on top of a Gibson girl style hairdo, and her dress covered multi-layers of petticoats.

As we lurched out of Snohomish City the train headed north and followed a small river in a narrow valley. I saw an Indian family walking along the tracks headed back to town and soon there was another Indian camped on the river bank. He had a fire going with a blackened coffee pot next to it, some rainbow trout were hanging in the smoke. We rolled past a few small farms and went over a short bridge and then another. There were less trees in the bottomland of this valley, a good number of homesteads and I noticed a white church with a steeple to the right. I'd been enjoying the sights for a mile or more when the man and woman in front of me started talking.

"Looks like the river is up," the man said, gazing at the water.

"Yes, it sure does," the woman replied.

"Must be spring run-off from the snows."

"I suppose, but what about the hotel we stayed in last night? Did you like the Penobscot?"

"Oh, yes. It was elegant. I loved the parlor on the second floor, and those views of Mount Rainer were absolutely magnificent. Did you like it?"

"Quite a lot. I think we should have a home someday with wainscoting like they have," the man replied.

"Yes, well, that's all in the future. Now, when we get to Tante Anna and Oom Harmen's farm I don't want us to announce that we're expecting immediately. Let's wait for the right moment to tell them. Maybe at dinner."

"Okay, that sounds good. So, how long have they had their chicken farm?" the man asked. The lady looked up at the ceiling and thought for a moment.

"Let's see. They came over from Holland in '88 and to Seattle in '90. They got the farm I think two years later, so that would mean they've been in Hartford for about four years, more or less."

Outside we began to pass more trees. Douglas-fir and cedar, wider and taller than the ones in Everett, with thick scaly bark defined in vertical grains of brown fiber. The forest got thicker as we traveled north until the close-in trees disappeared and we came upon a clear-cut piece of ground with only stumps and smoldering slash piles. A crude shingle operation in the middle of it, two men were hand splitting shakes. There was a skid road coming off the hill behind it where a team of oxen were pulling cedar logs down a primitive road grade. A man carrying a whip was walking beside them.

Soon we rolled back into forest, about a mile later the river we'd been following turned to the east out of sight and not long after that we began to slow. The air brakes went off and once again the door to the coach opened, the conductor stuck his head in the car and hollered, "Hartford!"

We passed a long wooden warehouse, over a couple of track switches and crossed a gravel road. The tracks made a slight turn and the train stopped beside the depot, a gentleman was waiting on the platform. Across the way a horse and buggy were tied to a post next to a two-story hotel over on a dirt road. The building had an upper level balcony with a sign that read, 'Meals At All Hours.' The couple in front of me got up to disembark, I followed them. Stepping off the train I ran over to the hotel and went inside, where a lady wearing a long white apron asked if I'd like a table.

"No thank you ma'am. Do you have any sandwiches ready-made? I'm in a hurry."

"Why, yes, we do," she replied. "I have some ham and cheese and roast beef lunches for ten cents."

"Great! How about a ham and cheese?" I quickly said. She walked back to the kitchen while I dug in my trousers and found a dime. Just as she was coming back the bell on the locomotive rang.

She held out a brown paper bag, I handed her the coin and bolted for the train.

I opened the door to my car, walked down the aisle and past an older man sitting in the seat in front of me. I nodded a hello and he nodded back. As I sat down I asked, "Headed to Monte Cristo?"

"Nope, not today," he answered with a voice that sounded like his throat was filled with rusty nails. Then he slightly turned his head and added, "Just goin' to Granite." He had a shortly cropped grey beard, a black fedora on his head, and wore a red and black Mackinaw. I opened the lunch sack and pulled out a sandwich wrapped in wax paper. In the bottom of the bag was an apple and a piece of hard candy. I smiled, took one bite of the sandwich and since it was going to be a long ride I folded the wax paper back around it and placed it in the backpack for later. I looked outside from my open window.

We'd left the trees and rolled into a flat valley of small farms. To the east I could see the mountains that I saw from Everett, we were much closer to them now. The same pyramid shaped one was a lot bigger and another had three peaks and thick snow on it. We rolled by a homestead where a zig-zag split cedar rail fence encircled a garden in front of a sturdy log house. There was a woman hanging laundry on a line strung between the home and a fruit tree and two children in hand-me-down clothes were playing fetch in the yard with a setter dog. A few miles later we slowed down again.

"Granite Falls," the conductor said into the car, then added, "fifteen minutes!"

As we eased up to the new looking two-story board and batten station house there were town-folk all about, almost like it was a big event to have the train arrive. Railroad ties were strewn around and bundles of cedar shingles were stacked in sheds next to the tracks ready for loading. An antique speeder car was sitting on a side track up ahead that looked like it was built before the Civil War. It had a brass boiler and stack, and a dark stained wooden box seat. There were multiple raw-wood frame buildings in the center of town, all of them so freshly built that I could smell the scent of fir sap still on them. The two fellows that hopped on at Snohomish City disembarked. I saw them head up the tracks towards a building and decided to stretch my legs and take the air.

Out on the depot platform there was a slight breeze. The scent of bacon and eggs wafted over from a hotel on the main street that paralleled the tracks. A boardwalk ran from the depot and up the tracks towards what looked like a saloon and to some other businesses so I thought I'd head that way. Strolling by the bar I looked inside and saw the two fellows but continued walking. Up ahead was a stable with a sigh that read 'Earl Livery' and as I got closer the stink of horse manure replaced the scent of the forest. There was a bald man in overalls shoeing a fine-looking chestnut mare in the entrance of the barn, the horse had its head in a box full of oats on the ground, and there was a watering trough next to them. Just past the livery was a general store, I started to walk towards it when the train bell sounded.

As I turned around the two fellows from the train quickly walked out of the saloon. The one bringing up the rear swiped the hat off the other with a swing of his hand, it landed in the mud just off the boardwalk.

"Le-Roy!" the hatless man barked, "Yah! Youse darn good for not-ting!" he hollered at his buddy. LeRoy started running while the other stepped off the boardwalk to retrieve his cap. He picked it up and brushed it off on his leg.

By then LeRoy was climbing aboard the train. He turned to his friend and boasted, "Yer' gonna have to be a lot quicker to keep up with me, Strom!"

Back on the train I found my seat and sat down. There were a good number of new riders, a couple was now sitting in front of me and the conductor showed up right away to check tickets. Excited children ran up and down the aisle and climbed over vacant benches.

As we left Granite Falls it looked like there'd been a forest fire, blackened stumps and the bark on the sides of the trees had been scorched. The underbrush was burned back to stubbly stems and roots and in some places the forest floor was covered in blotches of black, but soon enough we were back in healthy woodlands.

We began to climb a slight grade that soon leveled out and started an extended turn to the right that passed a small lake as we ringed the base of a mountain. In no time we were out of the thick forest and following a river in a canyon, rolling along a ledge with the waters swirling just below me to the left. The color of the water was a milky emerald green and I became mesmerized. I thought, *a mild green with some white and a little bit of black but not too much would reproduce that.* We crossed a series of bridges that spanned ravines and creeks when we crossed over the river on a truss bridge when the car went dark. We were in a tunnel, the couple in front of me turned to each other and started kissing. Seconds went by and we came out the other end into the sunlight, the two stopped and looked around while the woman fixed her messy hair.

Now we were on the opposite side of the river so I got up and moved to the other side of the car where I could see the water. The canyon narrowed and so did the river, we were in a gorge of granite walls. Immature cedar trees gashed out from fissures in rock cliffs, their trunks bending at the base, turning upward, staying vertical. The river was steeper, crashing around boulders and picking up speed. I could hear the sound of the turbulent river over the rumbling of the train then we rolled into and out of another tunnel. The boulders on the bank are covered in moss and the surface of the water danced and splashed with waves of whitish-green water. At one rocky notch the river at the waterline looked to be only thirty-feet wide from bank to bank.

I could see high up into the cliffs and outcroppings surrounded by evergreen canopies with a joyous background of blue skies. Inspired, I opened my pannier and dug out a sketch book and pencil. As soon as I did the car went black again.

"Criminy, another tunnel," I said out loud. The woman in front of me turned her head and gave me a quick, nasty look for my comment.

The train came out the other side and began a long sweeping turn to the left, then everything went dark, then light. A series of tunnels were upon us, so I set down the sketch pad. In between two of them I caught a glimpse of an eddy pool. I spied some large logs wedged between rocks on the bank, the ends of them sticking up in the air. After one last tunnel that turned to the right I could see up ahead that we'd been traveling on top of a rock and log retaining wall. Then we came out of the gorge and into a wide valley with a timbered ridge in the distance. The river widened and the water looked like it was running slower. We rolled by a marshy area and a grove of spruce.

Up ahead I saw black smoke, soon enough we rolled by three men working a rudimentary saw mill with a wood-burning boiler engine. The tracks turned to the right, then straightened out and there was a small town. The train began to slowly come to a stop next to a water tower. A string of buildings rested comfortably along the railroad line, bordered by a hedge of low bushes growing between the tracks, and a worn wooden sidewalk ran in front of the buildings. An unpainted building with a flat false front was next to another with a covered porch and one had a sign reading, 'Robe Post

Office.' One building looked like a hotel, two older men sat in chairs on its porch; they were leaning up against the building smoking pipes. I saw two men in work clothes jump aboard. I sat and waited gazing out my window at the scenery while the train took on water, and we were off again.

As we picked up speed I thought, *this sure is a smooth ride, I won't have a problem drawing.* I picked up my sketch pad and looked out the window. The river turned away from us and we were back in the burgeoning forest. I glimpsed three black-tailed deer eating ferns, lowering their heads and taking one long bite of each green leaf at a time, then they were gone. But soon enough the train made a turn to the right and there was the river again. Two massive peaks rose up from behind the trees, it felt like I was riding a train through the Alps. I began to capture the landscape on my pad, sketching the river, mountains and sky. Concentrating, I glanced back and forth from my drawing as I worked, trying to get as much detail as I could. Many miles later the rendering was finished.

There was a tap on my shoulder. "Hi mister," a young girl in a green calf-length dress said, it startled me.

"Oh, hi there," I replied.

"What-cha doing?" she asked in a happy tone.

"Oh, just drawing the scenery."

"Can I see?"

"Sure," I answered, turning the pad so she could view it. She smiled, looked at me, and ran back up the aisle to her parents. Interrupted but trying to grin at her I reached over to my pannier, pulled out the sandwich and began to finish it and the apple.

I gazed out my window and watched the wilderness roll by. We were back in the forest and always seemed to be climbing a hill. I watched with glee as one grey, bushy-tailed squirrel chased another one around the circumference of an enormous limbless fir tree, then I popped the piece of hard candy in my mouth and saw a tote road paralleling the train tracks. We passed a few shacks with railroad ties and equipment strewn around them and soon leveled out.

I noticed that the forest kept changing, in some places there were stands of spruce which would be replaced with wide, tall cedars, or fir. In a grove of hemlocks, tendrils of pink flowers burst out from the green limbs on every tree, wisteria vines had encroached upon the grove turning it into a colorful vision the likes of which I'd never seen before. The angle of the sun brought out the contrast of colors before me, my eyes sparked and my heart jumped. I flipped over the earlier sketch on my pad. *I have to get this!* I turned my head and focused my eyes to see and soak in as much as I could of what I'd just witnessed, and attacked the paper in earnest.

For miles and miles I worked at my task as the train went up and down grades, over bridges, around sharp corners and along the river. Invigorated I labored away, numb to the constant click-clacking sounds of the tracks and conversation, only stopping my sketching to reach into my pannier for a small box of colored pencils once the forms were outlined. Multiple shades of green, pinks, brown, grey, yellow, and lavender consumed my strokes of line until, all of a sudden, the air brakes went off again and we began to slow down.

"Silverton!" the conductor cried into the car. I looked out the window. There were a few small buildings to my left over against a hill and on the other side was a depot next to a bridge perpendicular to the tracks that crossed the river and into a small town. I saw a 'No Chinamen' sign nailed to a tree and on the other side of the bridge sat many buildings and what looked like street lamps planted on a wooden sidewalk. There were piles of split stove wood strewn all along the main road that continued up through the town. The two men that got on at Robe got off and the train jerked forward, I turned back to my sketch pad.

As we rolled away we began to gain some elevation, but then we flattened out and rolled into an enormous meadow of wild flowers; white and purple, green and yellow. Marshes filled with tall shoots of cat tails and stunted, twisted trees, their limbs covered in moss.

On the south side of the valley was a magnificent singular snow-covered mountain, a half-mile wide at its base that must have risen thousands of feet from the valley floor. I was astounded. From top to bottom was a vertical glacier that bulged and grew at the base from avalanches. *But it's June*! At the summit I saw four or five linked granite peaks, each crest hundreds of yards apart from each other. Creeks and streams ran down the front of it, crevasses of ancient rock ran up and down its front. I wanted the train to slow down or stop so I could get a longer look at the magnificent grandeur of it all. But a moment later it was gone. I closed my eyes and tried to burn the sight of it in my memory. I opened my eyes, flipped over the page in the pad and drew it as quickly as I could, losing myself in the moment.

I could feel the train climbing again while I sketched. As we did so the river kept getting smaller, soon enough we were at the top of a pass where a wood frame building with a steep pitched roof was right next to the tracks. The train took a turn to the right and we began to go into a valley that held another river then down a gradual slope. Finishing the quick sketch, I couldn't help but hear my neighbors talking.

"We are getting close," Strom said to LeRoy.

"Yep, and boy do I need a drink."

"Yah, and I is hungry, but we have to get back to da' mine. And I bet-cha old Comins will be waitin' at the depot when we get there," Strom said.

"To hell with that kinda talk. Martin Comins is always thirsty. He'll have a belt 'er two before we hike up the Mystery!"

I couldn't believe the natural beauty of the wilderness that surrounded us. The train turned to the left and we rolled over a trestle bridge that spanned the river and crossed over to the other side of the valley where the tracks began to straighten out. A few miles later I could see some ramshackle cabins that looked like they were built of scrap-lumber and a few canvas tents, stumps and trees slash lined the train tracks. A sign on a cabin read 'Rattler Claim' and a muddy trail peeled off from the tracks and up into the hills.

The train turned and before my eyes was a jagged mountain that jutted up like a gigantic bear's tooth of granite, capped with a dusting of snow, I was awestruck. On a ridge line of crenelated rock coming down its side I could see a spire of stone, like a wide monolithic finger, balanced, pointing straight up. *A place like this has to be seen to be believed!* I shook my head in wonder. I felt the train slowing down, the air brakes went off and we rolled across one final trestle bridge that crossed the river and into a level switching-yard.

The immediate valley was stripped of trees, slash and broken limbs, stumpage and rotting wood was scattered on the slopes of the close-in hills. I saw a plume of white smoke, or perhaps steam, rising from a large building up the hill at the base of the spire mountain and there was a plank road lined by wood frame buildings of different sizes and shapes running up an incline. Way up on the side of the mountains were tall towers made of timbers with cables strung between them, buckets hung from the cables. The train came to a stop on the only level ground there was, we were at the end of the line. Passengers stood up from their seats and the car became lively with talk.

"Monte Cristo!" the conductor hollered with gusto into the coach.

I picked up my easel and pannier, then looked around on the bench and floor to see if I'd left anything behind and picked up one of my pencils. Stepping from the train and into the sunshine I was surprised to see a man walking around playing a fiddle, there were lots of people with children running around chasing each other. A few boys had wooden boxes against their chests suspended from straps around their necks, they called out to the disembarking travelers.

"Get your own sample of Monte Cristo ore!" one hollered.

"Only five cents, take home some real gold and silver ore!" another loudly said. He picked a piece from his box and held it up in the sun, showing its sparkles in the reflected light.

The man with the fiddle walked over to LeRoy and Strom. He stopped playing and started talking to them.

"Comins is around here somewhere lookin' for the two of you. Where ya' been?"

"Oh, criminy Doc, I had to see a man about a horse," LeRoy said, grinning.

"Aw, bullshit! You boys went on a bender, and I know it," Doc spat.

"Martin knows damn well we was down in Snohomish gettin' more black powder and new bits," LeRoy offered.

"And I had to see da' dentist," Strom said.

"But Comins told me ya' been gone for days!" Doc countered. Just then a man who I guessed was Comins walked up. He was tall and lean, a pair of spectacles rested on the bridge of his nose, and a bushy reddish-brown mustache covered his upper lip.

"Well, well, well. Tiz about time ya' two devils got back," he said in a thick Irish accent. "Was it not said ya' would be but two days?"

"Yah, yah," Strom said. "The dentist was busy and we had to wait an extra day for more powder. They were all out."

"Okay, alright. How about if I buy a round?" LeRoy offered.

Comins eyes sparked, and he nodded, "A wee dram on yee, tiz it?"

"If a shot a whiskey will keep me in the good graces of the Duke, then by God, I'm buyin'!" LeRoy remarked with enthusiasm.

"By God ya' say?" Comins remarked, his eyes mused. "I'll be tellin' ya' right now that if God was the one that invented whiskey then he did it so we Irish wouldn't be ruling the whole entire world, don't ya' know?"

LeRoy and Strom looked at each other and grinned at the same time. Then Strom said, "Yah, yah! You yust be rulin' all of us and da' rest of Monte Cristo, then!"

"But it'll only be one, ya' hear me? Then it's off to the Mystery," Comins proclaimed then added, "We'll get the box of powder and bits from the freight car on the way back." They all walked away, slapping each other on the back and headed to the other side of the tracks and over a footbridge that crossed a creek down below the depot.

I took a breath of fresh mountain air, but there was a taste and smell of burning coal to it, then I looked around. We were in a valley surrounded by rugged steep peaks with what looked like glaciers on the top of some of them. I could hear the sound of the rushing river but there was a drone of machinery mixed in. Then a blast of black powder boomed out in the distance. I flinched at first, and remembered I was in a mining camp. I'd heard and read stories of wilderness towns, but seeing this place with its craggy peak surroundings; the high streaming clouds moving overhead against such a clear cobalt blue sky made me feel like I was on another planet, or in some ancient wilderness, in a different time and place.

I felt like I was being watched or in the presence of some entity, almost spiritual, maybe mythical. Was I in the presence of the Creator? Was God looking down on me here high in the mountains, my being so much closer to heaven now?

Then I remembered the trunk, so I walked back to the last train car where the clerk was pushing open the large door from inside. He was a small older man and wore a neat black vest over a white collarless shirt. I noticed a large bin of block ice behind him and crates of food and vegetables.

"Hey there," I said to the fellow.

"Howdy," he replied, "do we have something for you?"

"Yes, there should be a green trunk with black banding and the name Oliver Cohen on it."

"Cohen, you say? Might you be relations of Jacob and Eva?"

"Why yes, they're my Aunt and Uncle," I replied brightly.

"Ya' don't say! I'll tell you what, I'll have the supply wagon haul it up to the Pride Hotel for you."

"Thanks Mister," I said and turned to walk away but stopped. "How do I find their place?"

He pointed up the hill, "You see that two-story building at the very top?" I looked where he was pointing and saw it.

"I do."

"Just head up the hill and take a right on 1st Street."

"Okay, appreciate it."

Near the depot I walked across a short but sturdy wagon bridge with layers of thick wooden decking and log railings on each side. It crossed over a small creek that flowed into a larger fast-moving creek that had silty, pale looking water running in it. The larger creek ran behind the main buildings of the camp and came down from a mountain valley high above the town. Once over the bridge I turned to the right and headed up a planks-on-the-ground thoroughfare that was lined by rough-cut board and batten buildings.

I climbed the hill past a saloon and a meat market with whole chicken carcasses hanging in the window. Across from it was an unpainted frame home where a man with a beard was sitting on the porch whittling wood.

A little log cabin next door had 'Printing Press' in big bold letters on a sign with 'Monte Cristo Mountaineer' stenciled in the window, then a large mercantile. I looked into the false-front building and saw a fully lit six-lamp chandelier hanging from the ceiling. *There's electricity up here?* I kept walking. Past it was the Monte Cristo Hotel; it had a wooden boardwalk that split off from the main planking and went over to a set of stairs that climbed to a wrap-around landing and front door. Up ahead was another log cabin, a stump in front of it had a crude wooden sign hanging on it that read, 'Barber.' The planking stopped and the street changed to dirt, I turned around and looked back down the plank road.

The rear portion of each building was built on tall posts and beams cantilevered out over the slopes behind them. Then I noticed all the carved-out earth and axed stump roots removed for the wide planked street, each plank pitted and scared from use; it traveled in a serpentine path, dodging still standing stumps, buried boulders and terrain as it made its way up the grade. Across from the hotel another plank road angled to the right over a retaining wall of log cribbing. I saw two makeshift street signs, I was at the corner of Dumas and Mercedes.

I had arrived.

II

THE PRIDE

Sequestered in these lonely mountains, I've found both solace and folly in the comings and goings of the residents in this camp. The miners with their foul language and black boots walk by with daily coarse stories while the tourists offer a level of decency that seems to help balance my framework and settle my dust. My interest always piqued when I could see someone approach and then enter my frame.

Above me, granite cliffs are blasted and mined for gold and silver, they loom over this steep valley like hollowed out edifices, corrupted and extracted, their rich ore a tonic for eastern greed. Below me, down valley, I can see the swirling, fast moving river, and the single straight stretch of railroad tracks leading to town. There's the wooden water tower down in the small level area where the trestle crosses the glacial fed waters, the locomotive turntable and the end of the line. From my location up at the top of the hill I look over this young camp, but it was never my idea to end up this way. I was logged, milled, and built by my owners to house them and their guests.

Monte Cristo had two parts, upper and lower; the lower part of town was split in two by the river, upper town was across the wagon bridge and up a short incline. Across from the depot and below the tracks was the main part of lower town, and a blemish on the land; a maze of sin and misfortune. Stumpage, garbage, and piles of tree slash were strewn between a smattering of hovels and shacks hastily built from used or scrap lumber scrounged from the town saw mill or brought into camp by wagon. Rickety wooden sidewalks ran from cabins to shanties to outhouses built on stumps and posts, elevated over knee deep mud and swamp water that never seemed to dry out. On the opposite side of the river, between it and the tracks was another row of lower town but one had to walk the trestle tracks on the way out of Monte to go there. I was built at the top of upper town.

Whenever it rained the water washed over my cedar shingles and clung to tree needles, casting a shimmering, silvery glow when the sun broke through. I took great pride in protecting my inhabitants from the wet weather and providing shade from the summer heat. I loved those days of warmth when the air was so fresh and clear, I could swear they were scented with a touch of tranquility.

In the morning, when the children walked by on their way to the schoolhouse, I could hear their footsteps on the dirt and duff street. Some would skip or run up the thoroughfare past the homes and businesses on their way to class, as the clang of a steel hammer on metal sounded from the blacksmith's anvil and would ring out from below me.

Last winter I damn near froze to death. Hell, the cold bit so deep that granite shattered and the smoke coming out my chimney turned around and headed back inside. But now the warmth of summer is so soothing and delightful, I don't want it to ever end.

From my vantage point near the top of Dumas Street I see it's the highlight of the day, the train has arrived. I prided myself on recognizing the familiar faces and quickly learning the new ones. I'd count them off as they climbed the hill, many of them here for the day to see the sights, others here to stay. Some would stop at the bottom of Dumas Street at the Pioneer Market to get groceries or maybe buy milk from Arthur at the condensery. Others would sit down for a game of cards and a jigger of rye at Cobb & McRae's saloon or head to the Royal or Washington Hotels. I could see Frank Peabody sitting and whittling wood on his front porch watching the people walk by.

I spied a new young fellow coming up the hill — he was medium height and stout, wearing brown trousers, a plaid shirt and he had a box on his back covered in green canvas. His black hair was pulled to the back of his head tied in a cropped pony tail and was carrying an odd looking three-legged wooden frame that had a chain dangling from it. The young man had a different look and a quiet demeanor in the way that he walked and carried himself than all the others. He seemed mindful in how he took in his surroundings. I watched him stop in front of the Monte Cristo Hotel and look back down the grade, then the new young fellow started walking uphill towards me and I knew he'd be staying under my roof.

As he approached he called out, "Uncle Jacob! Aunt Eva!" then sprung up the stairs and onto the covered porch, rang the bell and returned to the street. He looked up at my frame of weather-beaten clapboard siding and tall false front with the hand-chiseled hotel sign and grinned. A second later I could hear the rumbling of feet inside of me and the inn keeper's voice.

"Oliver?! Is that you?" the short, chubby inn-keeper cried, running outside.

"Yes! Jacob!" Oliver hollered and smiled. They hugged each other and then stepped back, each one looking the other up and down.

"You look good," a balding Jacob said, beaming at his nephew. "Good to see you again. How've you been? Huh?"

"I've been alright, I guess. Coming up here was a great idea, it's good to get away."

"You getting through it okay?"

"It was tough," Oliver replied, sorrowfully. "Losing Dad. I still have an emptiness inside."

"He was my oldest brother and I loved him, too. Miss him every day."

"I miss him too. But's great to see you, again," Oliver offered, "so you got my last letter, then?"

"Oh, heavens yes, just a week ago. We were going to write back but we figured you'd be here before a reply would get to you." Then Eva dashed out so fast that she darn near knocked her nephew over trying to hug him.

"You're here!" the woman of the house exclaimed. "I'm so glad you made it," she said, giving him a warm, welcoming hug. "So wonderful to see you!" she added, holding him close. Then she whispered, "I'm so sorry about your Father. I wish I could have traveled down for the service last fall. But I'm glad that Jacob went."

"Yes, I know," Oliver sighed, stepping back and shrugging his shoulders, a small frown forming on his face. "I understand, it was a long way to go and you had to run the hotel," he said, then broke into a grin. "But boy, this place is sure something! I've never seen such mountains before, not even in the Sierras!" he remarked, finally taking the big green box off his back. Miss Sheedy came out on the porch, she wiped her hands on her white apron, threw back her fiery red hair with a flip of her left hand and said, “Well, if it isn’t the blessed artist, come all the way from the fine state of California, is it?” She gave a wide smile and announced, “Welcome to Monte, Oliver, I’m Liz. Supper will be on the table in a bit,” and she spun around and went back inside.

“Good to meet you, Liz!” Oliver said, smiling at the front door. Then he looked up into the sky and turned his head. “What is that awful droning noise?” he asked. “It sounds like a train grinding its way over a bunch of rocks.”

“Oh, it’s the concentrator. It processes the ore for shipment to the smelter in Everett,” Jacob replied, pointing in its direction.

“How much does it run?”

“Twelve-hours a day, from six in the morning to six at night, six days a week.” Oliver shook his head.

“Don’t worry. You’ll get used to it,” Jacob said with a laugh. “How about if we show you around?”

“Yes, I’ll show you your room,” Eva added, and they walked inside.

The front door opened to an entry room, windows casting beams of light across the grey painted ship-lap fir floors and throw rugs, a pump organ was off the entry and a stair case climbed to the upper level. Around the corner was a large greeting room, in which a man was sitting in a red overstuffed chair reading a thick hard-bound book. He looked up through his pince-nez, grinned faintly, and went back to his story.

A mahogany honesty bar with ornate carvings was directly across from them; the room was furnished with two black velvet sofas, a walnut table and chairs. In the next room was the dining room, the table was set. The walls were covered in floral wallpaper and a potbellied stove rested comfortably in a corner. Pulley and sash windows were framed with chintz draperies, and a single light fixture with a pull string hung from the ceiling in each room. Jacob went up the stairs, saying, "I've got to go check on something before Henry shows up, go on ahead."

"How was the ride? I bet you're starving!" Eva said as they walked into the kitchen. Liz was preparing a tray of cups and saucers, busy at her task. Oliver looked around; on one wall was a long counter with a red coffee grinder mounted on the end, a sink in the middle with a hand water pump, the basin window had a mountain view. The rest of the wall was unfinished wooden shelving stocked with cans of fruit and vegetables, coffee, flour, and all the other kitchen accoutrements. Past it on the back wall was a built-in table with wrap around benches. The other side held white cabinets and overhead open finished shelving, in the center a black and chrome Majestic wood cook stove. A wood box for kindling and blue kerosene fuel can sat next to its legs. There was a hallway at the back wall that went down to the laundry and rear door.

"The ride was magnificent! The wilderness and scenery were unbelievable, I felt like I was riding to the last frontier and would never see anyone again. But then, of course, I knew where I was going," Oliver answered, but then quickly added. "I did have a little something to eat on the train." Eva went down the hall, stopped at a door and opened it.

"So, I've made a place for you. Take a look." He poked his head in the tiny room. A cot was up against a wall, a night stand sat next to it with a kerosene lamp on it, there were a few painted wooden boxes on the floor with a chamber pot next to them and a small dresser.

"This will be perfect! Thank you Aunt Eva!" Oliver said brightly.

"Oh, you're welcome. It's not all that much. In fact, I guess I should tell you — it was the pantry. Jacob built all that new unfinished cabinetry in the kitchen for everything that was in it so we didn't need it anymore. And please tell me you got our last letter."

"You mean the one with the chores?" Oliver said.

"Yes," she admitted, "Jacob wanted to make sure you knew what you were in for and that you could stay as long as you'd like. As long as you keep up on your work list, that is," Eva said firmly as she brushed back her wispy black hair.

"Oh, yes, I understand. I'm more than happy to cut and haul all the stove wood, run errands and to help out."

"Very good then," Eva approved, then rapped her knuckles on the door across the hall. "So, this is Liz's room," she said, "follow me and I'll show you the laundry."

"You have electricity?"

"Can you believe it? Upper town has power from the dynamo at the concentrator. It's great, since we put up with the noise and all."

Eva continued down the hall to a large back porch with wrap around windows. At one end was a white bath tub with claw feet and curtain around it with a washbasin beside it. A long low work table was against one wall with two tubs and washboards. Another wall held a tall folding table, and there was a good-sized parlor stove for heating water in the corner. Eva turned and walked to the back door, a clothes line with pulley was strung from the inn to an outhouse.

Outside, a rain barrel was next to the door and off to the side were two sheds. The first was smaller and full of tools; axes, hand saws, rings of hanging rope, rigging, and steel cans of kerosene and the other was a large and nearly empty wood shed, both of them were built of unfinished wood, the cracks and moss on the exteriors indicating that they'd seen better days. Next to them were two windowless outhouses of unfinished clapboard. One was two-stories and had a ramp from the second level of the hotel over to a small elevated porch that served two doors and on the bottom level of that one was another door. The other outhouse was raised with a single door, it had a few stairs that went up to it. Eva gestured at the steps and said, "For when the snow piles up." Then Jacob was at the back door.

"Looks like you found the facilities! Supply wagon's here," Jacob stated.

"Oh, my trunk," Oliver said, jerking around. "It has all my frames and canvas."

"Okay, well, let's go unload it," Jacob nodded with a quick grin. The three of them walked back through the inn and out onto the street, where a squat figure of a man wearing a rumpled slouch hat was sitting on a mule drawn wagon with its reins in his hands.

"Come on, hurry up! I've got better things to do than look at the ass end of this here mule. I still gots ta' get over to the schoolhouse and then down to the smithy and around the loop!" he exclaimed with a voice like sandpaper. He had a half-smoked cigar couched in the side of his mouth and a week's growth of salt and pepper beard on his chin.

"Yeah, yeah, Henry," Jacob said. "We'll have you on your way in no time."

The three of them walked to the back of the wagon, Jacob and Oliver unloaded the trunk and set it on the ground while Eva grabbed a crate of block ice.

Henry pointed out, "Those two small white boxes and the little tan one is yours, too."

"Okay, thanks," Jacob said, seeing his name on the packages. He quickly unloaded them and carried them over to the porch.

"What's the word on all the new Cornish?" Eva asked Henry.

He took the chewed piece of cigar stub out of his mouth and stiffly turned his head towards her.

"I guess Rockefeller and all a' his syndicate cronies got fed up with the strike. I heard some say that Colby's mines in Michigan are 'bout pinched out, so he's bringin' 'em to Monte. I hear they're good workers," he drawled, then released the brake, snapped his reins and smacked his lips, "Hupp mule."

"The mine manager that stays here sometimes on weekends says that too!" Eva hollered at Henry's back as she carried the crate inside for storage in the icebox. Henry and his team began to roll up the street and over towards the school. With every turn of the stiff wheels, they and the wagon raised a grating squeak and creak.

"Good Lord," Jacob said, helping lift the heavy trunk by its leather handles. "I never knew canvas and frames could weigh so much."

"I know, I'm sorry. I've got all my brushes and paints in it, plus all my clothes. But I took out some of the drawers to make it lighter," the young artist conceded as they carried the barrel-top trunk inside and to Oliver's room.

Setting it down in the former pantry Jacob remarked, "Took some of the drawers out, huh?"

Oliver laughed and said, "Well, you won't have to move it again for a while."

"How long do you plan on staying?" Jacob asked, but with a friendly smile. Oliver looked down at his trunk and opened it before answering. He grabbed an envelope from the lone drawer on the right side and handed it to his uncle.

"You can open it later, it's from my Mom," he explained, then said, "I'd like to stay as long as I'm welcome, maybe paint all the seasons." Jacob looked at his nephew with concern.

"But what about after Monte Cristo? Don't you have long-term plans?"

Oliver thought for a moment.

"I'd like to build up an inventory of landscapes and open a gallery. Maybe back in San Francisco, or who knows, Seattle's a possibility."

"You think you can make a living being an artist? In Seattle?" Jacob inquired.

"Oh, absolutely. I'm determined to."

"And raise a family?"

"A family?" Oliver said quickly. "I'm still young, I've got plenty of time to do that."

"Oh, okay. I guess you're right," Jacob said, nodding his head. He shoved the letter into a back pocket of his trousers and suggested, "How about some supper?"

"Sounds good to me."

They went back to the dining room where Liz and Eva had the table ready. Cornbread, chili, coffee, butter, and glasses of water and a freshly baked cherry pie were all set for the four of them and their lodger.

"Tonight, we have my famous five-way chili with Polish sausage and beans, and lots of fresh butter from Arthur's condenser. Please everyone sit and help yourselves," Liz announced as she wrung her hands on her apron and sat down.

"Oliver, this is our guest, Walter Maddox. He's come up from Seattle to relax and leave the exciting city life behind," Eva explained.

"Good to meet you, Mr. Maddox," Oliver acknowledged, ladling a portion of chili into his bowl.

"Yes, good to meet you, too," Maddox replied, not looking up from buttering his cornbread.

"So!" Oliver said, glancing back and forth from Jacob to Eva, "what's it like living here?"

"Well," Jacob answered, "the winters are long and cold, with lots of snow. A good number of folks leave in the winter. But those vacant cabins need to have the snow on their roofs shoveled or else they collapse."

"And there's plenty of avalanches, especially up high near the mines. We can hear them rumble down the mountains," Eva interjected.

"And the summers are short," Liz added.

"The townsfolk are friendly, most of the miners, too. And when the mines are running hard and everything is working I hear the syndicate is shipping as much as fifty-tons of ore a day. And well . . . of course, then there's the miners and their off time, when they hike to town, there's lots of drinking and gambling. In lower town that is," Jacob related.

"That a fact, huh?"

"On the weekends, especially down at Fred's, he's always busy," Eva chimed in.

"Fred's?"

"Why that'd be Frederick Trump's saloon," Liz replied. "He's got the other Monte Cristo Hotel but we just call it Fred's. He built it on some shady placer claim, I might add," she said, raising her eyebrows.

"But, I thought I saw a Monte Cristo Hotel on Dumas Street?" Oliver asked.

"Yep," Jacob said, "there's two. But he built his place down just below the tracks and put up a sign with the same name to get the attention of the new arrivals."

"Everyone who comes up here's heard of the real Monte Hotel, and that it's a fine establishment, so when they see the sign by the tracks they just head over that way and Fred gets them signed up for a night before they know it," Eva said.

"Except me," Mr. Maddox chimed in. Everyone laughed and went back to enjoying the meal.

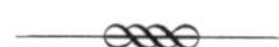

Later that evening, after the concentrator had shut down and all was quiet, Jacob and Eva were up in their room on the top floor. While Oliver busied himself getting organized in his room downstairs Jacob was at his desk and Eva was laying on the bed flipping through her latest copy of Harper's magazine, lingering about life in a big, bustling city with tall buildings and fancy stores to shop in.

"So how much longer before we can sell out and buy a real hotel in Seattle and leave this muddy dull place?" she said, looking up from her magazine.

"Seattle!?" Jacob exclaimed. "What about a town up north, like Anacortes, maybe?"

"Anacortes? Seattle is where I want to live," Eva said sternly.

"But I hear Anacortes is a great place and we could get a hotel up there for a lot less than in Seattle. I thought we already talked about this," Jacob replied.

"Well, you talked about it to yourself," she snipped.

"I thought you liked it here?"

"Jacob," she said firmly, "I said to you when we came here that I didn't want to live in this mining camp forever."

"Ah, yes, now I remember. But we've only been opened for barely three years."

"We should sell while business is good," Eva suggested. "That way we can get a good price."

"Sure, sure, but Oliver just got here and what about Liz? She should have a say in this."

"Oh, you know well and good that Liz will go with us to wherever we buy a new hotel, we're all she's got. And business is good now, so that means we should sell," Eva stated. Jacob paused and rubbed his chin for a moment to think about what she'd just said.

"Okay, alright. How about this, if we have a mild winter and tourists come up for the snowy weekends and we save enough money and our books look good then how about if we sell next spring?" Jacob said with his best attempt at a sincere smile. Eva looked away and thought about the proposal for a moment.

"Next spring, huh?"

"Yes, next spring."

"Well, alright, but I want to go to Seattle and see what's available sometime."

"How about in the fall?" Jacob suggested, turning his focus back to his desk.

"I'm gonna hold you to it," she said and went back to her magazine.

Satisfied that he'd kept the argument to a minimum, Jacob pulled the letter from his trousers that Oliver gave him earlier in the day and began to read:

Dearest Jacob,

I hope all is well and thank you so much for taking Oliver in, he needed to get away and find himself. By now you've found the money I included, it's to help with his room and board. I have no idea if he told you that he plans to make a little extra money sitting at the train depot selling sketches and paintings but he promised that he'd do his best with all the chores.

I must tell you though that Oliver hasn't been the same since your brother Joseph died unexpectedly last fall. The sudden pain we all had to deal with was more than we could almost bare. After the passing Oliver took to drink but then his sweetheart left for a job with a relative in Chicago. He didn't want to talk about it and I do believe he would have married her. I just let things run their course. He's a good kid and we all love him so much. Oliver's promised to not shirk his chores and keep a diary while he continues to work at his art, he's very talented!

As for me, I'm doing fine. I sold the jewelry store and keep busy with the garden club and my flowers during the week but my arthritis acts up every once in a while, other than that everything is okay. Please give my best to Eva. I'll stay in touch and please write.

Love you both,
Isabel

"What are you doing, reading?" Eva asked, getting up from the bed and walking over.

"It's a letter from Isabel, Oliver gave it to me."

"What's she say?"

"Well, she sent twenty-dollars to help with his room and board and she finally sold the pawnshop, thank goodness. But I guess Joseph's death was pretty hard on Oliver, as it was on all of us. He was someone special. No one will ever be able to replace him in Oliver's life, or mine really. It was a big loss."

"I know. Joseph was a good dad, and a good man," Eva said. Jacob shook his head and closed his eyes for a moment, then opened them and spoke again, looking at the letter.

"But she says his girlfriend left for Chicago, and he started drinking. So, I guess he's obviously had his share of heartache."

"What should we do?" she asked, placing a hand on her husband's shoulder.

"About what?"

"Well, if he's struggling, then we should help him somehow. He's probably protecting his grief, not showing it."

"Dealing with death is different for everyone. And besides, he's an adult now. He seems alright to me."

"Okay, but —"

"But what?"

"Jacob, you know as well as I do about all the drinking and gambling that goes on up here. What if he falls in with some of those miners and gets friendly with them?"

"And what if he does?" Jacob asked. But Eva didn't answer right away.

"Huh?" Jacob said.

"I just don't want to see him fall in with the wrong crowd, that's all."

"Eva," Jacob said with a stern voice, "he's old enough to make his own decisions, we should let him be. As long as he keeps up with his chores I don't think we should bother him."

Downstairs, Oliver had opened the trunk and was going through his particulars, unpacking. I watched him as he lifted the top drawer out, set it on the floor and took some shirts and a pair of wool trousers out, placing them in the little dresser; underneath the clothes were boxes of brushes and paints. Opening the lid of what looked like an extra-large cigar box he ran his fingers over the various tubes of oil paints, smiling. He closed the lid and set it down, then he pulled out a folded stack of canvases and a slotted pinewood frame. Oliver found a stretcher key in his trunk, a hammer, and glass container of small tacks, and set all the articles at his feet.

Taking a piece of canvas, he got down on his knees and slid the frame to the front of him. He tacked one corner of canvas to the backside of the wooden frame then wrapped the canvas around the edge of the frame and pushed the key against the canvas into the slot to stretch the surface. He worked his way around the frame, stretching and tacking, until the canvas was as tight as a drum. Once finished he placed it on the easel, found his sketch pad and flipped through the pages until he found a gigantic snow-capped mountain that he must have done on the train. He went to work. I watched him keep at it until he was finished. By the end he could barely keep his eyes opened. I was impressed.

This had turned out to be a very good day. For apparent reasons my bones and frame felt better than they had in months. This new fellow was a pleasant addition, I looked forward to having him under my roof.

III

A WORKING CAMP

B*lasts of hot steam. The vibration of machinery and crushing rocks. Mineral dust rising up and filling the air like a mist — not a dream, not yet wakefulness. The whirring drone of noise seeping through the walls. What's going on?* Waking I looked up at the white board ceiling and brushed the sleep from my eyes, then I remembered: the concentrator. I rolled over in my little cot and wrapped the pillow around my head, but the clamor kept swelling in my brain. I got up, pulled my trousers on over my long johns and went out to the kitchen.

The sound of kindling burning, snapping and popping in the cook stove crackled in the air and the scent of fresh coffee and biscuits filled the room. Liz was standing at the stove, a pan of sputtering grease and bacon before her.

"Good morning," I said.

"It's a fine day today, Oliver. Good mornin' to you," she offered. "There's coffee cups over in the cupboard."

"Thank you, that sounds good." As I stepped over to the counter I noticed a blank space on the wall. I grabbed a mug, poured myself a cup and took a sip, then went back to my room. The painting I finished the night before was still resting on the easel.

I held it up for inspection and then carried it out to the kitchen. Holding the painting against the wall where the blank space was I turned my head around.

"What'd you think?" Liz walked over and gazed at it for a moment, then she recognized it.

"Well I'll be! Is that the mountain down the tracks? Did you do that last night?" Liz asked with a smile. I nodded my head and grinned.

"Won't this be a great spot? Do you think Jacob and Eva will like it?"

"That's a pretty good painting, I'm sure they'll love it," Liz replied and went back to the stove.

"Where can I find some nails?"

Liz turned around, "Out in the tool shed."

I walked to my room and put on my boots, then went down the hall and outside. The early morning sunlight was emerging over the mountains across the valley, striking the shadows; another summer day in Monte Cristo was just beginning to shape itself forward.

In the shed I found a workbench and started rummaging around then found a jar with an assortment of fasteners. I started to head back when the sound of a voice startled me.

"Find what you were looking for?" It was Mr. Maddox above me on the ramp, on his way to a constitution. I stopped and looked up.

"Didn't see you up there, good morning."

"Yes, it is," he murmured as he opened the outhouse door, wearing a plaid bathrobe and carrying a magazine. I went back to my room for my small hammer. Returning to the kitchen, Liz was pouring hot bacon grease into an empty tin can.

"Any success?" she asked.

"Yep." I eyed the center of the wall, held the nail in place, and gave it a few quiet raps. I hung the painting and took a step back. Liz came over and inspected it. Taking a closer look, she made a smacking sound with her lips, stood back, and put her hands on her hips. She whispered with amazement, "That's not bad. Tiz a fine gift you've got, Oliver."

"I did it last night half asleep."

Liz shook her head and paused, then said, "The smallest thing can outlive the human race." I nodded my head in agreement and started to walk back to my room when Liz added, "Breakfast will be ready in another twenty minutes. The biscuits aren't done yet."

Stepping into my tiny space I glanced around. *I still feel a little tired. Should I lay down for a bit*? But the constant whir of the concentrator changed my mind.

"I'm gonna go for a quick walk," I said down the hall. Stepping out into the cool morning air all was silent — except for that incessant machinery noise.

I went out to the street, walked towards the concentrator and stopped, then looked down Dumas. A few people were milling about and a mangy old hound was slowly moving from person to person, hoping for a hand-out when a man wearing a white smock walked out of the Pioneer Market carrying two bottles of milk. I watched him go across Dumas to the mercantile and step inside. The dog followed him, but seeing the door close the hound yawned and stretched and then laid down on its side next to the entrance.

Below me was a huge five-level building with a long angled shed roof that ran down slope to near the larger creek. I followed a trail along the side of the hill through rock outcroppings and stumpage. As I got closer the noise grew and the ground began to shake. Steam poured out of a short smokestack and black coal smoke billowed from another. I could see railroad boxcars way below on tracks being loaded.

Hanging above and going up-mountain to the mines, buckets with wheels on the top of them ran along a continuous cable that was strung from one wooden tower to another. They were pulled through the air by a separate cable, all to be carried down where the ore was dumped on a metal grate to separate it by size at a bunker near the top of the building. The same cables went around a steel bull-wheel and back up the towers on the mountain. Iron carts loaded with ore were pulled by teams of horses from the bunker along a covered dirt road to a trestle that went into the top level of the building. Soon enough I was at an entry and poked my head inside.

The deafening roar of running machinery and rocks being crushed greeted me. A huge steam boiler with an enormous fifteen-foot-diameter head wheel with a wide belt spinning on it ran to generators and compressors through a series of pulleys; workmen were everywhere. Where I stood at the top level a flume of surging glacial water entered the building and washed the ore down through screens and crushers. Pulverized into smaller pieces by rollers, the stone was carried by the water down to the next level below through a series of machines where it was loaded into buckets and brought back up and fed through more screens and rollers and shakers. From there the tailings and water overflow was separated again into what looked like settling tanks and moved onto revolving tables washed by what was by now milky-white colored water at the bottom of the building where the material was loaded into boxcars and the transformed water flowed back into the creek. I was finally spotted and a man in grease stained overalls walked over to me. He had cotton stuffed in his ears.

"Somethin' I can help you with?" he shouted above the clamor. I shook my head.

"Nope, just wanted to see where all the noise was coming from."

"Okay, but you best be leavin'. United Concentrator employees only," he said, pointing at a sign behind me that read, 'Employees Only.' I raised my hand in acknowledgment and left to go back to the Pride.

The wonderful aroma of fresh biscuits and bacon welcomed me when I walked back into the kitchen. Jacob and Eva were sitting at the built-in booth warming their hands around steaming cups of coffee while Liz was setting plates on the table.

"Morning," Jacob said, his eyes still red from sleep. "Where ya' been?"

"I took a walk over to the concentrator," I answered.

"Oh," Jacob replied, nodding.

"Your painting is beautiful," Eva said as I sat down next to her.

"It's a gift for you two, I did it last night."

"Thank you," Jacob and Eva said at the same time.

"You're welcome. I'll be doing more soon," I said. Liz set a mug in front of me and poured some coffee.

"The miners call that mountain you painted Big Four," Eva offered.

"I can see why, with all of those peaks," I mentioned.

"Actually there's five," Eva added.

"Some say that four brothers, who used to trap in that valley long before the train was built, named it Big Four for the four of them. But from the south side of it in the summer after most of the snow has melted the snow that remains up in a snowfield shows the open number four on it," Jacob said. "I think that's the main reason why they call it Big Four."

"Really?"

"Yep," Jacob replied, "you can see the four from just a short way up the trail, on the way to some of the mines."

Liz brought over to the table a platter of biscuits and bacon and then a plate of scrambled eggs and bowl of gravy. She sat on the end of the bench, bowed her head, crossed herself and recited, "A cabin with plenty of food is better than a hungry castle, let's eat!" Loading his plate with eggs, Jacob asked.

"So, Oliver, what do you have planned for the day?"

"Well, I noticed the wood shed is about empty. I thought I'd get started filling it." Jacob and Eva both looked at each other and smiled.

"Have you ever cut down a tree?" Jacob asked.

"Can't say as I have," I answered, feeling a little bit raised in the city-like, setting a biscuit on my plate.

"Aw, it's easy. You just chop out an under cut on one side then chop at the other side and over it goes. You'll get the hang of it," Jacob said.

"But what trees do I cut?" I asked, reaching for the gravy.

"The closest ones to the hotel!" Jacob laughed. "We just hike up the hill and start cutting, then haul it down."

"Well, okay, if that's the way you do things around here," I replied.

After breakfast Jacob and I went out to the tool shed. He started gathering equipment; a short cross-cut saw with tall handles at each end, an ax with two blades and some hemp rope. He tightened the ax in a vise on the worktable with one blade pointed upward, picked up a file and started to sharpen it. I watched him closely to learn as much as I could. After a dozen passes he felt the edge with his thumb, smiled, and sharpened the other blade. When he was done he handed me the ax and the rope, then started walking with the saw in his hand.

I followed him out to Dumas and up the hill, we stopped at the tree line. He looked up a skinny hemlock and nodded his head up and down.

"This little one will work for starters," Jacob said, setting down the hand saw. "See how more of the limbs are on the downhill side." I looked upward.

"Yep, I see them."

"That means the tree is heavier on that side, so it wants to go that way."

"Okay, so we chop on the downhill side first?"

"You're a quick study! Go ahead with a few level swings and cut into it about here," he said, pointing to a place on the bark with his index finger. "Then cut downward just above where you started and that will be the under-cut."

I walked around the tree and set my feet. Jacob stepped away and I took a swing. I missed and hit the tree with the ax handle. I looked up at my uncle.

"That's okay, at least you didn't crack it. This time extend your arms and touch the blade on the tree where you want to hit it first," he said, nodding.

"That way you can get a feel for how far away the tree is before you swing. Like taking a measurement before you start."

I re-set my feet, extended my arms and touched the tree with the blade and swung. The cutting edge of the blade sunk deep into the wood, I levered out the blade and swung again, and again. I changed my footing and chopped some more.

"Looks good," he said, "now hit it downward, just above the cut-line." I set my feet again and did what he said. A chunk of white wood flew away from the bark. I swung again and another piece fell to the ground. I kept at it until Jacob raised his hands.

"Whoa! That's more than enough!" he hollered. "Now it's time for the back cut. Come over on the other side, uphill, and start just above the level part of the under-cut. That way the under-cut will act like a hinge and the tree will fall forward, down the hill."

"You're sure about that?"

"Go ahead, you should be okay," my uncle replied with an encouraging tone. I did what he said and took a few swings, with another swing the ax went all the way though the tree and the whole upper part of the tree dropped right off the trunk and landed on the ground at the base of the stump.

"Run!" Jacob yelled. "Run uphill!"

I dropped the ax and we both stepped uphill and away from the tree as fast as we could and turned around. The hemlock started to tip downhill and began to pick up speed as the limbs whistled and moved through the air, for a brief moment the drone of the concentrator disappeared.

"Timber!" Jacob yelled as the tree came crashing to the ground. I looked over to him. He had his hands on his hips, his mouth was agape and his eyes as big as saucers.

"By God," he exclaimed, "That was close. I think I let you cut too big of an under-cut. But still, you'll be a mountain man yet! Now, snip the branches off with that ax and we'll use the saw to cut it into lengths and pull them down to the hotel."

I felt like I'd conquered my own life-tree of self-discovery and an explosion of happiness burst in my stomach. Grabbing the ax I set to work.

IV

MYSTERY HILL

Perched on the descending ridge-line of a stand-alone hill in the heart of Glacier Basin, the miners were deep inside of a tunnel. Every day they bored and drilled, blasting away at my inner veins, taking what was mine. For thousands of years I've stood tall and proud over this valley, up until seven years ago when that one fellow showed up and took his pickaxe to me. Now all I can do is watch them dig out my gold and silver ore and send it down below to all that noise and racket, that smoke and steam.

For hundreds of years the Indians would come in the summer to hunt deer, pick wild berries and dig roots. I liked them. They only took what they needed to live and survive. They'd camp down in the meadow where the two creeks met and stay a month, then leave me be to sleep all winter under a blanket of snow. But for now, this Old Man of the Mountain waits, while I watch, and I listen to the miners in the tunnels as they work.

Eli Peet shined his candle head lamp at yet another triangle blasting pattern they'd drilled in the adit. He reached for the Jack-leg drill and turned to his partner and began to speak as he lifted the heavy tool.

"Give me a hand with this damn thing would ya', McGavock?"

"Yeah, yeah," Ed McGavock answered, reaching down and helping lift the heavy air drill.

"Yep, I'm tellin' ya', we were all kings back in the day at Cripple Creek," Eli said. "Hell, they said it was just worthless cow pasture but I knew better. Had myself a glory hole for two weeks, pulled a few thousand of gold out before it went dry, by golly," the old sourdough remarked.

"Oh, don't think I haven't heard it all before," Ed replied and added, "You were rich and now yer' broke. Ain't we all up here?"

"Well now just wait there a second," Eli snapped, "we're all workin' our —," he stopped talking and turned at the sound of boots. Sam Strom stumbled up to them carrying a wooden box and lantern. He hung the lamp from a nail on a support post and coughed.

"Ve' got da' powder and da' blasting contractor . . . is youse boys ready for another charge?" he asked.

"'Bout time ya'll showed up! We got holes drilled from Kingdom Come to China fer' Christ sakes. Of course we're ready, where the hell ya' been?" Eli barked as he positioned the bit of the drill against the spot he was about to hammer. He held it against the wall of the mine and said, "We was 'bout ready to give up and head to town an' find more powder ourselves." Dave LeRoy and Martin Comins were right behind Strom.

"Head ta' town? Sounds good to me! I still gots ta' pay my little sweetie a visit," LeRoy said with a grin.

"Aw, Libby Malone ain't ever gonna love you," Eli replied.

"That's a-right," Ed McGavock added, "she's too busy lovin' everyone else!" The three other miners laughed heartily.

"I'll tell you what," Comins started up, "if we blast and muck twenty-feet in four days then I'll be racing you to town, and LeRoy — then ya' can go fall in love with that dance hall gal."

Instantly Eli Peet pulled the trigger on the Burleigh Jack-leg drill and the sound of granite being bored echoed through the mine. A minute later he was done with the bore and the mine went silent, only the sound of dripping water could be heard.

"Alright, you got the needle and fuse?" Eli asked.

"I do," Comins answered, pulling a long rod shaped copper needle and some fuse cord out of a wooden tool box full of his blasting implements.

"And funnel?"

"Aye, right 'ere," Comins added. Eli stepped back from the drill holes.

Comins placed the needle into the first hole and put the narrow end of the tin funnel over the needle and into the bore hole. Strom stepped next to him and slowly poured some of the new supply of black powder into the funnel. Martin carefully rammed the blasting material into the hole with a thin wooden powder pole around the copper needle until he knew there was enough of it in the bore.

"And the clay?" Martin asked, tilting his head at the toolbox.

"Yep," Eli answered, reaching for and then handing him the can that held the material.

With his thumb and fingers, Martin shoved a plug of clay into and around the needle at the holes opening then slowly pulled the copper needle out without disturbing the clay. Once that was done he slid a length of fuse back into the small hole left by the needle. When they finished the remaining holes, Comins stepped back and turned to the other men.

"Everyone out!" he ordered as he pulled a tiny box of matches out of his trousers, "and leave me a lamp." McGavock and Peet carried the drill out of the way while LeRoy and Strom carried the powder, Martin's toolbox and the other tools and lanterns from the area. Once they were out Strom yelled, "All clear!" back into the mine from the headhouse that covered the entrance.

Martin nodded his head and grabbed the four lengths of fuse and banded them together in his left hand and cut them off with his pocket knife so they were all the same length. He lined up the ends, struck a match and lighted them at the same time. Seeing each one sparking he turned, picked up the lantern and quickly walked down the ore car tracks to the headhouse and daylight. Once outside he rubbed his eyes as he hurried away to a pile of timber support beams, turned the lantern wick till the flame was out and set it down next to his toolbox.

Ten seconds later a black powder explosion boomed deep inside the mine and a blast of dust and smoke poured out of the entrance, filling the headhouse with a cloud of grit. Comins walked over to the tailings pile, pulled a handkerchief out of his back pocket, and wiped the sweat from his brow. He gazed out to the craggy rocks of Cadet Peak across the basin and whispered to himself, "There's no better life than this."

Martin walked over to a trickling freshet of mountain water in a steep close by rocky ravine. He bent over towards the stream, cupped his hand against his mouth and took a long cool drink. Turning around he saw Eli and the rest wandering down the trail towards the cookhouse to kill some time while the dust settled in the adit.

"I guess it's break time?!" he hollered at them. They kept walking so he headed the same way.

The low-slung bunkhouse was a horizontal pile of logs resting on a ledge of rocks. It might not have looked like much but it was home to many a miner. There was a shed roof addition on the front and the main roof was built of long thin hand-split cedar shakes. A wisp of wood smoke curled out of the chimney. As Martin approached the cabin door he could hear Big Nelson inside playing cards.

"That's right by-gobs! I'll see your one and raise you another!" he bellowed. In his mind, Big Nelson had been in every card game and mine, in every state this side of the Rockies. Big was a no-neck, muscle-bound lummox with a nose that looked like it'd been broken in three places, his high forehead was a slab of yellowstone and his chin jutted-out like a smooth curving ridge of granite. When Martin opened the door Big looked up and grinned at him from the rough-cut plank table and turned back to his game of cards with George Pratt. Martin crinkled his nose — the room smelled of rancid lard, moldy cheese and spoiled milk.

George eyed the cards against his chest. "Damn it, Nelson!" he complained, dropping them on the table. "I'm done with you." Big Nelson swept up his winnings with ham-hock forearms and dirt smudged hands: two quarters, two dimes, three boxes of matches and a cut-plug of tobacco still in its wrapper. George dropped his head into his hands, let out a quiet low moan, and pushed himself away from the table and walked over to his bunk. Big cracked a smile and looked at Martin.

"How many more feet?" he asked.

"A wee bit, maybe two. Not sure yet," Martin replied on his way across the room to the kitchen where he found a tin cup and poured himself some black coffee. On the far wall in the main room were stacked bunkbeds where the night shift miners were asleep;

Sam Keeler, Billy Iverson, Al Croft, and Joe Digby. Dave LeRoy had already found his bunk, enjoying his break time. He stared up at the log purlins on the ceiling with a faraway look in his eye. Eli was sitting at the back table packing his pipe with tobacco while McGavock headed through the kitchen, where Chubb Purcell was busy making bread, and out the back door to the outhouse.

"I'll tell ya' right now, if we could get three or four feet in a week in the Victor at Cripple Creek we'd think it was Christmas morning," Big Nelson remarked. "And how 'bout the train yesterday? Any more Jacks?"

"Cousin Jacks ya' mean?" Comins replied. "There were, and I hear the O & B has new owners."

"Then I guess the O & B will be startin' up again?" Big asked as he pulled himself up from the table and walked over towards his bunk.

"Looks like it. Heard it at the Cleveland and Kline," Martin added.

"Well, we's a gonna need a little shut-eye since I'm on night shift this week," Big said as he rolled into his bunk.

Chubb was listening as he kneaded his bread dough. He pinched off a piece and saved it in a piece of cheesecloth for the next day and sprinkled a tiny bit of flour over his task. He checked the fire in the cook stove, added a few bits of limb from a fir tree, and wiped his hands on his filthy apron and went out to the main room.

"Cripple Creek, ya' say," Chubb broke in. "You ever hear of a miner named Crazy Bob? Heard stories 'bout him all the way up in the Dakotas."

Big Nelson lifted his head up from his bunk and turned his mouth towards Chubb. From the look on his face Chubb could tell that Big Nelson was working up a brag.

"If you mean Crazy Bob Rutledge! Hell yeah! Why he worked a vein that he holed into a cavity as big as rich man's bathroom. Yep, he showed his lamp into that vug and lo and behold its walls was a' covered in gold so damn bright he fell down in a tizzy, I'll tell ya' that!"

"Aw, yer' just talkin' through yer' hat again, Big," Chubb boomed, laughing.

"I'm tellin' ya' right now Old Bob had gold fever so bad that he built a vault door on it. An' then he locked that door and put armed guards in front of it!" Big proclaimed while George Pratt lay in his bunk with his feet crossed and his arms behind his head, the faint play of emotion showing on his face. He chimed in:

"Yep, the gold fever will overtake a man and drive him to the bottle even if he hits a strike. Why I heard that Old Virginny City Finny stayed drunk for two years straight after he sold his share in the Comstock. Last I heard he fell off his horse and cracked his skull, died right there on the spot, the whiskey flowin' through his veins like the silver in his lode. Hell, even Henry Comstock his-self went broke after he sold his share and done shot his head off in Bozeman. I'm here to tell ya' the gold fever is a curse, we's better off just a workin' here in Monte for wages." Martin spoke up:

"Well there's more to this world than being a miner. Oscar Wilde once said that if you know what you want to be then you inevitably become it. Because if you never know what you want to be, then you can be anything." He slowly nodded his head and added, "There's a truth to that."

"For criminy sakes. Who the hell is Oscar Wilde? Some rummy ya' met in a bar?" Big Nelson chided.

"Don't tell me you've never heard of the finest Irish playwright in the world?"

"Aw, you and yer' educated talk. If yer' half as learned as you think you are then what 'er you doin' out in this wilderness workin' with us miners? Huh, Martin?"

Comins paused, grinned and said, "When I was a young lad I felt the hand of God touch me wee brow in church. I studied in seminary to be a priest for a number of years and even taught at university for a wee bit. But me mum, God-bless her soul, questioned me at home. In the years that followed I believe I embarrassed the family with me fondness for the rye so, I came to America and ended up out here. Then built my cabin below town and homesteaded a fine spread down on the glistening waters of—"

"Yeah, yeah, we've all heard about yer' place down on the lake," McGavock chided.

"Wish I had myself a little land," Chubb said, turning back to his bread dough and stove but then added. "Martin, make sure you check the tram buckets comin' up today for any grub an' supplies. Train came in yesterday and my load of eatables still ain't here yet."

Martin nodded at Chubb then finished his coffee and set the cup on a table while Big Nelson and George Pratt rolled over in their bunks to get some sleep.

"Eli and Dave, get Strom and Ed and meet me in the mine. You've got to get that ore mucked out and loaded out to the tram before I can blast again," Martin said, leaving the cabin. He headed up the talus rocked trail, past stunted snow-bent and windswept Alpine and Pacific fir, as his trousers brushed against red heather and copper bush; then he stopped and picked some salmonberries. Spitting them out, he muttered, "Bitter, too early." As he hiked he pulled a red handkerchief out of his back pocket and tied it around his neck.

At the headhouse he lit the kerosene lamp, grabbed his toolbox and headed inside, ducking his head to miss the support timbers and cross pieces. The rubble of ore was piled knee high at the blast site: galena, chalcopyrite, and pyrite. Martin held the lantern up to the blasted-out wall and grinned at the sight of a vein of galena. The sound of metal wheels broke the silence.

"How's it look?" Eli said, pushing an ore cart, his lantern hanging on the front of it.

"Good," Comins replied. "We've got a vein of galena, so I think we'll do a drift and follow it."

Over the course of the next few days I watched the crews work day and night as they blasted away at my insides, taking more and more of me out. Some worked mucking ore out of the adit and hauling it to the terminal in carts, while others loaded the ore in the tram buckets, letting gravity pull them down to the bunker at the concentrator. Other men carried timbers inside the mine and built support columns to prevent cave-ins. By the following Monday two of the crew must have been restless, I saw Strom and LeRoy wander down the trail to town. Soon after they left the cookhouse I saw LeRoy stop to pull something out from underneath his vest and check it, then he shoved it behind his belt. Once done he reached down to grab a handful of columbine and hurried to catch up with his friend.

V

THE PEDDLER

It was another blue-sky day, I was pleased to see that the string of clear beautiful days had continued while I worked cutting wood. Setting another big round on the chopping block, I aimed for a small crack in the grain and pop! It flew apart with just one nice blow.

After cutting a dozen more rounds I took a break and walked into the kitchen, Liz was taking inventory after the busy tourist weekend. She stood at the counter with a piece of paper in front of her and a pencil in her hand making a list.

"What-cha doing?" I asked from the sink, pushing the hand pump down and then pulling it up, getting a drink of water.

"Well, Saturday is the 4th of July, and after this last weekend we're going to need more flour, since I made so much bread for the guests."

"Oh, that's right," I replied, taking a long drink. "The 4th is coming up."

"Sure is, and there's a big celebration with fireworks planned this year," Liz said as I made my way over to the table. Eva came in and walked straight to the cupboard.

"How's the wood going, Oliver?" she asked, grabbing a water glass and filling it at the sink.

"Oh, pretty good. The shed is starting to fill up," I answered. "Does the train come today?"

"Yep, every Monday, Wednesday and Friday," Eva replied. "At about 2:30, as long as there's no delays," Liz added.

"Okay," I said, pulling out my pocket watch. "That's pretty soon. I think I'll be there when it does, maybe do some sketches of that big mountain above town or of the people getting off the train."

"Good for you," Jacob approved from the kitchen door. "We don't expect you to cut wood every day and not be an artist anymore."

"Yes," Eva affirmed, "you've got a lot done in the last few days."

"Thanks, I'm actually starting to enjoy it, I like swinging an ax. Splitting's the best part," I offered.

"I always thought burning it was the best," Jacob said, laughing and slapping his knee. Eva took a drink and looked at Jacob.

"There you go again," Eva remarked, "laughing at your own dumb jokes."

After refilling my glass with water I headed out to the front porch to sit in Jacob's rocking chair. Just as I was lifting the glass to take a drink a brown and black furry creature jumped out of some rocks across the way at the base of the hill. It hopped up on a small boulder with a few sprigs of grass in its mouth and began to feed on them, jamming them into its mouth and chewing vigorously. It looked like a rabbit but its ears were too small. I rocked forward to get out of the chair and take a closer look. As soon as I stood up the little thing began to stomp its rear feet and started chittering and chattering when it let out a high-pitched bark, as if it was mad at me. Then it scurried back down in the rocks so I returned to the chair.

I could hear faint voices talking. I turned my head to Dumas Street and the two fellows I rode on the train with days before, Strom and LeRoy, were coming down from the mountains. LeRoy had one hand in a vest pocket and a bunch of wild flowers in the other, his bowler hat was down on his brow and he was strutting along with a big grin on his face. As they got closer I could hear them speaking, deep in conversation.

"Yah, yah," Strom said, "just a couple of belts at Fred's and den I'm headed back to the bunkhouse."

"Fine by me. Do what ya' want," LeRoy replied. "Libby and me, why we might just pull up stakes and say so-long to this town. It's her birthday next week and who knows, maybe we'll celebrate down in Snohomish City and never come back."

"And den what? Find a job somewhere else?"

"All I know is I'm gonna get my baby doll anything she wants, and if she wants to leave then we're gone. That's all I care about," LeRoy said as they continued down the street. I pulled my watch out again, saw what time it was and decided to get ready before the train arrived.

In my room I opened the trunk and thought about what I should take to the depot, my paint supplies or sketch pad and pencils? I quickly decided that trying my hand at both was the best option, so I opened the field box and made sure I had a small paper pad and everything else I needed.

Coming down Dumas carrying my easel and field box I wondered how much I could charge — that is, if I actually sold something. I knew I couldn't just give my work away, and decided that a painting should be at least two dollars while a sketch should sell for fifty, no, better yet, seventy-five cents, since the tourists should have plenty of money to spend. Then I decided to stop in the mercantile and set my gear down on the porch.

A man behind the counter with a handlebar mustache nodded at me as I walked in. He had dark hair parted in the middle, a long aquiline nose and wore a white apron tied at the waist. Behind him rows of shelving from floor to ceiling were stacked with canned fruits and vegetables, tobacco, boxes of cartridges, spools of yarn, sundries and all kinds of merchandise. Sacks of flour, and bins of sugar and salt were stored in a long cabinet behind the counter and stacks of catalogs were opened for review and ordering. In one back corner was the framed-in post office room with a mail slot and a wicket clerk window. In the front of the store was a sitting area with tables by the windows, two old-timers sat at one having coffee and playing checkers.

Women with baskets hanging from their forearms moved through the room. Crates of fresh fruit and vegetables were stacked in the center of the store on long tables. On the other side was hardware and rigging; shovels and hand tools, saws, rope, nail boxes and lanterns; axes and hammers hung on the wall. Stuff was everywhere. There was some hard candy in jars behind glass in a cabinet near the front where I stood. I stepped over to them and waited until the clerk was done.

"Yer' new in town?" the man with the mustache said, strolling over.

"Yes, as a matter of fact," I answered.

"What can I get you?" he asked. I dug in my trousers for some money.

"How about five of that hard candy, the cinnamon ones."

He moved his head up and down and reached under the counter for a small brown paper bag. Then he shoved a big metal spoon in the jar and scooped up a good number, poured them in the bag and handed it over. I held the coins out for him to take.

"Nope, not today Oliver. On the house," he said with a grin and a quick wave of his hand.

"How do you know —?"

"Jacob and Eva's nephew, right?"

"I am."

"Son, everybody knows everybody here in Monte — I knew who you were the moment you walked in, and you bear a resemblance I might add. Jacob told me all about you." He stuck out his hand and smiled.

"I'm Charlie O'Connell, the manager of this fine establishment," he said, lifting his left arm and sweeping it to the side of himself. I shook his right hand.

"Good to meet you! Thanks," I said, popping a piece of candy in my mouth. "You've got a great store, I'll see you soon, Charlie." I turned and left the store.

Outside I picked up the easel and field box. Looking around there were a good number of people milling about, the sound of their shoe and boot heels scuffing the wood planking. Farther down at the wagon bridge two kids were throwing rocks in the creek as a couple of workingmen walked across it and towards the depot. Two gentlemen in suits were talking in front of the Pioneer Market when another black powder Boom! blasted up in the hills. Everyone on Dumas looked in the direction briefly, and then went back to what they were doing.

I heard someone humming and looked uphill. A tall fellow with glasses was coming down the street — I recognized him, it was Martin Comins, the man I saw with those two miners the day I arrived. As he walked by I said, "Hello," and he looked over at me.

"Yes, lad," he responded, raising his hand as he tromped by. The bottom of his brown trousers were tucked into the top of worn, black brogans and there was a red handkerchief tied around his neck. The blue homespun work shirt he had on was covered in dust, and he seemed to walk like he knew where he was going. I followed behind him, down to the depot.

A few town folks and some teenage boys selling ore samples were beginning to gather around the station in anticipation of the train. I watched as Martin walked past them and the depot, across the tracks past the turntable and water tower, and over the footbridge that spanned a small creek. Then he turned and ducked into a board and batten sided building with a steep pitched roof of cedar shakes. There were some benches leaned up against the depot around the corner from the tracks — that's a good spot to sit and paint, I thought, but I had some change in my pocket and there was no sight or sound of the train, so I thought I'd see what lower town had to offer.

I set down my easel and walked across the footbridge carrying the field box. I could see the rest of lower town over on the other side of the river, between it and the railroad tracks. Rows of slip-shod buildings ran parallel to the tracks. There was one building painted green built on stilts out over the riverbank, the front of it clinging back to the ground. It had tall foundation posts going down to the river bed and a man was under the building working on its foundation, nailing lumber cross pieces to the posts.

Ambling down a boardwalk I went past slip-shod buildings, shanties and a rough-hewn outhouse. A few steps later I could hear loud voices, men quarreling and laughing nearby. There was a hand-painted sign over a door where all the noise was coming from: The Monte Cristo Hotel, I poked my head inside.

Framed, unfinished walls with thin gaps but just wide enough for slits of sunlight to come through, sawdust covered uneven wood floors, and a string of barrels with planking on top served as a bar with a makeshift counter behind it holding bottles. Some tables and chairs were close to the front and a battered old upright piano stood in a corner. There was a barber's chair off to the side, a staircase climbed up one wall and a buxom woman with coal black hair sat by herself at a table fingering her necklace while she gazed out a window.

Martin Comins was leaning up to the bar with a few miners next to him, Sam Strom was at a table wolfing down a pile of pancakes with a miner I didn't recognize that was nursing a glass of flat beer. LeRoy was nowhere to be seen. I took a seat near the door and set my field box on the table. I could hear Martin talking.

"Fred around, yet?" he asked a cadaverous looking man behind the bar with grey skin and bags under his eyes.

"Nope, still back in the old country at some wedding," the bartender said, drying a glass with a rag that looked like it was more dirt than cloth.

"And here I was hoping to get me ears lowered before the big weekend!" Martin remarked as he lifted a jigger of whiskey to his lips. He downed the brown liquor and set his glass back on the bar. "Pour me another wee dram and then I'll try Ned over in upper town, see if he can get me cropped before the fourth." He set a quarter on the bar, the bartender poured Martin a shot then set a dime in front of him. A moment later a miner slammed his fist down on the bar and commenced to hollering.

"Damn yer' parsimonious ways, Shamus O'Dowd! This ain't no high-falootin' six-bit hotel! Yer' a two-bit shop and that means *I still get a second full shot of whiskey*. EVEN WHEN I PUT MY DIME BACK DOWN!" The bartender wheeled around and glared at the miner, then at the tiny glass in front of him and finally saw the dirty little dime.

"Yeah, yeah! I see can yer' damn dime now that ya' put it *back* on the bar. Ya' should-a just left it there after yer' first pour," the barman said, topping off his drink. But the miner didn't touch it, choosing instead to glare at the back of the bartender's head as he walked away, both of the men scowling.

The ceiling above me started to creak and footsteps sounded out, someone was coming down the stairs. It was Dave LeRoy, I recognized him from earlier. He walked over to Sam Strom with a sideways grin on his face and sat down.

"Yah, and how's yer' little Libby doin'?" Strom asked, his mouth full of syrup and cake.

"Aw, she ain't happy. Business is slow and we're both broke," LeRoy said, adjusting his belt, trying to get comfortable. "But I still need to get her something," he said, scratching his stubbly sideburns.

"Yep, well, at three bucks a day that's how the syndicate wants us, broke 'er starvin' 'er both," the miner sitting next to Strom said.

"Yeah, you might be right about that," LeRoy said in a disgusted tone to the miner, his eyes narrowing. LeRoy turned his attention back to Strom and spoke in a quiet tone.

"Some caller last week gave her a fancy necklace so I need to get her something better." He got up, fussed with his belt again, pushed up the back of his bowler hat and moved over to the bar. The faint rumble of steel wheels and the chugging of a locomotive could be heard coming up the valley. I grabbed my field box, popped another piece of hard candy in my mouth and headed out the door.

More people were at the depot standing around talking while waiting for the train. In the distance a plume of steam could be seen above the trees and the rumble of the train was getting louder. Some kids started pointing in its direction and the station master stepped out on the platform, pulling his watch piece out of a vest pocket. Looking at it he nodded his head and looked back down the tracks.

I walked over around the corner to the benches, sat down and gazed up at the bear tooth mass of granite above me. Grabbing a pencil I took a small framed canvas from the field box, set it on the easel, and began to lightly draw the outline of the mountain. Next I got the palette, started mixing paint and went to work on painting the mountain. Soon shouts of joy and the clapping of hands filled the air as the train chugged across the trestle and rolled into town.

Glancing back and forth from my canvas and the subject, I could hear the happy passengers disembarking around the corner. Two couples with children walked by talking with thick Cornish accents followed by a short man with a leather satchel at his side, hanging by a strap slung around his neck. He clutched the satchel tightly with his left hand as he put his right hand on the top of his floppy cloth hat and looked up at the mountains. As the fellow stepped back over to the station master, I could hear them talk as I worked away.

"Excuse me, sir. I'm here today to make my timepiece rounds. How's your watch running? Keeping time alright?" he asked. His extra-long trousers were bunched up above his worn-out shoes, there were holes in the elbows of his suit coat.

"Running fine, thank you," the station man said. Just then Strom and LeRoy walked around the depot corner. The fellow with the satchel approached them.

"How about you gentlemen? How are your watches running?" he asked.

"Yah, no, mister," Strom answered. "No watch here, don't need one. I've got the boss ta' tell me what time it is."

"And how about you?" the peddler asked LeRoy.

LeRoy's eyes sparked and he looked down at the man, grinned at his locked satchel, and adjusted his belt.

"No timepiece on me but, a, my gal's birthday is next week. Would ya' have anything bright and shiny in yer' bag?" The peddler looked the dusty, dirty LeRoy up and down and rubbed his chin and crinkled his nose, then quickly shook his head.

"Sorry, don't think I can help you, today," the watchman sniffed. He started to walk away but LeRoy grabbed him from behind and spun him around.

"Listen, fella, I need to buy a little somethin' for my gal," LeRoy said with a firm quietness. The peddler jerked his arm from LeRoy's grip and clutched his satchel.

"I'm sorry but I only have items for people that can pay. Now good day."

LeRoy quickly pulled a few crumpled-up coin notes from his trousers. "See, I've got plenty of dough," he said, holding up his thin wad of multi-colored bills. The peddler frowned at the small sum of money.

"I already said I'm sorry, sir. I don't have any '*shiny items*' for that amount," he replied and walked away towards Dumas Street, gripping his leather bag tightly.

The corners of LeRoy's mouth turned downward. He poked Strom in the shoulder, tilted his head to lower town and said, 'To hell with that little twerp," and they left.

I went back to my canvas and decided to paint the mountain as if I was farther downstream with the train in the foreground heading across the trestle into town. I had the bulk of the painting done when an older man and woman came around the corner. They stopped and took in the views, both were well dressed. He had a stove-pipe hat on and was wearing a black suit and carrying an ivory handled cane. The woman wore a long yellow dress with black piping and had a white parasol and black leather purse.

"Such beauty," the man said.

"Yes," the woman replied, "I just love coming up here."

I picked the painting up off the easel and stepped away from it — my thin sable haired brush in one hand. I was tapping my chin thoughtfully, walking directly in the path of the approaching wealthy couple so they might by chance catch notice of me or my work, but they didn't. I walked past them, holding the canvas up in the air as if I was trying to get a better angle. This time the man saw me. I could feel him come up behind, looking over my shoulder.

"Beautiful work, son," the man said with a deep voice. "Honey, come and look."

"Thank you, sir," I replied, turning around.

"Are you an artist by trade?" he asked. His wife came over, I turned for her to see the painting and said to him, "Why yes, I am."

"That would be a fine keep-sake. Will you sell it?"

"I would! Each painting is . . . two dollars," I said with a touch of apprehension, hoping I hadn't asked for too much.

"Excellent. I'll take it," he said, digging into his pants pocket.

"Do you know the date?" I asked him.

"Why yes, it's June 29th," the man said handling over two silver certificate dollar bills just as Martin Comins strolled by.

"Thank you. I appreciate it!" I replied shoving the bills in my pocket.

"Could you do me a favor and deliver it for me at the Monte Cristo Hotel?" he asked.

"I'd be happy to."

"Excellent! Please drop it by for Mr. Nickolas Rudebeck. Thank you," he said, and they walked off towards upper town, following Comins.

"That's a wonderful painting," the man said.

"Yes, I believe we should hang it in the library," the woman replied.

The crowd had by now disbursed and left the station, but I saw Henry down the way getting his wagon loaded at the freight car. I looked up the hill to the Pride and then down at lower town. I smiled. *I think I've earned myself a drink.* I dated and signed the painting, then picked it up along with the easel with the field box and went down to lower town.

Stepping back inside Fred's I saw Strom and LeRoy bellied up to the bar, both of them talking loudly. Strom was motioning with his hands as he spoke.

"Yah, yah. I tell you right now that the great commoner will win. Come November he is going to be the next president!" Strom proclaimed to the room.

"Aw, that what-cha call it, bi-metal-lism, ain't gonna work," LeRoy drawled.

"Yah, it will," Strom retorted, "and when it does silver will be worth the same as gold. We'll all be rich!"

"That's a, bunch a . . . baloney," LeRoy slurred.

I set everything on an empty table and made my way over to the end of the bar and put down a quarter while the two miners argued. The bartender walked over.

"What'll it be?" he asked as he wiped the area in front of me with a wrinkled dirty towel.

"Got any cold beer?"

"Not today, just warm stuff."

"Well," I said a touch nervous, "How about a shot of whiskey, then. Thanks," I said. Turning around to the room I saw a set of legs coming down the stairs. It was a young and thin, almost waif-like woman. She had a red and white print dress on with layers of petticoats underneath, a few wild flowers were behind her ear and her yellow hair was hanging down around her shoulders. When she sat down at a table near the piano there was a pouty look on her thin lips, she stared out a window, mute. Dave LeRoy saw her and went over and asked her to dance — I figured she was the one he'd been talking about when I saw the two miners walking past me earlier. The bartender came back over with a shot glass, poured the whiskey and picked up the quarter and set down a dime.

This time I wasn't afraid. I knew I could handle it. *Just one and that's it.* All those nights I'd spent falling down drunk, trying to fill the void of losing my Father, and staring up at the ceiling with one eye closed, watching it spin and getting sick from the booze and having hangovers. Those drunken days were gone, just like my dad was now.

I picked up the whiskey and looked at the brown liquid, then put it back on the bar and took a breath. I picked it back up and threw back the shot, grabbed the dime and left. As I did I walked by LeRoy and his girl, they began slow dancing, he was holding her close and whispering in her ear. Then he spun her around and picked up the pace and yelled at the bar, "Come on Strom, let's have us a dance!" The bartender went over to the piano and started to play it while Strom stood up and began to shuffle his feet.

Strolling out of Fred's with the painting and my gear I could hear the piano in the background and decided to take advantage of the clear day and do a quick pencil sketch this time of just the mountain. The whiskey activated my brain and I went to work on drawing the same bear's tooth mountain again. This time I added some clouds and included the thumb shaped vertical rock on the ridge line.

Thirty minutes later the conductor walked by. I recognized him from the ride up last week. He stopped at the edge of the platform, looked up at the view, yawned and stretched out his arms. Turning around he noticed me.

"Afternoon, young fella," he said.

"Nice day, huh?" I answered.

"Always nice to be up in Monte," he noted with a smile.

Just then LeRoy and Strom stumbled past. I could smell the booze as they went by and heard just a little bit of what they were saying.

"I'm tired . . . too much dancing," Strom said walking slowly. "And . . . another shift."

"Not me . . . you go . . ." LeRoy stammered. "I'm . . . get . . . somethin'. Even if'n I gots to . . . that . . . with —," he added, grabbing his belt.

"What, no," Strom slurred. "You be . . . yah?"

"I'm good," LeRoy said with a grin, catching his breath, "I'll catch up with you." Was all I could clearly heard him say. I wondered just what it was they were talking about as they walked away towards upper town.

Satisfied with the sketch I got up and thought I'd run the painting by the hotel and then walk around before heading home. After I stopped by the hotel I went back down Dumas. Near the wagon bridge I noticed a road going behind the buildings that followed the creek upstream, I headed that way. The water was running fast and had the milky-white color from the concentrator runoff. I passed some foxglove and thistle growing along the edge and saw a stable with a few milk cows and two mules and horses, there was a ramshackle shed-like barn at the far end. A tall fir tree was near the barn next to the creek bank, it was the only tree still standing in town and made a good background, so I set down the easel and field box.

One white mare with a black mane saw me approach. It tromped over and held its head out and over the fence rail, she seemed friendly. I reached out to pet her when she let out a loud snort and shook her head violently.

"Easy. That's okay, it's alright," I said in a soothing voice. I held out the palm of my hand, "I bet you'd like it if I had a carrot." But then she shook her neck and head again, a cloud of dust rose up around her while one mule clopped over and dropped its head to graze on some weeds.

I walked back down the mud-rutted road and sat on a pile of white boulders where I left my gear across from the corral. I opened the field box, took out a sketch pad and a pencil and started to draw.

All was quiet and peaceful as I worked away on the lone tree, barn, and the creek on the other side of the stable. Two birds called out. I raised my head to listen to the fluid call and response . . . *whit* . . . *whit* . . . of two wood thrush on separate stumps and smiled. I turned back to the pad and reinterpreted the actual slip-shod fencing and made it look better than it was, then I worked on the ruts in the road and the foliage on the hillside, the stumps and debris on the mountains. Soon I'd finished the rendering and —

Ka-POW!

I looked up from my sketch. It sounded like a gun shot. Then silence.

Someone screamed. Seconds went by and —

Ka-POW! . . . *Ka-POW*! The echoes of the shots reverberated off the surrounding cliffs.

I leapt to my feet, the pad spilling off my knees and onto the ground. The sound came from below town, down the tracks. I started walking quickly back down the wagon road. Between the buildings I saw a few men running on Dumas. Two were yelling and waving their arms. I picked up my pace and got to the trestle then headed down the railroad tracks beginning to think that something had possibly gone wrong.

When I saw blood on the tracks a cold shiver went down my spine. Then I saw someone lying on the ground over on the tote road across from the Rattle Claim sign moaning in pain. A group of people had already gathered around, including Charlie O'Connell from the mercantile.

"I've been . . . robbed," the man was mumbling as I came up. It was the watch peddler from the train station. "I was . . . sell a watch," the peddler stuttered, "and he shot . . . me!"

"Somebody go get Dr. Miles!" O'Connell yelled at the people coming up. "Nathan Phillips has been shot. Hurry! Bring a stretcher!"

Two men ran away to fetch the doctor just as Martin Comins showed up, breathing heavily with a bit of shaving cream on his neck.

"What happened here?!" Martin yelled, pushing his way through.

"He shot me," Nathan replied, "and ran . . . into the hills."

"Who? Who shot ya' lad?" Martin asked, bending over towards the peddler.

"Somebody, a guy. I was going . . . he said a friend, wanted a watch . . . but I wouldn't sell . . . he didn't have, money . . . pulled out a gun."

"What?! Oh, for the love of Christ," Comins said. His face went pale as he put his hands on his head and quickly looked around, then he kneeled down next to him, beginning to mutter something under his breath.

More people came running up, shocked at what was happening. Nathan was bleeding heavily. He had a bullet hole in his left hand and a wound in his left shoulder.

Martin righted himself with a determined look, ripped off his shirt and began to apply pressure to the man's shoulder wound.

"Someone else work on his hand," Martin barked. "Yee'll be okay, help's on the way."

Another man took off his shirt and wrapped it around Nathan's hand. When he did the peddler let out a bloodcurdling scream and tears began to roll down his face. He started shaking, and moaned between tears, "He took all my money, he got everything!" Minutes ticked by. Somebody reached down with a cup of water and tried to give him a drink, but spilled most of it on his shirt when the peddler's bobbing head tipped the tin cup.

Two men from town on horses galloped up. I recognized the one horse from earlier at the stable. Its rider pulled hard against the reins as the mare snorted and nostrils flared, its head bobbed up and down as it pawed the road with a heavy hoof. A big fellow on another horse who I guessed was the leader spoke up.

"Which way? Where'd the guy go?!" he hollered.

Nathan raised himself up from the ground on his one good elbow and feebly tilted his head at the ridge, to the north and said, "Up the mountain."

"Looks like he's headed for Goat Lake! Let's go!" one yelled. The riders galloped off on the tote road and up a side trail in pursuit just as Dr. Miles showed up, another man had a stretcher.

"Out of the way!" the doctor hollered as people immediately parted to make room. The man placed the stretcher on the ground next to the peddler while the doctor set down his small kit bag and opened it. Unwrapping the bloody makeshift shirt bandage from the wounded man's hand the doctor grimaced, and then pulled a roll of gauze from his bag. The doctor re-wrapped his hand and applied pressure, then looked up at the faces staring down on him.

"We've got to get this man on the train to the hospital right now," Dr. Miles said with a concerned look on his sweaty face. "Somebody run up to the depot and tell Conductor Speer to hold the train. I can give him an anodyne but I can't treat him here, he's got a bullet hole clean through his hand and is gonna need surgery right away."

I watched a fellow head off to alert the train, running past the girl I saw earlier in the bar. She was walking towards the commotion with a look of shock on her face and holding up her dress as wildflowers fell out of her hair. Once she got close the expression on her face worsened and she stopped. When she saw the peddler on the ground, covered in blood, her face turned to terror. Creeping slowly towards the crowd of people she put her hands over her mouth and stood still. All the color drained from her face, then she looked around at everyone, like she was looking for someone. She quickly turned around and ran back to town. Jacob and Eva showed up.

"Good lord!" Jacob exclaimed, seeing the peddler on the ground, "What happened?"

"He was robbed . . . and shot," I said, tense and concerned.

"But why . . . why would anyone in Monte shoot him?" Eva said, her voice quavering.

"Move! Everybody out of the way! Now!" Dr. Miles hollered as Martin and three other men lifted the stretcher and carried Nathan up from the tote road.

"Careful," the doctor said, following alongside, now applying pressure to his shoulder. When they got him on the tracks and off towards the train the rest of the crowd slowly walked behind and around them, wild with talk and speculation as more people showed up.

"Who would do such a thing?" someone asked.

"A thief and a criminal would, that's who," another replied.

"If the syndicate would pay us a decent wage this kind of thing wouldn't happen around here," a man dressed in work clothes said.

"I want to know who did it."

"Yeah, me too!"

"We need to get the sheriff up here, and soon!"

"Well, we need a Town Marshal!"

"We need another jail!"

Up the tracks I could see Conductor Speer running across the trestle towards us with a scowl, his jacket half on and a sleeve billowing out behind him. Everyone in town was already at the depot, waiting. All of them with their heads turned towards us, moving around, talking and pointing.

As the group walked by lower town there were men and women standing outside of saloons and shacks watching us carrying the wounded man. There was one saloon with a sign above the door that read 'Cleveland & Kline,' it was the same saloon built out over the river bank and painted green I saw earlier. A middle-aged man of medium height and dark hair stood at the entry with his hands on his hips, our eyes met and he nodded, a sour look was on his face.

"How's he doing?" Conductor Speer asked.

"He'll make it but he needs to see a surgeon," the doctor replied.

"We've got a place set up for him in the baggage car with plenty of room," the conductor offered as he turned around and walked with the doctor. "Will you be riding along?" The doctor thought about the question for a moment.

"Yes . . . yes, that'd be good. I can tend to him on the way."

"I've sent word out through town that the train is leaving right away." I heard the conductor say. I watched as Dr. Miles nodded in approval.

As the doctor and his patient approached the hundred-plus depot crowd some of them who could see the peddler on the stretcher began to turn away and shield their eyes from the blood and gulped while most swarmed around the wounded man as they walked past to the baggage car. Some of the crowd craned their necks to catch a glimpse as others at the far edges of the burgeoning throng jumped up to see over the mass of people now filling the depot area. Everyone murmured amongst themselves with questions about what had happened.

At the baggage car the four men lifted Nathan up as two train attendants pulled him aboard, the doctor climbed the stairs and entered the car.

Conductor Speer walked back to the locomotive and gave the engineer the all clear. The bell rang and the whistle sounded as he looked out over the mob of town folk.

"Since we've got an emergency the train is leaving now! Is there anyone here that knows of someone that's still over in town who needs to get onboard?" Speer asked and waited a moment. No one spoke. "Okay! All aboard!" the conductor hollered. At the same time that the conductor was speaking I caught a glance of someone walking on the other side of the train and climbing aboard.

As soon as the locomotive pulled out from the depot I saw Martin Comins briskly walk away and head across the footbridge to lower town. I followed him thinking that he was up to something and quickly realized that he was going to Fred's. I kept my distance. Approaching the building I could hear loud voices, so I stood outside.

"What ya' mean she's gone?" Comins hollered.

"Yep, just now," the bartender replied, "Libby came down the stairs with a suitcase and left without a word, just took off. Why?"

"Didn't ya' hear what happened? A man just got shot!" I heard Comins say. Realizing what I'd heard, my heart sank. *What if she knew who robbed and shot him?* I dropped my head and walked away. As I did I felt the pull of drink. My mind turned in the direction of lower town across the river, and my feet followed.

VI

CLEVELAND & KLINE

Walking over the trestle bridge with my head down I couldn't seem to get the image of the peddler lying on the ground and bleeding out of my mind. Once across I looked up and saw the green building over on the river bank, it didn't look like most of the others, since it had a coat of paint. Bright green siding with white trim boards around the windows, it was tidy and neat in a neighborhood of downtrodden structures and living arrangements. I left the trestle and started to walk down the embankment.

The same middle-aged man I saw earlier was walking back into the building from a small hand-drawn wagon sitting outside that was filled with blocks of ice from a fresh, cold shipment on the train. Then a woman walked out, picked up a block and went back in. I poked my head inside. The place was empty, smooth floors painted brown, card tables up front, wainscot bar with a brass foot rail, finished white interior walls, and a wood stove in the corner — overall it was a fine-looking establishment. The middle-aged fellow saw me at the door.

"Yep, the Cleveland and Kline is open," he said, standing up from behind the bar with a block of melting ice in his gloved hands. He glanced at me — then bent over and stored the ice away under the bar in an icebox.

"Come on in, and don't worry, we won't shoot you. We've had enough of that today . . . and we sure don't need any more days like this," he remarked, standing back up. The woman I'd seen earlier walked out from a back room and stood by the door.

"Yes, quite a day," I said, stepping into the saloon. The man looked me up and down.

"Well, if you're a tourist this kind of thing ain't normal round these parts, never has been and never will. Your first time to Monte?" he asked. He was medium height and wore a black vest with a white collarless shirt underneath, his hair was parted in the middle.

"Umm, yes. Got here last week," I replied walking up to the bar. "I'm Oliver."

"Good to meet ya', Oliver," he grinned and put his hand out.

"Pleased to meet you," I said, shaking it and sitting down.

"I'm Addison Cleveland," he said, and then motioned to the woman saying, "and this is my wife Elizabeth. What can we get you?"

"How about a shot of whiskey?" I asked.

"Sure," he answered, setting a glass in front of me and filling it. I set a quarter on the bar.

"Welcome to Monte, Oliver," Elizabeth said, stepping over to the counter, her voice calm and soothing. She was short with auburn hair pulled into a tight bun and wore a blue gingham work dress.

"Our business partner Jacob's around here somewhere," Addison said.

"Oh really, that's interesting. My Uncle's name is Jacob, too. He and my Aunt Eva have the Pride Hotel."

"Well I'll be, no kiddin'," he remarked, picking up the quarter and putting down a dime.

"Okay, Addison," Elizabeth broke in, "I'm headed home. This day has given me a really big headache. Good to meet you, Oliver."

"Good to meet you too," I said.

"Alright, I'll see you soon," Addison said to his wife. I looked over to him.

"So, you know my uncle?"

"Sure, sure. Everybody knows everybody here in Monte. How they been?"

"They're good," I replied.

"Is Liz still up there cooking for them?"

"Oh yeah, she's a great cook."

"What are you doing in Monte? You a miner?"

"I'm a painter."

"Painter, huh? Sorry, we just put on a coat a month ago."

"No no, I'm an artist. Landscapes mostly, and portraits."

"Well, I'll be! We could use an artist around here. Bring a little culture to the place. How long you plan on staying?"

"I'd like to see every season. Paint them all," I replied, throwing back the shot of whiskey.

"Even winter? Not many stick around for the cold season," he said just as two men walked in and up to the bar. Both of them were bellowing away, frantic in conversation. I recognized them right away from earlier.

"What's this world coming to, anyway? How could this happen?" one said, his hands moving in rhythm with the words he spoke.

"I guess we're just like the big city now. Robbery, shootings. What's next?!" the other grumbled, shaking his head. He was heavy-set, wore a grey suit and white ruffled shirt with a black cravat tie. The other was wearing a collared shirt and trousers, looking more like a workingman.

"I just can't believe this!"

"Me neither . . . And that poor peddler lying there shot, bleeding to death."

"I know, I know. I can't understand it."

"Ah, Mr.'s Baker and Bartholomew," Addison said, gesturing towards each one as he said their names. "What'll it be? The usual?"

"Yes, please," Bartholomew muttered, fussing with his tie, "I've got plenty of time until the posse gets back before I start in on an article. Need to get all the facts."

Bartholomew was an older gentleman with a squished-up face and fleshy jowls. Wild bits of white hair, like short feathers, stuck out above his ears and the back of his head from under his homburg hat.

"I've got time for a quick one," Baker said. "But I will need to get to my key machine soon and send a report to the sheriff. Give 'um a heads up on today's activity." Baker had a round face, thick mustache, and wore a felt hat with the front rim turned upward. They both set quarters down on the bar.

Addison stopped pouring Mr. Baker's drink, the corners of his mouth turned downward and his jaw tightened, he looked agitated. He set the bottle on the bar and stared at Baker.

"For some of us this is still a make or break town, so how about if you try to remember that the Fourth of July is soon and those in business like me don't need the tourists alarmed. We've got a big weekend coming up and no one can afford to have people think they're going to get shot if they come up here, Ed. And the same goes for you too, Bartholomew." He finished pouring the two shots.

"Yes, but," Ed Baker replied, "I'm required to make a report to Sheriff Hagan. We did have a shooting today, after all," he said, downing his drink.

"I understand that, but we don't know yet who the shooter was, or the circumstances involved," Addison said. "You need to be careful with what you report. Can't you maybe wait a day or two so's you can get the facts straight?"

"No," Ed Baker quickly replied, starting to get up, "I could lose my telegraph license."

"Okay, but. Can't you go easy on the way you word it?" he pleaded.

"Well, he was still alive when they loaded him on the train."

"Exactly!"

"So, I guess I could say someone was injured." Baker said, walking towards the door. "But you owe me one!"

"Thanks, Ed," Addison said with a smile. He turned his attention to Bartholomew and held the neck of the bottle over his glass but didn't pour.

"And what about the newspaper, Jim? How are you going to report it?"

Bartholomew tapped the rim of his shot glass with a finger. Addison poured the drink.

"Well, the readership of the Mountaineer is pretty much confined to here in the community, and the whole town probably already knows what happened today, except the miners up in the hills of course," Bartholomew stated.

"Yes, but, I'm more concerned with the tourists this weekend buying the paper once they're here and reading some frightening story about that poor fella getting shot."

"Okay, alright. I see your point. But I do need to sell the news. And after all, there's nothing that inspires a newsman more than a good story and, this is a frontier town, as you know. Why, you could put up a sign that says, 'Famous saloon where the peddler took his last sip of whiskey,' and they'll be lined up outside the door!"

"Damn it Bartholomew! Can't you see my point?" Addison snapped, glaring at him.

"Alright, okay, I get your meaning," Bartholomew said, giving in just as a group of town folk walked through the door.

"Hey Jacob," Addison said to a fellow who walked around the bar and nodded at Bartholomew and Baker.

"Oliver, this is my business partner, Jacob Kline. Oliver is Jacob and Eva Cohen's nephew," he said, introducing us. I recognized him from earlier as one of the men that helped carry the stretcher.

"Good to meet you, Oliver," he offered, putting out his hand. He was tall and dark haired with a goatee. "Hell of a day, huh?"

"Yes, I know. Good to meet you," I said, shaking his hand.

"We got the peddler loaded on the train and I stayed and talked with Charlie for a while," he said to Addison. Then he looked back at me. "What brings you to Monte?"

"I'm here staying with my aunt and uncle at the Pride, for a spell."

"No kidding? Haven't been up to see them lately, how are they?"

"Good, I think they're full this weekend."

"Are you helping them at their inn?"

"Oh yes, cutting cord wood and doing whatever. Plus, I'm trying to paint."

"I didn't know their place needed it."

"Oh, no. I'm an artist, I do paintings," I replied. He looked confused for a moment.

"Ah, one of those. Well good, we could use an artist around here."

Just then I remembered that all my gear was still over at the stable and picked my dime up from the bar.

"I've got to get going. Great to meet you folks," I said, turning to head for the door.

"Don't be a stranger, we're always open," Addison said.

"Yeah, stop by anytime," Jacob added.

"Okay then, I'll see you later," I replied and headed back to the stable then home to the Pride of Monte Cristo.

VII

GLASS EYE

I never miss a thing in this town, everything that happens I see from the upstairs windows or hear from the attic. Oh we've had our share of fist fights and brawls in lower town over dance hall girls and gambling and the like over the years, but I knew something was up when I saw that dusty, well-dressed familiar miner with the bowler hat and blue pin striped vest following the jeweler around town. Never trust a fella that doesn't wear what he does for a living, that's what I say.

I'd see him waltz on down from the hills every Saturday night, and others in between, headed to lower town for a drink and a roll with his gal. The one with the thin lips and yellow hair. He may have loved her, but so did everyone else. She showed up in town like so many of the others, looking for fortune in a boom town. But Monte ain't a gold rush town, it's a company town, owned and run by the Rockefeller syndicate and his investors from the east coast. They all thought they'd get richer than they already were, except for me and my mountains, we knew better. Just like I knew better about Dave LeRoy. Knew it the day he showed up and conned his way into a job.

Earlier today when he came a strutting down Dumas Street like some cocky barnyard rooster with Sam Strom, a good citizen of fine Norwegian stock who'd been fooled into the friendship and taken up unknowingly with a lout, I knew it was gonna go bad. Just by the way he walked and with his hat down on his brow and a hand in his vest pocket, I could tell he had something else in mind. But I've only got these windows to look through, why if I had a voice I would have screamed out loud and told the whole darned town that Dave LeRoy was a comin', so watch out!

I recognized the peddler right away getting off the train. He'd come up from time to time to make his rounds and sell his watches and rings and bracelets. I saw him give a line of talk to LeRoy and a few people at the depot, none of whom seemed interested, then head over to the wagon bridge and into upper town, the whole time clutching his satchel. I saw him stop at the meat market, and the mercantile, then sell a watch to a businessman from Everett wearing a stove pipe hat.

My suspicions came to a head when Strom came a-stumbling drunk and tired back up Dumas and into the hills all alone muttering about his next shift, his companion evidently having independent plans for the day. Shortly thereafter I spied the peddler move on up to the Royal Hotel and go inside. Then, sure as the wind, Dave LeRoy came a strolling up the hill looking in store fronts, asking questions and pointing in one direction and another. He found the peddler in the lobby of the hotel and smiled that smirk of his, telling that poor merchant how he had a friend who wanted to buy a watch and that he could make a sale, only the friend couldn't get away from the mine where he worked, see, so they'd need to go out together into the woods to meet him.

For those who saw the two men walk back down Dumas nothing seemed out of place, and when they got to the tracks I saw LeRoy point down the line, across the trestle, and they continued. Once they were down near the Rattler Claim LeRoy pulled his six-shooter from under his vest and lunged for the peddler's satchel. But the peddler quickly turned and began to run away, back to town. But LeRoy quickly grabbed him from behind, lost his balance and fell to one knee, holding a weak grip on the little man. The peddler struggled and freed himself of the determined miner.

Next LeRoy gets back to his feet, cussing and waving his pistol all over. The peddler makes to flee and Pop! The gun goes off. The peddler falls face first onto the rails and gravel bed of the tracks. LeRoy took a moment then, maybe trying to think this new development through, but it's only that one moment that he needs to decide, and soon enough he's moving again, scrambling along the tracks towards the peddler, who's by now gotten to his hands and knees and is doing his best to crawl away off the tracks, screaming bloody murder while LeRoy is wavering drunk and flashing the six-gun at him. LeRoy sees that he had winged the fellow in the shoulder but it doesn't stop him.

Most of those in town thought it was just a black powder blast or a less loud misfire from up in the hills as the seconds ticked by.

LeRoy lunged again and pulled at the satchel and a struggle ensued, but the peddler held fast. He tried to move away from him, fell off the embankment and onto the tote road.

Then LeRoy aims and shoots at him but missed. And another gunshot rings out and echoes over the valley. The peddler screamed for help. This time there was no mistake. Everyone close enough to hear the second shot leapt to their feet and began to run in the direction of the sound.

LeRoy scrambled down and went and shot him in the hand, the hand the peddler was gripping his satchel with. He took the satchel and climbed back up on the tracks. I watched him run off like the devil, down the line then north up a trail through the woods. He kept looking over his shoulder the whole time, tripping and stumbling, terror on his face. I could tell his mind was racing, thinking about where he'd hide and if he'd ever see his dance hall girl again.

Soon dozens of men and women were running down the trestle, yelling and waving their arms. The first few to get to his side were shocked at the sight of the bleeding man. Two men ran back for Doc Miles and a stretcher.

Then I saw LeRoy's girlfriend. She came running up and her face turned to panic when she realized what had happened. Covering her mouth, she turned and fled.

Martin Comins ran up and took off his shirt and placed it on the peddler's shoulder wound while others brought him water. In no time the doctor was there and they carried him to the train, I watched the whole thing unfold. I sure hope they catch that worthless lout LeRoy.

In the meantime, I stay vigilant and forthright at the top of the hill. Aligned with the trees and the stars, I'll just sit here and wait for what tomorrow may bring.

In the morning, Liz was up with the first sounds of the concentrator, starting a fire and making coffee. Opening the icebox she found the bacon and a bowl of eggs, but the milk and cream bottles were empty, the butter depleted.

Oliver was awake in his room, scratching his head and rubbing his eyes, he lay on his cot for a few minutes, then got up and slapped on his trousers. He lumbered out to the kitchen where Liz reached up to the cupboard for a coffee mug and set it on the counter for him.

"Morning," Oliver said, yawning and stretching his arms.

"Yes, good morning," Liz replied. "Once you're awake and have a cup of coffee in you do you think you could do me a favor and run down and get us some milk and butter?"

"Sure," Oliver agreed, filling his mug with steaming coffee. He slowly walked over to the built-in and sat down. "You mean the dairy at the bottom of Dumas?"

"The dairy is in the Pioneer Market, you'll find it. Have Arthur put it on our bill," Liz explained, opening the firebox door and adding a handful of split hemlock to the flames. "He should be open by now, and if you could, get us two quarts of milk, a pint of cream and a pound of butter."

"Okay," Oliver quickly replied. "Did any one find out if the posse found that guy?"

"I guess they came back empty handed, he must have gotten away," Liz remarked, cracking an egg over a mixing bowl.

"Any idea who it was?" Oliver asked, sipping his coffee.

"Jacob thinks it was probably some hard-up miner, but I haven't heard anything else."

"Has this kind of thing ever happened before, up here?"

"Oh gosh no, well wait, yes, now that I think about it. They found a dead man out on the tote road a couple of years ago and buried him right there where they found him," Liz related. "But I don't know if they ever figured out how he died, or was killed. Oh, we've had a few brawls and knife fights in lower town but no blatant shootings and robberies like this." Oliver stood up from the built-in and downed his coffee.

"I'll be right back." He went to his room, strapped on his boots, then walked on down the hall and out the back door.

Outside the air was crisp, and the sky was clear, the din of the concentrator was the only thing to keep Oliver company as he made his way down Dumas. Up ahead at the mercantile, Charlie had stepped out onto the porch and was sweeping.

"Hey Charlie, good morning," Oliver offered. Charlie looked up and grinned.

"Mornin' Oliver. How are you?"

"Very well, thanks," Oliver replied. "Any news on the shooting?" Charlie stopped his task and looked at Oliver.

"I heard a telegram came back from the authorities and Sheriff Hagan is hot on the trail now," he said.

"So, the sheriff knows who did it?" Oliver asked, stopping in the middle of the street.

"Word has it that a fellow by the name of LeRoy might have done it," Charlie answered.

"No kidding," Oliver replied with a nod.

"Yep, I believe it. He's a trouble maker, for sure. He beat up some poor drunk down in Snohomish last winter, beat him to a pulp. Had to spend a month in jail for it down there."

"Oh really? Hadn't heard that."

"Yep, he's all kinds of bad," Charlie added.

"Okay, thanks. See you later," Oliver replied and started to walk away. Charlie went back to his sweeping.

Up ahead there was an open sign in the window of the Pioneer Market, a rough-hewn board and batten building with a pitched roof. A small sign painted on the side of the building read 'Star Dairy.' Oliver stomped the dirt off his boots on the porch and stepped inside.

The store was dark but clean, metal jugs of milk stood gleaming behind a counter that was stacked high with wrapped wheels of cheese and cartons of eggs. Next to the dairy counter a glass cooler held blocks of ice, bottles of milk and piles of butter on wax paper. Behind the counter a man dressed in a white smock was sitting on a stool and busy turning the handle of an upright separator machine as a stainless-steel bowl full of milk spun on the top of it.

"Morning, are you Arthur?" Oliver asked, shoving his hands in his pockets.

"That'd be me, Arthur Thrall, proprietor," the man replied, turning around to see who was at the counter.

"Could I get two quarts of milk, a pint of cream and a pound of butter? It's for Liz Sheedy."

"Oh, Liz sent you, did she," Arthur said, standing up. He had brown hair parted on the side, a mustache upturned on at the ends and a square jaw. "You must be Oliver."

"Yep, Oliver Cohen."

"Jacob told me all about you. The artist, right?" Arthur said, stepping over to the counter and putting out his hand. Oliver shook it and grinned.

"Yep. Liz said you could put it on the hotel's bill."

"That I can do," he said, grabbing a wooden box with Star Dairy written on the side of it and placing it on the counter. He opened the glass cooler to get the milk and cream and set the bottles in the box, then took a few spatula's worth of butter from the cooler and smashed them into a wood press. Once done he slapped the press down on a piece of wax paper and lifted the press, a square puck of butter with a star shape molded on it appeared. Arthur wrapped the butter in the piece of wax paper, placed it in the box and slid the box across the counter.

"I hear the sheriff is after that gunman now," Oliver commented.

"I heard that same thing," Arthur replied. "And I heard that Dave LeRoy did it."

"That's what Charlie O'Connell just told me."

"Yeah, I guess the dance hall gal that he was seeing ran off yesterday. Someone said she was in on it."

"No kidding?"

"Yep, all kinds of rumors flying around town. Some say they're on their way to BC or Alaska with thousands of dollars of loot. I sure hope Sheriff Hagan catches them."

"Yeah, me too."

"Okay, so there you go, one pound of unsalted raw butter, a pint of cream and two quarts of milk. Anything else?" Arthur said.

"That's all we need for now. Thank you," Oliver said. He walked out of the building carrying the box of dairy goods and headed up Dumas.

Along the way Jim Bartholomew was out in front of the *Monte Cristo Mountaineer* tacking a poster to the side of the log building near the front door. Oliver walked over to him and got a better look at the flyer.

"Morning," Oliver said. Bartholomew turned around.

"Yes, good morning," the newspaperman replied.

"Is that a wanted poster?"

"Not yet, it's a notice for information leading to the whereabouts of a fellow by the name of Dave LeRoy, about the shooting yesterday."

"So, he *did* do it?"

"From the peddler's description he gave the sheriff in Everett and the fact that a young lady, who some say he was seeing, flew the coop yesterday, we're pretty sure it was him," Bartholomew said.

"So the sheriff talked to the guy that got shot?"

"Yep, Ed Baker got a telegram from him last night. He interviewed the peddler and Doc Miles," he said, stepping towards the doorway. Before he went inside he turned around and looked at Oliver.

"I just wish that damn LeRoy would have found some other town to fall into his wickedness. A man like him is innocent of knowledge, and only sees the world in a vile and corrupt way. Why, back in the used to be, I never thought I'd see the day that a person of such foul and sinful behavior would violate the laws of man and God here in our little Monte. But now a-days . . ." he said, looking down, his voice trailing off and shaking his head.

"Oh, yes," Oliver replied, "apparently he was a devious fellow with no regard for life, or the law."

"I just can't understand the world today," Bartholomew said, glancing up and raising his head. "Why anyone would disrupt the good nature of our town with such a vicious and intemperate act is beyond me, and beyond any form of constructive or normal thought for that matter. And really," Bartholomew said, staring over Oliver's shoulder with a distant look in his eye, "when it gets down to it, I guess we should have seen something like this coming, with us not having a jail and being all the way out here in the wilderness. Let's just hope the law catches up with him, and soon."

"Yes, I know. I sure hope they do before he does something like that again," Oliver said, walking away and back to me, the Pride of Monte Cristo.

VIII

INDEPENDENCE DAY

The day began with grey overcast skies, but by three o'clock the sun was beginning to break through. Upper town was decked out in colorful red, white, and blue bunting and banners, American flags flew and hung from every porch and window, I'd never seen so many stars and stripes. Every hotel and inn were filled with tourists who'd arrived on the train the day before, and most of the miners had come down from the surrounding hills to join in the festivities.

As I came down Dumas I could see below in the clearing that a long row of tables was set end to end near a barbeque pit, all of them covered with plaid cloth, and a ten-foot-tall pile of cord and junk wood for a bonfire was off near the creek. A few men were setting up an infield for a baseball game using the side of the depot for a backstop with sandbags for bases, benches and chairs had been brought down and placed near the baselines for bleachers.

Charlie O'Connell was up ahead, standing on the porch of the mercantile with another gentleman taking the air. He saw me approaching and waved, beckoning me over.

"Good morning! Happy 4th of July!" he brightly said.

"Yes, and a happy fourth to you, too!" I answered, walking over.

"Oliver, this is Frank Peabody. Frank's been in this valley from the start," Charlie said, introducing us. Peabody was tall and thin, he had the look of a miner. Dungarees with suspenders, black cotton work shirt, and a long full beard on his face, reminding me of Rip Van Winkle. He smiled and stuck out his hand.

"Good to meet you, son," Frank said with a voice that sounded like two pieces of granite being rubbed against each other.

"Very good to meet you too, sir," I replied and shook his hand. His grip clamped down on my hand like a vise.

"Aw, no need to call me sir, young fella. Call me Frank."

"Okay, Frank," I said, shaking my hand after he let go. "Looks like we'll have a fine day to celebrate after all," I added, looking up at the now ice cream cloud covered sky. Charlie and Frank did the same.

"Yes, indeed it does," Charlie replied. Frank nodded and said, "Them clouds will burn off soon."

"So, Frank, do you work in the mines?" I asked, not really knowing what else to say.

"Oh, I'm done with most of the hard labor," Peabody quickly replied. "I sold most of my claims to the syndicate but I've got one I'm still workin' by contract. Comins handles my blasting now a days so generally I spend most of the time at my house down the street, pay the bills and once in a while spend a little money if'n the thing pays out."

"Sounds like the good life alright," I said.

"Nothin's better than livin' in Monte."

"Well, I best be on my way. Good to meet you!" I said, stepping back out onto the street.

I could see the newspaper office up ahead in all of its log and sap encrusted glory, the door was fixed open and I could see Mr. Bartholomew inside talking to someone. Down the way some kids with packages of Chinese sparklers held tightly in their hands were sitting above the creek with an old grey dog that had red, white and blue bandannas tied around its neck. They watched me walk by while they waited for the merrymaking to begin.

Once I crossed the wagon bridge I stopped and took in the coming festivities. It was an eclectic mix of people; young and old, native and tourist — there was one miner wearing dirty torn trousers, food stained long johns and open boots without laces standing next to a man in a black-as-coal suit coat, silk tie and homburg hat, talking to each other like they were long lost friends. Under the shade of a festival tent a clutch of men were trading mining stories, embellishing away and laughing, slapping their thighs. A woman with a wrinkled bonnet and three children in tattered clothes chatted with a lady wearing a full-length store-bought lace dress that was fanning herself while a grouping of Cornish families talked in heavy accents close by.

On one side of the clearing Eva and Liz and a number of other women were arranging the food on the tables for the meal. Pies, cakes, pitchers of lemonade, heaping bowls of baked beans and corn on the cob, potato salad, crocks of soup, fresh bread and biscuits, and strawberry shortcake. The smell of barbequed ribs, chicken and brisket wafting through the air from the fire pit had combined with the sounds of happy people making me feel right at home. A makeshift speaking platform of pallets and scrap wood had been built off to the side near the baseball diamond.

At the depot I found the telegraph office and was surprised to see it open for business. Ed Baker was sitting at his key machine with a notebook, taking down a message as the *dit, dit, dits* sounded. He was wearing a corduroy suit coat; a hat was on his head with the brim turned up. His desk was covered with piles of paper and there was a cabinet of shelves with bits of paper notes tacked all over it. When the *dits* ended he stood up and came over to the counter.

"Mornin'," he said with a smile. "Need to send a telegram?" When we made eye contact he recognized me from the other day.

"Did I see you at the Cleveland and Kline earlier this week?" he inquired.

"Yes, you did, when the peddler was shot."

"Um, yes, very unfortunate. What's your name again?" he asked.

"Oliver Cohen. I'd like to send a message to my mother in San Francisco."

"Oh, sure, sure. You staying long in Monte?"

"Yes, for a while, I live with my aunt and uncle at the Pride."

"Oh, Jacob and Eva, huh?"

"Yep. My Father was Jacob's brother."

"Well, good to have you here, Oliver. I'm Ed Baker."

He went back to his desk and found a form for me to fill out, then handed it to me with a pencil. It was about the same as the one in Everett with the to and from lines and all. I started to fill it out:

'At Monte Cristo. All okay. Happy 4th. Love you, Oliver.' I gave it back to him and he counted the words.

"Okay, that'll be one dollar," he requested.

"Yes, right," I replied, digging in my trousers for the money.

"Looks like we're in for a big day," I said, handing him eight-bits. "I'm surprised you're opened."

"Oh, I'll be closing real soon. It's gonna be one heck of a smoker!"

"Sure looks like it! See you soon," I said, nodding. I went back out to the level area and glanced around when I heard some voices hollering, it sounded like it was coming from down the tracks. I walked back through the depot and out on the platform only to see a handcar coming up the line with three men on it. Ed Baker came out and stood next to me.

"Well, well, well, looks like the boys from Silverton found out about our little soirée!" he said with a sideways grin on his face. I looked back down the tracks.

Two of them were standing on the handcar, but only one was pumping the handle. The one doing the work wore a black vest with a silver fob, was tall and sweating profusely. The other was a burly heavy-set fellow wearing a red silk vest and white ruffled shirt and the third was sitting down holding on to a cocker spaniel and a red setter. They were all wearing their worn out and dirty best sets of clothes, all with wide brimmed hats.

As they rolled closer the tall one stopped pumping and side-stepped to face us and threw back his head. He let out a, "Whoop," and stood at attention with his eyes focused straight ahead. Then he did a little one-two skip-hop step and clicked his heels while doing an open hand salute.

"To Uncle Sam and the Red, White, and Blue!" he proudly cried, pulling a pumpkin seed shaped flask from his back pocket and taking a swig. He handed it over to the fellow with the silk vest who lifted the bottle to his mouth.

"Sperry! You know better, hand me an empty, why you!" he bellowed and tossed it over his shoulder to the side of the tracks. He raised his fist and shook it at Sperry.

"Damn yer' hide!" Sperry yelled. "That was my favorite flask!" They finally stopped a little farther up at the freight dock. They slowly got off the handcar then Sperry walked up the tracks to retrieve his flask.

"You know them?" I asked Ed.

"Oh, yeah. That was Dick Sperry, Frank Kazenski and Five-Finger Lewie. They're a low-down bunch from Silverton . . . whatever you do, don't get in a card game with Lewie. He'll rob ya' blind. But they'll all drink ya' dry."

"Which one was Lewie?"

"Lewie? He's the one wearing the silk vest, Sperry's the tall one," Ed said. He turned around and headed back to his office. I watched them saunter over to the footbridge and down to lower town. The cocker spaniel and red setter dogs followed right along like they knew exactly where they were going, tails wagging.

A ringing hand bell pierced the air. I walked back through the depot and saw men in suits and top hats standing on the make-shift platform. One was ringing the bell over his head, getting the affair started.

"Good afternoon everyone!" the man hollered. "Can I get your attention? Please everyone gather round so we can get this celebration going!" he said as people stopped what they were doing and slowly walked over nearer the speaker.

"I'm T. J. McBride, the general manager of the railroad, and I'd like to welcome everyone here today to Monte Cristo!" McBride said to applause as people waved streamers and hooted and hollered.

"Today our great nation is one-hundred and twenty years old!" he said to even bigger cheers. Once the crowd settled down he added, "And counting!" Just as he was about to start up again a miner close to town lit a black powder charge and an appropriate Boom!

echoed out over the valley. The crowd cheered even louder. McBride looked up in the direction of the blast and took off his top hat.

"Thank you, to whoever made that fine miners salute!" he shouted.

"Aw, you can thank old Charlie Packer for that one," a man yelled to great laughter.

"Oh, yeah, old Charlie will be boomin' all day long up on Toad Mountain," another miner smoking a pipe hollered.

"Very good, very good," McBride said, raising his hands, and continued. "But now I'd like to introduce the man that has made all of this possible, the man who we all owe a great depth of gratitude to, Mr. Fred Wilmans!" Most of the crowd cheered and clapped their hands as Wilmans stepped to the front as he waved to the crowd while a few miners covered their mouths and made coughing and grumbling noises.

"Thank you, thank you," Wilmans said with his hands up in the air. He was medium height and build, and wore a finely cut grey suit and tie.

"I'd like to take this opportunity to say to all of you here today; happy Fourth of July! Now, before we get started I wanted to thank all the hard-working men and women and families that have helped build this town and these mines, the tramways, and the railroad!" he remarked to cheers. "Even though my brothers and I sold all our claims to the syndicate except the Comet I'm here today to celebrate our nation's birth with the people who I want to celebrate with! You! The great people of Monte Cristo!" he said to thunderous applause. Once the cheers and clapping died down he started up again.

"Seven years ago today, this valley was discovered by the great Joe Pearsall and shortly thereafter he brought Frank Peabody and my brother Mac and myself here to start staking claims. Is Frank here? Where's Frank?" Wilmans asked, scanning the crowd.

"He's right here!" Charlie O'Connell hollered as he pushed Frank Peabody towards the speaker.

"Come on up here Frank," Wilmans said, waving him forward. Peabody shrugged his shoulders and slowly walked up to the platform.

"Everyone fresh in town, this is Frank Peabody. Why I wouldn't be here today if Frank hadn't brought me up here. Yes sir, this man is the living proof of this place you've *all* built! How about if you say a few words?" Wilmans requested, looking at Peabody. Frank nodded and looked out to the crowd, then stepped forward.

"Well, folks," he started, looking a bit flushed in the face with his hands at his side. "I ain't never done much public speaking before, but I will say this. I'm just damn sure glad that Joe Pearsall found this place and let me in on it. I wish Joe was here today to see all this but he's either up in Alaska or in Kellogg workin' his diggings. But I do want to say to everyone here today, I wish you all a happy Independence Day!" Peabody said as he waved to the crowd and stepped off the platform.

"Thank you, Frank," Wilmans said. "Today, thanks to men like Frank Peabody and Joe Pearsall, Monte Cristo is bigger and better than it's ever been! We are now shipping more tonnage of concentrated ore to the smelter than any operation in the Pacific Northwest, and this celebration today is the syndicate's way of saying thank you to *you*! The people of this good town!" Wilmans took off his top hat and raised it to a huge crowd of cheering people.

"Today we've got plenty of food for everyone, all the merchants have done a great job of working with the mining company to help put on this extravaganza and I say thanks to them and all the partners. There's barbequed ribs and brisket, corn on the cob, apple pie and even turtle soup! And the concentrator is shut down for today, so I want all those men that work the concentrator to enjoy their day off, because it's costing the company thousands!" Wilmans said to laughter.

"Later on, there's gonna be a bonfire and fireworks but for now, before we dig in, I wanted to remind everyone that we've got a baseball game starting!" Wilmans remarked with a broad smile as he swept his arm back towards a group of miners standing off to the side.

"It's the miners verses the railroad! Anyone who is not a miner or a railroad worker can play for either team and the winning team gets to boast about it for the year! So, everyone have fun and have a fantastic Fourth of July!" Wilmans finished and stepped down to the crowd to shake hands and socialize.

I went over to the food tables just as two of the fellows from the handcar showed up, Sperry and Kazenski. Doc Welch and some of the town folk recognized them behind me in line.

"It looks like the Silverton contingent made it up today," Doc Welch said.

"That's right by-jiminy," Sperry said, wavering in his stance. "We ain't gonna miss out on any Monte fun, especially when it's offered by the graces of John D. Rockefeller! How ya'll doin' Doc? Are ya' still makin' fiddles and canes and such?"

"Oh, things is good. I'm still building all my creations and runnin' the Penn mine," Doc replied.

"Haven't seen ya' down our way since when, last winter was it?"

"Nope, that would have been last fall, I believe. Back when I traded a fiddle for a little shine from Andy Hawks."

"Ah, yes. Mr. Hawks, a man of fine breeding and enterprise, I'd say," Sperry said stroking his mustache.

"How's he been anyway?" Doc inquired.

"Well, he's okay. Nearly got his-self shot walkin' up to the 45 Mine the other day when he didn't call out."

"Didn't call out? He must be losing some sense, maybe he had a head cold 'er something. But good to hear he's still walking the planet. Old Andy, always liked him," Doc said as he grabbed a plate and started to fill it.

I made my way down the table and piled my plate with fried chicken, baked beans, and apple pie, but I passed on the turtle soup. Down at the end a man was slicing beef brisket — he gave me an ample portion. I went and found a place to sit and watch the baseball game near the depot and eat just when Jim Bartholomew walked by.

Before me was a scene of movement and color: the line-ups for the baseball teams were taking the field as people talked and watched while children ran around. What a fine subject for a painting, or maybe even a watercolor I thought, even though watercolors weren't my strong suit. The railroad team was up to bat first and Martin Comins was on the mound wearing his finest suit of clothes with a black four-in-hand tie, spit shine Sunday boots and a big smile on his face.

"Here's a strikeout waiting to happen!" Martin said to the batter, grinning wide.

"Just pitch the ball Comins, there's no easy out here!" the railroader responded.

Martin wound up and made the pitch. The batter sent the ball flying high towards the creek but a fellow as big as a tree caught the ball in his bare hands and tossed it back. Martin caught the ball on the bounce, and cheered his teammate.

"Way to go Big!" Martin hollered as he pumped his fist. Just when I took another bite of brisket I felt a hand on my shoulder.

"Mind if I join you?" a voice behind me said.

"Sure," I obliged.

"Thanks," Dr. Miles said as he sat down. "You were in the crowd at the shooting last Monday, right? I don't think I got your name."

"Yes, that's right. I'm Oliver Cohen," I answered. "How's the peddler doing?"

"Good to meet you, Oliver. The peddler's good, he should recover. We got him down to Everett and then to Providence in Seattle where he lives. He's got family there."

"That's good to hear," I said and continued eating.

"I guess the posse never found the bastard that shot him," the doctor said, taking a bite of barbequed chicken.

"Yes, my Uncle said the same thing to me later that same night after they got back."

"Well, the county sheriff got a full description of the shooter from Nathan when we got to Everett, so they'll find him. I guess he got away with a thousand dollars worth of merchandise. Watches and rings, even a few diamonds."

"There's all kinds of rumors about who shot him going around," I said.

"Yes, and by the description Nathan gave they're pretty sure it's a fella by the name of Dave LeRoy. You know him?"

"Oh no, no. I don't know anybody. Just got here last week," I answered.

"I didn't think so but thought I'd ask," the doctor said. I finished my meal and stood up, then looked around for where the used plates went.

"Nice talking with you," I related. "I need to go and walk off all this food."

"Okay, happy 4th!"

"Same to you," I said, walking away.

As it happened, my feet turned in the general downriver, lower town direction. Halfway to the depot my mind told me to go pay a visit to my new friends, and see if they had any cold beer. Walking across the trestle I could hear a big cheer rise up from the ball game and guessed that a run had scored. Over on the other side of lower town the hazy particulate of cigar and wood smoke rose up from Fred's and the building next door like a chimney. People were all over on the elevated wooden sidewalk carrying on, dancing to a piano playing a syncopated rhythm and waving hats and bottles in the air. The sound of them and the ball game echoed off the cliffs of the valley and Boom! another black powder blast when off. After an odd quiet pause, everyone in town cheered in unison and the party across the way resumed with vigor.

The Cleveland and Kline was jam-packed with patrons raising glasses, gambling and carousing, it was thick with smoke. Addison and Jacob were behind the bar pouring whiskey and beer as fast as they could manage, the bar covered with coins and spilled liquor. At a poker table Five Finger Lewie was holding court with a smoldering cigar couched in the corner of his mouth. Around his table reigned the noisy merriment of miners free of manners, cursing and making bets. Jim Bartholomew sat at the end of the bar. I made my way over to him and stood against the wall.

"Afternoon," I said. "Busy place."

"Yes, indeed," Bartholomew replied, raising a hand, trying to get Addison's attention.

"Happy 4th," I offered, digging in my pocket and fishing out some change.

"What's it take for a fella to get a drink?" he yelled in the bartender's direction. Addison heard him and raised a hand in acknowledgment, saying, "And a happy 4th to you, too."

"Do we know each other?" Bartholomew asked.

"No, but I was in here the day when the peddler got shot," I answered.

"Oh yes, of course. What'd you say your name was?"

"Oliver Cohen."

"Jim Bartholomew, here," he said and held out his hand. I shook it as Addison came over with a bottle. The fellow sitting next to Bartholomew got up and left so I sat down at the vacant stool.

"Here ya' go, Big Jim," Addison said, filling his shot glass. Bartholomew grinned, reached into a vest pocket and placed a quarter on the counter. Addison looked at me and drew a blank at first then smiled.

"Howdy . . . Oliver, right?" he asked. "What'll it be?"

"Got any cold beer?"

"Yep, I do if you've got a dime." I quickly slapped a ten-cent piece on the bar. He stepped over to an extra-large open stainless steel bowl full of beer that was inside of a larger barrel full of ice and dipped a glass mug into it. Addison carried over the mug and set it down on the bar.

"We only have ice cold beer once a year during summer, so today's your lucky day. Paint any pictures yet?" he asked, sweeping the dime off the bar and into his hand as he started to walk away.

"Yes, sold one the other day!" I said happily. He stopped and turned around.

"Good for you . . . maybe, um —"

"Maybe what?"

"Maybe you might want to hang some here on the walls, we could sell them for you," he offered, grinning. *I liked the sound of that.*

"Sure."

"Okay, come by again in a couple of days," he said and went back to tending his customers.

The taste of the cold lager was a joy. Cold, clean, and refreshing — beer had never tasted so good. I lifted the glass to my mouth again, I enjoyed the drink and the thought of selling my work made me smile. Setting the mug down on the bar I looked over to Mr. Bartholomew, he was grinning.

"How'd that taste?" he asked. "Good I bet. Sounds like you're an artist?" When all of a sudden, a commotion rose up in the room.

"Duke!" hollered most of the patrons with glee, when another added, "It's the Duke of Monte Cristo! Make way!"

I turned and there was Martin Comins standing at the door huffing and puffing, clearly winded from running down the trestle. His suit coat and tie were gone and the tails of his shirt were hanging out. Chairs legs moaned and screeched as they scraped the floor as many a man quickly stood to greet him and shake his hand. Others smiled and gave him a wave or a sign to acknowledge his presence. He started towards the bar.

"How in the name of Jaysus is everyone on this fine holiday?!" Martin hollered. The room boomed with laughter and applause.

"Better than yesterday!" one man said, raising and downing his drink.

"Best day all year!" another answered.

"Quick and pour me some rye!" Martin cracked. "We're halfway through the game and I need me a wee dram!" Instantly the whole bar erupted in laughter.

"Who's ahead?" one patron asked.

"Big Nelson just hit one across Glacier Creek to tie it up, but the miners will win it!" Martin replied as he turned to the bartender. Addison handed him a jigger of whiskey. He turned back to the room and held the small glass high above his head. The bar went silent as he thought for a moment, then Martin let loose with a thick Irish accent:

"Here's to those who wish us well, and as to the rest of the blarney, and that railroad team, they can all go to hell!" The room boomed with cheers as he downed his drink.

"Give us another!" a voice cried out. Martin looked out over the room, then gazed up at the rafters and paused.

"Okay, here's one, by Richard Roesiger, my neighbor down at the lake. Are ya' ready?!" Martin hollered. Addison quickly filled his shot glass then Martin raised it high.

"Here's to yee as good as ya' are – and here's to me as bad as I am. But as good as ya' are and as bad as I am – I am as good as ya' are as bad as I am!" He downed his drink as the room howled with laughter once again. I noticed that Martin had a certain kind of rhythm and poetry in his speech and that his eyes shined like polished glass when he spoke in the presence of friends.

The Duke wiped his mouth with his forearm, slammed the glass on the bar upside down, and marched out the door while everyone close enough to him patted him on his back on the way out.

I went back to my beer, holding the cold glass felt good and everything seemed right. I felt right at home in this mining camp and life was good. I took another sip and turned to Bartholomew.

"So, why do they call him the Duke?" Bartholomew raised his glass to get Addison's attention. Once he saw him Bartholomew set the empty jigger on the bar and turned to me.

"Martin, you mean?"

"Yes, everyone called him the Duke when he came in."

"Well, you've heard of the book, *The Count of Monte Cristo*, right."

"Oh, yeah, sure."

"So Martin, he's our Duke of Monte Cristo."

"That's a great name. Have you read the book?"

"By all means, I've read the finest adventure novel of all time. You?"

"Haven't. But still, why do they call him that?" I asked again. Bartholomew looked up at the ceiling and thought for a moment.

"Because he's a finer man than any man in this camp, I'll tell ya' that right now . . . and, he was a Catholic Priest in Ireland for Christ sakes, even though he doesn't always talk or act like one sometimes. And for another, he's educated, and funny, and I'll tell ya' this; he'll save yer' bacon any time of the day or any day of the week. Why once he saved a dying man who got stuck in an ore chute and another he dug out of the freezing snow on the side of Cadet Peak after an avalanche — *That's* why we call him The Duke."

"Saved lives? Sounds like he's a fine fellow."

"The finest there is," Bartholomew said as Addison poured his drink.

"Thank you, sir," he said to the bartender.

"Yer' welcome. That's your second on a quarter, so that'll be a dime," he said setting the bottle down. Just as she did the room boomed again.

"Duke!" exploded from everyone's lips. And there was Martin standing with Big, the outfielder at the door, their arms around each other's shoulders, each with smiles as wide as the Sauk River.

"Big Nelson hit another homer across the creek and we lost the ball this time in the boulders, so the miners won 2 to 1!" Martin hollered out over the room. "The syndicate was too cheap to buy more than one ball so it's over!" Everybody leapt to their feet cheering and Jim Bartholomew immediately stood up, waving his hands over his head.

"The Mountaineer is buying a round!" he hollered and slapped a handful of silver dollars on the bar as the place thundered even louder than before. The patrons parted and Martin and Big strolled up to the bar arm in arm, both smiling broadly. Addison set two shot glasses on the counter and filled them. Martin and Big lifted their drinks to the crowd.

"I'd like to make a toast to the losing team, they being admirable ball players and all don't ya' know!" Martin said with a grin. "So here goes," he said, raising his glass higher.

"Those railroaders can't win them all, not when Big hits the ball, so they should stick to the rails, and try to stay out of jail, since none of them can catch or run either!" They downed their drinks as the crowd bellowed and stomped their feet against the floor. The rafters shook and my ears started to ring it was so loud in the place.

"Tell us another Duke!" someone yelled above the din. Martin set his glass on the bar and Addison automatically filled it. Big did the same and Martin raised his glass again.

"Okay, alright, alright," Martin said and thought for a few seconds, "a time honored traditional it'll be." He grinned and started.

"On the chest of a barmaid in Sale, were tattooed the prices of ale, and on her behind, for the sake of the blind, was the same information in braille!" he crowed. The place boomed with laughter, like a cannon had just gone off and I laughed so hard I nearly peed my pants.

"Again!" another patron yelled. But Martin shook his head.

"No, no. That's enough for now boys. Me belly is empty and I need to get back up and in the food line before dinner's all gone. But we'll be back!" he said as he raised an eyebrow and headed for the door with Big Nelson while a few others followed.

Hours later, as dusk turned to darkness, I sat up at the inn with Jacob and Eva and watched the fireworks light up the town below. Streams of bright, multi-colored hues in life-affirming colors arched and cascaded earth bound as they crackled and banged and whistled. Slow burning stars floated down leaving trails of sparks behind them as more fireworks rocketed up into the sky over and over again, only to explode in circular forms in delightful tints of colorful parabolic arrows. As I watched I burned the images of the afternoon events and the night sky lighting tones into my brain so I could revisit them later when I had my palette filled with paint and a fresh canvas before me. The day was complete, and my quest of self-discovery continued in Monte Cristo.

IX

EN PLEIN AIR

The smell of fresh coffee and biscuits had drifted into my room, waking me to a new day. Laying on my cot I rolled over and gazed at the ceiling, rubbing my eyes, the thought of trying to sell my work and making a little money entered my mind. I grinned and rolled off the bed, slipped my trousers on over my long johns and walked out into the kitchen.

"Mornin'" I said, scratching my head.

"Ah yes, top of the morning — or should I say late morning, to you, Oliver," Liz replied, reaching for a mug from the cupboard and setting it on the counter.

"Oh, a," I responded, "What time is it?"

"Just past 7:00," she said. "Since its Sunday you didn't have the concentrator to wake you up."

"That's nice for a change, two days in a row," I said.

"That was quite the celebration yesterday, huh?" Liz offered.

"Plenty of drinking going on, and those booms in the hills sure added to it."

"A little too many of them for me," she observed.

"You ladies sure did a great job on all the food."

"Well, thank you, that's nice of you to say," Liz said with a smile. "One woman from Everett said that my potato salad was the best she'd ever had. Did you like it?" Liz asked as she pulled two tins of hot biscuits out of the oven.

"Oh, was your potato salad the one with the celery and red peppers?"

"It was."

"Then yes! It was much better than the others."

Liz set the biscuits down on the stove next to a kettle of gravy with sausage in it. I poured myself a steaming cup of coffee and sat down at the built-in.

"Where is everyone?" I asked, taking a sip.

"Jacob and Eva will be down shortly, but the guests will be up soon and I've got to get ready for all of them. What are you going to do today?" Liz asked, cracking an egg over a bowl. She mixed the yolk and whites with a metal whisk into a froth then poured the mixture onto a hot griddle. I could hear it sputter and pop, she sprinkled some salt and pepper over it.

"Well," I said, taking another sip. "I thought I'd go for a hike, maybe paint some landscapes."

"Ah, en plein air," she said with a clumsy French accent. I turned my head around with surprise.

"You know about painting outdoors? In natural light?"

"Oh, yes," Liz quickly replied but then admitted. "Well, I've read about it. You?"

"All the greats like Monet, Renoir and Degas painted outdoors. I studied it."

"You did? Where?" Liz asked, her interest piqued, as she stirred the frying eggs with a metal spatula.

"At the art association back home."

"Art association, is that a school?"

"Oh yes, first class. I graduated with an art education degree last spring and could teach art if I wanted to, but all I want to do is paint."

"You're certainly good at it," she said and turned her head towards the painting on the kitchen wall. "Sometimes I stop and just stare at it."

"Thanks, I haven't done anything for a few days. I feel like a failure if I don't paint every day," I said.

"Well, you've got a good day of sunshine for it," Liz remarked just as Jacob and Eva came in to the kitchen.

"Good morning everyone," Eva said brightly. "The guests should be up soon. I'll get the table set."

"How's Liz today?" Jacob asked, then added, "And how are you doing Oliver?"

"Me? I'm fine," I answered. "This town sure knows how to put on a party."

"Yep, we sure do," Jacob said, pouring himself a cup of coffee.

"That was the best one yet," Eva added, pulling dishes down from a cupboard.

"What do you have planned for the day?" Jacob asked, sitting down next to me.

"Well, since I've got a good jump on the wood pile I thought I'd go for a hike and take my box easel along. Paint some of the mountain peaks," I said. Jacob took a sip of hot coffee.

"Sure, since the weather's good you should do that."

"Thanks, the light should be perfect today. I thought I'd go up in the mountains somewhere," I said, pleased to know that Jacob was okay with me taking another day off.

"You should head up Glacier Basin, there's some craggy peaks with some meadows and wild flowers along the way. Seen 'em with my own two eyes. Ain't that right Eva?"

"Oh yes, it's beautiful," Eva added, coming back in the kitchen from the dining room.

"Glacier Basin it is." Liz set a plate of scrambled eggs with a biscuit covered in gravy in front of me. "How do I get there?"

"Just head up from the top of Dumas and take a left where the path splits or you'll end up at the Justice Mine, then follow the main trail. Plus, there's the tram towers to follow if you lose the way. You'll figure it out," Jacob replied.

The sound of multiple sets of feet coming down the stairs sounded out through the inn as a family of hungry guests clambered through the living room and into the dining room signaling Liz, and Jacob and Eva to work. Jacob picked up the coffee pot and walked out to the big table as Liz carried two platters of eggs and biscuits while Eva followed holding a porcelain tureen of gravy with ladle. Wanting to get an early start I wolfed down the rest of my meal and headed back to my room to prepare.

Opening the trunk, I found my field box and opened it. Inside was everything I'd need: tubes of paint, brushes, small square frames of mounted canvas and the matching square palette. Double checking that I had all the necessary supplies I put on my boots and looked to the kitchen before heading out the back door. I saw some extra biscuits on a plate on the stove keeping warm, Liz and Eva were busy with the guests in the dining room so I quickly grabbed two, shoved them in a trouser pocket and walked out the back door, carrying the box by its worn leather attaché-like strap.

All was quiet outside, I looked up and down the street and then up the hill, no one was about. I set out and followed the extra wide trail that I'd seen all the miners using, then it narrowed to a trail that went past rotting stumps, slash and brush which eventually changed to a healthy forest of hemlock and fir. Across the valley was a steep, timbered ridge line that ran up to jagged, snowy peaks.

Heading up the trail more tram towers came into view. The cables strung between each tower held motionless ore buckets, stopped by the power of Sunday. Two lines of towers ran alongside each other, the downed trees that were once in their path had been left where they fell by the construction crew and were now on the ground decomposing. Broken tree limbs and slash were scattered all around, then the pitch got a little steeper.

As I hiked along, across the valley was a mine with rocks strewn all about below it, a couple of rough built structures were close by. A man came out of a hand-hewn cabin and tossed a pail full of kitchen scraps on a pile of garbage. I kept hiking and came upon a rocky area of large and small boulders, when a dozen high pitched calls filled the air. A family of those same small brown and black furry creatures were running around and standing on the rocks barking at me. I watched them for a little bit and then dug out one of the biscuits. I tore off a small piece and pitched it at them. They instantly dove down into the rocks after it.

Up ahead I heard the sound of rushing white water cascading over rocks. I stopped and saw a smaller trail that turned back to the right and figured it was the one for the Justice. In every direction the views were stunning, but I wanted to be up on the top of a ridge, somewhere that I could paint multiple views from different angles with more color and mountain-top scenery, something really spectacular.

The trail got closer to the falls then it began to turn to the right, around the base of the hill that was covered in yellow and purple wildflowers. Coming around the bend I saw a tram loading station up above me, a small trail snaked off and upward towards it. Then I saw a good-sized log and frame structure with a cedar shake roof and a single chimney, smoke curling out of it. It rested on the side of a slope and had a foundation built out of rocks making it look like it grew right up out of the ground. There was a miner sitting on some boulders out in front of it. I split off from the main trail and walked up and over to him. As I got closer I recognized the man, it was Martin Comins.

"Good Morning," I said, raising a hand. He was leaning back with a cup of coffee in his hand. When he heard my voice he looked up quickly, I think I startled him.

"Yes, lad. Good morning," he replied and smiled. "Out for a hike on this fine morning are ya'?" He was wearing the same clothes as the day before, albeit more wrinkled, dirty and worn. I could see he was sweating a little and his dark red hair was matted and oily, stuck to his forehead in damp bunches.

"I am, good day to be out in the hills," I said. "Do you live here?"

"No, no, I've got a little cabin downriver from town, but I decided to come up here last night to continue the celebration." He looked a little tired as he sipped his coffee when he started coughing. It got worse and he began hacking. A minute later he stopped and turned to the side and spit out some red-looking sputum.

"You all right?" I asked, taking a half step towards him. He raised up a hand.

"I'll be fine, lad. Just a wee bit of the illness this morning." Martin glanced at my box easel.

"I've never seen a lunchbox like that before," he remarked, nodding at my field box. His eyes were red and he looked paler than yesterday.

"Oh this," I said, looking down at it. "It's my painting kit." Martin tilted his head and grinned, then took another sip.

"Ah, a painter?"

"I do landscapes," I replied with a nod. "I thought I'd climb up higher and find a place to paint these peaks."

"Well, lad, yee have come across the best landscapes in the world," he said. "The glaciers and wild flowers farther up the path will dazzle the mind and eye. Have ya' a name, son?" he asked.

"Oliver Cohen."

"Cohen, is it? Would ya' be relations of Jacob and Eva at the Pride, then?"

"Yes, sir."

"A fine people they are. I'm Martin Comins."

"Good to meet you, too," I said, and took a full step forward and stuck out my hand. He looked up at me, adjusted his spectacles, and shook my hand while still sitting down.

"How about a bit of breakfast? Chubb should have things ready inside," he offered. I looked over his shoulder at the low-slung cookhouse then back at him.

"Thank you, but we just had a big breakfast at the inn. I'm still stuffed," I said.

"Ah, yes. Liz Sheedy is a fine cook," he said, standing up slowly like his legs were stiff.

"Oh, you know Liz?"

"Yes, indeed, lad, everyone knows everyone in Monte. But please excuse me now, me bellies rumblin' and me cup is empty.

Maybe I'll see ya' on the way down," he said as he turned around and headed over to the bunkhouse.

"Good to meet you," I said to his back. He raised a hand, opened the door and went inside.

Turning around I looked out over the basin. It was ringed by sharp granite peaks with snow still clinging to them in places. The debris of broken granite rock slides piled up and fanned out at the bases of ridgelines and trees were now at a minimum. Higher up a half dozen adult mountain goats with two little ones were clambering up a steep slope. I watched with amazement as they jumped from rock to rock and walked up the side of a steep granite face, then I started out again.

Just above the creek the defined trail began to disappear. I stopped and looked around for a way to go. I decided to go up a short slope and came upon a snowfield where the creek began, the water streaming out from the bottom of it. I stopped and took in the sights. Turning around the miracle of nature surrounded me; lofty mountain peaks, some with massive white glaciers topping them off, rock fields of giant boulders, and the air was so incredibly fresh, almost sweet. Across the divide it looked like I was staring at the back side of the same bear's tooth mountain that loomed over town. But I wanted to be higher. Scanning the slopes, I saw a lower spot on the ridge above me. It looked like the closest and easiest route that would take me to the top so I headed that way.

For what seemed like an hour or more I climbed higher and higher, over acres of rock fields and around outcroppings. At one point I stopped and looped my belt through the leather handle on my box easel so it was hanging behind me, giving me two hands to grab onto stunted trees and cracks in rock faces to pull myself up and over. I'd get through one difficult area only to find another series of tightly placed boulders, or more slopes of rocks. The final pitch was steep and short but not otherwise difficult. Somehow, I found the top of a ridge that looked out over a glacier. Winded, I walked out onto it. The surface of the snow was soft but it had solid footing underneath.

Below me was a 350-degree cirque of two basins ringed by jagged peaks with a tall mountain between them. As I stood in awe of the vistas before me I gathered that the two creeks down in town were the ones that streamed through both bowls that were before me now, which came together to form the river that flowed through the narrow notch of lower town. Every bit of snow, rain and glacial runoff from the two enormous basins before me had nowhere else to go but down through town. I tried to imagine how many feet of snow must pile up here in these two gulches and on these mountain tops during winter, all of it melting in the spring, running down and under the trestle bridge.

Turning around, jagged peaks and mountains went as far as I could see. I felt like I was the only person in the world. For minutes I burned the image of unlimited mountain tops in my mind and told myself to embrace and remember them for the rest of my artistic existence.

Satisfied that I had found what I'd been searching for I went back over to the edge of the glacier, sat down next to two flat boulders in the sunshine, and opened the field box on my lap. First, I took out the square palette and set it aside. Then I set a framed canvas in the upper inside half of the box and placed a series of paint tubes on the boulder next to me. Picking up a tube of white I squeezed out a small portion of it at the top corner of the palette, and beside it a dab of black, then green, red, and yellow. Finding a thin sable-hair brush I mixed some black and white at the bottom corner of the palate and made a start.

After many hours and three paintings later, the light was becoming difficult and my stomach was rumbling. A breeze picked up and blew a tube of paint off the boulder next to me. Reaching down to pick it up I remembered the biscuits in my pocket. Taking a bite, I looked to the west, then pulled out my pocket watch. It was past five o'clock. I closely inspected the three finished paintings, each of different views. The one that I liked the best was with the glacier in the foreground and the basin showing Mystery Hill and a mountain peak.

Gathering up the assortment of used brushes I set them on the rock beside me, found the small bottle of solvent and rag in the field box and got the brushes as clean as I could. I placed the paint stained palette against another in the box. While I waited to make sure the three works were dry I finished the biscuits and enjoyed the views. Then I headed back the way I came.

X

MATTIE

Over the course of the following weeks I fell into a pattern of cutting wood during the morning hours then heading up into the hills to paint in the afternoon. I added back straps to my field box so I could climb more easily and each time up I'd take a different route to find new locations to work from. Or, if the train was due to arrive I'd carry my easel and supplies down to the depot and do portraits of tourists for some spending money.

Often times, during the evenings after supper, I'd reproduce the small field easel paintings I'd done out in the hills onto large canvases. I hung as many kerosene lamps as I could in my room and even used an old mirror to help reflect the light on my work. In what seemed like no time I'd amassed a nice collection of landscapes and had begun to fill a jar with paper and silver dollars and lots coins from depot sales. One cloudy afternoon I decided to take a couple of the smaller paintings down to the Cleveland and Kline saloon.

Once there, I hesitated at the door, poked my head inside and glanced around — since it was a week day there were a couple solitary old timers nursing whiskeys, positioned as far away from each other as they could manage. I slowly and quietly walked in carrying my paintings in the field box. I recognized Jim Bartholomew and Ed Baker at the bar with coffee cups in front of them, Addison was pouring a shot of whiskey for a man at the far end. When he was done Bartholomew tapped the rim of his coffee cup and coughed. Mr. Cleveland looked up, saw his signal and walked over.

"How 'bout a touch of the Irish for my coffee?" he said, reaching into his vest pocket and setting a quarter on the counter.

"My pleasure," Addison said, but then noticed me.

"Oliver, how are ya'?"

"I'm good, and you?"

"Never better," he answered. He saw the field box. "What-cha got there?"

"Well, I thought I'd bring some of my smaller paintings by for you to see. Maybe take you up on your offer to sell them."

"Okay, let's take a look and see what you've got," he said and walked around the bar. "How about if we go outside where the light is better," he suggested, "and where we can talk."

"I did them up in Glacier Basin," I said, turning and heading for the door.

"I ain't leaving," Addison said over his shoulder to his patrons, "Just yell if anyone needs something."

Right outside the door I turned to face him, opened the field box and showed him the first one, a landscape of mountain peaks and glaciers. "Good," he said, nodding appreciatively. I placed it behind the next one and his eyes opened wider at the sight of a mine bunkhouse and tunnel entrance.

"Oh, I like that better," he said, smiling. Then I showed him the third, of a mountain meadow with wild flowers, jagged peaks and a stream.

"These are good! I had no idea you were so talented."

"So, you like them?"

"Oh, yeah!" he exclaimed. "If you do more like the mine building and tunnel they'd sell all day long, the tourists would buy those."

"Really? You think so?"

"Absolutely," he insisted. "Jacob needs to see these. Let's go back in and sit down, I'll get him."

"Okay," I said, following him inside and putting the field box on a table near the door. I took the paintings out, set them on the table and sat down. A few moments later he emerged from the back room with Jacob.

"Oliver, how are you?" he said pulling up a chair. Addison did the same.

"I'm well. You?" I replied.

"Very good. Thanks," Jacob replied, seeing the paintings. "You did these?"

"Yep. I did."

"I think we can sell them," Addison suggested.

"How much do you usually sell them for?" Jacob asked. He looked at each one as I considered his question for a moment.

"Hm, well," I said, "how about two dollars for each? And three for five dollars?" Jacob and Addison looked at each other.

"Two dollars to you? For each one?" Jacob said, starting the negotiations. I nodded my head up and down.

"Okay," Addison said. But Jacob raised his hand.

"Hold on," Jacob countered, "how about if we sell each one for three dollars, since you'd be showing them here in our building but we'd be doing the work to sell them. And we'd keep one dollar and you get your two? How's that sound?"

"Sounds good to me," I quickly agreed.

"And, I'll have to build some shelving to display them on," he added. I nodded my head again.

"But we'll just leave it at that price, three dollars each with no multiple discounts. How's that?" Jacob said and stuck out his hand. I quickly shook it.

"Fantastic, we've got a deal," I said, smiling. Jacob grinned, got up and walked to the back-storage room.

"Great," Addison added, then quickly said, "But I think we should have them behind the bar, so as they don't get stolen."

Jacob returned with a piece of blank paper, a dip pen and a glass inkwell. Across the top of the page he wrote in big black letters 'Contract to Consign and Sell.'

"It's always good to have a written agreement," Jacob said, not looking up.

"We like to put pen to paper for stuff like this," Addison said, assuredly.

"Fine with me. It's probably a good thing," I said as Jacob finished writing. He turned the paper around for me to go over. It was simply and quickly written; items, price, names, and lines for signature. We all signed it.

"Okay! How 'bout a drink to celebrate?" Jacob suggested, offering his hand.

"Great idea," I said, shaking it. Addison went over to the bar and got some shot glasses, a bottle and came back, setting a glass in front of each of us. It made me a bit jittery at first, then he poured the whiskey. I stared at the brown liquid while they raised their glasses.

"A toast," Jacob said. "To Oliver's paintings and some quick sales!"

"Yes," I said, quickly latching onto the tiny glass and downing it.

"Good for us," Addison said. "But now it's back to business," he said and we all got up. Jacob grabbed the contract and the paintings, his fingers touching the painted surface, and went behind the bar while Addison picked up the pen and ink. He moved some bottles on a shelf to make room and propped the paintings on it. I noticed how Jacob handled them and spoke up.

"Um, when you carry these small paintings its best if you only touch them on the edges with your hands flat. It's not good to touch the surface," I cautioned.

"Oh, okay. Sorry," Jacob said. He reached up and held one the right way. "You mean like this," he said, turning around and showing me.

"Yep, that's good. Thank you," I replied. Jacob set the painting back on the shelf then held up the contract.

"We'll put this agreement and any sales money in the safe in the back room," he stated.

"That's a good idea," I said to him with an approving nod. "I'll be on my way, nice doing business with you. See you later," I said and headed for the door with my field box.

"Okay, see you soon." I heard them both say.

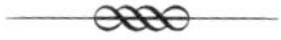

I got set up near the depot and the angle of the sun was perfect. I could see on the downward ridge of the bear's tooth mountain, the pinnacle of rock that stood out like an enormous thumb and the tramway that came across the face of the mountain down to the bunker at the concentrator. It was an exceptional backdrop for a painting. I got started.

Mixing black and white to get the right color of granite, I did the basic outline then blended green with some white to soften its boldness for the trees. The towers I did in with a combination of brown and white. I was about to start on the cables when I felt someone come up from behind.

"Nice work," a voice said. I turned around, it was Ed Baker, the telegraph man.

"Thanks," I replied.

"You're doing Wilmans Peak?" he asked.

"So that's what it's called."

"Yep, since the day Mac Wilmans named it."

"And what about that big piece of straight up rock?"

"Oh, yes, that's the Old Man of the Mountain, he's been up there watching over us for a long, long time. And if you look close enough you can see the ore bunker for the Comet Mine, right there on that tiny, little ledge," he said, pointing. I got up and stood behind him.

"Would ya' look at that," I said. "I can see it!"

"I need to get back to my key machine. Nice work," he said and left.

"Thanks, Ed," I answered and returned to painting. A few minutes later I could hear in the distance the faint sound of steel wheels and rumbling. The train had entered the valley and as it got closer the whistle sounded — town-folk and children started showing up in anticipation.

As the train rolled across the river trestle the air brakes went off and the bell began to clang. People started clapping and cheering, welcoming the locomotive and its passengers. I turned in my chair to watch as Conductor Speer stepped from the front car and onto the landing, helping each passenger disembark. Henry and his supply wagon came rolling up just as a young woman stepped from the car by herself.

She gazed towards Dumas Street then looked up at the craggy peaks that surrounded town. Opening a parasol, she swung it up over her head and glanced around. The young lady wore a full-length blue dress with white pin stripes and lace up brown leather shoes. She was a stunning picture and had the look of an ingénue; blonde hair swept up in a bun under a powder blue felt hat, cheeks sporting a rosy glow. An older couple that I'd seen before but had never met walked up to her. I was close enough to hear them talking.

"Miss de Graaf? Is that you?" the older woman said, walking over to her.

"Yes, are you Mrs. Chapman?"

"I am, and this is my husband Mr. Hiram Chapman," she said and continued. "We are so excited to have you! Thank goodness we've got another week to set up for the school year," Mrs. Chapman said, then added, "and the children are so happy about you coming to Monte!"

Behind me the train was backed up on the main line then driven forward onto one of three tracks in the switching yard, where a railroad crew uncoupled the locomotive and tender from the cars. Next the locomotive was driven forward and then backed up and switched to the track that was connected to the turntable while a railroad boss barked orders at workers. The engineer ran the locomotive and tender onto the turntable where the crew had him stop right at the center balance point, the crew began to physically push it around by hand on the turntable. Once turned around the engineer drove it off the turntable past the cars then backed it up and recoupled the locomotive and tender to the cars. The whole train was maneuvered forward off the spur and finally backed up into position next to the depot on the main track again, ready for the return trip hours later.

Just then a man and woman came up to admire the painting. They were well dressed, obviously tourists.

"Very nice, young man," the lady said. Her husband took a closer look holding his pince-nez up with the lanyard attached to them.

"Yes, indeed. Very nice. Do you have a gallery in town?" he asked. I was flattered to hear a comment like that and thought how to answer.

"Not yet," I said, smiling.

"But are you selling?"

"I will be, when it's done."

"I'm interested and I'll take it right now. How much?"

"These larger ones are five dollars," I replied. He put his hand to his mouth and coughed.

"A-hum. Five dollars you say," the man said, raising his eyebrows. His wife leaned over to him and quietly said in his ear, "That's far too much, Abraham."

"I have some smaller ones over at the Cleveland and Kline for three," I quickly said, trying my best smile.

"Oh, I see. And where would that be? The Cleveland and what'd you call it?"

"The Cleveland and Kline is over across the trestle," I answered, pointing. He looked in the direction but the depot was in the way.

"It's a saloon, a nice tavern I mean, over by the tracks," I offered.

"Very good then, thank you. By the way, could you tell me where the Monte Cristo Hotel is?"

"Yes, it's," I said, glancing over my shoulder to lower town and then looking and pointing at upper town, "just across the wagon bridge and up Dumas Street. Very easy to find."

"Thank you young man," the fellow said and they walked away. I glanced around, looking for the young woman. The Chapmans and her had already left, I saw them walking across the wagon bridge with Henry and his wagon loaded with a trunk following them. Most of the passengers had gotten their baggage and drifted off in different directions but a few people were still mingling around the depot. I went back to work on the painting and soon finished.

The light had begun to change so I gathered up my tubes of paint, brushes and easel and headed up to the inn. Walking past the mercantile store I looked inside and saw that it was busy with customers. I thought about going inside for a piece of hard candy but decided against it and kept going until I got home. I walked into the kitchen, Liz was at the sink doing dishes.

"Hey Liz," I said as I went by her. She noticed the painting and my gear.

"How'd it go today?" she inquired, rubbing her nose with a forearm.

"Not many tourists and business was slow. I did finish this one of Wilmans Peak though," I replied, headed to my room to store everything away. "Where is everybody?"

"I'm out here," Eva's voice sounded from the laundry room. "Jacob's down at the newspaper office. What're you doing?"

"Not much, just gonna go sit on the porch and then maybe cut some wood," I said as I closed the trunk and set the fresh painting on the easel. Walking through the kitchen I grabbed a cinnamon roll and continued out to the front porch and sat down in Jacob's rocking chair. The drone of the concentrator sounded in the background and a few Steller's jay birds cawed and landed in the road when I saw the Chapmans again. They came out of the schoolhouse just up the street with the young woman and started walking in my direction. Mr. Chapman had what looked like a sack of groceries in his arm and the young lady was carrying a small cloth overland suitcase. Eva came out on the porch.

"Good afternoon," Mr. Chapman said as they approached.

"Yes, hello Hiram," Eva replied. She walked out into the road to talk to them. I got up and followed her. "How are you folks doing?"

"Eva, hello. We're good, thank you," Hiram said.

"Meet my nephew, Oliver. He's here staying with us," Eva said.

Hiram Chapman held out his hand. I shook it, saying, "Pleased to meet you, sir."

"Yes, hello, Oliver, and pleased to meet you, too. This is my wife, Jean Chapman, and the new schoolmarm, Miss Mattie de Graaf." I nodded a greeting to the two women.

"Nice to meet you," I said to Miss de Graaf, her eyes were like sparkling blue diamonds and her high cheekbones flush with rouge. Not looking directly at me she nodded a hello but when her eyes shifted and met mine, the corners of her mouth curled upward.

"Yes," she said. "Nice to meet you," her voice rising. I smiled my best smile.

"We were just down the street showing Miss de Graaf the schoolhouse," Hiram said.

"Yes, it could use some cleaning," Miss de Graaf added, turning her attention to Mrs. Chapman.

"Maybe we could attend to that tomorrow," Mrs. Chapman suggested.

"How many students will you have this year?" Eva asked.

"As of yesterday, we've got almost thirty students registered," Hiram replied. Then he turned and looked towards Dumas Street. "Good to meet you," he said and they started to walk away.

Once they were out of hearing range Eva leaned over to me and whispered, "You need to mind your manners with her, mister."

"I know how to mind my manners," I said, walking back over to the porch.

"I saw the way you looked at her," she said, following me.

"Yes, and?" I replied, sitting down.

"And, this isn't Paris, buster. You need to watch your Ps and Qs," she added, walking back inside.

The next morning, I could hear the wind and rain when I woke up, a storm had swept in overnight. I rolled over on my back, knowing in all probability that I'd not be doing any painting outdoors. I didn't mind too much, the late summer rain was needed to quench all the dried-out plant life in the surrounding hills I'd seen on my hikes, plus I needed to build more canvas frames.

The sound of Liz opening and closing the oven door and the smell of bacon frying enticed me into rolling out of bed. Pulling on my trousers I walked out into the kitchen and yawned as I stretched my arms out to the side.

"There's Oliver," Liz said, standing over the cook stove flipping pancakes.

"Hey Liz, how are you today?"

"Good," she replied. "Looks like a rainy day."

"Yep. Think I'll take it easy today, maybe do some canvas or go down to lower town and check in with Jacob and Addison."

"You mean at the Cleveland and Kline?"

"They've got a few of my paintings for sale, thought I'd see if any have sold."

"You've got some of your art for sale?!" she exclaimed. "Good for you!"

"Yep. Gotta start sometime."

"Well, I think that's great."

"What's great?" Jacob asked, walking through the kitchen door. He set an opened copy of a newspaper on the built-in table in front of me and tapped his index finger on an article that was circled in pencil.

"Oliver's got some of his paintings down at the Cleveland and Kline for sale," Liz remarked.

"No kidding! That *is* great!" Jacob said. "For how much?"

"Three bucks each. For the small ones, that is," I answered, pulling the newspaper closer and looking at the article.

"Well those should sell. We should be selling them too," Jacob suggested.

"Selling what?" Eva asked, floating into the room with a brown house dress on. She stopped on her way down the hall to the laundry.

"Oliver's paintings," Jacob said. "He's got them for sale down in lower town. So we should be selling them too, for him."

"Fine by me," Eva said, turning and walking away. Jacob looked at Oliver.

"Are they charging you a commission?"

"We did a consignment agreement. They're selling each one for three dollars, I get two and they get one," I replied, trying to read the newspaper.

"And you're happy with that?"

"Oh, absolutely," I said, looking up from the paper. "I sold one to a tourist for two and besides, I hear the miners do hard labor all day long for three dollars, so if I can get two dollars for one of my small ones, each of which only take me an hour or two, then yes. Very happy here."

"But you have some expenses, though."

"That's true, but still. It's good, I'm happy with the arrangement. Did you read this about the guy that shot the peddler? Says it was Dave LeRoy," I said.

"I did, sounds like the sheriff finally got him." Jacob said, rubbing his chin. "I'll tell ya' what though, I won't charge you a thing and you can sell 'em for three dollars each here at the inn. That way you won't be undercutting them, if they ever find out." I looked at him and smiled.

"Great! Thanks Uncle Jacob," I said. "But, so, where did you get this paper?"

"A guest brought it up on the train and showed it to me, then left it. It's the *Arlington Times*," Jacob answered.

"It says here the sheriff and his posse went after LeRoy and caught up with him at a place called Wilson Creek, and they had a shoot-out."

"I saw that," Jacob replied.

"A shoot-out?!" Liz interrupted, her voice peaking, turning around from the stove.

"Yep," Jacob answered. "He shot at the posse, then they shot back and got him."

"Oh my lands! Well, serves him right," Liz said.

"Where's Wilson Creek?" I asked.

"The fellow that brought the paper up said it's in the Pilchuck drainage, somewhere near Ashland Lakes," Jacob answered. I looked back at the article.

"They cornered him in some boulders and killed him," I said, reading the text out loud.

"He should have raised his hands and given up," Jacob surmised.

"Yep, I guess there just wasn't any quit in him," I replied. "Did anyone else see this?"

"I took it down to Bartholomew to show him, plus I took it to the mercantile and showed it to anyone that was interested," Jacob answered.

I finished the newspaper story and shook my head.

After breakfast I went out on the porch with a cup of coffee to sit and contemplate the day. The breeze had died down but the sky was still drizzling. A couple of miners walked by over on Dumas, heading up the mountain soaking wet and I could hear the blacksmith down below pounding steel on an anvil. I looked the other way up 1st Street and saw some dust fly out of the schoolhouse door, and some more. *Is that the new school teacher?* With my interest piqued I took a sip coffee, set the mug down on the porch, and decided to see what was going on.

On the school steps I hesitated and nearly turned around but my heart pulled me up to the landing, where I reminded myself that after all, we were neighbors. Not bothering to knock on the door I called out instead.

"Hello, is anybody here?" I asked into the dust filled room, and hearing no answer, stepped inside. It was an open room with a high ceiling and a good number of desks. On a raised platform at the far end was large desk with a blackboard on the wall behind it, an empty wood box sat next to a Roxbury wood heater in the corner and an open door led to a back-storage room. Portraits of George Washington and Abraham Lincoln hung on a wall.

"Who's there?" an alarmed woman's voice replied from the storage room.

"It's your neighbor, from down the street. Do you need any help?"

"Why, just a minute," the voice answered. I smiled with anticipation but Mrs. Chapman came out of the room carrying a bucket and broom, wearing a green plaid gingham dress.

"Oh," I said, no longer smiling, "I saw the opened door and thought I could help. Yesterday when we met, it was mentioned that the school needed to be cleaned."

"Yes, yesterday. I remember now," she said, eyeing me with suspicion. She walked over and handed me the empty pail.

"Could you go and fill this with water?"

"Why . . . I'd be happy to," I said, trying not to seem surprised at seeing her instead of Miss de Graff.

"Uh, thank you —" she said insincerely, not remembering my name.

"Oliver," I reminded her, feigning a smile.

"Yes, Oliver."

I nodded and said, "Okay, I'll be right back."

Going down the schoolhouse stairs I headed for the inn's front door and grabbed the mug. Coming into the kitchen Liz was at the sink doing the mornings dishes. She looked at me and noticed the bucket.

"What-cha got there?" she asked, raising an eyebrow.

"Just need to fill it for the school," I said, setting the mug on the counter.

"Ah, helping the new schoolmarm are you," she said wistfully. "Heard all about her."

"You did, huh," I replied. "Just doing my civic duty."

"Civic duty?" she coughed.

"Yeah, okay," I said. "Can I get some water, please?"

"Sure, anything to help the school board," Liz said, giggling. She stepped back from the sink and dried her hands on a dish towel.

"You're a funny one," I replied, grinning and filling the pail.

"Eva said she's about your age," Liz offered as I finished. Without replying I walked out the door, bucket in hand.

Out on 1st Street I caught a glimpse of Miss de Graaf walking up the schoolhouse stairs. She was wearing a dark blue work dress, brown leather lace up shoes and white scarf, her shoulder length blonde hair was in a braid. As I got closer I could hear Mrs. Chapman inside.

"Oh, Mattie, there you are."

"Yes, good morning. Sorry I'm late," Mattie said. "I stopped by the post office on the way to get my new address taken care of." I heard her say as I came up the stairs and stood at the door.

"I've got some water," I offered. The two women turned to face me.

"There's our volunteer," Mrs. Chapman said, beckoning me with a hand. "He offered to fetch us some water." I walked over to them.

"Mattie, you remember . . . Oliver from yesterday," Mrs. Chapman said. I set the bucket down and stuck out my hand and smiled at Mattie. Her cheeks were not as colored as the day before, they looked even better, like soft white silk.

"Yes, thank you, Oliver," she said and shook my hand. "Good to see you again."

"You, too, Mattie," I said, holding my grip.

"Do you work in the mines?" she asked. I grinned and let go of her hand.

"No, not me. I'm a painter," I boasted. A confused look flashed across her face.

"I do landscapes," I quickly added.

"You do landscapes here?" she asked.

"Oh yes, up in the mountains and I do portraits."

"A painter?" Mrs. Chapman questioned. "That's doesn't sound very productive."

"Oh, I can do a few a day and I've sold a good number of them," I replied.

"How long have you been painting?" Mattie asked.

"For about five or six years. I studied it at the San Francisco Art Association, back home," I replied. She grinned.

"Oh, I love San Francisco!" she exclaimed. "You're from there?"

"I am, I grew up in the Excelsior District. You?"

"Bellingham, Washington, up north. Well, Lynden really," she replied. "But I graduated from the Northwest Normal School, it's called the New Whatcom now, though."

"So, you've been to San Francisco?"

"I wish. I've just seen pictures and read stories," she said.

"You'd love it there! The weather is perfect, and Woodward's Gardens is the —"

"Okay, that's enough you two," Mrs. Chapman said, interrupting. "That's enough talk about faraway places, we've got work to do and don't have time for silly chit-chat." Mrs. Chapman said, staring at me. "If you're interested in talking the whole day long maybe you'd be interested in coming to our community quilting social this weekend? There's lots of talk that goes on there," she suggested, but the tone of her voice had changed, it wasn't very friendly. *And quilting? Oh, I can't quilt. Don't even want to!*

I feigned another smile and said, "That sounds wonderful, but I'll be hiking up into the mountains to work this weekend."

"Oh, I'd like to go on a hike," Mattie said, but quickly added, "sometime."

"Hiking!" Mrs. Chapman interrupted again. "There's far more important things to do right now than go on some walk in the woods."

"Okay," I quickly said. "I best get out of your way so you can keep at your chores. See you later, maybe," I said and smiled at Mattie. She returned it.

Sitting down in the rocking chair the sky was getting lighter and the drizzle had ceased. I thought I might be able to spend my day doing some painting or sketch work when another idea came to mind.

In the tool shed I grabbed the ax, rope and buck saw and headed for the slope above Dumas Street. I picked out a smaller sized tree that had dead brown needles on it, knowing it was already dry and seasoned. I set my feet and started an undercut. Ten minutes later I had the tree down and the limbs off when I saw Mrs. Chapman leaving the schoolhouse. I cut the top off, cinched the rope around the limbless log and dragged it down to the schoolhouse, where I started sawing it into shorter pieces and splitting them. In no time I was carrying an armload of firewood up the stairs. This time the door was closed, so I knocked.

"Oh, hello there," Mattie said, opening the door with a surprised look.

"I noticed the empty wood box earlier," I replied, walking inside.

"Please, by all means," she said with a sweeping movement of her arm. I walked over and dumped the load into the box. "Thank you, Oliver," she said. "That was really sweet of you."

"My pleasure, and that's just the start. There's more," I said, heading outside.

"Okay, I'll leave the door open," she said. "Can I help carry it?"

"Oh no, I'm fine. You've got more important things to do," I answered, going down the stairs. I gathered up another armload and went back in. She was going through some books on what I figured was her desk.

"Where'd Mrs. Chapman go?" I inquired, dumping the load.

"Oh, she forgot the soap for the windows, she'll be right back."

"So . . . do you like to quilt?" I asked. Mattie stopped what she was doing and looked up at me.

"Well, since I'm staying with them for this first bit I guess I do," she said with a sheepish grin. I thought about her answer while standing at the door.

"I guess that's the polite way to say no," I surmised. She shook her head side to side and smiled. Then she flicked her fingers at me and made a funny, whimsical sound.

"Phssst, phssst," she smacked her lips like she was scolding a student, "I thought you were going to fill my wood box."

"Like I said, my pleasure," I gibed. Going down the stairs I saw Mrs. Chapman coming up 1st Street carrying a bottle of soap and some rags, she noticed that I was cutting them some cord wood.

"Well, I guess we could use some stove wood," she said, walking up, her words like ice. "But we certainly can't pay you."

"No problem. That's okay, I like to help," I replied, gathering up another armload. I followed her inside.

"How come the school doesn't have a wood shed?" I asked.

"And why do you ask?" Mrs. Chapman replied curtly.

"I noticed there wasn't one outside, and was just wondering. That's all."

"Well, the school only operates five or six hours a day and not on weekends or holidays, so we don't go through as much as a household normally would," she explained.

"That makes sense," I agreed and headed outside for another armload. When I came back they were busying themselves with washing windows so I continued loading in the rest of the stove wood until the last pieces had been brought in.

"Okay," I said, slapping my hands together over the box, wiping them off. "That's the last of it." Mattie turned around from washing a window.

"Thank you so much Oliver," she said. "I really appreciate it."

"Yes," Mrs. Chapman said quickly, not bothering to look at me.

"You're welcome, I'll cut some more when I can. See you later," I said, looking at Mattie.

"Yes, see you soon, maybe," she said.

"Good-bye," Mrs. Chapman added loudly, her back to me.

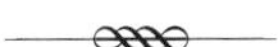

After dinner Jacob, Eva and I were sitting at the built-in enjoying some of Liz's fresh baked oatmeal cookies and orange spice tea with honey. Jacob set his cup down on the saucer and turned his head towards me. I didn't look at him, but I could tell he was grinning.

"So, did you sharpen the ax today before you used it?" I turned my head towards him.

"Boy, oh boy," I sputtered. "A fellow can't do anything in this town without somebody finding out about it." Everyone laughed.

"I guess you were in too big of a hurry to get started, huh?" he said.

"Alright, okay," I groaned.

"Aw, I'm just teasing ya'," Jacob sassed.

"Maybe you could teach an art class for her?" Liz suggested with a grin. I liked the sound of that.

"We'll see. Maybe I will."

XI

INDIAN SUMMER

Walking down Dumas I could feel a coolness to the morning, more so than the day before. Even though the sun was out it felt like summer was beginning to fade, the slow march towards fall was hanging in the air. The greenery on the mountain sides was turning yellow and gold and purple, it was an artist's dream come true, there was nowhere else I wanted to be.

There were some kids sitting on the porch of the mercantile, so I waved and grinned.

"Just a few more days till school starts," I reminded them.

"I know mister," a boy said.

"We got a pretty new teacher this year!" a freckled face girl added.

"I heard that too," I replied with a nod, and kept walking. At the depot I found Ed Baker in his office, I walked in and set a dollar bill on the counter. He stood up from his chair.

"Mornin' Oliver. Telegram?"

"Yes, please." He handed me one of his forms and a knife-sharpened pencil, I started to fill it out.

"Cooler out today," I offered.

"I noticed that," Ed replied, stepping back to his desk. Sitting down he said, "I was over at the Cleveland and Kline yesterday. I think they sold your paintings."

"No kidding!" I said, looking up. "That was going to be my next stop. Guess I should have brought some more with me."

"How's things up at the Pride?" he asked, and pushed his hat up on his forehead.

"Good, thanks. I've got all the wood in for the winter, so now I'm painting as much as I can while the weather's still good," I answered, then finished filling out the form and pushed it across the counter. Ed got up, walked over and looked at it.

"Think yer' mom will ever come up to visit?"

"Maybe next spring," I replied, and added, "Thanks, see you later." Walking away from the office I could hear Ed pounding away on his key machine. On the trestle I noticed how low and slow the river was running, and over across on the other side of lower town no one was about. I walked down the embankment trail and over to the tavern. The door was open so I poked my head inside — the place was empty. I walked in and stood at the bar then noticed that my paintings were gone, a second later I heard glass clinking in the backroom.

"Anybody here?" I called.

"Oh yeah, we're here," Jacob replied. He walked out of the back carrying a wooden box full of whiskey bottles.

"Hey Oliver, how are ya'?"

"I'm good. You?"

"Very well, thanks. We sold yer' paintings, I've got six bucks back in the safe for ya'," he said, putting down the box and returning to the backroom.

"Great," I replied. "Thank you."

Addison came around the corner.

"Howdy," he said. "Did Jacob tell you? About the sales?"

"He did . . . and you were right that you could sell them."

"Better bring us some more," he laughed. Jacob came back and put six dollars on the bar in front of me. Then he set a dip pen, inkwell and piece of paper on the counter. Bending down, he spoke as he began to write.

"So, where have you been going to paint?" Jacob asked.

"Mostly up the trail from Dumas."

"You should try this other side sometime, the Toad Mountain side," Jacob suggested, quickly pointing with the pen at the wall towards the different location outside. "It's got some great views. Silver and Cultus Lakes, or Sunday Falls over by the pavilion."

"Oh, okay."

"It's quiet and there's only the O & B and one other mine up there. Not as many people around."

"I'll try and get up there sometime," I said.

"Great, so, I'm making out a receipt of sale for both of us, that way we can keep the contract in place and keep going. That is, if you'd like to?"

"You bet I'd like to keep going, I'll bring you three more before the weekend," I said, folding the bills and stuffing them into a trouser pocket.

"If you'd like, you can bring us more than three and we'll adjust the contract."

"Sure, I'll get you more! And you can start hanging them on the wall, I don't think anyone will steal them."

"You sure?"

"Sure I'm sure, and since Labor Day is coming up I bet town will be packed with tourists. You'll sell out!" I said brightly. Jacob nodded and kept writing out the receipt.

"So, what are you doing today?" Addison asked.

"Well, ordering more paint, I guess," I replied. They both chuckled. Jacob handed me the receipt.

"Thank you!" I said. "I'll be by tomorrow with more."

I raised my hand and waved as I walked out the door. Crossing the wagon bridge, I thought about how many tubes of paint I'd need to order. Up at the mercantile the same kids were still on the porch but now a golden retriever dog was lying next to them, it raised its head up panting with its tongue hanging out. I almost reminded them about school again but decided not to needle them and walked inside. I went up to the counter where all the catalogs were laid out and started flipping through the pages. Manager Charlie O'Connell, came over.

"Oliver! How are ya' today?"

"I'm well, and you?"

"Very good. What-cha needing?"

"More paint and canvas."

"You should be finding that under art supplies," he said, right as I found the page.

"Yep, here it is. Have you got a form to fill out?" I asked. He raised a finger, turned around and went to get one. Just then the bell over the door sounded and Jim Bartholomew came in.

"Greetings everyone," he announced and headed back to the post office. Charlie set a form in front of me and went back to take care of him. While I was filling out my order the bell rang again and a few Monte women in long dresses came in with baskets on their arms. Two of them wore bonnets but one had a fancy hat with silk flowers, they started walking through the aisles. Just as I was adding up the order Charlie came back and Bartholomew went out the door carrying his mail.

"All finished?" he asked. I handed him the completed form, he checked my math.

"Yep, you got it right. That'll be three dollars and thirty seven-cents with the shipping charge," he said. I dug in my pocket, pulled out the folded bills and handed him four of them. He handed me a receipt and my change.

"Thanks. How long do you think it will take to get here?"

"It should be here in a little over two weeks. That is as long as a mountain slide doesn't come down and knock out the tracks again, then it'll be longer."

"Mountain slides! That's sounds dangerous, has one ever hit the train?"

"Not yet but a couple of avalanches have come close," Charlie replied. He went to put the order in the ledger, then added, "And there's no refunds for any reason, by the way."

"Okay, I should have enough paint on hand for now. Thanks again," I said and left for home.

Since the sun was still out I snatched an apple and a few of Liz's muffins from the counter and loaded them in a paper sack. In my room I opened the field box and checked to make sure I had everything I needed, then I flung it over my shoulder and headed out the door. As I was turning up Dumas to head into the hills a voice called out behind me. Turning around, I saw Mattie walking down the schoolhouse stairs.

"Hey Oliver! Where're you going?" she hollered, holding up her blue and white plaid dress as she started to scamper over, smiling. Her blonde hair was cascading down past her shoulders, she was a joy to behold.

"Going for a hike," I said, stopping and slowly walking back towards her.

"How far do you go?" she asked.

"Well, I've been up to the very top of a ridge in the basin before but today just a mile or two," I replied.

"That's not too far," she said, her bright blue eyes penetrating mine. "Care for some company?"

"Don't you have to get ready for classes?"

"That can wait," she said, waving a hand back at the schoolhouse when a mischievous grin swept across her face. "I'd much rather go on a hike with you."

"Oh. Okay!" I automatically responded. "You need to get anything?"

"Nope," she said, looking back at the schoolhouse. "I'm ready."

"Very good then," I said, and I tilted my head towards the way to go. "The first part just runs along this road then it narrows to a trail, there's a waterfall farther up." We started walking, side by side.

"I love waterfalls," Mattie said.

"We'll be there in no time," I said, walking past the concentrator.

"What goes on in that big, noisy thing?" she asked.

"That's where they crush the ore and ship it, six days a week," I said. We kept walking.

Across the valley was the steep timbered ridge line that ran up to jagged mountain peaks, and above us the ore buckets creaked and moaned as they moved along on the tram tower cables. Below us the bunker was nearly overflowing with ore from the buckets being unloaded.

"How do those work?" Mattie asked, pointing upward.

"Well, I don't know too much about all of this, but I believe the force generated by the heavy full buckets coming down from the mines then turns around and sends the empty, lighter buckets back up, like a big waterwheel."

"Gravity can be pretty powerful," she replied. We hiked past broken tree limbs and slash that were scattered all around from the tram towers construction, when the pitch got steeper. Across the valley was the mine with rocks strewn all about with a cookhouse and storage building. I pointed at it all.

"Over there's the Rainy Mine, I think it's called," I said, stopping. Mattie put her hand on her forehead to shield her eyes from the sun and looked across the valley. Just then a series of close-by high-pitched calls came through the air. It startled Mattie, she latched onto my arm and squeezed.

"What on earth is that?!" she exclaimed, glancing around. I pointed over to a pile of large boulders.

"Those are just Pikas, they're harmless," I said, turning to where a group of the little brown and black creatures sat stomping their rear feet and screeching in thin high voices. Mattie relaxed.

"Look how cute they are," she said, smiling.

Up ahead we heard the sound of rushing water and glimpsed the waterfall through the trees cascading over rocks. We took the trail down to the waterline, I looked over my shoulder at Mattie, her eyes were as big as saucers.

"Great spot, huh?" I asked, stopping at the pooling waters.

"Fantastic," Mattie replied.

As soon as we got there she went down to the waterline, took her shoes off, found a flat slab of rock that protruded out over the water to sit on and put her feet in the creek. While she did I went just upstream and opened my field box, found a sketch board and paper behind the canvas frames and began to draw.

I could see the mist of the falls land on her face, the moisture making her silky skin glisten. The sound of the falls enveloped us and the surface of the water sparkled and gleamed from the sunlight. Mattie was resplendent, leaning back with her hands behind herself, smiling and kicking the cool water up in the air with one foot, she had her dress pulled up to her knees so it wouldn't get wet.

"Oh, my, gosh, this is so beautiful," she said throwing her head back, her golden hair spinning through the warm air. She turned her head to look at me.

"Come and sit with me." It was a tempting request.

"Okay, just a minute," I replied, raising a finger and pointing at my work. She smiled and turned back to the swirling waters at the base of the falls. A number of minutes later I was done and took the drawing over to her, sat down and held it up in front of her.

"It's for you."

"You just did this?" she remarked gleefully. "It's wonderful! No one's ever drawn a picture of me before."

"So you like it?"

"It's really, really good! Thank you, Oliver," she said and placed her hand on my thigh, then patted it. Mattie gazed at me with her diamond blue eyes, almost to the point of where she was looking into me.

"You're welcome," I said. She kept her eyes focused on mine and . . . Boom! A huge black powder blast thundered across the basin. Mattie's fingernails instantly dug into my thigh, she yelped and both of us were so startled that we nearly bumped heads.

"What on earth?!" she hollered. I got to my feet.

"It's okay, just a normal mine blast, maybe from the Mystery, going deeper in the mine," I said and grinned. "Are you alright?"

Mattie stood up, gave me a long-suffering look and put her hands on her hips. "That scared the living daylights out of me!" she laughed, brushing off her skirt with one hand while she held the sketch of herself with the other.

"Should we hike up farther?" I asked, looking towards the trail then up the basin.

"Sure," she said. "I'm game for just about anything after that!" she replied as she glanced at the sketch again with a smile and rolled it up and held it in one hand at her side. I went back over to the field box to get it and the lunch sack. Mattie came over and watched.

"That's a neat little thing. What's it called?"

"It's a field box, some artists refer to it as a painter's box or field easel. It was invented in France, but I added the shoulder straps," I said. "People say that Claude Monet invented it and I like to think that's true."

"I've heard of Monet," Mattie said. I threw it over my shoulder, picked up the sack and said, "Shall we?" And made a sweeping movement of my arm towards the trail, we started out again with Mattie in the lead.

"I think Monet was the greatest of the impressionists, I studied him a lot in art school," I offered. "Monet once said that it's important to think in terms of color and shape instead of scenes and objects," I said as we walked along the trail. Once we got back up to the main trail Mattie looked back at me and I pointed to the left, up the basin.

"He's still alive and painting, right?" she asked.

"Oh, yes, very much so."

"What else did Monet say?"

"Okay, well — I'm not sure what else he said but I do know that he was somewhat eccentric. By the time he became successful and had money he built his own landscapes on his property. He had workers build settings in precise designs for the plantings he wanted to paint, you know, like lily ponds and water gardens. His best works I think are the ones with water reflections that take on a mirror-like quality with alternating light. But as his wealth grew, his gardens evolved and he became more extravagant. I read that he has seven gardeners," I explained. We kept hiking as the trail slowly began to turn to the right around the base of the hill that the tram towers went up and over. A fairly level area was coming up.

"Did he have children?" Mattie asked.

"He did, two sons," I answered. "And he had two wives. His first died of tuberculosis and cancer in her early thirties, I think, and after she died he did some of his best work."

"Really?" Mattie asked.

"Yes, he loved her deeply and her loss motivated him. Then he married a woman who had six children. So I guess he had eight children altogether." We walked a little further and I remembered a well-known Monet quote.

"He used to say, 'I like to paint as a bird sings.'" Mattie stopped and turned around. She took a step back towards me.

"Say that again, to me," she said, her bright blue eyes shining in the sun. My heart skipped a beat. She held the rolled-up sketch up to her heart and closed her eyes.

"Okay," I said, and decided to change the phrase a little. I reached down and grabbed her left hand and held it in both of mine, and paused for a moment.

"I'd like to paint *you* as a bird that sings a song." And I looked down on her face. She was smiling. Mattie opened her eyes and gazed at me then gave me a big hug. I embraced her.

"Promise," she said into my chest.

"Oh, yes. I'll do your portrait," I replied.

"I'd like that," she said. She let go and turned back to the trail. We started hiking again. Coming around the bend we saw the tram loading station up above us, a small trail snaked off and upward towards it. There were some wild flowers growing along the side of the trail. Mattie reached down and snatched a few with her free hand.

We could see up ahead the cookhouse where I met Martin Comins before, but no one was around.

"Is that a miner's house?" she asked, pointing.

"It's a cookhouse, I think they call it. Or maybe a bunkhouse," I said.

"Well, it looks like it would be a good painting, the way it looks sitting there."

"That's a great idea, you've got a good eye," I commented. "How much farther do you want to go?" I asked. Mattie glanced down at the sack in my hand.

"Well, what do have there?"

"Lunch! How about if we sit for a spell?" I suggested, looking around for a spot.

"That sounds good," Mattie said. We found a small level meadow area just above the trail and sat down. I opened the sack and handed her a corn muffin, she took a bite and grinned.

"Who made these?"

"Liz did, at the Pride Hotel where I live with my Aunt and Uncle. Liz runs the kitchen," I said.

"Your uncle owns it?"

"Yep, and built it. You met my Aunt Eva the other day, remember?"

"Oh, yes. And what about your parents? Where are they?" I looked away and thought about my Father for a moment.

"My Mom still lives in San Francisco, but my Dad died last fall, about a year ago."

"I'm so sorry to hear that."

"Thanks," I replied. There was a moment of silence and I had the feeling she wanted to know more. "It was an aneurysm, so it happened suddenly, his loss left an emptiness inside of me, like a void in my soul," I said.

"Oh, Oliver, that's so sad. I'm really sorry."

"Yeah, thanks, my Father meant the world to me. He was a smart guy and really good at business, he owned a jewelry store, that my mom just sold, and he was funny, too, always joking around. Right after I graduated from high school, he had me down at his store working with him, he sold other stuff besides rings and watches, but I didn't want to do that all my life. It wasn't that I was afraid of hard work and long hours, because I'm not. I put myself through art school working for him weekends. In college I made jewelry, mostly rings and I sold them in Dad's store, but I was painting too. I liked that better. In fact, one of the first paintings I did that was any good was of all the tall ships along the waterfront. My Mom still has it hanging in her parlor, she always said that the clustered masts were like limbless trees in a forest," I said and paused for a moment. "But I just felt that there was more to life than working in a jewelry store. I wanted to be a painter."

"Why's that?" Mattie asked. I looked off to the distant peaks and smiled then turned back to her.

"I found it far more challenging and gratifying, besides, have you ever heard of a famous jeweler before?" I asked. Mattie though about the question for a moment.

"Gosh, I guess I haven't."

"Exactly," I replied. "And how about you? Tell me about your life and family."

"Me?" she said, sounding surprised. "Oh, I'm not one to talk about myself."

"I'm not asking you to brag about yourself, just tell me a little bit about where you grew up and what your family is like."

"Okay, if you insist," Mattie said, clasping her hands on her lap. "I grew up on a dairy farm east of Bellingham up north of here in a town called Lynden, lots of Holsteins and pasture and we just started a few acres of raspberries, they grow really well in this climate. But it was pretty boring really, milking cows and baling hay. Don't get me wrong, I love the farm and my family. I've got two older sisters and a younger brother. My Mom and Dad still run the place, my little brother will get it when they retire since none of us girls are interested in it."

"You're lucky to still have both your parents," I said.

"Oh, I know, they're wonderful."

"So, what made you want to be a teacher?" I asked. Mattie looked up at the sky and smiled.

"Well, the New Whatcom teachers' school I went to was started in my hometown so it was close and very convenient but by the time I was a junior it moved to Bellingham so I moved too, and lived there until I graduated. But to answer your question I wanted to teach because I *love* children, and want to have a family, someday," she said. I nodded my head and out of nowhere my mouth opened and I blurted out, "Me too."

Mattie's head jerked around like someone had pulled it by a string. She looked at me and smiled. Just then a far-off Boom! sounded from another mine in the distance. We both turned our heads in the direction.

"Boy, it just never stops up here," she commented. I pulled the apple out of the sack and handed it to her. Mattie rubbed it on her dress and took a bite, then she held it out for me.

"No, you go ahead. I'm good."

"I'll eat half, then you can have the rest," she suggested when the sound of voices came up the trail. It was Martin Comins and another fella, Martin had a blue flannel work shirt on and black trousers, he was carrying a long steel drill bit on his shoulder. The chap he was with was short and wore baggy trousers, a brown vest and he had a pannier just like mine on his back. They were deep in conversation and it sounded like the fellow with the pannier had a German accent.

"Yah, well, I is still owed money from last summer," the German said. "Remember?"

"I know, I'm working on it," Martin replied. They saw us as they approached.

"Afternoon," I said, waving at them. It looked like Martin recognized me.

"Yes, lad," Martin replied, raising a hand, "and lass," he added. "Tiz a fine day to be out and about," he said as they walked by.

"Indeed, it is," I replied. "I've got a pannier just like that," I quickly said to the other man. He looked over at me as they continued towards the cookhouse.

"Yah, it's a daisy," he replied.

"Who's that?" Mattie asked quietly, once they passed us.

"The tall fellow is Martin Comins, they call him the Duke of Monte Cristo."

"The Duke of Monte Cristo? You mean like the Count of Monte Cristo? How come?"

"He's well thought of by the townsfolk, kind of revered. I heard he saved some miners' lives before, and I saw him make a few toasts on Independence Day, he was pretty funny." Mattie nodded her head up and down and handed me the rest of the apple.

"And the other guy?" she asked.

"Never seen him before. There's lots of miners that work up here." After a moment of silence Mattie stood up.

"Well, this was a great way to spend the morning. But I should probably get back to town, work on my lesson plans."

"Oh, okay, sure. I'll walk you," I offered as I got to my feet.

"No, no. That's okay. I know the way now. You stay up here and work, do some painting."

"Are you sure? I can come up here anytime."

"I know, but the weather is going to change soon and you won't be able to. We'll do it again, this weekend maybe, how about that?" she said, holding the sketch up to her heart. She took a half step towards me and stared deep into my eyes and smiled. Then in a flash she rose up on her toes and gave me a shy little kiss on my cheek. I was stunned. She pulled away but I grabbed her by the arms, pulled her close and we embraced for a wonderful moment.

"When can I see you again?" I said. Mattie pulled her head back and gazed at me.

"Anytime you want," she said and smiled brightly. She pulled away, turned and headed back down the trail.

"Promise?" I said. She stopped and turned around fast. Her dress hem spun up like a wheel and she waved.

"I promise," Mattie replied, and off she went clutching the rolled-up sketch in her hand. I watched until she was out of sight.

Taking a moment to look around I contemplated the rest of the day. Gazing at the log bunkhouse with its rock foundation I realized that Mattie was right, it was the perfect subject. It looked like it was built right up out of the ground that surrounded it: natural and organic. I headed up the trail and past it, knowing that I needed to search out the best angle and continued walking until I found just the right spot amongst some red heather, with a view of the cookhouse and mountain above it.

I opened the field easel and unpacked everything, mixed some colors, then made a start. I could feel the sun on my back and a slight breeze moved through the few trees that were near me, providing a calming effect that I liked. Some miners came and went from the building without noticing me and a fly landed on my neck, I swiped it off, and another one lit on my arm, I shook it off too. Soon the flies became bothersome but I was determined. Five minutes later a rock slide sounded over across the basin, I looked up but couldn't see where it came from. I continued working.

Once I had the outline of the mountain and ridge I worked on the sky then the foreground and building. Two hours later the painting was beginning to take shape and my stomach began to rumble. I worked a bit longer to finish it just as the sun began to set on the ridge behind me. I looked at my pocket watch, it was nearly four-thirty. The light, and hence the scene, began to change dramatically as the sun sank below the mountains. While I let the paint dry I cleaned the brushes and gathered up everything and had a thought — not storing away the painting in my field box I carried it by its edges towards the bunkhouse.

As I approached I could hear, and then see, someone in the covered entrance. It was the man who was with Martin earlier, he was down on his haunches filing a long steel drill bit he had supported on his knees. I went over to him.

"Evening," I said. "Is Martin around?" The man looked up from his task.

"Yah, he is inside," he said, pointing with the file at the door. I glanced at the closed wooden entrance then at the work in my hands.

"Could you open it for me?" I said, holding the painting up and tilting my head at the door.

"What ya' got der, sonny?" he asked.

"It's for Martin, and the miners."

"That thing is for da' miners?" the man asked, pushing himself up off the ground and opening the door. He yelled inside, "Somebody here!"

"Great, thank you," I said and walked inside. The stench of the place hit me square in the face. Wet, moldy clothes and moldy food, rotten wood, smoke, sour milk, and just plain old general stink filled my nose, it almost burned my eyes. There were a few men sitting at a rough wooden table near the door playing what looked like pinochle and other men were either asleep or lying in filthy bunkbeds that ran along both walls. A few old hunting rifles were leaned up in the corner.

"Is Martin around?" I asked, trying not to breathe through my nose.

"Right here," a voice from a bunk said, as faces poked out from beneath blankets. Martin set the book he was reading aside, hopped down from his bunk and came over.

"Hey Martin," I said. "I thought you and the rest of the men might like this?" I offered, holding the picture of the bunkhouse up for him to see.

"What have ya' there, lad?" he said, pushing the bridge of his spectacles up on his nose. He squinted at the work when a look of surprise swept across his face.

"That's this," he remarked and pointed at the floor. "Tiz a fine rendering yee've done!"

"It's for you, and the men," I said.

"What 'er ya' saying?" he asked. His jutted chin protruded when he spoke and I noticed that his eye lids were like thin little apertures. I could barely tell if he was looking at me, but I knew he was.

"I want you to have it," I insisted, pushing it towards him.

"Boys, gather round! Strom, Digby, McGavock, everybody, get up!" Martin said to the room. "The cookhouse has its own work of art! Chubb!" Martin hollered, "Get out here and see what we've got!"

I looked over Martin's shoulder and saw an overweight man with a dirty food stained apron materialize at the doorway of what I guessed was the kitchen, with a large wooden mixing spoon in his hand.

"What now?!" he belched. "I'm busy damn it, can't ya'll just leave me alone for once!"

"No, no, come over and have a look," Martin said, stepping to the side so Chubb could see what I was holding. The men at the table started to get up while others jumped down from their bunks to come over and stand with Martin. I recognized Big Nelson and the rest of them from the baseball game.

"Lookie at that, would ya'," a miner with a few missing teeth drawled.

"I'm seein' it," Big Nelson coughed, rubbing the stubble on his grizzled face. He switched the quid of chewing tobacco from one cheek to the other and gazed at the painting with the look of wonderment on his face.

"Aw, who cares about somethin' like that," McGavock scoffed and went back to his bunk.

"By golly, dis' place never looked so good," Strom commented.

"Ed's right," Joe Digby snapped. "We don't need something like this."

"Outta the way," Chubb bellowed as he approached, walking bandy-legged with a little half-step hitch. He slowly leaned down and stared at the painting. Then he pointed his spoon at it.

"Well I'll be, there's even a little smoke coming out of the chimney," he crooned like a child.

"Dick! Get in here and see this!" Martin yelled at the door. A few seconds later the man that was filing the drill bit came in and joined the crowd looking at the painting.

"Oh, that's a . . . wait, dat's da' bunkhouse!" he said with vigor and smiled.

"We should take up a collection," Martin suggested.

"Collection!" one miner blurted.

"I ain't got no money," another moaned.

"Oh, no, it's a gift. I want you to have it," I said to everyone.

"Thank you, Oliver," Martin said, sticking out his hand. "Tiz a fine thing to be inspired and create something like this."

"Well, you're welcome," I said, gripping and shaking his hand. The rest of the miners started to pat me on the back and thank me. I nodded and smiled.

"Where should we put it?" Big Nelson asked the room.

"It should go in the kitchen," Chubb replied.

"Oliver ain't givin' it to you, he's givin' it to *us*!" Big said.

"Yeah, that's right," another miner piped up. "It goes out here."

"That's right."

"Yep, he's right."

"Out here," the other interested men added.

"It's still needs to dry and harden," I pointed out.

"May I?" Martin asked, putting both hands out to accept the gift. I nodded and lifted it, showing him that he should take it the same way I was holding it.

"It should be propped up on a shelf, if possible," I suggested. Martin nodded and grinned as he took it. He raised it up and walked to the only shelf in the room near the kitchen door. It was covered with empty whisky bottles and piles of mining contract papers.

"Somebody move this stuff," he said over his shoulder. Chubb walked over and swept the papers off the shelf and onto the floor, scattering them all around. Martin gently set the painting on the shelf like it was an infant child swaddled in blankets. He stepped back and gazed at it with satisfaction, his eyes pinching into tiny thoughtful slits while everyone else gathered round and admired it.

"Nobody touches it!" Martin ordered. "Never! Ya' got that? Oliver says it needs to dry and harden, ya' hear me?" All the men nodded their heads up and down in agreement then wandered back to their bunks and card games.

Martin stood and continued to gaze at the painting, his eyes taking in every detail, mesmerized in admiration.

"Okay, then," I spoke up. "I'd best be going." Martin turned and grinned.

"Thank ya' Oliver."

"You're welcome, my pleasure," I replied and started for the door.

"That's a fine thing," he said, following me. "Yee've got a talent, lad, so don't ya' be wasting it."

"Oh, I won't. Thanks," I replied, turning to leave.

"Maybe we'll see ya' in town?" he added. "Buy ya' a drink." I jerked my head around.

"Sure, I'd love to have a drink with the Duke."

"Aw, sure 'in ya' will, lad. I'd be a wee proud to be spilling the whiskey with the best artist in the valley!" Martin said with a wry Irish grin.

"Alright. I'll look forward to it!" I turned again towards the door and felt the hand of the Duke of Monte Cristo pat me on the back. Without turning around I walked out the door of the cookhouse, shook the life back into my limbs as the clean, cool mountain air poured into my soul, and started back down the mountain, home to the Pride.

XII

PRIDE OF THE WOODS

Everyday I'd watch the bone-tired miners trudge to and from the cookhouse to the tunnel. They'd bring up their picks, sledgehammers and lamps, and drill their holes to black powder blast my veins. Then they'd swing their picks at the tunnel walls, like fearless soldiers fighting against the granite fortress I've been building for a million years. Deeper and deeper, tunnel after tunnel they'd bore into me but less and less they'd find. The realization that my gold and silver was only superficial was lost in the blackness that consumed the miners drive for their meager survival, only to find the color the industrialists coveted. This Old Man of the Mountain's bone to pick was with the eastern investors, not the miners. I'd come to recognize and understand the men that toiled and endured in these mines.

Hundreds of feet below daylight Sam Strom hacked at the wall of a drift with his pick, freeing up the last bit of loose ore from the previous blast. Working by the illumination of a few candle lamps he wore a felt skullcap on his head and a bandanna covering his nose and mouth, a pile of rubble at his feet waited for loading.

The dry, ungreased wheels of the ore cart squeaked and moaned along the narrow gage rusty rails and over uneven rock floors leading down the tunnel, flickering candles and kerosene lamps fastened to every support timber casting barely enough light to see. Black air pipe hung from support timbers or ran along the ground beside the narrow gage tracks and went for hundreds of feet. In between the strikes of the pick the steady sound of dripping water was the only thing that could be heard, until the tromping feet of Ed McGavock and Big Nelson echoed through the mine. They pushed the heavy wheeled ore cart up to their fellow miner and stopped.

"What'd you do, get lost 'er somethin'?" Sam Strom asked through his dust covered handkerchief.

"Hey, we're all workin' here," McGavock snapped, his face covered in black soot and mine dust.

"I was yust makin' a yoke," Strom replied, pulling the handkerchief from his face.

"Well, I'm *just* glad we're still makin' wages," Big Nelson said, "even if there ain't much color showing."

"Yah. Yust like the Mystery, the deeper we go, the less good ore we're finding," Strom added.

"Don't they know the ore is only on the surface? You'd think the syndicate would've figured it out by now," McGavock remarked.

"I know, I know. But since they've spent so much money on this whole operation they're determined to make it work," Nelson said, picking up a large piece of ore and dropping it in the cart as McGavock began to muck up the smaller pieces of rock with his shovel.

"Martin said dat dey're thinking about starting another tunnel across the basin, he said dey're gonna call it, *The New Discovery*," Strom said with a grim laugh, putting a sarcastic accent on the title.

"Fine by me," McGavock said, scooping up another shovel-full, "as long as it keeps bringin' me a payday."

"Yah, well. I hear dat since the syndicate gave us da' raise to tree dollars a day dey are going to charge us more for room and board at da' cookhouse," Strom said.

"Yep," Big Nelson broke in, lifting a huge piece of ore with both hands and dropping it in the cart with a loud clang. "I heard that too."

"If they're gonna raise our room and board then they should feed us better, and give us somethin' to sleep on like mattresses instead of nothin'," McGavock said.

"It is still better dan' starvin'," Strom said.

"Not by much," McGavock replied.

"Hey! We all know we're stuck here with no way out, and if we complain or go on another wild-cat strike the syndicate will just fire us like all the others and bring in more Cornishmen. So let's get this cart loaded!" Big barked.

"I hear we might get another hundred-foot contract," Strom offered.

"Who told you that?" McGavock asked, "Martin I'd guess."

"Yep, Sam's right, Comins told me," Big admitted, "last week."

"Yah, he'd know," Strom said, throwing the last few pieces of ore to the cart. Big went over and picked up the heavy pneumatic Jack-leg drill like it was a toothpick, spreading the support Jack-legs with his foot so they were stable on the ground and held the drill bit up against the tunnel wall. Once done, Strom and McGavock pushed the cart down the tracks and out of the way. Big Nelson leaned against the end of the drill, pulled the trigger and started to bore another black powder blast hole.

Later that evening, with deliberate slowness, the cook attempted to salvage some chicken-bone leftovers from days before while he listened to the men in the front yak as they played pinochle. He commenced to shake his head from side-to-side, tossed a pinch of salt over his shoulder and stepped away from his task.

"Aw, Dave LeRoy was nothin' but a chiseler, and a worthless drifter with a dumb eye for floozy women," Chubb said from the kitchen doorway. "And I'll tell ya' what else, a true miner takes his time and thinks things over and a miner like LeRoy, well, a miner, I mean a man like him thinks things up! Now that's a fact," he added before disappearing back into his primitive cook room.

"Yah, well, Dave was a good friend, and I do not believe dey killed him. He was too smart to get caught like dey said dey did. He's still out in da' woods," Sam Strom said, looking up from his dictionary, lying in his bunk. "He got away and I don't believe what dey print in 'dose newspapers." George Pratt, who'd never had the chance for any book learning in his life, glanced over at Strom and sniffed.

"Aw, you know, I'm one to believe that Dave LeRoy's life was marked by misadventure the day he was born," George flatly stated. "But tell me square, Sam. Do you still think yer' gonna learn how to read and be lettered by poking yer' nose in that word book?" Pratt asked from the front table, he looked over at Big Nelson and smirked as he put down another card.

"Yah, sure you-bet-cha," Strom quickly replied, a sparkle in his eye, "and when I do I'll be smarter dan' youse." Big, McGavock and Joe Digby burst out in howling laughter.

"Hell, we're all smarter than Pratt already," Big Nelson cracked, slapping the edge of the table.

"Don't sass me, damn it," George snapped.

"Aw, Georgie, I was just hackin' on ya'. I darned well know yer' far above yer' fourth grade education, these days," Big said. Just then Martin Comins opened the cookhouse door and walked into the room.

"Duke!" everyone said at the same time.

"Evening gents," Martin replied.

"Whar' ya' been?" Big Nelson asked.

"Had to go over to the O & B and help with some blasting."

"Any news on the next contract?" Ed McGavock asked, looking up from his cards.

"We're in luck boys! The syndicate wants another hundred feet in the Pride of the Woods before they're convinced it's pinched out. So that will take us into the fall, and maybe some more," Martin declared.

"I'm guessin' you didn't tell them we knows it's already out of good ore?" Strom asked.

"Oh, they know it's getting thin. They just want to make sure," Comins said.

"Fine by me," Big Nelson said. He laid down a club card and hollered, "trump!"

"Hold on, you didn't follow suit!" Joe Digby snapped.

"That's a club, damn it," Big snorted. Digby looked closer at the card, saw that it wasn't a spade, and warily nodded his head up and down.

"Speaking of trump cards," Martin said with a smirk, "Frederick's gonna be back in town, soon."

"How'd you come by that?" Big asked. All the players stopped and looked up to Martin.

"Oh, I stopped in there before I headed up the hill. Shamus told me, he got a telegram from him. He's got new barmaid, too," Martin disclosed.

"Is she working upstairs?" Joe Digby quickly asked, both his voice and his eyebrows rising.

"Oh, lad, I wouldn't know about that," Martin said.

"I bet she's churnin' butter. Hell, all the girls there are sportin' women," Joe bellowed, a lascivious smile forming on his ruddy face.

"Aw, you don't know squat Digby," Chubb chimed in from the kitchen door again then added. "Why, you wouldn't know the difference between an honest woman and a painted lady."

"Do too!" Joe replied. "I've spent more paydays at Fred's than anyone here. Hell, I've been all around this world!"

"Aw, baloney," Chubb said. He threw his hands at Digby and went back to his chores.

In the morning, George and Joe were out working the tram station while Big Nelson and Sam Strom pushed the loaded ore cart back and forth from and to the mine, loading and unloading ore.

"Come Sunday I'm headin' straight for Fred's," Joe said, standing by the bull wheel and waiting to pull the brake lever as the next tram bucket slowly moved closer into position.

"And then what?" George asked, "Spend yer' pay on some doxy tart and whiskey?"

"Damn rights, what else is there?" Joe replied, watching the next tram bucket come into position. Right when it was next to the elevated loading dock he pulled on the steel lever, engaging the compressed-air valve and triggering the hardwood brake pads on the bull wheel. They let off an awful high-pitched wail, instead of the normal screech, and the whole apparatus shook to a stop.

"It's never sounded like that before," George said, surprised. Joe walked over and looked up at the brake system.

"That one leather pad is shot," he said, staring up at it. George walked over.

"Yep," he observed, gazing upward and seeing where the leather was torn and hanging from the hardwood brake shoe against the bull wheel. "When you go down to town this weekend you can stop by the syndicate office and tell them we need one."

"I suppose," Digby replied. Just then the sound of squeaky ore cart wheels came through the air, they turned their heads at the same time to see Big and Sam pushing the full ore cart up the ramp to the loading dock next to the cable system.

"Dar' ya' go," Strom said, winded and sweating hard, taking a dirty handkerchief from his back pocket and wiping his brow.

"I'm thinkin' it's about time to switch," Big said, stopping and leaning up against the cart. "We've done our ten trips, now it's your turn."

"Ten?!" Digby snapped. "I've been a countin' and you've only done eight!"

"Aw, bullshit!" Strom said, picking worthless rock out of the cart and throwing it onto a close-by tailings pile.

"Yeah, I say bullshit, too! And since when did you learn how to count!" Big hollered.

"I can count all the way to a-hun-ert," Joe replied. George put a hand on Digby's shoulder.

"Hold on, Joe, there's no sense in arguing with Big. Why he'll just as soon pound all of them numbers you learnt right on outta yer' head," Pratt said. George grinned while Digby stared at Big Nelson, sizing him up.

"Oh, yeah, right. You know I was just pulling yer' leg, Big. Yer' right, that's ten loads," Joe agreed, nodding.

"That's better," Big said. He looked over at Strom, set his feet behind the end of the cart, reached down while inhaling a deep breath and lifted the whole thing by himself, dumping the ore into the tram bucket. A billow of rock dust flew up in the air just as Big righted himself, his large forehead and biceps gleaming with sweat. He put his hands on his hips and glowered at Digby, then he shoved the cart and let it roll back down the ramp towards the mine.

"There ya' go," Big said, pointing at the ore cart as it squeaked its way down the tracks. Strom and Big took a break and sat on the edge of the dock-like loading ramp while Joe and George walked over and began to push the cart back to the mine for another load.

"I'm here ta' tell ya' right now . . . that little fart is gonna push me too far, and POW!" Big said, striking a clenched fist into an open palm. "I'm gonna deck him so hard he'll be seeing stars for years!"

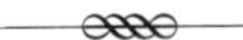

The following Sunday evening Chubb worked his way around the table with an iron kettle of steaming potato stew and ladled it out to hungry miners who sniffed at the contents in their bowls. Eli Peet quickly ate his portion, lifted his wooden bowl, and spooned the remaining bits into his mouth, then set the bowl back on the table.

"Ah," Eli sighed, his chin dripping with broth, "I'll take another, Chubb." George Pratt gaped at Eli, sniffed his stew again and frowned.

"Jesus, how can you eat this stuff? It's rancid!" George cried.

"Oh, a-huh," Chubb snapped. "So, you're not appreciating all my hard work, are ya'? And by the way Eli, if you'd like more, the proper term to use would be?"

Eli turned to look at Chubb as the corners of his mouth turned downward, his face in puzzlement.

"What 'er ya' wanting now?" Eli asked.

"He thinks yer supposed to say please for this crap!" George barked.

"Hey!" Chubb bellowed. "I do what I can with what I have!"

"Not if it's rotten!" Sam Keller said, pushing his bowl away.

"Oh! And I'm not a good enough cook?"

"Hell, anyone with half a brain could cook better 'en you!" Sam replied.

"That's it! I'm done!" Chubb hollered, stomping off back to his stove.

"Yeah, well, I'll believe it when I see it!" Pratt hollered.

Just then the cookhouse door opened and everyone turned their heads, Martin Comins walked in.

"There he is!" Big Nelson said.

"How goes the battle?" Sam Keeler asked.

"Tiz a fine evening me friends," Martin answered, walking straight back to the shelf and checking on the cookhouse painting. Seeing some dust in front of it on the shelf he carefully brushed it away with his hand, then he gazed at the painting for a moment.

"Looks good," he said, heading back to the table and pulling up a chair. Chubb came back out, set a bowl in front of him and filled it with his foul-smelling stew. Martin dropped his head down and sniffed the unpleasant fragrance then crinkled his nose. Everyone was looking at him, waiting with baited breath to hear what he'd say.

"That's okay Chubb, I stopped at Fred's for a wee bit on the way up and had some dinner," he replied, looking up and glancing around at the miners.

"Yeah! Ya' see! He's just being all nice and everything," George said. "That stuff is unfit for human consumption. Ya' know, I hear the cook at the Comet is making some pretty damn good grub — maybe we should all go to work there!"

"Maybe you should!" Chubb roared. "Maybe ya'll should!" He dropped the kettle on the table and stormed off while the cookhouse went quiet for a moment. A second later the sound of commotion and movement came through the air from the backroom as Chubb tore the room apart.

"So! Martin, what's new down in town?" Sam Keeler asked.

"Oh, not much. I worked Saturday at the O & B and stayed the night at my cabin then like I said, stopped by Fred's on the way up," Martin replied. "Thought I'd sleep here tonight so we can get an early start tomorrow."

"You see that new barmaid at Fred's?" Eli asked, his eyes as big as a cow's.

"Aw, I can't be peeling me eyes at a lady like that," Martin said.

"What about Digby? You see him down there?" Keeler asked.

"Oh yes, he's down there," Martin answered.

"We got the rest of that ore mucked out yesterday," Big said.

"Good," Martin replied, looking over at him. "We'll be blasting again in the morning."

Chubb walked back out into the room with his little bandy-legged half-step waddle wearing a coat, a frumpy felt hat and carrying an overloaded beat-up cloth suitcase with bits of clothing sticking out from it.

"That's it, I'm headed to town and catchin' the train, tomorrow! You bunch of hoople-heads can cook yer' own breakfast in the morning! And every other meal in-betweens as far as I'm concerned 'cause I quit! I'm goin' back to the Black Hills!" he hollered, slamming the cookhouse door behind him. Once he was gone everyone slowly turned and stared at George in disbelief.

"Don't be gawkin' at me," George said. "It ain't my fault he can't cook." But the men's stares turned to glares. "What?!" George alarmingly asked.

Martin leaned back in his chair and looked up at the rafters for a moment then cast a quick gaze at each man at the table, eventually settling on George; with a sparkle in his eye he finally spoke:

"Well, Georgie me boy!" he said with wry grin, "It'll be a fine day in the morning ta' wake smellin' flapjacks and bacon an' then seein' the sight of ya' at the stove with an apron 'round yer' waist!" The cookhouse instantly came back to life with bawdy, out-of-control laughter.

XIII

FALL COLORS

A shiver of cold was snaking its way up the valley, running upstream and pushing through the trees, winding around and over the ridgelines and mountains. The chill in the air reminded me that fall and winter were close relatives, every day seemed to be colder than the one before. Yesterday there was frost on the ground, and today I woke up to find a dusting of snow. I took my pair of wool pants out of the little dresser, put them on and my boots and went outside.

Standing up from dropping an armload of cord wood in the box I brushed off my shirtsleeves over the top of it and glanced at Liz, she was at the counter preparing breakfast. I poured myself a cup of coffee and sat down at the built-in.

"Good morning! And what's Oliver doing today?" she asked, cracking an egg over a bowl.

"Looks like I'm gonna make a snowman," I replied. "Did you look outside?"

"Oh, this," Liz groaned. "It'll melt off in a hurry, it's not out of the ordinary for us to have snow in the middle of October."

"Good thing my paint order came in with plenty of white," I mentioned.

"So, you're gonna stick it out, then?" Liz asked.

"I'd like to," I said, taking a sip.

"It gets pretty cold and lonely all the way up here during hibernation season," she replied. I took another sip and tried to think about what it'd be like.

"I can imagine this place covered in snow drifts. Does the creek freeze?" I asked. Liz laughed, turned her head around and looked at me.

"Oh Lord yes. Last winter the creek froze, we froze, and this place darn near turned into an igloo!" she laughed. "I've never been so cold and I've even spent winters in North Dakota!"

"Well, I'm still going to paint all the seasons," I said. Liz stared at me.

"How on earth are you gonna hold a paint brush when your fingers are frozen? And besides, won't your paint freeze?"

"Oh, jeez," I mumbled. "I guess I hadn't thought a' that."

"Have you ever even seen snow?" Liz said with seriousness.

"Yes, of course I have," I replied, proudly. "Like today!"

"But have you ever lived in snow?"

"Well, no," I answered. Liz laughed.

"It sure looks like you're a-gonna," she chuckled. Just then Eva walked in the kitchen.

"Mornin' all. You look outside?" she asked.

"Oh, good grief yes," Liz answered. "Oliver here thinks he's gonna paint with frozen fingers."

"Does he now?" Eva said, glancing in my direction.

"Aw, I'll figure something out," I replied. "Maybe I'll just look out the window and paint from inside."

"So, what are you doing today, Oliver?" Eva asked.

"Since it's a train day I was gonna go down to the depot and set up the easel," I replied, glancing at Liz as she looked out the window from the sink.

"It's already getting brighter. The sun will break through, it'll melt off by afternoon," Liz said optimistically.

Walking down Dumas the sunshine was bursting through the clouds, its bright light reflected off the coverlet of snow that hung on the town and the hills surrounding the valley, everything looked new and wonderful. The mud and dirt of the town was now covered in white, all of it looking fresh and clean. In the distance, the backdrop of fall colors from leaves hanging in the tress combined with the brilliant snow and the dank organic smells of wood smoke; it all produced a sense of wellbeing to me. The steel rails of the train tracks gleamed like silver streaks of lightning zooming through the woods across the trestle and out of town, they looked magnified and powerful, and I realized how much the town relied on them. Without the railroad we wouldn't be here and, couldn't live here without the supplies it brought.

Carrying my equipment, the fresh inch of snow crunched beneath my boots. At the newspaper office I saw a paper handbill tacked by the door and angled over in its direction. At the top of it was a notice for the period of filing for candidates in the election of Justice of the Peace that was now open. I wondered if Uncle Jacob would be interested.

I stood the easel up at my normal spot next to the depot, set my sketch pad on it and went over to the building. Stepping inside,

I could hear Ed Baker tapping his key machine, keeping us tethered to the world. Without him we'd be lost in the wilderness, void of any kind of quick communication with the rest of society, and mankind for that matter. I found comfort seeing him there at his desk, ever vigilant, on the job. He saw me when I came in, I pointed to the straight back chair and he nodded an okay that I could borrow it.

Walking out to my regular spot I glanced around. The water tower still had some snow on it, the melting snow dripping off the roof and running down its sides showed different lengths and widths of watery streaks. It was a great subject, especially with the pitched roof lines of the buildings in lower town behind it. Once I found the perfect angle I moved the easel, got everything set up and made a start.

As I worked away the ever-present drone of the concentrator in the immediate distance was the only sound to be heard in the valley since school was in session, until behind me I could hear Henry's wagon approaching. The heavy sound of his mules' hooves sloshing through the wet mud soon mixed with the rumble of the train as it pushed over Barlow Pass. I continued to draw the water tower and added a few roof lines of lower town in the background.

The whistle sang as the train rolled across the trestle, the bell clanged and the air brakes went off. When the train pulled up to the depot it chugged to a stop just past the water tower, the front of the locomotive engine and its bell, steam and smoke added to the scene, so I began to draw it in.

Like always, Conductor Speer was the first to disembark. A few townsfolk had come to greet the passengers and a contingent from lower town strolled up. I recognized the tall, cadaverous looking bartender but not the others who were with him. They stood off to the side and waited until a man of abbreviated height with a dark well-trimmed beard wearing a suit and derby hat got off. He brushed his suit coat with a couple of strokes of his hand and flicked at something on his sleeve with a finger, then casually glanced around with his nose tilted upward. The bartender and his group walked over to him. I kept drawing as I listened to them.

"Frederick!" the tall one said. "Good to see you, good to see you."

"Shamus! Yah, is good to see you, too," the fellow replied with a German accent.

"How was the wedding? How was the trip?" Shamus asked. Just then Ed Baker walked up. He glanced at the rendering and then at all the disembarked passengers.

"Looks like Fred's back," Ed acknowledged.

"Who's back?" I asked, working on the train's coal tender.

"That's Frederick Trump, but everyone just calls him Fred," Baker explained. "He owns the Monte Cristo Hotel, in lower town."

"Oh, yes, I've heard of him."

"Have you now?" Ed noted as the group headed to the baggage car.

"Liz mentioned something about him once," I said, trying to concentrate on the sketch.

"Well, Fred showed up a few years back. He got here before the railroad did and made a placer claim on the land where his place sits. But he didn't buy the land, just made a claim and built on it," Ed stated dryly.

"Isn't that what everyone does here?" I asked, putting the final touches on the smoke above the locomotive, finishing the rendering. Ed smiled tightly.

"Uh, no. Everyone else had to either buy their lots from the mining company or rent. It's not legal to build on a claim unless it's patented," he said. "A man in Everett owned the lot he made the claim on, I think I heard that a few others tried doing the same thing in lower town, back then, but I'm not sure. He owns it now though, bought it from the gentleman. So, he proved up."

Apparently, word had spread quickly through town that Frederick Trump had arrived. More people were joining the group at the baggage car and soon two men had Fred up on their shoulders and were carrying him down to his establishment. It looked like a celebration was to ensue. I turned to Ed.

"Is it okay if I store my easel and drawing in your office for a little bit?" I asked, thinking I'd like to get in on the festivities that appeared to be happening.

"Sure. You goin' down to join them?"

"I don't know about joining them, maybe just check it out and see what's going on."

I could hear them carrying on as I strolled up to the door of Fred's place and poked my head inside, it was full of miners drinking and playing cards. The same buxom gal I'd seen before with the black hair was sitting at a table but this time she wasn't alone and staring out the window, she was with a miner having at tête-á-tête. The top of her blouse was unbuttoned and her hands were fiddling with a silver pendant lost deep in the crevasse of her substantial cleavage. I walked over near them and took a seat at a table, she leveled her dark eyes at me as I went by but quickly took back up with her caller.

The room was alive with talk and mirth, men lined the bar as shots of whiskey were poured by Fred and Shamus. I recognized some of the miners from when they walked by the Pride but wasn't fully apprised of who the rest of them were. Jim Bartholomew walked in and joined everyone at the bar and a woman I hadn't seen before came over to my table, I guessed she was Libby's replacement.

"What'll it be?" she asked. She had a look that made me think that she was a stylish woman and high-born, her coarse wavy hair hung down to her shoulders and she wore a full length pleated black dress over a high collar white linen shirt.

"Whiskey," I answered automatically, not thinking. I reached in my worsted pants pocket and began to search for a quarter —

"Hurry up!" the waitress snapped, "can't you see I'm busy!"

"Oh, sorry," I replied, pulling out a quarter and setting it on the table. But the lady glared at me.

"What's this? No tip?"

I dug back in my trousers for a nickel and placed it on the table and grinned at her. She swooped them up and turned for the bar. I glanced around the room and listened to the revelry.

"How was the wedding?" Shamus asked Fred.

"Oh, yah, the wedding was in September and a good one. But I could only stay for the first two days of Oktoberfest since I had to get back. Oktoberfest was much better den da' wedding! I had lots of lovely little fräuleins to chase around! And serve me beer!" Fred replied to laughter with a sly little smirk. Jim Bartholomew spoke up.

"So, Fred! No one is running for Justice of the Peace yet and I've kept the filing open until this Thursday. That is, if you're interested?" he said, placing a quarter on the bar, adding, "How about a little of the cure-all?" Fred came over with a glass and bottle and poured him a shot, then gave him back a dime.

"What's this now?" Fred asked, setting the bottle on the bar. He twisted the end of his mustache while he waited for an answer, watching the newsman down his drink.

"Well, whoever wants to run for Justice of the Peace has to file to be a candidate by Thursday, three days from now," Bartholomew said. "I'm retiring so I'm not filing." Fred thought about his statement, and started pulling at his dark mustache. The barmaid brought over my shot, set it and a dime on the table without looking at me. I strained my ears and let the whiskey sit.

"And what does the Justice do?" Fred asked, raising an eyebrow. Shamus came over and stood next to him with an interested look.

"Pass judgement and make rulings on disputes, things of that nature."

"And dat is a paid position? Yah?" Fred asked.

"Well, not yet," Bartholomew replied, "but eventually it will. For now it's a position of stature within the community, you know, it's prestigious." Fred nodded and thought about the idea.

"A position of stature?" Fred responded.

"Absolutely, all judges are looked up to," Jim pointed out.

"You should do it," Shamus said, nudging him with an elbow.

"Oh, no. Not me," Fred replied. "I'm too busy."

"Too busy to be the Justice!" Bartholomew exclaimed. "There's not that much to do."

"You'd be good at it," Shamus said. Fred pulled his mustache some more.

"Has anyone else signed up?" Fred asked Bartholomew.

"Nope, nobody. Everyone I've asked to run has turned me down so you'd probably run unopposed," Bartholomew replied. Fred kept pulling at and then twisted his mustache with a distant look on his face, finally he turned to Bartholomew and smiled.

"Okay, I'll do it," Fred said. He looked out over the bar and raised his hands.

"Everybody listen!" he said. But nobody noticed. "Listen up!" he hollered, as a few men turned their heads towards him. "Everybody shut up!" he screamed, waving his arms. Finally the room quieted down.

"Today I've decided to run for the highest position in Monte Cristo and become the Justice of the Peace! So! The drinks are on me!" The whole place erupted in cheers and huzzahs as everyone crowded up to the bar. As they did I looked at my whiskey still on the table. Just then Fred yelled out over the room.

"Anyone who downs a drink on me, votes for me!" Fred hollered out as he raised his glass. Shamus quickly filled the empty shot glasses as they landed on the bar.

"To Monte Cristo and Frederick Trump for Justice of the Peace!" Shamus yelled, raising a glass. Every miner with a free shot downed their drink and let out a holler.

Since I'd paid for my shot I downed it and headed for the door and my drawing.

Walking across the footbridge I glanced over to the Cleveland and Kline and decided to check on any sales before I went back to Ed's office to collect my things. I looked over at Dumas Street and saw Henry and his wagon heading up it, making deliveries. I went across the trestle and down the embankment. The door was closed but a hand-made open sign was in the window, I walked inside. There were two fellows I didn't recognize sitting at the bar and Jacob was down on his haunches feeding a small fire in the wood stove. He looked up as I approached.

"Oliver, how goes it?" he said brightly, standing up. He slapped his hands together to wipe them off, saying, "We sold all of your paintings."

"You did! That's great, thanks," I replied. Addison walked out of the backroom.

"Hey Oliver," he said. "We need some more paintings."

"Okay, I've got plenty," I replied, taking a seat at the bar. Jacob walked by and into the back room.

"What can I get you?" Addison asked, wiping down the bar.

"How about a cup of coffee?" I asked. He nodded and went into the kitchen. I set a nickel on the bar. A moment later Addison returned with a small mug and pot of coffee, pouring it. Then Jacob materialized from the backroom and set a pile of bills in front of me.

"There ya' go. Twenty dollars for ten paintings," he said with a grin.

"Wow! That's great," I said, grabbing the bills and counting them.

"As long as the weather holds there should be plenty of tourists still coming up, so we can sell more for you," Addison suggested.

"That sounds good," I said. I took a sip of coffee then folded and stuffed the dollars in my trousers.

"What're ya' gonna do with all that money?" Jacob asked.

"Oh, save it for a rainy day I guess," I replied, sipping more coffee. He laughed.

"Have you been over to Sunday Falls or up to Silver Lake?" Jacob asked.

"Haven't yet."

"Well, ya' better hurry," Jacob said, tilting his head towards the window and the melting snow outside.

"Oh, I know," I acknowledged, finishing the coffee.

"In another month or two we'll be buried in the stuff," Addison added.

"Okay, I best be on my way," I said, standing up to leave.

"Bring us as many paintings as you can," Jacob said, reminding me. "We'll sell them all."

"I've got a bunch."

"Sounds good, thanks," Jacob said with a smile.

"Alright, see you soon," I replied grinning, heading out the door.

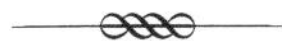

Stepping through the backdoor, the scent of cinnamon and brown sugar filled the hotel and welcomed me home. I put the easel and field box in my room and went to the kitchen. Liz was at the cook stove, feeding bits of wood into the firebox. The fire crackled and popped as the kindling exploded into flames and lapped at the stove top, warming it and the room.

"Hey Liz," I said. She jumped back from the stove.

"Oh, Oliver!" she gasped. "You startled me, I didn't hear you come in."

"Oops, I'm sorry. What-cha makin'?" I asked, sitting down at the built-in.

"I'm making my famous cinnamon buns for tomorrow's guests," she replied, wiping her brow with her forearm then opening the oven door to check on them.

"They sure smell good," I offered.

"Thanks, but I'll be needing a bit more wood, soon," she said with a grin. I hopped back up and went outside for an armful of cord wood, brought it inside and returned to my seat.

"The Cleveland and Kline sold all my paintings," I related. Liz spun around.

"They did? Good for you!"

"And they want more."

"That's fantastic," Liz said. "I told you before, you've got a gift you do."

"Thanks," I replied. Just then Jacob walked in the kitchen, carrying a small package wrapped in brown paper.

"I guess Henry just dropped this off, I found it out on the front porch," he said, setting it down on the counter. "Did he even knock?"

"I didn't hear him," Liz replied.

"Me neither," I said. "But I came in through the back door." Jacob walked over and sat down at the built-in.

"It's addressed to Eva so it's probably something she ordered through the mercantile, or it's just mail that Henry decided to deliver instead of leaving at the post office," Jacob said. Just then Eva walked into the kitchen and saw the package.

"Oh goodie, they're here," she said, grabbing the delivery and heading back through the dining room.

"What is it?" Jacob asked.

"Just some Seattle magazines," she replied over her shoulder. Jacob looked over at me.

"Her and her magazines."

"Say, did you hear Jim Bartholomew is taking candidates for the Justice of the Peace?" I asked.

"I know, saw the flyer," Jacob stated.

"You should run," I suggested. Jacob quickly shook his head.

"Nope, no politics for me," he croaked.

"But you'd be good at it. Fred Trump is running."

"What? Fred's back?"

"Saw him get off the train today, and I heard Bartholomew taking to him about being a candidate."

"Boy, you sure get around," Jacob laughed.

"The town isn't that big, after all," I said. "But why won't you consider it?"

"Nope, no thanks. Politics isn't for everyone, especially me," Jacob reasserted.

"I saw Fred pour free shots at his bar for anyone who said they'd vote for him."

"That's about right. I've heard that's tradition in some parts of the world," Liz said.

"Sounds like something Fred would do."

"Yep, saw it with my own two eyes."

"He buy you one?" Jacob asked with a touch of concern.

"Nope, not me. Well, I've got work to do," I said standing up. "The Cleveland and Kline sold everything I gave them and they want more."

"That's great news! Good for you, Oliver," Jacob said.

"Between the sales from here and down there I'm gonna be busy for a while."

That weekend I was sitting on the front porch, taking a break from reproducing paintings and watching miners come down from the hills as tourists went up into the mountains. I found it interesting to see the contrasts as the ragged miners walked downslope past the smartly dressed tourists huffing and puffing their way up, when I spied Mattie turning from Dumas Street. I smiled at the sight of her, she was wearing a blue bell-shaped dress and a blue and white striped long-sleeved blouse with a white V-neck collar and locket, her hair was down past her shoulders. I jumped up from the rocking chair and stepped out on the road.

"Hi Mattie," I said, smiling and putting my hands in my pockets.

"Oliver, how're you doing?" she replied brightly, stopping in front of me.

"I'm good, busy. You look wonderful today," I said. She glanced down at herself.

"Oh this," Mattie said, blushing and brushing her dress, "I was just at a morning tea. Have you been busy painting?"

"Oh yes, quite a bit. The Cleveland and Kline has been selling as many as I can bring them."

"That's great news! They should be selling, you're a good painter. You know, you still owe me a portrait," she said, reminding me, her bright eyes sparkling.

"That's right," I replied. "I do."

"Well, how about today?" she suggested with a grin.

"A portrait today?"

"Why not?"

"Okay, but where?" I asked. She glanced over my shoulder.

"How about the schoolhouse?"

I turned around and looked at it, nodding. "Right now?"

"Sure, are you busy or something?" she asked with a smile as warm and bright as sunshine.

"Alright, sure! Let me get my stuff and I'll meet you over there."

I ran over to the inn and ten minutes later I walked out of it carrying my easel, canvas and paints, just as Martin Comins was coming down from the mines.

"Oliver, lad! How are things today?" he asked, stopping.

"I'm well thanks, it's good to see you," I said. He looked at all my gear.

"Where ya' headed? Can I buy that drink?" He asked, laughing and smiling.

"Oh, boy," I said, glancing at the school. "I'd like that, but I don't think I have time right now."

"What's the hurry, lad? Let's go have us a dram," he said. I looked down at everything I was carrying and back at him.

"Canna' the mountain wait a wee bit for two friends to share a bit of rye? Where ya' off to?" he asked.

"Over to the schoolhouse," I replied, struggling to hold all my stuff. He instantly smiled and glanced at the school.

"Doing a class painting?" he asked. I thought about how to reply to his comment

"Yes. A group painting . . . for this year's class."

"Ah," he smirked. "Don't see any kids around."

"Oh, um, I guess they're not here, yet," I said. "I'll catch up with you another time."

"Very good, lad," Martin said, walking away.

Climbing the stairs, I noticed the door was cracked open. I nudged it wider with my foot and saw Mattie sitting at her desk. She'd already built a fire, it crackled and popped in the wood heater. Mattie looked up at me and grinned as I entered the room.

"There you are," she said with a bright smile, standing up and walking towards me. "Here, let me help you."

"Thanks, we should probably set up near a window — so we have plenty of light," I said. "What kind of portrait are you thinking you'd like?" I asked, swallowing hard.

"What kind?"

"I mean like a close up or a full body, where either you'd be sitting at your desk, or standing at the blackboard. Maybe something like Madame X?" Mattie looked at me with a confused smile.

"Madame X?" she asked. "That doesn't sound right."

"I didn't mean anything out of sorts. We could do a half-length with you sitting down, like Mona Lisa," I suggested.

"Oh, I've heard of the Mona Lisa but, tell me about Madame X though," she said, stepping over to the window and pulling back the curtains.

"Well, let's see. Madame X is a portrait John Sargent did of a woman that's standing at a table and looking away from the artist, to the side of her. She had alabaster skin and wore a black satin dress with jeweled straps. It was done as a study in contrasts, black on white, that kind of thing," I explained, setting up the easel near the desk.

"Well I like the idea of me standing. Maybe I should stand by the desk with the blackboard behind me?" Mattie suggested.

"Well, if that's what you want —"

"But you're the artist. What do you think?"

"I think we should do a half-length, with you sitting at your desk and the black board behind you. Maybe we could have a math problem in chalk on the board and some books on the desk, a few props to add to it but not too much. And, we should have a lamp on the desk to help with the lighting, but have it out of sight. How's that sound?"

"Okay, I think that would work," Mattie said with a smile.

I went over to the desk and stacked some books while Mattie worked at the blackboard, then got a chair and my paints set up.

"So, how do you want me?" Mattie asked with an elfin grin, sitting down at her desk.

"How about if you, just, ah . . . smile! Yes, you smile and look at me. There, good. Maybe have your hands on the desk, or you could hold a pencil like you're correcting a student's paper. How's that?"

"Okay. Whatever you say," she said.

I started with pencil and worked on getting her centered on the canvas. Then I began on Mattie's features, her chin and high cheekbones, lips, mouth and smile; her nose and then the basic shape of her eyes, forehead and brow. Once I'd got her outline done I reached for a brush and my palette.

"So, can we talk while you work?" Mattie asked.

"Oh, a little. I do need to concentrate, though," I said, blending paint.

"Okay, I'll try not to bug you," she replied. I looked at her and grinned.

Glancing back and forth, from the canvas to Mattie, I fell into a rhythm and she settled into her pose. I defined the contours of her face and hands and blouse and decided on my own to not include the props on her desk or math problem on the blackboard.

"How's it going?" Mattie asked after a while.

"Good, I've got the basics done and started working on your contours," I said, taking a quick break to scratch an itch on my nose.

"My contours?" she said, twisting in her chair.

"The contours of your face. You know, your nose and chin."

"Oh, those contours," she concluded, smiling.

"Also, I'm concentrating on just your face."

For over an hour I worked on defining her features in sepia tones, adding shadow to her nose and under her chin. I worked the brush strokes in different directions to smooth out the appearance of the paint layer, adding vibrancy to her portrait.

"My legs are getting stiff; can I stand for a minute?"

"I'm almost done," I replied, dabbing at the palette for some more blue.

"So . . . can I please at least stand up, maybe take a quick peek?" she asked. But I kept working away, trying to finish.

"Please?"

"Okay, sure, I could let it dry for a bit," I said, exhaling, finishing the shadow under her chin. Mattie got up and walked around to view her painting. I got up and pulled the chair across the floor and out of the way for her. She stepped in front of it and leaned over to take a closer look.

"Oh, my, gosh. It's fantastic! I love it!" Mattie said. She turned to me and grabbed me by my forearm, she squeezed and smiled brightly. Mattie turned back to the painting and gazed at it for another minute.

"Is it done?"

"Almost."

"Okay, happy to sit some more," she said, scurrying around the desk and sitting back down, with a grin from ear to ear.

"The last thing I need to do is your eyes, so look directly at me the whole time," I said. She was still smiling.

"By all means," she replied, trying not to move her lips or snicker. Her eyes were like a window into her being; bright, and bluer than I'd ever witnessed, or painted for that matter. I paused and got lost in them for a moment.

"Well? Aren't you going to paint?"

"Oh, sorry." I focused on my task because I knew that the eyes were the most important aspect of any portrait.

Once she was ready I fixated. First, I tried to pay attention and figure out if Mattie had one reflection on her pupil, or two. I reminded myself that one reflection is always brighter than the other, but I looked for that one reflection and tried to capture it with just the right mix of color. Glancing back and forth her sparkling eyes became mesmerizing jewels, her gaze bore into my soul and I fell into a working trance.

The iris is always darker on the side of the reflection and lighter on the opposite side, so I paid close attention to that. Then I worked a little more on her eyebrows, trying to get the correct shape as well as how close they were to her eyes to get the exact likeness. I made one last pass of light brown on her eyebrows and stopped to review the painting as a whole and was satisfied. I pushed my chair back and stood up.

"I think it's finished," I said, looking at Mattie then setting down my palate. She hoped up out of her chair and scampered like a gazelle around her desk over to the easel.

"Oliver," she said softly, "It. Is. Absolutely. Perfect! I love it!" Mattie looked back and forth from the painting to me for what seemed like minutes.

"So, you like it?"

"I just said I love it!" Mattie repeated. She stepped closer, grabbed me by my forearms and rose up on her toes. Then she kissed me on my cheek. I wrapped my arms around her and hugged her tight until we pulled away from each other. Time stood still for a moment.

"How about if we go down to the mercantile for coffee? On me," Mattie suggested, her face a touch blushed.

"Okay, that sounds great! But what about your portrait?"

"We can leave it here," she said.

"What about the school kids?" She looked over her shoulder at the painting.

"How about if we put it in the storage room for now?"

"Sure, is there a shelf for it so it can dry?"

"There is, follow me," Mattie said. I carefully picked the painting off the easel by its edges and carried it to the room. Mattie moved some boxes from a shelf and I set it down. We both stepped back and looked at it.

"You are a very talented man, Olive Cohen," she said with wonderment. "That's the nicest thing anyone has ever done for me."

"Aw, quit it some more," I said. We both chuckled as we left the schoolhouse side by side.

XIV

AUTUMN CHILL

Rolling over on my cot I stared up at the ceiling and listened to the rain for a moment, I could hear it pound against, and run down the outside of the building. Getting up, I pulled my trousers on over my long johns, walked down the hall to the laundry and looked out the window. An almost unimaginable sideways rain was slashing through the air and pelting anything in its way. Across the valley I could see the trees bend and sway from wave after wave of wind, a menacing blanket of black clouds was pressing down upon the town and ridge tops.

I went back down the hall to the kitchen, Liz was already up and at the counter with an aura of powdery white floating around herself. She reached into a bin of flour and sprinkled a dusting over the bread board and the dough she was kneading then wiped her brow with a white forearm.

"Mornin'," I said. Liz turned her head.

"Oliver, good morning," she replied, blowing a wisp of scarlet hair from her eyes.

"Nice day, huh?"

"Oh, this," she scoffed, "the rainy days are when the real work gets done."

"It's a good day to stay indoors, looks like we're in for a big storm."

"Oh, this is nothing! Just you wait, pretty soon we'll be up to our necks in snow and sleet," she said, dividing the dough in half and forming it into two loaves, then gently placing them in lard greased bread pans.

"Be a dear and open the oven door for me," Liz said, carrying the tins to the stove.

"Sure, happy to help," I said, and walked over to open it. Liz slid the two pans onto the rack, then I closed the door and poured myself a cup of coffee when the sound of muffled voices came through the ceiling. It sounded like someone was arguing but I knew there weren't any guests.

"I guess my Aunt and Uncle are up," I said, sliding into the built-in. "Sounds like they've got a little disagreement going on." Liz turned to me and frowned, shaking her head before going back to the counter.

"What's going on?"

"Oh, probably nothing," she said. The voices got louder.

"Nothing, huh? Doesn't sound like nothing to me," I asserted. But Liz kept her back to me and didn't say anything while the yelling continued.

"Liz?"

"Okay, but you can't tell them I told you," Liz said quietly, turning and glancing around the room, her mouth tight and serious. She walked over and sat on the edge of the built-in.

"So," she whispered, "Eva wants to sell the hotel." My ears perked up.

"And do what?" I asked. Liz put a finger up to her lips.

"Buy another one in Seattle, or one somewhere else, maybe Anacortes," she said quietly. I took a sip of coffee and thought for a second.

"And I guess Jacob doesn't want to?" I surmised.

"That's right. They've been going around and around about this for a while."

"Really?"

"They have. And . . . they haven't been getting along, lately."

"Oh! Well, as far as I know the thing about mining camps and gold rushes is that they never last," I said. "So, Aunt Eva told you already?"

Liz nodded.

"But Jacob asked me if I'd like to be partners in this place, a couple of months ago. I'm not sure if Eva wants me as a partner. She hasn't approached me about it. I don't even know if Jacob told Eva he asked me. So, I haven't said anything."

"What'd you tell Jacob?"

"That I'd think about it . . . You see," Liz said quietly, "Jacob's a silent partner in the Monte Cristo Hotel and I'm not sure if he's told Eva about that, yet."

"No kidding. I had no idea," I replied. "So then, what's going to happen?"

"Well, back when all this was going on Eva asked me if I'd go with them when they sold, and I said I would," Liz answered, standing back up.

"Well, that was good of her to ask you."

"Oh yes, it was," she said. Then she put her fingers to the side of her mouth and ran them across her lips. "But you need to keep your lips zipped, mister. This is all very private."

I nodded my head and whispered, "Okay, don't worry. I can keep a secret." Liz went back to the counter and I sipped my coffee.

A moment later Eva walked into the kitchen dressed, but her hair had been quickly done, strands falling from her normally tight, neat bun, and she wore an uncharacteristic scowl on her face, although upon seeing me she adopted a quick smile, yet her eyes remained dark.

"Good morning, everybody," she said, grabbing a coffee cup.

"Mornin'," I greeted her, smiling.

"Good morning, Eva," Liz offered. When Eva's back was to her Liz glanced over at me and made a *you keep quiet* look on her face.

"Yes, good morning, Liz," Eva replied, pouring herself some coffee. She sat down at the built-in across from me.

"Looks like another rainy season is here," Eva commented.

"Yep, pretty wet out there," I added, sipping my coffee.

"Spring can't come soon enough for me. So! What are you up to today?" Eva asked, looking at me.

"Oh, the usual rainy-day stuff, I guess. Reproduce some paintings. Maybe go down to the Cleveland and Kline. Take a nap," I said, laughing.

"Reproduce paintings?"

"Yeah, the ones that sell the best I do again from memory."

"Oh, that sounds like a good thing to do. Have you seen Mattie, lately?" she asked. I took a sip before replying.

"Yep, a couple of days ago."

"You've seen her around then?"

"I did a painting for her last week."

"A painting?" Eva asked. "What kind of painting?"

"Her portrait," I said. As soon as I said it Liz scurried over and sat down next to Eva. Liz's eyes grew eager and she grinned at me but the scowl on Eva's face returned.

"Did she ask you to do her portrait?" Eva asked, her voice rising.

"Yes, she did."

"And you did one for her? In private?" she asked, frowning. I looked at her.

"I did, over at the school."

"Well, that sounds a bit too forward, and way too *personal*," she replied.

"Oh, not me," Liz said. "You're both adults now, college graduates and all."

"You see," I said, looking at Eva. "Liz approves."

"But I don't," Eva said coldly. "How did this happen?"

I looked down at my coffee.

"So?!" Eva snapped.

"What?" I replied.

"So, tell me about it!"

"Aw, there's nothing to tell," I said, rubbing the stubble on my chin. "It was no big deal. I painted her portrait and gave it to her. That's all. I painted it then we went down to the mercantile and had a cup of coffee and cinnamon sticks. That was it."

"Ooo, I think he likes her," Liz laughed.

"Well, you need to take it slow, buster," Eva suggested. "And what do you think her parents would say, or think, about something like this?"

"Yeah, yeah," I said, sipping my coffee.

"Oliver? Answer me."

"I don't know what they would think but since it was Mattie's idea I would guess that her parents would be fine with it," I said, looking at my Aunt.

"You two would make a nice couple," Liz offered. With that I got up and stood over the two of them.

"Okay. I think I need to leave now," I said, walking down the hall and out to the privy.

Hours later in the afternoon, the wind and rain stopped, the clouds turned to greyish white and the sky began to lighten, but even then, the clouds still seemed to hang around. They had shape-shifted into long and flat, low-slung sky shutters that scraped across the tops of the mountains, the black coal smoke from the concentrator rose up and stained them producing a dark grey horizon, and the cool damp air prickled the skin on my face.

Coming down Dumas I was careful not to slip on the slick mud; rivulets of rain water had carved out the dirt and duff in the road, leaving tiny canyons ready for more water run-off. Up ahead was the log cabin with the barber shop, a new sign on the stump read 'Shave and Hair-Cut 25 ¢.' I rubbed the stubble on my chin and then felt in my pocket for some change. Finding a few coins, I went over, scraped the mud off my boots on the edge of the landing in front of the door and walked inside. The front room was dark and tiny, not much bigger than the barber chair. Past the chair was a half-closed curtain that separated the business from a living area, the barber materialized from behind it.

"Afternoon," he said, closing the curtain behind him. "Hair-cut for ya' today?" The fellow was medium height with salt and pepper hair cropped short, and wore black suspenders and a white shirt with the sleeves rolled up.

"That and a shave," I replied, glancing around. I took off my wool coat and the slouch hat that I'd borrowed from the hotel and hung them on a nail. The place was small, across its rough-hewn log walls there were tacked pictures cut from magazines, fashionable looking men in cities with fashionable looking haircuts and waxed mustaches. Behind the barber chair was a large mirror and a counter full of scissors, straight razors, and a glass jar of combs with blue water in it.

"I'm surprised it took you so long to stop in," he said as I sat down in the swivel chair. He pumped the lever and spun the chair around so I was facing the mirror. Our eyes met in the looking-glass.

"Surprised?"

"I've been watching you walk by for the last few months and wondered if you'd ever come in the door," he said, tossing a white sheet of cotton over me and tying it around my neck.

"Oh, sure, right. I guess you see everybody that goes by," I replied.

"How do you want me to cut this . . . a . . .?"

"You can just trim the ponytail. Snip it about three inches below the banding, okay?"

"Sure, sure, I can do that after the shave," he said, picking up his long razor and stroking it back and forth on a wide leather strap then setting the blade on the counter below the mirror.

"You're Oliver, the artist, right?" he asked, working up a lather in his shaving cup with a brush.

"I guess you know everyone, huh?"

"Jacob told me all about you," he replied, smearing white foam on my chin and face. He turned and grabbed the sharpened straight knife from the counter. "I hear you came up here all the way from San Francisco."

"Yep, and this is sure different than the big city but I like it. So, what's your name?"

"Ned Berwyn's the name. Been here since the summer of '93. Came up from Seattle by way of Newcastle."

"Newcastle? Where's that?" I asked, right as Ned began to shave my neck.

"It'd probably best if I do the talking right now, son. So! Newcastle is a coal camp east of Seattle. Had a shop there for years before I came up here," Ned related. "I grew up in Seattle and graduated from the Sixth Street School back in '78, I think it's called the Central School now. Then I had a shop in the Madison District but got tired of that. Wanted to see more of the world, so I headed out to Newcastle." Ned stopped to wipe the foam from his knife.

"You like this better than Newcastle?" I asked, raising my hand under the sheet, attempting to possibly scratch my nose. Just then Ned brought the knife up to my face.

"Oh," he laughed, "we're pretty far out in the sticks and could use a jailhouse. But we've got an election coming up for Justice of the Peace so maybe that will get us a new one, which I would hope keep the miners in line." Ned stopped again to wipe the foam off his knife.

"I didn't know there was a problem," I quickly said. Ned brought the knife back up to my face.

"Every once in a while, there is. Hell, a few years ago when Joe Conner was found dead out on the wagon road some said he was bushwhacked and strangled but others claimed he choked on his lunch, like on a chicken bone 'er somethin' an' more said he just died a natural death, like a heart attack. But when it happened it caused a lot of concern around here, people got worried, myself included, so a jail was built. Then once it was a couple-a liquored up boys, we guess from the mines, tore up that brand-new jailhouse and pushed the whole damn hoosegow in the Sauk River, by-golly. Deputy Wesley and Constable Brookings never did find out who did it," Ned said, wiping his knife off again.

"No kidding?! I hadn't heard that one. How does a jail get pushed in the river?"

"Aw, it was a flimsy thing and built out of crap-wood right on the riverbank, it weren't no brickhouse. I think it got used once or twice for a brawl 'er two down in lower town. I doubt if Fred gets elected that'll change. He's the only one signed up so far I hear."

"So, Trump's running unopposed?" I asked.

"Yep, and I hear his whiskey's been doin' all his campaigning for him," Ned stated matter-of-factly. I wanted to say something, but he was right in the middle of scraping my face with a very sharp object.

"Brookings comes by every now and again but I'll tell you right now, if I was the justice around here any foul behavior would not be tolerated, and there sure wouldn't be any more shootings or robberies like we had back in June," Ned said as he worked his way around my face.

"By-God I'll tell ya' this too, Newcastle was a lawless camp until we got old Grady Brown as Marshal. He cleaned up that town and set it straight, it's all civilized now! But answer me this son, does that whiskey slinger down in lower town seem like any kind of lawman or justice-dealer to you?" Ned asked, stopping and holding the knife away from my face so I could respond.

"Well," I replied, "now that you mention it, I guess not."

"That's-a right," Ned quipped, bringing his knife to my face again. "Never cared much for the man myself, but if he gets elected we'll see what he does for this town. I hear Sunday is the election rally, the only one scheduled. It's going to be at the pavilion, Sunday afternoon that is, two o'clock sharp I guess . . . yep, sure hope the weather holds off," Ned said as he finished up. He handed me a towel to dry my face and grabbed a pair of scissors.

"What'd you say? About one or two inches below the band?"

"Cut it off a little longer than that," I replied, reaching back and showing him with my hand. Ned lopped off the back of my hair with a quick snip and took the sheet off.

"Thank you, sir," I said, reaching into my pocket for a quarter and dropping it in his open palm.

"Stop in again," Ned replied with a friendly nod, grabbing a long-handled broom. I stepped back out onto the street and took in the air.

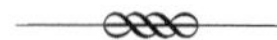

The following Sunday afternoon, Jacob, Eva and I stood next to a husband and wife with two young girls both with toy jig dolls hung by string that they each held in their hands. The dolls had jointed arms and legs attached to the strings that the girls would move to make the little toys dance as they waited for the big event to begin. A minute later Jim Bartholomew strode out from the side of the open-air pavilion stage.

"Welcome everyone to our election program!" Bartholomew proclaimed from the podium as everyone cheered. Hanging behind him from the rafters were the same red, white and blue bunting from the 4th of July that lined Dumas Street. Most of the citizens from town and a good number of miners had jam-packed the wood frame structure.

"Although a big decision will be made in a few more days to the east, that being the presidential race between Mr. McKinley and Mr. Bryan, today we are going to hear from our one citizen that is running unopposed for Justice of the Peace, Frederick Trump. Let's hear it for our candidate!" Bartholomew hollered out over the crowd. Almost everyone clapped and cheered while a few miners and railroaders coughed and murmured amongst themselves.

"Now then, before we start I do want to say that if there is anyone here who would like to be a write-in candidate then they can come up and make a speech for why they should be elected. Okay? Everyone got that? But first we've got a little bit of entertainment," the newspaper man said, motioning over to the side of the stage. "Doc Welch is here and he's going to play us some fiddle music while Danny MacFarren and Lila Crabtree do a buck dance. Come on kids, let's go!"

The two teenagers walked out to the front of the stage in wooden shoes. She wore a colorful print dress, and he was in a grey flannel shirt, dungarees and suspenders. The fiddler counted off and commenced to saw away on his strings, playing a lively version of 'Turkey in the Straw.' The boy stepped to the front and bowed to the audience then started by bending his knees and dragging the toe of one of his shoes across the floor. The girl watched with her hands to her face and a look of astonishment. Most of the crowd began to clap and stomp their feet in unison to the fiddler and called out in whoops and yahoos.

Next the boy did a quick skip-hop and a run of quick heel stomp shuffles, causing the floor to vibrate, the sound from his wooden shoes ringing out through the structure. He turned and faced his dance partner, put his hands on his hips and clopped away with a big smile. He danced towards the young girl, stomping away as she gawked back and forth from the crowd to him while pointing at his moves. Gradually the boy backed away from her as he danced then moved back towards her again. The whole time Doc Welsh played on, his bow running back and forth across the neck of his violin as he moved around the stage wearing a black vest and felt hat with the front brim turned up. Finally, the boy danced off to the side. With that the girl did a twirl and bounded to the front of the stage.

She did a quick curtsy at the boy and the crowd, hitched up her long dress and dragged the toe of her shoe across the floor. Then she did a little skip-hop and commenced to sashay in shuffles back and forth across the stage, following that she did light on her feet tap-steps while the boy glanced back and forth from her to the assembly, smiling with glee.

The boy started dancing again, he shuffled over to the girl and held out his hands. She grabbed hold and they danced together, hand in hand facing each other, smiling like they'd just won a county fair contest, they broke free and danced side-by-side. In syncopated rhythms they slammed the floor hard with their wood shoes on the downbeat; *clip-a, clip-a, boom! clip-a, clip-a, boom*! Over and over. The crowd clapped and stomped until finally the fiddler slowed down and the two dancers stopped, the entire room erupted in cheers.

Jim Bartholomew stepped back to the front of the stage, clapping while the two young and breathless dancers took a bow.

"How about that, folks!" Bartholomew stammered, his hands held out towards the teenagers. "Keep it up!" He hollered at the throng. "Let's hear it for Danny and Lila!"

As everyone clapped and yelled I glanced around the pavilion, there near the entrance was Mattie, she was looking right at me. I pushed and shoved my way through the crowd over to her.

"Hey Mattie!" I said, smiling.

"Hi Oliver," she said, grinning from ear to ear.

"Did you get to see most of that?" I asked. Mattie nodded.

"I did, I got here right as they started," she replied, trying to be heard over the applause still happening.

"Weren't they great?" I asked, leaning over so she could hear me.

"Oh, yes, I loved it," Mattie replied, smiling. Just then Jim Bartholomew started up again.

"Okay everybody, settle down! Now it's time for our candidate. In just over a week election day with be here and all ballots will have to be properly marked at my office by 6:00 p.m. on Tuesday November 3rd. So don't forget all you men."

"Now then, like I mentioned earlier. Is there anyone here that would like to be a write-in candidate?" Bartholomew asked, when a voice called out.

"Yep! Right here," a man spoke up and raised his hand. He started walking up to the front as the crowd whispered amongst themselves.

"It looks like we've got a second candidate," Bartholomew said with his hands up over his head, clapping. The crowd responded with a few cheers and yahoos, some pumped their fists in the air. The newspaper man nodded his head up and down and grinned.

"It looks like we have . . . Ned Berwyn everyone! Let's give him a round of applause! Come on up here, Ned!"

The barber made his way through the crowd to the podium as a few folks slapped him on the back and wished him luck. He wore a bowler hat, a dark suit with a white high collared shirt with a blue cravat and brushed boots. Just as he was about to mount the stage a lone voice called out:

"That guy can't even cut my hair right, how's he supposed to ta' lay down the law?" Ned turned around and saw the man's face.

"Aw, shut up Digby! Ain't no one can cut that scruff of hay you call hair!" Ned yelled to scattered laughter. Ned walked across the stage and grinned at Bartholomew as he shook his hand and turned to the gathering.

"Alright everybody," Bartholomew said, "quiet down so we can hear what Ned has to say." Ned pulled a slip of paper from an inside coat pocket, glanced at it and looked out to the crowd.

"Good afternoon everyone," he began. "Seems to me there should be two of us running, so as of right now, I'm throwing my hat in the ring for Justice of the Peace!" he said to cheers.

"As most of you know, I'm Ned Berwyn and I've been here cutting hair since '93. I consider most of you my close friends," he said, glancing at the slip of paper, "and over the years I've watched this camp grow into what it is today. A fine town with nothing but *fine citizens*!" he exclaimed. When he got to the fine citizens everyone cheered.

"But I will tell you this. I will try my very best to make sure that we get a new jailhouse and I will hold all lawbreakers accountable. Because if you elect me to be your justice then I will make sure that this fair town is rid of all ruffians. And I will not tolerate someone like that Dave LeRoy fellow who chose to shoot and rob or the like of those that ruined our jail and tossed it in the Sauk River!" he shouted, as nearly every miner booed and every shop keeper cheered. I looked over at Mattie and we both started clapping.

"Mark my words, those that break the law under my watch will find themselves behind bars or run out of town on the rails!" he boomed, while the pavilion fell into a smattering of boos and hurrahs.

"It is my pleasure to be here today, and if elected it would be my honor to serve you, the fine citizens of Monte Cristo! Write-in my name and I will do you right!" Ned exclaimed, stepping from the stage.

As some in the room clapped I leaned over and said to Mattie, "It sounds to me like the miners won't be voting for him."

"Maybe," Mattie said, nodding.

Jim Bartholomew walked back up to the podium and waited for everyone to quiet down.

"Thank you, Ned," Jim said, clapping his hands. "Alright everyone. Next we've got our formal candidate Frederick Trump!" Every miner and most of the others in attendance cheered and clapped as Fred made his way up to the podium.

He had a stove pipe hat on his head, and wore a finely cut jet-black suit, a white high collared shirt with a four-in-hand tie, his boots were brightly polished. Once in front of the crowd he beamed with delight, his hands behind his back as he twisted his body back and forth, taking it all in. Then he raised his hands until it was quiet.

"Fine citizens of Monte Cristo!" he said, his voice resounding out over the hall. "I cannot tell you how happy I am to be here today! Now, as you all know I am running for Justice of the Peace, which is an important position, a fine position, and I believe that you, being my neighbors, already know how well suited I am to such an honor," he said, turning his head and body as he spoke, gesturing with his hands.

"But it is my pleasure today, nonetheless, to say that, if elected, I will make it my duty to see that all laws are abided by because there will be no more shootings and robberies if I am in office! And I agree with my new, last minute write-in competitor about having a jail, we need one," he said, raising a hand and pointing finger upward, "Because I will now make an absolute promise that I will build us a new jail!" he said, projecting his voice out over the crowd. The business owners in the room burst into cheers, while just a few miners clapped.

"Now then, on a national level, I believe in everything the great William Jennings Bryan believes. If you agree with him, then you agree with me. Because if we expand the gold standard and bring in silver, then we'll see an enormous increase in the money supply and, with it, benefits for all. There will be higher wages and more sales for businesses. The gold standard for our monies must be changed!" he yelled. Everyone in the pavilion started clapping and cheering. Trump raised his hands until it got quiet.

"If you elect me I will deliver justice to all on an equal basis. I will treat the businessman the same as the miner, and the same as the railroader. Just remember, if you're going to be voting for Bryan, then vote for me!" Trump yelled. He doffed his top hat, held it in the air and began to step away from the podium. Taking slow measured steps, he put his hat back on and clapped with the crowd as he left the stage.

Men tossed their hats in the air as Fred made his way through the crowd, people patted him on the back and shook his hand. Mattie and I watched him walk by and followed him outside. A horde of miners and railroaders surrounded him.

"Alright all you men," Fred said, looking around the group, "free shots for everyone at my place!" Big Nelson and George Pratt hoisted him on their shoulders and carried him off to lower town. I looked over at Mattie.

"Should we join them?"

"Oh," Mattie said, surprised by the idea. "No thank you. I'm alright."

"Don't care for politics?"

"Well, I mean—" Mattie looked away.

"Or is it because women don't get to vote?" I asked, but Mattie didn't answer right away. "You know my Aunt back home in San Francisco pickets political rallies for not including women, you should see her letting them have it, yelling and carrying on. Why once she tossed her sign at a commissioner!"

"You see! That's a problem," Mattie snapped.

"What's a problem?"

"Picketing in the streets! All of those women screaming and carrying on as they do. So, when women do get the right to vote you'd want all of us to act just as bad as you men, drinking and quarreling and such."

"But I thought you'd —"

"Just look at all of you, ready to go drink yourselves stupid with Fred Trump! And all for politics! You turn into animals when it comes to political dealings and you want to drag women into that kind of behavior!" Mattie said loudly, flushed as she spoke. I stared at her in silence for a moment, my mind thick and confused.

"But I thought you'd want the right to vote?"

"I do! I do want the right to vote but I will not allow myself to be dragged down into the gutter with screaming and rioting in the streets." The corners of her eyes sparkled with moisture, she turned away from me so as to dab at them.

"So, you do support a woman's right to vote?" I asked, relieved.

"I do, absolutely," Mattie replied quietly, turning back to me, her eyes still red.

"That's good to hear, because most contemporary women think they should."

"Well, I'm a woman who lives in the contemporary world and I think we should," she said. "I just don't want to see women behave like drunken fools," she said, her face still red from her speech.

"Well, I'm a big believer in the suffragist movement. Someday soon women everywhere will have the right to vote," I replied.

"That's nice to hear because Susan B. Anthony's a champion, and a tireless leader of women's rights," Mattie said. "But let's not talk about this now. How about if we go for a walk or something?"

"Okay, alright. How 'bout, if ah, we go over to the falls?" I offered.

"That sounds better," she agreed. "But I do need to get back, soon."

"Okay," I said, standing in front of her.

"Alright, then . . . what are we waiting for? Let's go," Mattie said, flicking her fingers at me to start walking, her blue eyes bright again, sparking with interest.

"Sure." We headed back past the pavilion then silently hiked through an area of flat meadow land along the creek. About half way there I finally spoke up.

"Those kids were sure good dancers," I offered.

"Yes, they were great. And those shoes they had were loud!" Mattie replied.

"They were, weren't they," I said. "So . . . how are the classes going?"

"Great! Most of the kids are well behaved and good learners."

The falls ran down a granite face beside mossy boulders and ferns. We stopped and found a couple of flat rocks to sit on.

"You know, I sure like my portrait," Mattie said, brushing and flattening her long dress. "I look at it every day."

"Do you still have it at the schoolhouse?"

"Oh, yes. Mrs. Chapman saw it the other day."

"Did she? What'd she say?"

"She kind of scoffed at it, but she's blind as a bat," Mattie said, laughing.

"Ah, ha, you're funny. But, I don't think she likes me," I said. A moment of silence came over us as the waterfall gurgled beside us.

"She is kind of grumpy, well, they both are really."

"I can see that." Another moment of silence occurred, then Mattie spoke again.

"Tell me, Oliver. What do you want out of life?" I thought about what she'd asked before I answered.

"Well, the same thing as any young man would," I replied, looking at her. "A wife and children, a house and home, money, all those things . . . And lots of happiness, you?" Mattie blushed.

"Oh, I want all of that, too," she said, then smiled. "So, you *do* want to have a family someday?" she asked, looking warmly at me with her penetrating eyes.

"Absolutely," I replied, not hesitating.

"That's nice to know," she said, smiling. "This is a great little place, but it's getting late. We should be heading back."

"Okay, I guess it's suppertime," I said, standing up.

Mattie started out, leading us away from the falls. She had her dress hitched up so it wouldn't drag along the ground. I tried to think of something to say.

"What's it like living with the Chapmans?" Mattie instantly stopped, spun around and looked at me.

"Very boring," she replied, with a funny little smirk on her face. "She's a terrible cook and all he does is complain." I smiled as an idea developed.

"Well, let me check with Liz and my Aunt Eva and Uncle Jacob first, but, how about if you come over for dinner some evening soon?" I asked. Mattie broke into a wide, glowing smile.

"Oh, my savior! Yes, that'd be wonderful. I hope they says it's okay," she said. Mattie gathered up her skirt, turned back around towards the pavilion and started skipping.

XV

HIGH WATER

It was a crisp fall evening when I found myself standing with Jacob and Eva and a gathering of town folk in front of *The Monte Cristo Mountaineer* waiting for the election results. The crowd eventually spilled out onto the street planking and into the mud as more people showed up and waited. Fred Trump stood with a kerosene lamp next to Shamus O'Dowd while Ned Berwyn was off to the side with Arthur Thrall and Frank Peabody, over in the shadows.

"This is kind of exciting," Eva said, a bonnet on her head and wool coat wrapped around herself.

"Yes, it is. In a way I guess we're making history, this is the first presidential election we've ever had in Monte Cristo," Jacob added, his breath clearly visible in the chilly mist.

"So, who do you think's going to win?" I asked, shuffling my feet, trying to stay warm.

"For President or between Trump and Berwyn?" Jacob asked.

"Both."

"Oh, well, hands down Trump will win here. But I'm not sure about Bryan. I'm thinking that McKinley will probably win the presidency, having whipped the rebels such as he did," Jacob said.

"Yeah, I agree with Jacob," Eva said, then added, quietly, "for once. But Trump will win because there's more miners than businessmen." Just then Jim Bartholomew and Ed Baker stepped out of the little log cabin and into the street. I could see that Bartholomew had a slip of paper in his hand.

"Can I get everyone's attention, please?" the newsman asked. Ed Baker raised a lamp for Bartholomew to see what was written on the paper.

"Listen up everybody! The votes are in and counted and . . . by the margin of 32 votes to 5 . . . Fred Trump has won and is now the Justice of the Peace in Monte Cristo!"

Trump instantly threw up both his arms in victory and a cheer went up in the crowd surrounding him. He stepped out from his group and said, "Thank you everyone! At this time, I'd like to thank Mr. Berwyn for being an honorable opponent and I'd like to also thank all of my supporters. Right now, everyone come on down to my fine establishment, where it's nice and warm, for a little victory celebration!" The bulk of the people followed him to lower town as we watched them trudge away.

"What about Bill Bryan? How'd he do?" one man called out.

"I don't know about how he did nationally," Jim Bartholomew replied, "but I can tell you he won here in Monte Cristo by a 2 to 1 margin, 25 to 12." The crowd began to murmur between themselves as most followed after Fred and the rest thinned out.

"Did you vote, Oliver?" Jacob asked, as we began to walk up the hill.

"Nope," I replied, after a few steps. "I didn't think I should."

"Why's that?" Eva asked.

"Well . . . because I don't really think of myself as a permanent citizen," I said. "I'm not gonna live here forever."

"Let's all hope we don't have to," Eva said dryly. "At least Oliver is smart enough to know that there's no future here."

"Oh," I said, then thinking about my private conversation with Liz. "Don't get me wrong, I think Monte Cristo has a bright future."

"Yeah, that's because you're just visiting! We're stuck here," Eva put out from the side of her mouth. She started walking faster up the hill, away from us. Jacob glanced over at me with a tight frown.

"She's a little tired tonight," he said, shaking his head and hurrying after her.

"Well, at least we can all rest assured knowing that Fred's in charge!" I laughed coldly.

Looking out from the laundry room window the next morning a layer of snow covered the valley, the hotel floors felt colder than the day before. The temperature had plummeted overnight. I went back in my room, slipped on a pair of shoes, and went out into the kitchen.

"Mornin' Liz," I offered.

"There's Oliver," she replied. "Good morning! Can you do me a favor and get some cord wood?"

"Sure, be happy to," I said, going back to my room for my coat.

Outside, a thin layer of ice floated in the water barrel and there was about three inches of fresh snow, it crunched under my feet on the way over to the wood shed. Loading an armful, a tiny mouse scurried out from under the pieces. It ran up and along the top of the front pile and to the back. “You need to find a new home little guy, because this one is gonna disappear sooner than you think,” I said to the little fella.

I went back inside, dropped the load in the box and brushed off the arms of my coat over it. Liz was over standing in front of the sink, rinsing her hands.

“Thanks,” she said, drying them on a plaid towel. She took a mug down from a shelf and set it on the counter, I knew it was for me.

“So, Fred Trump’s the new justice,” I said, since she wasn’t up when we’d gotten home the night before. I walked over to get my mug.

“Oh, I figured as much,” she grumbled. “I don’t know if it even matters. Anyway, I was going to make oatmeal this morning.”

“Sounds good to me,” I replied, pouring a cup of coffee. I went over and took my coat off and set it on the bench, then took my normal seat at the built-in and took a sip of hot coffee.

“Looks like winter’s here,” Liz offered. She filled a large tea pot full of water at the sink and carried it over to the stove, then fed the fire.

“Liz? You ever have guests over?”

“Guests? Well, of course. This is a hotel, it’s how we make our living.”

“No, no, I mean like a friend from town.”

“You mean like to see the place?”

“No, I mean like a person from here in town that comes over for a visit.”

“Oh, like a miner? Never. Absolutely not, they’re all filthy.”

"No, uh, I mean . . . I'm talking about Mattie. I was wondering if she could come over for dinner sometime," I said. Liz jerked her head around to look at me and grinned.

"Ah, so you do like the girl," she laughed. "I think that'd be grand, let's have her over!"

"Do we need to make sure it's okay with Uncle Jacob, and Aunt Eva?"

"Check if what's okay?" Jacob asked, strolling into the room. Liz turned around and looked at him.

"Oliver was just asking me if you thought it'd be okay if we had Mattie over for dinner," Liz said. Jacob thought about it and nodded his head.

"Sure, I think that's a great idea. Invite her over. How about after the weekend, when guests aren't here?"

"Okay, thanks," I said. "But what about Aunt Eva? Do you think she'll be okay with it?" Jacob paused for a moment.

"She'll be fine," he said, then thought for a moment. "I'll tell her."

"Thanks Uncle Jacob. Mattie told me how Mrs. Chapman's not much of a cook so she'll be thrilled to have some of Liz's cooking. You look outside yet?"

"Oh yes," Jacob replied, sitting down with his hands wrapped around a steaming cup of coffee.

"I'm guessing the train runs all winter?" I asked. Jacob looked at me.

"As long as there's no floods to wash out the bridges or avalanches covering the tracks with tons of snow," he stated.

"Avalanches?"

"Sometimes they come down and carry trees and rocks down on the tracks. When that happens it takes a few days or more to reopen it," Jacob replied, sipping his coffee.

"Do they just shovel the snow off the tracks?"

"Well, yes, and no. They've got a rotary plow, a real big mechanical thing they push in front of the engine that throws the snow a-hundred feet. But when there's an avalanche they have to bring in one or two section crews to remove all the trees and debris first by hand. That takes a while."

"Sounds like quite the operation," I said.

"Oh, it is, alright," Liz added.

Eva walked into the kitchen with a sour look, her hair messy and eyes dark. She said, "Well, it looks like old man winter showed up last night! I wish I was a bear so I could sleep through the whole thing." She kept walking towards the hall. I looked over at Jacob. He rolled his eyes.

"Don't worry honey, it'll be spring in no time," he said. Eva stopped in her tracks and turned around to the kitchen.

"And then what Jacob?!" she snapped, glaring at him. Jacob met her gaze silently, then took a long, slow sip of coffee. Eva spun on her heel and stomped off, slamming the back door. The room was quiet for a moment. Jacob looked over at me.

"Oliver," Jacob said quietly, "you're a young man and that's a good thing, since you're not married. But when you do get married, just-a, well, make sure you plan everything out in advance because Eva wants to sell this place and buy a new hotel in the city," he said to me, his voice quiet and firm.

"Oh, really," I answered, trying to sound surprised.

"Yep, she's tired of Monte and wants to sell in the spring since business is good. So, I told her we would," Jacob said. "It's either that or build a new one that's bigger and better than this one, here in town. But that's just me talking." I nodded and took another sip of coffee.

"You've both agreed to sell then? Possibly?"

"Like I said, in the spring. Maybe. But for now, we should enjoy it while we can and have Mattie over for dinner."

A week later Monte was covered in a thick blanket of white from blizzards of snow. I found myself shoveling over a foot of the stuff from the second-floor ramp and digging out a path from the back-door to the outhouse. Taking a break and wiping my brow I leaned on the old flat-head shovel my uncle had provided for the task, then gaped at the mountain across the valley. It looked like there was six or seven feet of snow covering the ridgeline, and the tree branches were covered in what looked like whipping cream, waiting in winter's frozen grasp until it was lapped up by spring.

Once I had a path cleared from the inn to the street I went back and sat down in the rocking chair to cool down from all the exertion. Over at the schoolhouse wood smoke curled from the chimney, the windows were spattered with frost and the cedar shingles were now covered over in a thick coating of snow. I was admiring the string of icicles that hung from the roof-line when the front door burst open and the sounds of happy kids instantly filled the air.

The building quickly emptied and thirty kids were out in the middle of the street, throwing snowballs and building snowmen. Mattie came out and stood at the top of the stairs with a shawl wrapped around her shoulders. She saw me right away and waved. I smiled and waved back. Then she made a beckoning move with her hand, signaling me to come over.

"Recess time, eh?" I asked, walking over to her.

"Two or three times a day," she replied. "Depending on how wound up they are. Come on inside and warm up!"

"Oh, I probably shouldn't."

"It's okay, just for a minute," she said, her eyes wide and bright.

"Well, if you say so," I replied, going up the stairs. As soon as I walked in the door she closed it halfway, pulled me out of sight behind it, and stared into my eyes. I never knew eyes could be so blue.

"So? Are we having dinner?" she asked, beaming at me. The corners of my mouth curled into a grin.

"Yep, Jacob thinks it'd be great. How about tomorrow?"

"Oh, perfect. Thank you!" she said. Just then a girl screamed outside. Mattie's eyes got big.

"Billy Jamieson just hit me with a snowball! Miss de Graaf!" the young girl cried.

"Not that Jamieson boy again," she muttered, turning towards the door.

"Billy, get in here this instant!" Mattie yelled, her voice sharp and clear. "This same thing happened yesterday," she said to me. Mattie stormed down the stairs and ran over and hugged the little girl. Then she pointed at the schoolhouse and stared at the boy.

"Back inside, mister," Mattie said. "Recess is over for you, again."

"But I didn't throw it!" Billy hollered. "Danny MacFarren did!"

"Don't talk back to me!" Mattie replied. "Now you march back in to your desk!"

"Okay, it looks it's time for me to go. I'll see you later," I said, walking back to the hotel.

The next evening Mattie looked magnificent wearing a powder blue dress with light grey pinstripes and a white long-sleeved blouse. She had her hair down and her eyes reflected the candle light. I pulled back her chair so she could sit down. Liz brought in a platter with a roasted chicken on it, she set it in front of Jacob and turned towards the kitchen. Eva carried in a heaping bowl of mashed potatoes then spun around and followed Liz.

"This looks wonderful," Mattie said, scanning the well-appointed table covered in bone china, silver cutlery, cloth napkins and candelabra. "Thank you so much for having me over."

"Well, we're happy to have you," Jacob said.

"Yes, it's so nice for a change to have a local guest, instead of a tourist," Liz said, bringing in two gravy boats, setting one at each end of the table. Eva returned with a bowl of roasted vegetables; red and green peppers, carrots and broccoli. She sat down in the chair next to Jacob.

"Should we say grace?" Eva asked.

"I will," Jacob quickly offered. He glanced around the table. Everyone lowered their heads and closed their eyes.

"Blessed are you, Lord our God, King of the Universe, by whose word all things came to be, who brings forth this bread and food from the earth. Let us say Amen," Jacob said.

"Amen," everyone added. Jacob stood and picked up a carving knife. He sliced into the chicken and I picked up the bowl of mashed potatoes, handing them to Mattie.

"Okay everyone, dig in and enjoy!" Liz said, opening a napkin and placing it on her lap.

"All this food looks fantastic," Mattie observed.

"Yes, thank you Liz, and Aunt Eva," I said.

"Yes, thank you both," Mattie added, spooning some potatoes onto her plate. Liz picked up a gravy boat and passed it to Mattie while Eva picked up the roasted vegetables and passed them to me.

"So, Mattie," Eva started, "how long have you been teaching?"

"This is my first assignment, I just graduated with a degree last spring."

"Where from?" Jacob asked, slicing away.

"The Normal School, in Bellingham. It's a small college but all the professors are top notch," Mattie answered, adding some gravy to her potatoes.

"I've been to Bellingham," Liz said. "Years ago. Before I came up here."

"Lots of coal mined up there, I hear," Jacob said.

"Oh yes, the coal mine has been in operation for a long time," Mattie added.

"I've heard good things about Bellingham and I understand Anacortes is a nice town, both on the water and all," Jacob related. "I'd like to see them sometime."

"Anacortes is great!" Liz remarked. Eva turned to Jacob and made an odd little smirk at him, then she changed the subject.

"So! What do your parents do for a living?" she asked, passing the bowl of mashed potatoes around.

"They're dairy farmers, and they grow raspberries," Mattie answered.

"Any brothers and sisters?" Jacob inquired, passing the plate of sliced chicken.

"I have two older sisters and a younger brother. My sisters are teachers, too."

"Where at?" Jacob asked.

"One teaches in Fairhaven near Bellingham and the other is in a tiny town north of there called Ferndale," Mattie replied.

"This chicken is sure good, Liz," I said, trying to break into the conversation.

"And what about your brother?" Eva asked, trying the vegetables.

"He enlisted in the state militia last year, right now he's stationed down at the mouth of the Columbia River building a fort. He wrote me last month and said it's going to be called Fort Columbia. These potatoes are delicious, by the way," Mattie said.

"Oh, thank you," Liz blushed, "I put butter in them and added some garlic."

"Yes, they're very good," I said.

"And the chicken is so moist but cooked through," Mattie said. "How do you do that?" she asked, looking at Liz.

"Oh, gosh, thank you," Liz said, blushing. "I use as low of a heat as I can on the Majestic, feed the fire slowly." Then Mattie smiled brightly and glanced around the table.

"Did you know that Oliver painted my portrait?" Mattie said.

"Oh, yes," both Eva and Liz said at the same time. Jacob looked surprised.

"But we haven't seen it yet," Eva said.

"It's beautiful," Mattie gushed.

"Well, we'd *all* like to see it," Jacob said.

"Mattie," Liz said, "you should have Oliver teach a drawing class, sometime." Eva glanced over at Liz, then looked down at her plate.

"Ooo," Mattie quickly replied, "I like that idea."

After dinner Liz brought out a piece of peach pie for everyone, each with a dollop of whipped cream. When Mattie tried a bite, I could tell by the look on her face that she liked it.

"Oh, my, gosh — this is terrific," she said with relish.

"That's nice of you to say," Liz replied, "but I must admit, they're canned peaches."

"Canned peaches are fine by me," I said, and everyone laughed.

On the walk over to Mercedes Street, without saying anything, Mattie grabbed my hand and held it tight. A light snow was slowly falling like floating tufts of cottonwood seed in the spring. It was a perfect winter night, the air was cold and crisp, just cold enough to make your face tingle. It almost felt like Christmas Eve, although it was early December.

"Liz sure is a fabulous cook," Mattie said. "That was a great meal, and the pie was wonderful."

"Yeah, we're pretty lucky to have her," I replied. We walked on, the darkness of the night only broken by the dull red windows of homes with bright lanterns sitting in their windows. Surrounded by the high peaks of the Cascades, in the dim light of the sleepy town, and amongst the soft, fluffy snow of early winter, Monte Cristo felt like the most peaceful place on earth.

"Well, this is me," Mattie said, stopping in front of a two-story frame home with white paint and blue trim. A lamp shown bright in a porch window and Mrs. Chapman could be seen sitting next to it staring out the window. Mattie quickly let go of my hand.

"Thank you, Oliver," she said. "You sure have a nice family. Maybe I'll see you tomorrow?"

"At recess, right?" I replied. Mattie nodded and turned for the door. I watched her glide up the walkway and go inside the house. I stood there for minutes staring at it, wishing the house was ours.

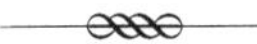

I awoke to the pleasing aroma of coffee and bacon and the sound of Liz's feet scurrying around the kitchen. Opening my eyes, the events of the night before brought an early morning smile to my face. *Mattie's such an unbelievable woman.* My thoughts quickened to the notion of spending the rest of my life with her. I laid on my little cot thinking about the possibility.

Finally rolling out of bed, I noticed that the floors were warmer than the day before, which was a pleasant surprise after the previous cold. Out in the kitchen Liz was tending the snapping, crackling fire; next to the percolating coffee pot on the stove a cast iron skillet held sizzling bacon and an empty but warming griddle.

"Mornin' Liz," I said, coming into the room and grabbing my old coffee cup.

"Oliver, how are ya' today?" she asked, bright and cheery.

"I'm good! That dinner last night was somethin' else, thank you for that."

"My pleasure. Mattie sure is a sweetheart," she offered. I poured myself some coffee and went over to the built-in.

"Yes, she's great. I really like her."

"You're a nice courting pair," Liz said, placing the cooked bacon on a plate and draining the grease into a tin can. She stepped over to the counter and measured the last of the flour into a bowl. Added salt, mixed in baking powder, pinch of sugar, egg and milk.

"Are you thinking about a serious courtship?" Liz asked, mixing the batter with a wooden spoon.

"Do you mean am I thinking about marriage someday?" I asked. "Were you ever married?"

Liz looked away and carried the mixing bowl over to the stove. She spilled a bit of bacon grease on the griddle and spooned in the batter for pancakes.

"Yes, once. For a little while when I was younger," she said, not turning around. "But it didn't end well. He had a hard time staying in work and turned into a drunk, and got himself killed in a bar fight."

"Oh, my-gosh. I'm sorry to hear that,"

"It was a long time ago, it's no trouble anymore. So! What are you going to do today?" Liz said, turning around.

"Not sure yet," I replied, taking a sip of coffee.

"Do you think you could run down and get me a couple of sacks of flour at the mercantile today?"

"I'd be happy to."

Walking down Dumas an hour later wearing my winter coat and a slouch hat that a guest had forgotten at the hotel the air was noticeably warm, the snow of the days before had changed to rain, and the sky was dark and heavy. The town was lively with the sound of snow sloughing off trees and sliding from roofs, the ground becoming slushy with melt-off. I scraped the mud off my boots on the edge of the porch at the mercantile, and headed inside; the little copper bell mounted on the door ringing out and announcing my arrival.

Charlie O'Connell was behind the counter, adjusting the inventory on his shelves. No one else was in the store.

"Charlie, how are you today?" I asked, closing the door. He stopped what he was doing and turned around.

"Oh, hi Oliver, life is good today!" he replied, grinning.

"It's raining pretty good out there and it feels warmer, too," I commented.

"Yep, that's life in the Cascades, even if it is December. Cold and snowy one minute and warm and rainy the next. How can I help you?" he asked.

"Liz needs two sacks of flour," I said.

"Okay," he said, turning around and opening a bin. The bell above the door chimed.

"Mornin' you two," Jim Bartholomew said. "Looks like it's warming up outside."

"It does," I replied, nodding at him.

"Yep, creeks up I see," Charlie added, setting the sacks of flour on the counter.

"My ink come in?" Bartholomew asked.

"It did, all three bottles," O'Connell replied, walking to the storeroom.

"And you get any tooth powder?"

"Didn't," Charlie said, over his shoulder, "next train maybe."

"Bacon?" the newspaperman added.

"Nope," Charlie replied, disappearing behind a curtain.

"Hmm, maybe I'll try the Pioneer," Jim mumbled to himself. He looked over at me.

"How've you been?"

"Good, thanks. You?"

"Fair to middlin' I'd say. I hear you're courting the schoolteacher," Bartholomew said, raising an eyebrow — his owlish white hair sticking out from under the sides of his hat.

"We're just friends," I replied.

"Oh, a-huh," he grinned. O'Connell came back and set the large ink bottles down on the counter.

"There ya' be," Charlie said. "Three dollars and seventy-five cents plus shipping, comes to four dollars an' fifteen-cents."

"Such a deal," Bartholomew replied, rolling his eyes and digging into a trouser pocket.

"Can I pick the flour up on my way back? In ten or fifteen minutes," I asked, looking at Charlie.

"Sure," he answered. "I'll put it on the Pride bill and leave it behind the counter."

Down at the wagon bridge the creek was noticeably higher, and louder. The earlier rain had given way to a hard, pounding rain, and a warm wind was beginning to blow in from the west. I walked over to the depot, where I stomped the mud off my boots before stepping into the telegraph office.

"Ed, how are you?" He spun around in his swivel chair.

"Good, Oliver, good. Need to send something?" he asked, standing up.

"I do, haven't sent my Mom a telegram in a while, I need to let her know all's well." He reached under the counter and set a form in front of me, then gave me the pencil from behind his ear.

"Raining pretty hard outside," he commented.

"I'll say," I replied, jotting down a quick note to mother.

"Snow's melting fast. I don't know if I've ever seen the river so high."

"No kidding," I said, handing him the paper and a dollar. Ed looked at the form and nodded.

"Okay, see you soon," he said and went over to his key machine. I headed out the door by way of the mercantile.

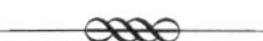

I was sitting at the built-in chatting with Liz hours later in the afternoon when there was a rush of hurried footsteps, Jacob came storming into the kitchen dripping wet.

"There's a log jam at the main trestle!" he yelled, his voice cracking and his hair wild beneath his soaking hat. "Come on! Hurry!" I set down my glass of water and stood up.

"What's this?" Liz asked.

"A log jam?" I said.

"Yes! The rain melted all the snow and the river is bursting. It's a flash flood! The trestles might go!" Jacob hollered, the look of horror in his eyes. He ran out to the staircase and yelled up it, "Eva! There's trouble! Hurry!" Then he bolted out the front door.

Liz and I looked at each other. She jumped up and ripped off her apron, ran down the hall to her room and grabbed her coat, then ran for the door without putting it on, breathlessly muttering, "If we lose the trestles . . ." and off she went. I slapped on a coat and the same slouch hat then jumped into my boots, running out the door without even bothering to lace them.

Down near the depot a crowd of people stood in the hard driving rain, all of them pointing and yelling at the newly formed pile of logs that had crashed up against the main trestle and its supports. The river was a raging torrent, brown water pushing against, over and around the jam, shaking the bridge. More limbs, debris and log supports from the already collapsed upper concentrator trestle and switch-back were rushing up against the jam-up by the minute as the river's force thundered against the main trestle's uprights. I could hear boulders in the river bed rolling and rumbling under the weight of the water's energy. Just then a railroader started to drive a handcar away from the depot, pushing the handle up and down in a frenzy across the trestle bridge.

"Look!" someone in the crowd yelled, "he's taking the handcar across!"

"No! Don't!" another hollered, pointing at the railroad worker.

"Stop! It's too much weight!"

"No! No! No!"

"Don't do it!" others in the crowd hollered and motioned with their hands.

I looked over at the Cleveland and Kline. Jacob and Addison were standing up on the tracks above their building, clutching their coats around them and watching up stream with all their neighbors. Over on the other side of lower town people were scurrying around and watching the rising river, it was already over the footbridge. Sunday Creek had jumped its banks and was flowing freely under all the structures making lower town look like a floating island of shanties.

Once the handcar was across the trestle the man hopped off and ran back over, stumbling along the way when the sound of children's voices came up in the air behind me. I turned and there was Mattie with her class, the look of shock and horror on their young faces, their mouths agape. Ed Baker showed up.

"The telegraph's out, poles must be down farther down the river, we're cut off!" I heard him say. A jolt went up my spine when one of the middle timber supports gave a loud crack and began to give way, falling into the water and floating downstream. Seconds later some of the heavy cross planking was pulled under and down into the swirling crashing waters, in an instant the steel rails were hanging suspended. When another support moved.

"Oh no! There it goes!" someone yelled.

"No! No!!" someone else moaned in agony.

"Please no! Not this!" a woman cried.

The river forced an opening under the bridge and it took full advantage. One by one the timber supports fell into the cold, brown maelstrom when the log jam freed itself and gushed downstream, making a thundering, crashing sound of logs banging into each other. The rushing log jam instantly took out the tall corner posts of the Cleveland and Kline, toppling the whole building into the horizontal geyser of cascading waves when somebody screamed; "AAAAYYYEEE!! NO! NO!! NO!!!" at the sight of the structure being swallowed in the rushing tide, the building breaking apart instantly, with only the roof on the surface of the surging river floating downstream. When another, bigger jolt shocked my spinal cord.

"*MY PAINTINGS*!!!" I screamed, rushing forward towards the crashing bank of the river. Someone in the crowd held me back as I watched everything I'd done that year be destroyed by the river . . . I put my hands on my head and bent over, staring at the ground, not believing what I'd just seen. All my work and effort and creations were swept away in the blink of an eye, gone. My heart stopped and my mouth went dry. I didn't want to move. I couldn't believe it. It felt like a mule had just kicked me in the belly, all the wind went out of me. Finally, someone in the crowd pulled me up and I turned around.

Eva was running across the still standing wagon bridge, her coat streaming behind her off one of her shoulders. When she got to the edge of the crowd she stopped and saw what had just happened, then she began to wail, tears streaming down her cheeks. I saw Jacob go over to her. When she saw him approach she hurried towards him, he tried to hug and console her. But she threw up her fists and started beating his chest. Pounding and pounding, then yelling at the top of her lungs as her fists flew.

"You bastard! Now we're stuck here! Stuck here! Do you hear me?! What are we going to do?! What am I going to do?! I hate this place! I hate you! I hate everything about you!" Eva screamed so loud she collapsed to her knees in the mud, delirious and moaning, her energy and emotions spent.

Liz rushed over to her. Jacob tried to help her but Eva just pushed him away. He looked up, shaken and pale. He looked like the ghost of a man, dazed, and unrecognizable. Liz pulled Eva up by her waist and they began to walk slowly across the wagon bridge and back up the hill. Everyone stood motionless, confused and lost in their own town. I didn't know what to say or do, my mind was thick and cold with the loss of my work. Then I looked back across the river.

Addison and Jacob stood with the rest of their stranded neighbors, all of them pointing at the river and walking over to where the building used to be. Someone in the back of the group was motioning with their hands and talking but I couldn't hear anything over the thunder of the river.

"Everyone! Listen up!" Ned Berwyn called out over the raging torrent near me, cupping his open hands to the sides of his mouth. "We all need to stay calm, we'll be okay. All of us need to go home and get out of the rain. Then we should have a meeting."

"Stay calm?!" someone hollered. "How are we supposed to stay calm for Christ sakes?!"

"We don't need any blasphemy!"

"Yeah, well, why didn't the Lord stop all this rain!"

"The savior's not at fault here!"

"Our town's stranded and the railroad's gone!"

"That's enough and Ned's right!" Charlie O'Connell hollered. "Let's all go up to the mercantile, then we can figure out what we should do. We'll figure it out, together!"

"Somebody needs to get up to the Mystery and all the other mines, let 'em all know what happened," Arthur Thrall added.

"Alright," Ed Baker put in. "I'll go, the wire's down, so I'll run up there right away and be back in no time."

"Why did we ever come up here to work in the wilderness anyway? This whole idea of having a town up here at the top of the Cascades is crazy!" someone was saying as I came into the mercantile.

"It's them east coast big wigs!" another man said, "It's easy for them to have other folk come up here and hack it, but you'd never see any of them up here with us in the mud and the snow and now this!"

"Aw they're not to blame! It was the chinook I'm telling you!" Jim Bartholomew said, trying to get his point across. People were moving all the shelving and merchandise, pushing it up against the walls to make as much room as possible for everyone.

"All that rain and warm wind hit the snow up above like a summer storm and melted everything, and fast too," Bartholomew added, shaking his head.

"You mean a Washoe Zephyr, that's what we called it in Virginia City," Henry the wagon master insisted.

"It doesn't matter what you call it," Hiram Chapman snapped, sitting next to his wife. "The trestles are all down and there won't be any trains here for months."

"Yeah, well. At least the wagon bridge is holding," Arthur Thrall said.

"But that's because it free spans '76 Creek from bank to bank without support posts," Bartholomew said. "Too bad we don't have one like it that spans Glacier Creek to get us over to the railroad grade side of the valley and back to civilization."

"First, we need to find out if the next river bridge below us at Weden Creek is down or not," Charlie O'Connell suggested.

"Good idea, Charlie," Ned Berwyn asserted. Just then Martin Comins, Ed Baker, and a few of the men from the Mystery walked in the door sopping wet.

"We need to get somebody down to Silverton right away, see how they're doing," Ed Baker said.

"Who's here from the railroad?" Martin asked the room. He walked towards the back of the store and stood near the post office facing everyone.

"I'm the only one," a railroader answered.

"Okay, and what's your name, lad?" Martin asked, his face calm and determined.

"Ben McDonough," the young man said. "I took the handcar over the trestle just before it went down."

"You're lucky to be alive son," Hiram Chapman piped up.

"No kidding," another man said. "If that bridge would've gone down with you on it . . . Hell, just the weight of that maintenance car and you could have brought it all down."

"Alright, okay. Thanks for taking that risk, Ben. That handcar should come in handy," Comins said. He paused for a moment while

ome in the room murmured with low talk and everyone else hung
n silence for Martin's next words.

"So, let's hope to never see the likes of this again, and losing the Cleveland and Kline, well," Martin said, pausing, his eyes downcast momentarily. "We need to give praise to the Lord in Heaven above hat there wasn't any loss of life and be thankful that Addison and is wife Elizabeth, and Jacob all have their own cabins to stay in. But we need deal with the fact that we're stuck over here with two reeks on each side of us and we need to get across Glacier Creek to he railroad side of the valley, somehow, since the other concentrator restles are damaged too. Anyone got any ideas?"

In a flash of consciousness, I remembered back to drawing the arn and lone tree in June.

"How about if we fall that tree over at the stables for a temporary bridge?" I said. Everyone turned their heads towards me.

"That's a good idea, Oliver," Martin said, looking directly at ne. "Can ya' fall it?"

"I can," I said, automatically volunteering without even knowing it.

"Okay, thanks," Martin said. "Then we'll need Ben, to take he handcar downriver to the Weden bridge and see if it's still up or not, and come back and give us a report. But two people should go, n case something happens," Martin said. Looking larger than life.

"I'll go with him," my uncle said. I hadn't even noticing he'd walked into the building.

"Alright, thank you Jacob," Martin said. "Good, now we're getting somewhere."

The room sat silent, patiently waiting for guidance. Martin gazed out over the room as if he was about to give a Sunday sermon, his face calm and benevolent.

"So, the train won't be here to save us, this we know. That means we have to save ourselves, and we will. How are we doing for food?" Martin asked, looking over to Charlie O'Connell.

"Well, I've been thinking about that already," Charlie began, "and I'd say there's about a month of can goods and staples here in the store for maybe two dozen people — maybe a little longer if it's rationed."

"And Arthur," Martin said, looking around the room for him, "what about feed for your milk cows?"

"Well," Arthur said, gripping his hat tightly and looking at his feet, "About that, uh, I've got a problem. Last week I discovered that my roof's been leaking, so now most of my hay's gone to mold. I've got about twenty or thirty days of good hay left in the shed for maybe one cow. But in a month the trestle might be repaired and they can bring more in," he replied.

"What?" a man asked, loudly.

"Aw, jeez Arthur," someone moaned.

"That's okay," Martin said, rubbing his chin, "We'll deal with it. We can't depend on that with winter coming on. Plus, there very well could be more damage down the line with more bridges out and we won't know until we get down there."

Ben McDonough spoke up, "I'm gonna make a guess and say that the railroad won't be up and running for about two months."

"You don't know that," Hiram Chapman piped. "It very well could be longer."

"No, no. The railroad will have it up and running in no time, they've got to," Frank Peabody said.

"Okay, well, we'll figure all that out. And what about the telegraph wire, Ed?" Martin asked.

"That depends on the damage down the way. I'd say it'll be a while," Baker replied. "For now, we have no telegraph communication with the outside world, but the mail can be walked up the valley as soon as the bridges are passable by foot."

"Well, at least we all have our homes with wood for the fires. It could be worse, folks," Martin said.

"And how could it be worse? Huh?" a man with two crying kids said. "Tell me!"

"Listen," Martin snapped, the look of seriousness on his face. "We are gonna get through this, and we all need to pull together right quick. Okay? . . . Now then, I think the most important thing we need to figure out is how much food we have on hand. Let's all go back to our respective homes and do an inventory of what each home has, then figure out how long each of us can hold on with the staples ya' got. And we should all meet here again tomorrow morning. How about 8:00?" Martin suggested, scanning the room as he spoke.

"Well I'm not sharing any of my food," the man with the crying kids said.

"Me neither," another man said.

"Hold on here! Nobody's asking anyone to share their food," Martin replied.

"And where's our new justice Trump? Why isn't he here?" Hiram Chapman asked.

"Fred's stuck over in lower town since the footbridge is down," Jim Bartholomew said.

"Okay everybody, we need to take things one at a time and try our best to deal with everything that's happened, so let's get started. Oliver, how soon can ya' have that tree down and spanning the river?" Martin asked, looking right at me.

"I'll have it down in no time," I replied, standing up. Martin nodded.

"Okay, sounds good. The sooner that tree is turned into a bridge the sooner Ben and Jacob can get across the river to the pump car. So get after it, lad!" Martin said, looking right at me with an encouraging grin, when he did a quickening rushed through my system that I'd never felt before.

The meeting ended and everyone made their way to the door and shuffled out onto the street, except Jacob, Liz and a few others who stayed behind to go over things. I pulled out my pocket watch to check the time, 3:15 pm, and looked up at the sky. Black clouds were still stacked up against the mountains as the rain continued. I turned and headed up Dumas.

Looking up, I saw Mattie coming down the hill with a grim look on her face.

"Are you okay?" I asked. "Where's all the kids?"

"Schools done for the day, there're home now," she replied. "How was the meeting? What are we going to do?"

"Well, everyone is supposed to go home and take a food inventory. I'm on my way to get an ax to fall that big tree over by the stables," I replied, pointing in its direction.

"You need to be careful," Mattie said, looking into my eyes. "I don't want anything to happen to you."

"Don't worry," I said. "I'll be fine. I've got to get going."

"Okay. Are the Chapmans down at the mercantile?" she asked, glancing over my shoulder.

"Yes, I believe they still are. See you soon," I said. She touched me on my forearm then continued down the street.

I went straight to the tool shed, found the double bit ax and put it in the vise. I gave both blades a few swipes with the file for sharpness then headed down to the tree.

By the time I got there Ben McDonough, Ed Baker and Arthur Thrall were waiting with axes and a cross-cut saw.

"We thought we'd at least wait and give you the first swing," Ed Baker yelled, straining for his voice to be heard over the rush of the water.

"Alright," I said, walking past him and over to the base of the tree. I looked up the trunk and saw that most of the limbs were on the creek side. I nodded my head, knowing that it would fall in the right direction, then set my feet and started chopping.

XVI

EXODUS

In the morning, I rolled off the cot and stood up. Pulling on my trousers I glanced at my field box leaning up against the easel, the pain of losing all my paintings shot through my system again. I walked out into the laundry room and looked outside, it was still cloudy, a fine mist moved through the air. "This stuff is gonna have to stop," I muttered to myself. In the kitchen Liz was at the counter kneading bread dough with her back to the room.

"Mornin'," I offered, rubbing my sore biceps.

"There's the bridge builder," Liz said, trying to be cheery.

"Anyone else up?" I asked, reaching for a mug.

"Jacob's already out the door, went to take the hand car down the tracks," she replied.

"What time is it?"

"Quarter past seven," Liz said. "They shut the concentrator down."

"They shut it down? Oh, I guess it didn't wake me up."

"No train, no concentrator."

"Yeah, no paintings too," I said, pouring myself a cup of coffee.

"I'm so sorry about you losing all of them."

"Thanks Liz, plus they had some money in their safe for me."

"Oh, gosh, that's tough."

"I know, it's my fault, I never should have had so many of them in one place, especially on the river like that. But what can I do? I guess I could just blame Mother Nature. That's nothing though compared to the Cleveland and Kline getting destroyed. But I'll be okay, eventually" I said. "Is Aunt Eva up?" I asked, going over to the built-in.

"Ah, no," Liz replied quietly. "She's in her room."

"Did she ever come down for some dinner last night?"

"She didn't. I'm going to take something up for her in a bit," Liz said, not looking at me.

"I've never seen her like that, yesterday," I said. But Liz didn't reply.

"What's gonna happen?"

"You mean about her or about the town?"

"The town, for starters."

"Oh, we'll survive, we've got no choice. They'll get the train running again, but we might have to leave temporarily. It depends," she said.

"You mean on how much food we have on hand?" I asked. But again, Liz didn't answer.

"Not enough for all of us, I guess," I said.

"Like I said, it depends on the train, and on how much food Charlie, and everyone else has. How about some breakfast?" Liz asked.

"Sure," I answered. "But then I've got to get down to the meeting."

Coming down Dumas the roar of the river still sounded out over the valley. Up ahead I could see people filing into the mercantile and, in the distance, Jacob and Ben were coming back on the handcar. Glancing over at lower town it looked like Fred Trump, Shamus and a few others were sawing boards and nailing down temporary planking, attempting to repair the footbridge, which was barely above the water. Sunday Creek had gone down a bit but was still over its banks, flooding and isolating their portion of lower town. Stepping inside the mercantile the room was buzzing with talk. I saw Mattie sitting by herself at one of the front tables, I went over and joined her by the window.

"Hi, how're you doing?" I said to her, sitting down and placing my hands on the table.

"Good morning," she replied, with a tired strained look on her face.

"You okay?"

"Just worried," she said. "The Chapmans had a school board meeting last night. They're going to close it, I mean the school, for the time being, anyway. They think that because the concentrator and the mines are shut down that the kids should be home with their parents. Plus, they're pretty sure we'll all be hiking out real soon."

"That's too bad. You'd think they'd keep the kids in class to keep their minds off the flooding," I said.

"I know. It's just so troubling," she replied. "But how are you doing? I'm really sorry you lost all your paintings," she said, putting her hands on the table.

"Thanks, I still can't believe they're all gone. Washed away in just a second like that and I'll never have that many of my paintings for sale in one place again, especially in a building built out over a river, but what can I do?" Mattie looked at me with warm reassuring eyes.

"I know, it's terrible. We'll get through it," she said, placing her hands over mine and squeezing them.

"It's my fault, it'll never happen again."

From the front window we saw Jacob and Ben walk up and come in the door. They headed directly over to Martin and Charlie, who were standing by the post office window in the back of the room with Bartholomew and Baker. The room got louder with talk when everyone saw them come in. Comins finally stepped over to the main counter to address the citizens.

"Okay everyone, listen up!" he shouted, raising his hands. "Quiet down, please! Okay, thanks — Ben from the railroad says that the downriver bridge is too damaged for the train but repairable for foot traffic. He thinks it's going to be well over a month before the train is running up here again." The room bristled with dark, angry murmurs.

"What are we supposed to do until then?" Hiram Chapman said.

"Yeah, what about those of us without much food on hand? What are we gonna do?" another man added. Just then Addison Cleveland and a few of his neighbors from lower town walked in, their shoulders slouched, looking tired and worn-out, some folks got up to go over and talk with Addison.

"So, what should we do?" Arthur Thrall asked.

"Well, before we make any decisions," Martin said, pausing, "how many here have more than a month's worth of food on hand? Let's see a show of hands." Heads turned to look at each other and slowly a few hands rose in the air, far less than a quarter of those gathered. Martin counted the hands but stopped. He shook his head, looked back at Charlie and then turned to the room.

"Alright, so . . . it looks like we need to come up with an evacuation plan," Martin said. Instantly gasps and groans overtook the room.

"What!? Already?"

"Isn't there something else we can do?"

"Why should we leave so soon?!"

"People. People! We don't have a choice there's not enough food on hand," Martin pleaded. "I know that no one wants to leave their homes behind and besides, there's no deer to shoot, they've left to winter in the lowlands, which is exactly what we're all gonna have to do, too! There's no way around it. We'll figure it out, but we need to do so way before we run out of food. It will take a couple of days to get ready to hike out and days more to hike, especially if we have to go all the way to Granite Falls. Maybe longer depending on how rough it is."

"You're sure about this?" Jim Bartholomew asked.

"What other choices do we have?" Martin asked, his jaw tightening. "Everyone downriver for all practical purposes are stuck in this same situation. There's no train and that means there's no supplies, no nothing. And it's good that most of the town has already left for winter."

"Okay, so which way will everyone go?" Jim Bartholomew asked.

"We could take the old wagon road north to Sauk City," Sam Strom suggested.

"Yes, we could," Ed Baker said, "but we need to find out what kind of shape it's in first."

"But that's a tough way," Charlie O'Connell added.

"Most of the railroad grade and tote road to Silverton and beyond is still probably in place, I bet," Ben McDonough said, "and walking the track grade is more level than that old wagon road to the north. There's too many hills that way."

"But there's homesteaders down in the Bedal camp on that wagon road," Sam Strom replied. "They'll help us."

"Okay, alright," Martin said. "Before we decide about a route, it's plain that we need to do some reconnaissance. Sam, can ya' hike the old wagon road and check on its condition today?"

"Yah, I'll go," Strom said and headed for the door. But Henry the wagon master raised his voice.

"It's better if two go," Henry offered, standing up.

"Okay," Sam replied, stopping at the entry.

"Good, we'll be back before dark," Henry said.

"Before you go how about if we all meet here again at, let's say four o'clock?" Martin suggested. Henry pulled out his pocket watch, checked it and looked at Sam. He nodded in agreement, then they both left.

"And what about someone trying to reach Silverton?" Martin asked the room.

"There's no hope for that until the river goes down," Ben McDonough said. "Unless if someone wants to try swim across it," he said. No one replied.

"But if someone stays on this side they could hike through the woods to Barlow Pass, and down to Silverton, today. Both towns are on the same side," Martin reasoned.

"That's right!" George Pratt hollered.

"Yep," Ned Berwyn asserted. "All someone has to do is bushwhack their way downriver to where the other bridge is out and walk the tracks all the way to Silverton."

"Yes, yes," Ben McDonough jumped back in, "You're right. But I'll tell ya', Weden Creek will be difficult to get across, and taking the railroad grade when we all leave will be much better than that old wagon road north because there's nothin' but wilderness up there, even if Sam does have friends at the Bedal camp. The track grade has more towns and cabins along the way, there's more places to stay and get out of the weather," Ben said.

"Yep, Ben's right," Jacob Cohen quickly said. "And maybe more food."

"I agree," Ed Baker added. "The train may be washed out below Silverton and they very well could be in the same mess as us . . . it's still worth finding out what kind of shape the tracks and tote road is in. Especially if the river doesn't go down, and soon."

"So, George, are you willing to hike to Silverton today?"

"Yep, and I'll be back tomorrow for sure," Pratt said, heading for the door. "I'll follow Sunday Creek up the mountain first to find a place higher up to cross it."

"You'll never make it to Silverton today or even get back tomorrow," Hiram Chapman chided, then continued, "Why, that's nothing but a fool's errand." George stopped and turned around.

"Oh, I'll make it alright, mark my words," George said, heading out the mercantile.

"You're all dumber than the Donner Party for criminy sakes! And we all know that story," Chapman complained to the closed door.

"That's enough Hiram," Martin said coldly, glaring at him. "We're all doing the best we can, okay." Martin turned back to the room. "Then its set. Everyone go to their tasks and let's all meet back here at 4:00," Martin finished, ending the meeting.

Mattie and I followed Addison outside, I could tell he'd been shaken. I tried to console him.

"I'm sure sorry about your business and everything. I couldn't believe it when it happened," I said. "How's Elizabeth? Where's Jacob?"

"Elizabeth's good, she's doing fine and is down at the cabin," he replied, nodding. "Thanks for asking, but that gall-darned river," Addison said, "I can't believe the building and everything is gone. Jacob didn't feel like coming up, he's taking a break down at his place."

"So, a, I feel terrible about all of this. I've never experienced anything like this, ever," I said.

"Me neither and I'll never own a business on or live next to a river again," he said. "It's just too powerful, too unpredictable."

"Mother Nature's to blame," I said. "I couldn't believe it when I heard the rocks rolling downstream under the water." Then Mattie pulled on my hand.

"Oh, this is Mattie de Graaf," I said, introducing her. He nodded and feebly said, "Howdy."

"I can't tell you how sorry I am about your loss," she said.

"Thanks," Addison said and turned to me.

"Well, I'm really sorry about all your paintings," he said. "I don't know how I'll ever be able to repay you."

"I know, that's okay, it's a tough deal for everyone. All the time I put into those paintings," I said, exhaling. "It's hard to swallow, but I'll be okay. You've got far more important things to deal with."

"The river took our safe, too, just washed it all away," Addison said, sweeping his hand out to the side. "We had some money in it for you, too," he added. "Plus, most of ours."

"I figured, maybe someday you'll find it."

"Well, thanks for understanding, Oliver," he said.

"What are you going to do?" Mattie asked.

"Elizabeth and I are staying. I'll shovel roofs and work for the railroad, we'll be fine. Jacob's got a cousin in La Conner so he's gonna walk the old wagon road to Sauk City and then head down the Skagit. He doesn't care what kind of condition the road is in. He's going that way no matter what, so he says, he'll get through it," Addison said.

"Thanks for chopping down that tree. I'm sure glad you fellas did that, wouldn't be over here if you didn't," he added. "What about you? What are you going to do?"

"Not sure yet, probably walk out with everyone else but we haven't decided," I replied.

"Well, I should get back. See how the wife is doing."

"Good luck this winter," I said. "Do you think you'll open another tavern?"

"Maybe, but it'd only be in upper town, I'd have to borrow some money if I do," he replied. "Or I might go down to Granite in the spring, maybe try to get a job at the Wayside Mine. I hear things are going good there." Then he turned and walked towards the stables.

"Maybe I'll see you in a few months!" I hollered at him. Addison turned around.

"Okay! Maybe," he said. We watched him slowly walk off.

"I feel so sorry for him, losing his business and all. I just can't imagine that," Mattie said.

"I know, it's terrible what happened," I replied. "So, what do you need me to do?

"Oh, I'm okay. I'll just go home for now but I'll see you in a few hours at the next meeting."

"Alright, see you then."

Walking down to the next meeting the afternoon the sky had cleared and the sun was out, steam rose from the street planking and from every rooftop. Children played down on the flats in the railroad yard, oblivious to the trouble, but the crashing sounds of the river still sounded out over the town. Up ahead there were a few people out in front of the mercantile.

A new sign in the window read, 'No Food Sales until Evacuation Decision.' It was a surprise. Two men walked up and read it, then stared at it as the corners of their mouths turned downward into frowns.

"What the hell is this?" one man asked.

"I can't believe it, so now we're supposed to starve?"

"Nothing like a company town," the first one said, shaking his head. Another man heard them as he walked up.

"Charlie has no choice, he can't have a run of supplies on his store or let someone with plenty of money buy him out either," the fellow replied. Both men glared at him.

"Aw, ta' hell with you!" They turned and walked away.

I scraped the mud off my boots on the porch before I went inside. Mattie was already there at one of the front tables.

"I guess you saw the sign," I said, sitting down and joining her.

"Oh, yes, everyone's been talking about it since I got here," Mattie said. "You can't blame Charlie."

"Well I guess, but a few men were just out there arguing about it," I replied, "I don't really agree with it if someone's starving."

"I don't think anyone in this town is gonna let somebody go hungry."

"I should hope not," I replied. "So how're the Chapmans?"

"Not good. She's having a cold spell with a bad cough and sore throat. She's been in bed all day and Mr. Chapman, well, all he does is spend every minute complaining but then he doesn't do anything about it. I couldn't wait to come down here," she answered.

"How about Eva?" Mattie asked.

"Still pretty shaken up, I could hear Jacob and her arguing upstairs. I think he wants them to stay."

"What about Liz?"

"She told me she'd stay. They've got a fair amount of canned goods on hand because of the inn, but I don't think they've got enough for me, too."

"So, then what? What do you want to do?" Mattie asked, her penetrating eyes looking into me. I didn't have to think long about her question.

"I want to be with you and make sure that you're safe, help you get out," I said. Just then Henry and Sam Strom walked inside and went straight over to Charlie O'Connell at the main counter, we could hear them talking.

"Good to see you made it back! What'd you two find out?" Charlie asked.

"Them first two bridges is out and the banks 'er washed away and too steep for women and children unless we rebuild them, completely," Henry said. "The which-a-way of it is settled as far as I'm thinkin'."

"Yah, mud and rocks and trees all over the road," Sam added. "It'd be lots of extra work and weeks to open it up. The women an' kids, they wouldn't stand a chance, it's all kinds of rough."

Martin Comins came inside. He went back to the group and they started talking. I looked at Mattie.

"It sounds like everyone's gonna be going down the railroad. I guess we should pray for the river to go down," I offered. She glanced out the window.

"I've already been," she said, and we watched for more people to show up.

Town folk began filing into the mercantile full of talk and speculation. Fred Trump and Shamus O'Dowd walked in, sopping wet and covered in mud. They started asking questions and making comments to those that would listen. Then Hiram Chapman and Ed Baker showed up, Jacob and Liz walked in behind some miners I recognized but didn't know, then Arthur Thrall, Frank Peabody, Ned Berwyn and more. Once everyone was situated Martin stepped over to the front of the post office.

"Ben and Sam just got back from the old wagon road and it's not in good shape, they found two bridges down and a number of trees and mud slides are blocking the road," he reported.

"But we can move the trees," Frederick Trump said.

"Yes, we could, but they said that the bridge work is too involved, and the ravines and approaches are all washed out and the creek banks are too steep to get down, for women and children especially," Martin countered.

"But if everyone goes out the railroad grade there could be trees and mud slides downed on it too," Fred replied.

"Yes, we know, but the grade is flatter so it will be easier for walking, and there are cabins and towns along the way."

"You are making decisions too fast," Fred argued. Martin cast him a look of concern.

"No he's not!" Ed Baker piped up.

"I think Frederick's right," Shamus said.

"Well of course you do! You work for him," Jim Bartholomew said.

"I was the one elected to make these decisions," Trump barked. "And you are making them too fast!"

Ned Berwyn leapt to his feet and snapped, "Fred! Martin's been doing a great job; besides you were elected to uphold the law and no one's breaking any laws here! Are you gonna pass some ruling on who is leaving and who is staying?!" Ned chided. Fred crossed his arms and glared at Berwyn.

"Yah, well, I'm staying anyway," Fred croaked. "I have a building to take care of."

"Alright," Martin put in, "Okay. So! Let's get back to the food supply problem for those that do stay. Maybe once the water goes down we'll have a supply train of horses and mules go to Silverton for food. Build a ferry to cross the river, or something."

"And what if they're out of food?" Fred said, then he quickly mumbled, "*Wir warden alle verhungern*," and rubbed the side of his nose.

"Frederick!" Ned Berwyn boomed, glaring at Trump, "George Pratt headed out for Silverton this morning and he'll be back tomorrow with the news if they *do* have supplies *and if* the train can still get there. Martin's got things handled!" Ned kept his focus on Fred while the room went still.

"That's enough! Everyone, we've got to keep things on an even keel," Martin said, breaking the silence. "We're all in this together and we are going to get out of this together."

"Now then," Martin started again, "Charlie's put a sign up in the window, ya've all seen it, so we need to determine our exact food supplies and maybe, if we need to, allocate a rationing system so that we all have a little something to eat, equally. Until we leave."

"I'm willing to donate two of my three milk cows to those who stay until the train comes," Arthur Thrall said. "Like I said yesterday, my barn roof has been leaking and most of the winter hay I had stored has molded. A week ago I put in an order for more hay and feed but the train won't be making that delivery. There's only enough hay to last maybe a month but for only one cow. The other two will provide enough beef for those that stay to rebuild the railroad, all winter if they have to," Arthur said finishing with his hat in his hands.

"Here, here!" Jim Bartholomew cheered, as the room joined in. "That's the spirit!"

"Yes! Thank yee, Arthur!" Martin added, the sound of applause filled the room.

"But people! People!" Martin hollered. "That doesn't mean all of us can stay. I'm guessing that the railroad will hire as many miners as they can to start work on the bridges down below and up here, so those cows will have to go to the men that work to get the road running again as well as those that stay to shovel roofs."

"Martin's right," Frank Peabody said, "we need to come up with a proper plan to feed those that stay and an evacuation plan for those that leave."

"Let's see a show of hands of those who are leaving?" Martin asked. Almost everyone raised their hands. Martin started to count them but stopped.

"How about if we start a list of names for those that are leaving and those staying to work? Charlie? Canna' ya' get some paper and pencil?"

"You got it," he replied, searching for the items behind his counter.

"Once we get a list done we'll be able to estimate how much food we'll have left for the ones who stay for winter," Martin surmised. "That should do it for today. Let's meet here tomorrow for when George gets back with his report. And Charlie, how about if ya' just write down the names of people who are hiking out as they leave the meeting?"

"Sounds good," he replied, heading for the front of the room.

Once outside, I turned and looked at Mattie.

"Well, it looks like Martin's got everything handled. How about if I walk you home?" I asked.

"Okay," Mattie replied. We started walking towards Mercedes Street.

"Martin's doing a good job getting things organized," Mattie offered.

"Maybe he should have ran for Justice of the Peace?"

"Yeah, maybe. Fred doesn't seem to be doing much," she said, "except fix the footbridge."

"Well, his whiskey can't help him now," I replied. Once we were at the Chapmans I stopped and saw Mrs. Chapman sitting at the window staring at us, Mattie saw her too and kept walking up to the front door.

"So, I'll see you tomorrow," I said to her back. Mattie turned around and grinned.

"Okay, see you then."

The next day the sun was out but the temperature was colder, cold enough to refreeze the snow up higher and slow the run-off, lifting spirits. By three-thirty word had spread that George Pratt had returned from Silverton. Myself and everyone else gathered quickly at the mercantile for the news; buzzing with excitement and speculation.

Martin Comins, Charlie O'Connell and George Pratt walked out of the back room of the mercantile with sour looks on their faces. George had bags under his eyes and was walking with a noticeable limp, his clothes were sopping wet and covered in mud and mire.

"Okay everybody," Martin said, raising his hands for quiet. "As all of us canna' see, George is back after a long two days and . . . Lord, I wish I had better news. But not only is there no rail service to Silverton, the town of Robe is also without the train," Martin said, gasps and groans instantly filling the store.

"What?! Not even Robe?" someone cried.

"Holy Mother of God!" invoked another in the crowd.

"What happened?" Ned Berwyn asked, his voice calm and measured.

"Well," George said, stepping forward, "I was told by the railroad crew in Silverton that the tunnels below Robe are filled with log jams, and most of the bridges are out from there all the way up here." Just then Mattie came in with Mr. Chapman, I went over to stand with her, shaking my head as I approached. Hiram quickly understood what the news was.

"We're all doomed," Chapman moaned.

"That's right, we're finished," someone said.

"No," Martin broke in, "we'll be okay. We just have some work ahead of us. We'll get through it."

"That's right," Ned Berwyn quickly added, "we've got to stay positive."

"We just have to accept the situation and put our minds and backs into it," Arthur Thrall pointed out.

"Okay, alright," Martin said. "And what about our lists?"

Charlie O'Connell took a few folded-up sheets of paper out of a pants pocket and a pair of reading glasses. He put the spectacles on and looked out to all the faces, he started to speak.

"We've got one-hundred and sixteen men, women and children that are on the leaving list, and that doesn't take into account all the miners still up in the hills. And there are twenty-three people staying." He shoved the list back in his trousers.

"Okay, thanks Charlie, and George," Martin said, looking in his direction, "what about the way to Silverton? What's that terrain like?" George shrugged his shoulders and faced the crowd.

"It's difficult, and I can't see us making it that way in any kind of order . . . I was lucky to get across Weden Creek both times, the water is still running fast and I couldn't find a shallow spot to cross or jump from boulder to boulder. I'm afraid that's just not the way for anyone to go. But there were a few men from the railroad near Weden Creek today on my way back and they're thinkin' they'll have a temporary fix on that bridge right quick, said it'd ready to cross by foot in another day or so."

"Okay, that's good news! Hear that people? Thank you, George, for doing that, we all appreciate it. It sounds like the only way out then is the railroad grade and tote road," Martin concluded.

"That's it then," Ben McDonough added.

"Yes, we have to start making plans to leave," Martin agreed. "The creeks went down today and if this weather holds, and we all stay dry, we should be able to leave in a day or two. What if we build some railings on the tree bridge, so nobody falls and we make it safer?" Martin suggested. He looked at Ben McDonough with confidence.

"Ben," Martin said, "canna' ya' handle that?"

"Sure," he said. "I can do that."

"I'll help with that, too," I added. After the meeting I went up to Ben outside.

"The railroad has some lumber and all the tools we need down at the engine house," he said.

"Okay, let's go," I replied. We both headed towards the railroad yard.

XVII
THE MARCH

Opening my field box, I put in a sketch pad and as many small canvas frames as the lid would hold, then checked to make sure there was a palette and plenty of brushes, paints and other various supplies. Satisfied, I closed the lid and placed it inside the pannier, then I found my leather drawstring pouch in the trunk and put all my money from the jar inside of it: seventy-six odd dollars in a spread of crumpled old bills, silver dollars and dirty coins. A small fortune for a man whose only expense was paints and the occasional tipple. I tied the drawstrings to my belt and shoved the pouch in a front trouser pocket and set the easel on the floor next to the trunk.

After loading my pannier, I carried it out to the kitchen by its framework. Jacob and Liz were sitting with our empty breakfast plates in front of them and cups of coffee in their hands. Resting on the built-in table were one can each of beans, peaches and corn, a sauce pan, a bulging paper bag, pocket knife, and a bottle of water with a cork in it. The black slouch hat that a guest had left at the inn, which I'd used a few times, was on the bench seat.

"Well, this is it," I said, feeling anxious and trying to smile. Jacob stood up and put the hat on my head and handed me an envelope.

"It's a letter for your mom," he said. "Can you mail it when you get to a post office?"

"Sure," I replied, looking at my uncle, wishing I could stay. I know he knew how I felt, I opened my arms and we hugged. I closed my eyes.

"Thank you for everything," I said. "I'm going to miss you and Aunt Eva. Say goodbye to her for me, and, thanks for the hat." I opened my eyes, Liz had stood up from the built-in.

"Goodbye, Oliver. I'll miss our mornings," she said, her eyes a touch red. She picked the paper bag up and handed it to me. "Here, I made a few sandwiches for you. Plus, these cans on the table are for you, too."

"And that knife is for you," Jacob added, picking it up off the table and handing it to me.

"Thank you, Uncle Jacob," I replied, putting it in my pocket. "It'll probably come in handy."

"Thank you for the sandwiches, Liz," I said, putting the bag and cans in my pack. "I'll miss our mornings, too. But remember, I might be back in a few months."

"We sure hope so," Liz grinned. "I guess I'll have to go back to running down to Arthur's condensery or the mercantile myself now."

"And here, I figured you might get thirsty, plus the rivers are still running with silt," Jacob said, handing me the glass bottle.

"Thanks," I answered, opening the pannier and placing the water bottle inside.

"I'll ship your trunk and easel as soon as the train's running again, but only if you write and tell me to," Jacob related. "You've got it all packed and set for me, right?"

"Yep, I'll let you know when I'm coming back. Everything else is packed away in case I need you to ship it," I replied.

"Okay, I'm going to try and get Eva up and down to see you off. We'll be there in a few minutes," Jacob said.

"I'd like that. I'm going to meet up with Mattie at the mercantile, and you can keep all my other paintings you have on the walls for now."

"So, you're going to walk with her and help her along the way?" Jacob asked.

"Yep, that's the plan. I'm going to get her to Bellingham and find someplace for myself to stay, rent a room at a boardinghouse or something once I get there."

"You'll write to us when you get to Bellingham?"

"I will, you can count on it," I promised.

"Okay then, off with you," Jacob ended, gesturing towards the front door. "See you in a bit."

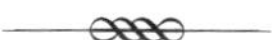

Coming down Dumas, the early morning sky was clear and cold. The street in front of the mercantile was overflowing with baggage and people. Some were carrying luggage across the tree bridge and the rest of town was walking towards the store. A few of the men were carrying rifles and others had pistols in holsters strapped around their waists. A pile of shovels, axes and hand saws were assembled next to the front door for the expedition to use.

I saw Mattie standing at the edge of the crowd. She had on a black work dress, high-top leather boot shoes and wool coat, a stiff winter bonnet was on her head and she carried a small, overland suitcase. I walked over to her and held out my hand, she grabbed hold and squeezed.

"All set?"

"I am, but the Chapmans have decided to stay," she said.

"Oh gosh, really?" I replied.

"They knew they'd be too slow. They'll be fine, they think they have enough food to get by," Mattie said.

"What do you think about them staying?"

"They've got a lot of salted pork laid up and a pantry full of canned goods, so if they're smart about it they'll be fine," she said. "Plus, there's just no way they can hike all the way to Granite Falls if need be, and her cold is getting worse by the day."

"Okay, then," I said. Martin was standing on the porch, facing the huddled mass before him, looking out over the crowd.

"We need some people to take a shovel, or an ax, or a hand saw if we need to clear out paths and open up trails. Is everyone set?" Martin asked. "Any last questions?"

"How long do you think it will take to get to Silverton?" one lone voice asked.

"That depends, we should get there by nightfall if everything goes well. It's about fourteen miles, I believe," Martin said.

"Now, we've got a long way to go and it being December I know it's not exactly hiking season. Everyone can choose to walk the railroad tracks if you've got good thick soles on your shoes, and if not then ya' can walk the tote road that runs close along the tracks. I know that we can't all walk side by side or walk at the same speed but let's all try to stay in sight of each other. Alright! George Pratt is going to lead the group for now and I'm going to bring up the rear, plus we all need to look out for one another. Everyone needs to be careful and kids," Martin said, raising his voice, "there'll be no leaving ya' parents or the trail, and no running at any time! We don't need any falls, or injuries, or anyone getting lost. Does everyone hear me?" Martin said, scanning the group with his hands on his hips. All in attendance nodded while staying silent.

"Let's take a moment of prayer before we head out," Martin instructed. He clasped his hands to his chest and closed his eyes.

"May the good Lord be our protector and guide during this journey we are about to make. Watch over us, protect us, and keep us free from harm to body and soul. Lord, support us with your grace when we are tired, help us be patient in any trouble that may come our way and keep us mindful of your presence. And may God be by our side as we attempt to hike down from these treacherous mountains . . . Amen." Martin raised his head and looked out over the mass of people, he smiled a benevolent smile and said, "Well, here we go!" and pointed downriver. I looked back up Dumas, Jacob and Eva were just walking up.

"Goodbye Aunt Eva," I said, opening my arms for a hug. But her eyes were dark and there was a look of concern on her face. I let my arms fall to my side.

"Jacob says you're going to Bellingham?" she said, her arms crossed.

"Yes, I'm accompanying Mattie to make sure she gets there safely."

"Well, you two need to be careful," Eva said, glancing at Mattie and back at me, "and *you, mister,* need to be a gentleman. Understand?"

"I understand *and* I know how to be a gentleman."

"Oh, don't worry. I can take care of myself," Mattie said. "I trust Oliver."

"You best be hitting the trail," Jacob said, tilting his head downstream. I looked at Eva and opened my arms again, she uncrossed her arms and gave me a hug.

"See you in the spring," I said. "I'll write."

"You can help us move when we sell," Eva said, glancing at Jacob. "Be careful," she added.

"So, here we go," I said.

"The sooner we leave the sooner we'll get there," Mattie added.

Everyone began to file away and over to the tree bridge while Jacob and Eva and everyone that was staying watched us walk away. There was already a good number of people over on the other side waiting and a few others slowly hiking away. Upstream a few men were working on the concentrator trestle supports and planking.

George Pratt got out front and took the lead down the tracks. I glanced over at lower town, Fred and Shamus were standing outside of his saloon watching us leave. Both of them were staring at the group, their faces hard and unreadable.

Some of the miners that were leaving had tattered rucksacks slung over their shoulders and carried lanterns and pickaxes. Young girls hugged dolls and boys held slingshots as parents walked beside them carrying what few things they could: backpacks of food and clothes, shovels and walking sticks. The tote road was a mess of deep mud so most walked on the rail line out of town.

"What's Bellingham like?" I asked as we headed down the tracks, taking measured steps, trying to step from tie to tie.

"Oh, you'll like it. It's a great town and the people are friendly."

"What will we do when we get there?" I asked, walking over a short plank bridge that crossed a small creek.

"Well," she said, then paused to think for a moment. "It would be best if you got a room downtown, and I stay with my sister Jocelynn in Fairhaven and look for work."

"What grade does she teach?"

"She teaches at the elementary level, she's my oldest sister."

"And what about your other sister?"

"Oh, Mary Anne? She's a teacher, too, but at the higher levels. I thought I told you all this, at dinner, remember?"

"Right, I remember, but I don't think you said what grade they taught." Then I changed the subject. "I have a feeling I'm going to like it there, in Bellingham," I commented.

"Already? How could you? You haven't even been there," Mattie said.

"I know I'm going to like it because you'll be close by," I replied.

We kept walking. About a mile downriver something caught my eye over on the other side, it was a big black box. I stopped and went over to the riverbank wondering about what it could be, Mattie followed.

"Do you see that over there?" I said, pointing across the water. Mattie squinted as she looked.

"Oh, yes. I do, that black thing you mean," she answered.

"It looks like a . . . oh wait, it can't be, it's, why I think it's Jacob and Addison's safe!" I exclaimed. "Well I'll be darned, the river carried it all the way down here. And there's some money of mine in it."

"We need to tell them, somehow," Mattie suggested.

"I can't believe it! The river washed it up on the bank. Imagine that, the strength of the river to do such a thing!"

"Well, you should write Jacob and Eva about it once we get back to civilization and they could tell Addison," Mattie offered.

"Right! As long as someone doesn't steal it," I said. We went back to the group and kept marching as a slight breeze began to move through the air.

Tell-tale signs of the wreckage of the rain and flooding were everywhere, freshly gouged out steam beds coming down from the mountain side, rain-washed piles of hemlock needles littered the ground and overflowing established creeks with new channels had changed the waterlogged landscape. All along the riverbank uprooted trees and cast up logs covered the rocks and boulders.

It didn't take long to hike the fairly level three miles from town to the damaged trestle bridge. There were a few sections of timber supports missing and a half dozen railroad men were fastening down planking over some temporary supports. I saw Big Nelson and Sam Strom working with them. George Pratt stopped and held his hands over his head.

"Hold up everyone!" George yelled, turning around.

Mattie sat down on a log at the edge of the river. Ben McDonough was there working on the repairs and came across to the exodus.

"We've got the bridge mostly passable but at that one section there," he said, pointing at a short span, "you can only cross one person at a time. No need to worry it's sturdy and safe."

"You sure about that?" one miner with a wife and kids called.

"Sure am," Ben replied. "We wouldn't let you cross it if it wasn't."

"So you boys been walking on it?"

"Yep, all morning. It's good and strong."

Martin walked up with more people and scanned the bridge from the river bank. Sizing things up he crawled up on a large boulder and watched over the crowd and gave instructions as people filed by.

"Everyone, take your time crossing! And only one at a time over that span," he said, keeping a keen eye on the situation. "Let's all form a line and watch your step." Ben McDonough went over and stood near Martin to watch.

Mattie and I got in line and waited as everyone slowly made their way across. When we got up on the bridge and it was our turn Mattie looked back at me and grinned a sly little grin, then said, "Don't fall in."

I nodded my head as I watched her start to walk across the planking. She held her arms out to the side, with one hand holding her case, like she was walking a tightrope in a circus. Once on the other side where it hadn't been damaged and was wide again she hopped over the last portion and turned around and yelled, "Come on! It's easy!"

"Be right there!" I hollered and started walking over to her, slowly. Halfway there I held my arms out like her and grinned but kept my eyes on the planking. When we were across we sat by the river and watched as one-by-one everyone got over safely. Martin was the last.

"Good job everyone!" Martin said. He pulled out his pocket watch and checked the time. "We've got about six hours of daylight left to get to Silverton. George! Lead the way!"

George started out and we all followed. Mattie and I hiked the gentle uphill grade of the railroad tracks still trying to step from tie to tie since the rocks between them were sharp.

"How are your feet and shoes holding up?" I asked Mattie, looking down at her feet.

"They're fine, they've got some good thick soles," she replied.

Not far from the bridge there was a mudslide covering both the tracks and the tote road; the mud and clay was about two-feet thick. Some chose to wade through it but we did fine skirting around the lower side. We hiked around a bend when, out of nowhere, I heard music on the wind.

"Do you hear that?" I said, stopping to listen as a few notes floated by. Mattie's eyes sparked.

"I do," she replied. "Is that a fiddle?"

"Sounds like it," I said. We started walking again. As we got closer to the top of the hill the fiddle got louder. Mattie smiled and started skipping a little ahead so I laughed and followed her, walking at a faster pace. When we got to the crest of the pass we came upon a board and batten structure with a steep pitched roof and platform landing. It was right next to the tracks with a sign that read, 'Penn Mining Company.'

Doc Welch was standing on the warehouse platform playing his fiddle as we walked up. He stopped sawing his bow and said, "Howdy folks! There's a rain barrel over 'round the corner with a dipper if anyone's thirsty," and went back to playing. Mattie and I went and enjoyed a drink of water then sat down on some boulders for a break.

Martin came strolling up with the rest of the group and started to do a jig, everybody chuckled at the sight of him high stepping and strutting, kicking up his heels. Finally, Doc stopped at the end of the tune and they began to talk.

"I figured I'd be seein' somethin' like this," Doc said, his eyes getting bigger by the moment at the sight of everyone.

"How's Doc holdin' up?" Martin asked, walking over to him.

"Oh, I've got plenty of grub inside," Doc said, pointing behind himself at the warehouse.

"Here all by yer' lonesome?"

"Yep, my crew's down below Robe, cleanin' out all the logs and such in the tunnels," Doc said. "Looks like you've got the whole town of Monte with ya'."

"Aye, me friend, I just about do," Martin said. "All one-hundred and sixteen of us."

"A fine lookin' group they are," Doc said.

"Not a finer group of citizens in the county!"

"So, are ya' staying at Silverton or headed down to the homestead?" Doc asked, placing the fiddle under his chin again.

"Oh, I plan on goin' home and checkin' on things. But first I've got to get everyone safely off the mountain," Martin said, then turned to the group. "Everyone! Let's take a five-minute break before we get back to hiking," he shouted. "Then it's all downhill!" Doc let out a little whoop and started playing his fiddle again.

"I've got some sandwiches, if you're hungry," I offered Mattie.

"That sounds good. How about if we split one?"

I nodded and opened the pannier, found the paper bag and pulled out one of three small packages wrapped in wax paper. Opening it, we found a pre-cut smoked ham and cheese sandwich with sourdough bread and a note that read, 'Thanks for getting the flour! Travel safe, Liz.'

"That was nice," Mattie said. I handed her half of the sandwich and bit into my own. We sat and ate while we watched and listened to Doc play his fiddle. A bedraggled family with two kids sat down close to us, the mother, looking like she hadn't slept in days handed out a few pieces of beef jerky, the parents started to bicker. The mother sent the kids off to the rain barrel and turned to her husband.

"So, what are we going to do when we get to Everett?" she said, frowning.

"I already told you, I'll find work," he replied.

"But where?" she asked, wringing her hands.

"Everett's a busy town, there's a nail works and a shipyard. You know as well as I do that they're always looking for workers down there. I'll find something."

"But you're a miner. You've never worked in a nail works or a shipyard," she continued.

"Damn it, Martha," he said, raising his voice. "Then we'll come back when the mines start up again. Or maybe we'll stay in Silverton and I'll work fixing the railroad." Just then their kids came back. They stopped arguing and Mattie looked at me.

"What are you going to do in Bellingham for work?" she asked.

"I can always paint, or I could teach art somewhere," I replied.

"Well, there's a good number of businesses downtown. I bet there's a jewelry store you could get a job at."

"Yes, maybe I will."

"Alright everyone!" Martin hollered. "George, let's get going!"

I stood up, strapped on my pannier and held a hand out for Mattie. She looked up at me, smiled and put her hand in mine.

"Here we go," I said, pulling her up. I watched her brush off her dress and we started walking but then I had an idea. I turned around and started walking back to the building.

"Oliver," Mattie said. "You're going the wrong way!" I turned around again and walked backwards so she could hear me.

"I'm gonna go and tell Doc about the safe, see if he can get word to Addison," I said. "It'll just take a second."

"Alright," Mattie replied, stopping. "I'll wait."

Once I got back to her side we started off down the tracks, the sky was beginning to be covered with high overcast clouds and there was a chill in the air. Above us to the south were granite cliffs with sparse trees. I started thinking about where we'd stay that night and if we would even find lodging. After a quarter mile and a few bends in the road I looked behind us, our group was strung out for as far back as the last turn, and as far in front of us to the next.

In the distance two peaks rose up above the trees, one of them coming to a sharp point. We walked over a good number of short bridges that spanned ravines and creeks that rushed down the mountainside. Below us to the left in the valley floor was a small creek that kept getting bigger the farther down the grade we got. Then the creek intersected with another and soon enough it turned into a small river.

We settled into a kind of automatic indifference and just kept putting one foot in front of the other in a mechanical rhythm, it brought me to a sort of lost detachment from what at this point felt like an endless route out of the mountains. I looked up into the craggy peaks then down at my feet, the steady movement of walking allowed my mind to fold into an area of thought never known to me before — I looked up again at the mountains and wondered: *Are the mountains more than just rocks and fissures? Do they have a living life that they only know of and understand? Can the mountains see us?* When all of a sudden I was shaken out of my reverie by *Ka-Boom!* The unmistakable sound of a rifle shot echoed through the air.

Mattie and I stopped and quickly turned around. We saw a man aiming his rifle up the slope of a hill about a quarter-mile behind us.

"It's a cougar!" someone yelled. "There's a cougar up there!" George ran past us and back up the tracks as the cries of cowering women and children were heard, a ripple of fear moved through the procession.

"Where?" George yelled.

"Up the mountain!" a man hollered.

"Oh my heavens," Mattie said, alarmed. "What should we do?"

"Just stop and wait, he's not going to go after the whole bunch of us."

"We don't need no cougar following us," a man near us said.

"That's for sure," Mattie added. We watched as George ran up to the man with the rifle and they started talking and pointing upward to where we guessed the cougar was. Then *Ka-Boom!* The man fired his rifle again.

More people screamed. Children that were walking ahead of their families ran back to their mother's side. We saw the man who fired the rifle unstrap his holster and hand it to George, he fastened it around his waist while they talked. Soon George was running back in our direction and up to the front of the group, keeping a hand on the revolver at his side.

"What happened?" I asked as he went by us.

"Joe Digby saw a mountain lion up above the tracks and fired a shot at it. He thinks he missed since he saw it run off. So, he fired again to keep it away."

"What do we do now?"

"We'll be fine but keep yer' eyes peeled," George said, patting the pistol at his side. "We spread the word to have all the men that are armed to be at each end and in the middle of the group." George went back to the front of everyone and we started walking again.

"That was a little scary," Mattie said.

"Yeah, but that cougar's probably more afraid of us than we are of him."

"Hopefully it's long gone."

"Yes, I'm sure it is."

After what seemed like hours I found myself in a neutral state of mind, it got to the point where I'd let my body fall forward only to catch up with myself with the constant pumping of my legs. Then I began to ask myself questions: *Was my body merely a vessel only to be used to bring myself down from the mountains? Or was my body being used to get to a new place in time and a new life?* Yes, I told myself, I was using my body for both of these things as long as it held up because my arms and legs were beginning to ache from carrying the heavy pannier. Soon the ache turned to pain and I told myself that I had to detach my mind from the hurt and continue to move forward one step at a time.

I looked up and saw that the train tracks had broken into a huge meadow. It seemed familiar from the ride back in June. I wondered if we were at Big Four Mountain, but the valley was covered in a multi-level shroud of grey clouds so I wasn't sure. I kept glancing in its direction and walking when finally, there was a break in the sky and there it was — a massive singular mountain of granite that rose up thousands of feet from the valley floor. I stopped and so did Mattie, gazing at the sheer magnitude of it.

The mountain was so incredibly impressive I found it inspiring. A concerto melody resounded in my head and my whole body instantly buzzed, it was breathtaking to behold. As I stood there, I came to the realization that I was witnessing something bolder and more beautiful than my eyes could take-in. I felt like a child of that mountain, a child of earth and heaven, and a child of God.

"Someday I want to come back here and camp and paint, and work for weeks," I said, staring up at it. "I could paint this mountain over and over: spring, summer, and winter."

"You should do that, it really is beautiful," Mattie said, stopping and enjoying the view. Droves of evacuees passed us by as we stood gazing. Finally, we started walking again. The sky started to mist and soon enough the fine mist grew into droplets that then turned to rain. In no time we found ourselves slogging forward through a driving rain storm.

All we could do was keep our heads down and our feet moving. One step after another, after another. On and on we walked as the pain in my legs shot up to my back and my imagination began to run again: *Was I going to be able to keep my legs moving? What will happen to me if the pain in my legs and back makes me stop?* But I can't stop in this weather, not now. Then my eyes started to see the ground move up and back away, up and down, back and forth. *Were my eyes playing tricks on me? What's going on?* I glanced over at Mattie. Her mouth was wide open and she was breathing heavily, her eyes unfocused and feet dragging. Just then a scrappy looking teenage boy came running back up through the crowd huffing, and puffing.

"We're here!" the boy yelled, running though the wet, rag-tag group. "We got to Silverton!"

XVIII
SILVERTON

I raised my head and a huge smile of accomplishment broke out on my face. I recognized the bridge that crossed the river and a few cabins over on the hill to the right, there was smoke curling out from every chimney. I looked over at Mattie, she was grinning ear to ear with relief. Up ahead people from our group were filing into the small railroad depot with more running up and standing under the eaves, trying to find shelter. We walked across the bridge and found the town overwhelmed with rain-soaked evacuees in the muddy street scurrying around and asking each other where to go and what to do.

"Am I ever glad to get here!" Mattie said.

"No kidding, my legs and back are killing me."

"Mine too."

"But I think we might have wasted too much time looking at that mountain," I replied, glancing around and worrying if we were too late to find a place for the night.

"Where should we go?"

"Well, first let's try to find someplace where we can get out of the rain," I said.

Our group filled the main street. There were a few saloons and a general store, a closed barber and cigar shop, a livery stable farther up. Cord wood was stacked in the street and in front of every building under covered porches. Everyone saw Martin walk up, he went over and stood on the planked sidewalk.

"Okay everyone, gather up!" he called out. "There are a few hotels here for those with money, and for those without there's a livery stable with a large barn up the way. And I'll check with the preacher, he's got the red house up at the end with his church next to it," he said, pointing in its direction. "It should be available to stay in and only a short walk up the way. Let's all meet back here in the morning, and I'll be over in the building across the street if anyone needs to find me later. In the meantime, let's go find the Minister," he said, and walked off up the main thoroughfare. The group began to disperse, most following him while others formed long lines at the general store and a hotel just up the way.

Of a sudden a man's sharp whistle sounded, then, "Haw," was heard in the air. We both turned to see a stage coach coming across the bridge into town, the driver sitting on the top bench snapping the reins to his four horses. They pulled up and stopped outside of a building where he hopped down and opened the door for his passengers. A few of our group ran over to him.

"We need to get down valley."

"How much for a ride in the morning?"

"Sorry, full up with Silverton folks for tomorrow and I can only go as far as the next washed out bridge." We heard the driver loudly say to them. I turned to Mattie.

"Well," I exhaled, rainwater pouring off the brim of my hat. "I guess we're on our own." She looked at me with latent urgency then glanced up and down the street. She started towards the hotel. I followed her.

"I need to get a room, I'm exhausted and my feet are killing me," she said, slogging through the mud, her dress a sopping wet encumbrance. "I've got the money for it."

At the hotel a long line of people stood in the rain from the door out into the mud filled street, men, women and children, all anxious and worn out. While we waited I noticed that only men were leaving the hotel and the line was moving faster than I thought it would, we were soon inside.

"Next!" the lady behind the counter cracked. She wore the trappings of a sporting woman, her robust bosom held back by a tight chemise under a white blouse unbuttoned at her throat. We stepped forward.

"I suppose you want a room, too?" the woman asked, her voice raspy.

"Yes, I'd like to see about a room for the night," Mattie answered, politely.

"No men," the woman quickly belched, looking at me, "women and children only. We don't have enough space for everyone from Monte. You men are gonna have to fend for yourselves." She turned back to Mattie, "One dollar for a room, two if you want board included."

"That's fine," Mattie quickly said. "What's for supper?"

"Beef stew and bread tonight, an egg and bread in the morning," the lady replied. "And that's a shared room, missy," she added, staring at Mattie, waiting to see her money.

"Do I get a bed?"

"Yep," the woman replied, "but you've got to share it."

"With who?" Mattie asked, her voice thick with irritation.

"You're from Monte, right?"

"Well, yes. I am," Mattie answered. The lady looked at her register. "I'll put you with a . . ." she said, looking at the page, "Mrs. Jamieson and her kids, how's that?" Mattie rolled her eyes and blanched at the thought; knowing that Billy Jamieson from her class could be a problem.

"Fine," Mattie exhaled, "I'll take it," she replied, placing two dollars on the counter.

"You'll be in room 2C, up the stairs. If ya' ain't blind you'll find it. Next!"

Mattie turned and pulled me by my arm over to the bottom of the staircase. She set her bag down and looked into my eyes.

"Where will you stay?"

"You don't need to worry, I'll be fine."

"But you'll need to find someplace. Where will you go right now?"

"Well, I'll take a look around, maybe try another hotel," I said. "Or go up to the church."

"Maybe my room will have a window. I'll look for you."

"Okay, but if you don't have a window I'll meet you in the morning. Right here."

"I promise," she said, her penetrating eyes boring into me.

"Alright, I'll be here then. Sleep sound," I said.

"Goodnight," Mattie replied, squeezing my arm. She turned and I watched her slowly climb the stairs, her small overland suitcase hanging heavy in her hand.

"See you in the morning," I said. She stopped and turned around at the landing and smiled, then trudged upward around the corner and out of sight.

I went back outside. The rain had let up but the town was a deluge of people. Over at another hotel there was a sign in the window, 'No Men,' so I walked up the street. At the livery barn there were at least forty fellows from our group waiting in ankle deep mud in a line. I stood and looked up and down the way, thinking I might be able to stay there but still wondering if there were any other options. I walked up to the tiny clapboard church and found it overwhelmed with evacuees. The preacher had his hands full: families with crying children were bedding down, every bit of floor space and every pew was already taken by those in dire need of a place to stay. I turned around and my feet started walking back to the main part of town and the building where Martin said he'd be.

Opening the door, I inched my way inside. It was a saloon, noisy and completely filled with local miners and Monte folks, cigar smoke hung thick in the air. I stood next to the door and scanned the room for Martin. Kerosene lamps and candle flames flickered off the embossed metal ceiling, granting just enough light to see through the haze. I spotted him leaning up against the end of the bar next to George Pratt and another man with a wide brimmed hat. There wasn't an empty chair in the place.

Maybe I can get something to eat?

I made my way through the crush of tables full of men playing cards and drinking. I recognized a few fellows at one table: Five-Finger Lewie wearing his red vest, Frank Kazenski and Dick Sperry. They were playing poker and carrying on, one hollow-eyed miner with a chiseled face sat with them, a halo of smoke ringed his head. I could hear them as I side-stepped by.

"Looks like there's money to be spent in town tonight," Lewie said, tossing cards around the table.

"With all these lost souls the hotels will be full in no time," Kazenski replied.

"What's, whit, all a, da' new . . . comers," the hollow-eyed fellow slurred. He was so drunk he could barely link his words together.

"When are ya' gonna catch up with the rest of the world, Curley? They've all come down from Monte because it's washed out, worse than us," Sperry replied.

I made my way over to Martin, he saw me approach.

"Oliver, lad, good to see ya'. Come and have a whiskey, it'll revive ya'!" he said, an empty jigger in front of him.

"Hey Martin," I said, taking off my hat and holding it in my hands but leaving my backpack on. "So, the hotels are already full, and the livery, too."

"Yer' looking for a place for the night, then," he quickly replied, as the bartender re-filled his shot glass and took a dime. "I've got some of us set up with the preacher and there might be a wee bit of room left in his church — that is, if you'd like to sleep in a pew with the others?"

"I was just up there and it's full to the rafters," I replied. Martin nodded.

"Well, I have to admit, I don't know what to do with everybody else. There's too many of us and Silverton is only a small village. There's not enough roofs to get under."

"I don't need much, just someplace dry," I said. The man next to George spoke up.

"You're from Monte?" he asked.

"Yes indeed," I answered.

"Have we met, before?"

"Andy, this is the artist I mentioned," Martin said. "The one that painted the cookhouse, remember?"

"Oh, yes," he replied, puffing on his cigar, "the artist." He pushed up the brim of his hat and stuck out his hand.

"Pleasure to meet you, I'm Andrew Hawks. Martin's told me all about you, you're one heck of a painter I hear," he said, grinning. I shook his hand and smiled.

"Thanks, great to meet you!"

"I'll tell you what, I've got a cabin up the gulch at my claim, and Martin and I just set up a tent right next to it for anyone from Monte to stay in." Right when he said tent I was jolted to the thought of spending the night under a canvas roof during a December rainstorm, but then I realized a tent would certainly better than nothing. I was about to accept his offer but he started up again.

"However, any good friend of Martin is a friend of mine!" Andrew said as a big grin broke across his face. "So, you're welcome to stay in my cabin with me and these two knuckleheads. It ain't much, but there should be just enough room on the floor for one more, it'll keep you out of the rain and be warmer than that old tent," he said. Then he pointed with a finger and said, "Just go about a quarter mile up the street till it turns into a puncheon road. Keep going and my place is the first one on the left after the road crosses the little creek, you'll see it. I've got a lamp lit in the window, just make sure you stir the coals and keep it warm. You'll find a key under the door mat. Maybe I should charge you a painting?"

"Oh my gosh, thank you. Thank you so much! I'd be happy to do a painting for you."

"You're welcome, son. You can make me a painting for Christmas," Andrew said with a sly grin.

"Ah, sure," I automatically replied, quickly thinking that I could maybe do one that night but wishing I wasn't so sore and worn out. Andrew's sly grin changed to a real smile

"Don't worry about it son! I was just kidding about the painting," he laughed.

"Oh okay. Maybe I can do one for you when I get back in the spring?"

"That'd be fine," he replied, puffing on his cigar. I was overjoyed to know that I had a place to stay for the night when my empty belly began to rumble. I glanced around to see if there was a cook and kitchen.

"So, do they serve food in here?"

"They do but the kitchen just shut down. They're out of food already," Martin replied, picking up his whiskey, Andrew and George did too.

"Here's to the finest things in life," Andrew said, raising his glass, "whiskey, cards, and swimmin' with bow-legged women!"

"I'll drink to that," George grinned, and they all downed their drinks. "Bartender!" George Pratt cried out, "Pour us another!"

"Oliver, how about it?" Martin offered. "I owe ya' one, remember?"

"Oh, that's right," I replied. It was tempting. I told myself I shouldn't but my mouth opened up, and instead of politely refusing, I heard myself say, "Sounds good."

The bartender poured us all a shot. Martin picked up his shot glass and looked at me.

"A toast to Oliver's spring painting!" We lifted our glasses and threw back our drinks, I set my glass back on the bar rim down.

"What's this?" Martin asked, eyeing my upside-down shot glass.

"Just one for me," I said, putting my hat back on.

"Ah, tiz' a brave man that turns away from the whiskey," Mar-n said wryly. I stepped over to Martin and patted him on the back ıen shook Andrew's hand again.

"Thank you, gentlemen. I've got to get going and stop at the otel to check on my friend, then I'll see you all in a bit at your place, .ndrew."

"See ya' soon lad," Martin said.

"Good to meet you, Oliver," Andrew replied. "Make yourself : home when you get there."

Outside the night sky was black as tarpaper, save for the side-alk oil lamps casting a shadowy glow on a few people still roaming :ound searching for a place to stay. Taking off my hat I looked up at ıe hotel but didn't see Mattie in any of the second story front win-ows. I slowly walked around the building twice calling her name ıd gave up.

Up the street, I passed the livery and came upon the puncheon oad built of wide split cedar planking. The darkness got thicker the ırther away I walked from town. Crossing the creek, I could hear oices ahead in the darkness, then saw the soft glitter of the lamp ı the window that Andrew mentioned. It cast a weak light on a :w moving figures. There was someone at the door of the Hawks abin! I walked slower. I could make out two larger and two smaller lhouettes, two adults and two children.

"Who's there?" I called. "Are you looking for the tent?"

"Tent! A tent won't do in weather like this. Are you the owner f this here cabin?" a man's voice replied. I paused.

"I'm not the owner. This is a friend's home," I said, stepping loser.

"Well where's the owner? We *need* a place for the night. I've got *two* kids," he replied, sounding desperate.

"I heard that," I said, stepping closer. I recognized them from earlier in the day, it was the husband and wife that were arguing about finding work in Everett.

"I believe there's a tent up here for folks that hiked out —"

"Too cold for my kids to sleep in a tent fella!" the man snarled.

"Well, a, there's still room at the hotels back in town for women and children," I quickly suggested.

"We can't afford a hotel either," he said, stepping closer.

"I can understand that . . . but I can't let you in the cabin, the owner is back down in town."

"We can't sleep out in the weather," he insisted.

"I'm sorry, I don't know what to tell you."

"How the hell are we supposed to get through the night, damn it," he barked. I took a step backward and thought about what I should, or could do.

"Okay," I said. "Give me a second." I turned and walked back a few steps into the darkness, then pulled out my pouch. I felt around inside of it for two silver dollars and walked back over.

"Here's two dollars for a hotel room for your kids," I said, handing him the coins.

"What?" the man snapped.

"Listen, I'm sorry. It's not my place and this is all I can do for you," I said firmly. The man shoved the money in his pants pocket and looked over his shoulder.

"Come on, let's go back to town," he said, motioning to his family. They all scampered away from the cabin.

"Thanks," the man quietly said, walking past me, heading into the darkness with his wife and kids. I squinted into the black void of night as they walked away and shook my head, not knowing what else I could do for them.

On the porch I took off my pannier, found the key under the mat and unlocked the door. I stepped inside and breathed a tired sigh of relief. I took off my heavy wet coat and found a nail to hang it up on the back of the door with my hat, then set the key on the counter and left the door unlocked.

There were plank floors, one window above the sink that had pans hanging over it, and a cook stove on one side of the room. Glancing around it was a cozy place: table with a plaid coverlet and two straight-back chairs, a rifle in the corner and there was a small half-loft up in the rafters. A box full of wood was on the floor next to the stove and a few jars of moonshine were on a shelf next to a piece of paper tacked to the wall with; 'Notice of Mining Claim: Maude Mine Silverton District,' written across the top of it. I opened the firebox door and tossed some dry pieces of cedar on top of the coals and blew on them, the kindling took to fire.

Opening my backpack, I pulled out the sauce pan and cans of beans and corn and set them on the counter. I looked around and found a can opener on a shelf and dumped both cans into the saucepan, in no time they were bubbling hot on the stove. After my meal, I washed my dishes, dug out a blanket from the pannier and collapsed on the floor underneath it.

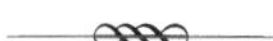

I awoke the next morning to a heroic level of snoring. Martin was half covered by a blanket and deep asleep next to me, his head turned in my direction and his wheezing directed straight into my ear. The place was cold and it was light out. I lifted my head and saw George

Pratt on the other side of him, mouth wide open but breathing quietly.

Sitting up, still in my boots and clothes, my back and legs were stiff and already starting to ache. I gathered my blanket, folded it and placed it into the backpack and put on my coat and hat. As quietly as I could I opened the door, but then had a thought and stopped. Opening the pannier outside, I dug out the field box and stepped away from the cabin and got a good look at the place. Quiet as a mouse I went back inside, pulled out the sketch pad and commenced to do a rendering of it. When I finished, I wrote 'Hawk's Nest,' on it and left it on the table.

Walking out into a grey and wet, comfortless morning I strapped on the pannier and pulled out my pocket watch, it was nearly eight. I headed down the gulch, crossed the creek onto the puncheon road and walked inside the hotel. No one was behind the counter but I could hear laughter emanating from the dining room off the lobby. I poked my head into the room, Mattie was sitting at the one long table looking refreshed and chatting with another traveler. There was an empty seat across from her so I walked over, took off my back pack, set it up against the wall and sat down.

"Oliver!" she exclaimed, smiling and twisting towards me in her chair.

"Good morning," I replied. "How'd you sleep?"

"Pretty good," she answered. "And you? Where'd you stay?"

"I stayed in a friend of Martin's cabin, it worked out fine," I said. Just then the same lady from the night before came into the room, she saw me right away.

"Breakfast for you?" she asked, pouring hot coffee into a customer's cup from a blue enamel coffee pot.

"Yes please," I replied.

"Okay, you get one fried egg and a piece of bread for fifty cents. It's all we got and we're running low."

"Alright, thanks," I said, thinking that I wasn't getting much for such a high price. She turned the mug in front of me right side up and filled it with steaming coffee while I dug out four-bits and handed it to her. Then I wrapped my hands around the warm cup of coffee and smiled at Mattie.

"How far do you think we'll get today?"

"I guess that depends if we run into difficulties or not," I replied, sipping as much as I could of the hot drink. "I think the next town is called Robe."

Another woman from down the table spoke up. "It is," she said, "and it's about fourteen miles to the west."

"Okay, thank you, Mrs. Jamieson," Mattie said, nodding and taking a drink of coffee. "Good thing it's all downhill."

"Yes generally," Mrs. Jamieson added, "but there are a few hills in between."

"Good to know," I replied, sipping more coffee. The hotel lady walked in from the kitchen and set a plate with one egg fried sunny side up and a slice of homemade white bread in front of me. Then she topped off my cup with more coffee.

"Anything else?" she asked

"No thank you. I'm good," I said to her, picking up a fork. A few people came down the stairs and even more showed up from outside, all of them waiting at the dining room entrance. Two of the customers at the end of the long table got up to leave, as soon they did two new ones took their places. I began to devour my breakfast.

"Alright, I'll be out in the lobby," Mattie said, getting up. Her seat was instantly taken by a man who looked like he hadn't slept in a month. I nodded at Mattie as she headed out of the room, shoveling the rest of my food in my mouth.

Carrying my pannier by its strap, Mattie followed me from the main entrance and out into the already crowded street. An unwashed old-timer wearing a bearskin coat and hat and charcoal stained buckskin pants wandered up to us as he glanced around at everyone with a puzzled look on his face, smelling of wood smoke, tobacco and plain old general stink.

"What in tarnation is goin' on?" he asked though missing teeth, a load of chaw bulging behind a scruffy cheek. "Whar all these-a people come from?"

"We hiked out from Monte yesterday," I replied.

"Ya'll headed down ta' the flatlands?" he asked, spitting a stream of brown goop on the ground. Mattie crinkled her nose and started to walk away.

"That's right," I said, turning and following her. "We gotta get moving!"

"Welp, good luck!" I heard him say.

"That man had a very odd odor about him," Mattie said.

I nodded and said, "Yes indeed, I noticed that too."

We headed to where we were going to meet Martin, a few of our group stood waiting in a light mist that was beginning to spray down from a gunmetal sky. I cupped my hands to my mouth and breathed warm air into them, then shoved my hands in my pockets. We both looked up and down the street. There was a small pile of cord wood stacked under the porch of a storefront, I pointed at it and we went over and sat down.

"How long should we wait for Martin?"

"He'll show up," I answered.

"Maybe we should get a head start?"

"Oh, I don't know about that."

"But all we have to do is follow the railroad. It couldn't be that difficult."

"Yeah but if we run into trouble, that wouldn't be good."

"What could happen?" Mattie said with an optimistic smile.

"Well, for one thing that cougar might find us again," I reminded her. Mattie's eyes got big.

"Oh, forgot about the cougar."

I looked across the street, a closed sign rested in the window of a general store. It gave me a thought as the mist turned into rain.

"You know, I wonder if I should go over to that store and buy a tarp when it opens," I said. "And get some rope."

"What for?" Mattie asked.

"If the weather turns sour or if we get stranded we could build a lean-to."

Mattie nodded, "Yes, maybe." We sat and watched as more and more people showed up looking for somewhere to take cover. I thought I might see the same family from Andy's cabin the night before when we saw George and then Martin stroll up wearing a rain slicker and hat. People started gathering and the open sign went up in the store.

"Okay, here we go," I said. "I'm gonna go and buy us a tarp," I said, standing up and strapping on the back pack.

"See you in a minute, then," Mattie said, walking over to where Martin was with her overland case. As I hurried across the street another sign from inside the store was placed in the front window that read, 'No Food Sales.' I went inside and the owner glared at me.

"Did you see the sign?" he asked in a dark voice, rough as tree bark, pointing at the window.

"Yep," I replied, walking down an aisle. "Not here for food."

"I can't allow all you Monte folks to be buying me out like ya'll darn near did last night."

"It was the same up in Monte, I understand. Where's your tarps and rope?"

"Next row over, you'll see 'em."

I found what I needed and set a small canvas tarp and roll of hemp rope down on the counter. There was a barrel of canes, walking sticks and umbrellas next to me. The man stood staring at me from behind his counter.

"How much for an umbrella?"

"Those are a dollar-fifty each," he replied.

"And the tarp and rope?"

"That would be another dollar and twenty-five cents," the man said.

"Okay, I'll take 'em all."

"That's two seventy-five."

I pulled the money out of my pouch, set it on the counter, and shoved the tarp and rope into my pannier.

Leaving the store, I walked over to the group where Martin was going over a few last-minute things, they were about ready to leave.

"Alright folks, let's try to stay together as much as we can. We've still got a long way to go and it won't get any shorter no matter how long we stand here, so let's get to it!"

Once he finished the already tired looking group began to slowly head down the muddy street towards the bridge, all of them as dirty and rag-tag as the day before. I saw Mattie waiting, standing off to the side. As I walked towards her she saw me approach so I opened the umbrella and held it out for her.

"For me?" she smiled.

"It will help keep the rain off your dress. Make for some easier walking," I said, handing it to her.

"That was sweet of you," she said. "Thank you."

We followed the caravan of evacuees across the bridge and down the tracks. After about a mile the group began to get strung out again as some people slowed while we kept up the pace with Martin in the lead. I didn't see any sign of the family from the night before and wondered if they decided to stay on in Silverton to work for the railroad or maybe even go back to Monte.

Up ahead, a well-worn trail split off from the tracks. I pushed the brim of my hat up on my brow and saw that it climbed a slight incline. Through the leafless trees on the hillside was a miner's cabin and a few outbuildings. Then I saw what looked like an old-growth hollowed out cedar stump with an outhouse built on top of it. A rickety set of make-shift stairs went up to a door with a half-moon cut in it when it dawned on me that the ground was probably too rocky to dig a hole, either that or the owner was too lazy to dig one.

I chuckled to myself and pointed at it for Mattie to see as we walke by.

"That's creative," I said.

"It's an outhouse, right?" she asked.

"I believe it would be!" I replied. We walked on.

"So! I wonder how everyone's doing back at Monte?" I askec

"I was just thinking the same thing," Mattie said, the shaft the umbrella resting on her shoulder.

"I bet the railroad crew is still working on the trestle belo town."

"Probably," Mattie responded.

"I'm not too worried about everyone in Monte, I think they' be fine. But what I'm more worried about is our evening meal. Wh did Martin say back in Silverton when I was in the store?" I aske as we walked over a short bridge that crossed a small creek that w undamaged by the flooding.

"He said that there's a settlement called Gold Basin befo Robe and he got a report that there's a bridge being repaired farthe down on the tote road, and that it might be passable by foot some time today."

"He say if there's a place to eat in Robe?"

"He didn't but I'm already getting hungry."

"Well, we still have two sandwiches from yesterday, and a ca of peaches, we'll probably go through that today."

"We'll make it," Mattie said reassuringly.

Up ahead, a blanket of fog was creeping up the valley toward us, soon the full weight of the murky haze had enveloped us lik smoke. It seemed to take me out of body and the meaning of lif began to cloud over, I began to lose all sense of place and time as w marched on. The thick mist made me feel like we were on the edg of existence and traveling into an unknown space where the meaning of life became a shadow, lost and hidden in a hazy wilderness where nothing made sense.

We walked with a rhythm that kept us in sync. After what seemed like a never- ending period of time we found ourselves even more strung apart from the group and still in the fog. We knew that Martin and a few were ahead and others must have gotten tired behind us who may have stopped for a break. Then we came upon a somewhat level area where a grove of sparse hemlocks grew between the tracks and a narrow portion of the river. Mattie stopped and grabbed my arm.

"What's the matter?" I asked.

"Look," she said quietly, "across the river over in the shadows . . . there's some kind of animal." Through the hazy mist I could make out the figure.

"I see it!"

"What is it?" Mattie whispered. It started to slowly creep towards the river bank. "What should we do?" Mattie asked, her voice quiet but intense. I looked behind us, there was nothing but fog. I turned back and focused on the dark shadowy animal when I realized what it was.

"It's a wolf!"

"A wolf!" Mattie cried.

"Let's keep going," I whispered, keeping my voice as firm as I could. As soon as we started walking down the tracks again the wolf did the same on his side of the river, right at the same pace while it kept its eyes glued on us. I stopped and turned around, Mattie did the same. We could barely make out a few figures of our group walking around the last bend behind us.

"I don't think wolves can swim," Mattie said.

"They might if they're hungry," I added. "Dogs can swim."

"Stop it, Oliver. I'm serious, what should we do?" she saic with a touch of panic. She grabbed my arm again but with a tighte grip.

"Well," I replied, glancing around, "let's see." The river wasn very wide but it was still loud and running fast, too fast and deep fc the wolf to get across. Then I had an idea.

"Wait here," I said, feeling a little uneasy.

"What are you going to do?"

"I've got an idea, you'll see," I answered, heading over to th river bank.

"You be careful, Oliver Cohen!" Mattie cried.

As I walked through the trees the old grey wolf lowered it head and watched my every step with it front paws wide apar When I got to the bank I slowly took off my backpack and lean it up against the closest tree. I looked around and found a baseba sized rock, pitched it at the wolf and started jumping up and dow and flailing my arms and screaming like a loon.

The wolf immediately rose its head and opened its mouth, began to howl!

"Oliver!" Mattie yelled. I turned around to look at her, sh was glancing back and forth, up and down the tracks. She starte waving her hands at someone back up the line. I picked up anothe rock and threw it at the wolf but missed. The wolf stared at me bared its teeth and growled and then started to howl again. I foun a good-sized piece of tree limb and picked it up, thinking I'd thro it to scare him away. I pitched it with all my might — it bounced of the ground and hit a tree near him.

The wolf ran off into the woods on his side of the river and u the mountain. I turned around and looked at Mattie.

"Did it leave?!" she yelled. I smiled at her and strapped on the back pack.

"Yep! It took off," I said, walking back over to her.

"Thank goodness," she replied.

"Oh, I don't think he could have made it through the river, its running way too fast. He's gone, and with all the people coming on behind us he'll keep his distance from here on out," I said.

We started walking again and the sky began to brighten, a mile later the fog had lifted but the high clouds remained. Wherever I looked there was only the vast green of the trees, shinning and brilliant with color from the rain. The low granite slopes rose to cliffs high above us as we plodded along in a kind of mental detachment from our sore and tired bodies. As we walked the tracks I studied the grey shadows cast from low lying clouds that hung against the hills so as to try and remember them for future paintings.

A few miles later we passed through groves of fir trees, they towered over our heads and must have been two or three hundred feet tall, like natural steeples — with the echoing sound of the river in the background it felt like we were in some kind of wilderness church. As we walked the tracks turned around the base of a hill and we came upon a railroad section crew repairing a good-sized bridge that was heavily damaged from the flooding, much more so than the Monte bridges. Martin was already there, breathing heavily and talking to the men — we were some of the first of the group to arrive. We went over to them and stood off to the side.

"Yesterday we fell an old growth just downstream," one of the section crewmen said to Martin. "We dumped it right around the bend," he explained, pointing downstream. "Then we snipped the limbs and nailed down planking where the top busted on the other side. It's plenty strong, we just finished it."

"But what about the stage coach?" Martin asked.

"Oh, you mean Gus and his drivers? They've got three coaches altogether, comin' up from Granite and Robe, going back and forth between them and Silverton and the all bridges that are down, so they've got a whole dang system figured out."

"Alright," Martin said, "sounds like yee've got everything handled."

"Just follow the trail downriver, you'll see the tree, cain't miss it," the fellow said, pointing again. Martin turned to the few of us gathered around him as others showed up.

"I'll stay here and wait for the rest of the folks. If anyone feels like heading down there go ahead, or wait with me," Martin said, the rain pouring off his slicker and the brim of his hat. I looked at Mattie, she tilted her head downriver.

We started walking the freshly bush-wacked trail as the rain began to let up a little, and soon saw the tree spanning the river. Standing on the bank it looked like something built during medieval times, where the tree landed the top had broken on the far bank, there was planking spanning the broken portion with bracing underneath it, it looked sturdy. The riverbank we were standing on was higher than across the river, so the log had a pitch to it.

"The guy said it was plenty strong," I said, trying to suppress a laugh, gazing at the ad-hoc creation.

"Maybe we should wait for someone else to go?" Mattie asked, raising her voice to be heard over the river.

"Nah, I believe him. He's a railroad guy and it looks plenty strong. It might look a little slip-shod but I don't think he'd lead anyone astray."

"I don't know about that," Mattie said, sounding skittish.

"How about if I go first to make sure it's safe," I said. Mattie nodded but then shook her head.

"I don't know if I can keep my balance on it with this thing," she said, lifting up her overland case. I looked at the suitcase in her hand and had a thought.

"How about if I make some back straps for your case?"

"Sure! That sounds like a great idea," Mattie replied with a smile.

I took off my pannier and dug out the rope then pulled the pocket knife from my trousers. I cut four lengths of rope and tied two of them tightly around her case, then I tied one length to each of the ones on the case making strap-like loops, turning it into a backpack of sorts. Mattie put an arm through a loop and slung the case over her shoulder then did the other, trying it on for size.

"This is much better, thank you," she said, adjusting the straps with her hands, getting the loops comfortable on her shoulders.

Climbing up on the five-foot wide log I could see that they'd axed notches cross-ways in it to provide some footing and cut it flush were the limbs were, as well as nailed a few short pieces of lumber cross-ways. But there was no railing like the one Ben and I had built in Monte, so while it did look pretty well-built and sturdy it still looked treacherous and slick from rain. I turned back to Mattie.

"It'd probably be best to close your umbrella for when you go across, okay?"

"I will," she replied, shaking it off and closing it.

"Okay, see you on the other side!"

I took a few steps — the log didn't bounce or move at all. When I got out farther and the rushing water was under my feet I started to creep along, as slowly as I could, while keeping my balance and staying upright. Where the tree's top had snapped they'd nailed planking down to span that broken underwater portion and cut notches for the planking ends so it was flush with the bark, to keep people from tripping. I kept my eyes focused downward where I was ever so slowly walking.

When I got to the planking I stopped and turned to check on Mattie when one foot slipped off the edge, luckily I didn't fall. I thought I could hear her yelling but couldn't understand the words. I took a deep breath and started again, holding my arms out to the side for balance. Exhaling, I stepped off and onto the riverbank — I made it across.

I waved at Mattie and cupped my hands to my mouth and yelled, "Its fine! Come on over!" She waved back to acknowledge me and climbed up on the log as more people started showing up. She started over, holding the umbrella out to the side in one hand and her other arm out for balance while keeping her focus on her feet. Stepping from notch to notch she was at the planking in no time. She looked up at me and grinned.

"Good job!" I hollered. She took another step on the planking and — crack! A big piece of drift wood floating downriver smashed into the rough-hewn bridge, shaking the planking and hitting her foot. She immediately stepped back, the piece of timber lodged up against the span becoming wedged in place. Mattie looked back and forth from the bridge to me. I started to walk back out on it but she raised her one free hand to stop me, then yelled, "I'm okay!"

She started out again, taking little steps. It looked like she was limping and I began to worry. Slowly but surely, she made her way over.

"Are you alright?" I asked as she got closer.

"That was close."

"Did it hit you?"

"A piece of it did in my foot," she said. I held out my hand and helped her.

We both looked down, there was a scuff mark on the side of her boot right above her left ankle.

"It'll be okay," she replied, reaching down and rubbing it.

"Should we sit for a while?"

"No, let's get going."

"Aren't you hungry? I've still got sandwiches," I reminded her. Mattie glanced at me and then nodded.

"You know, that sounds good." I took off the backpack, pulled out the tarp and draped it over a log.

"Do you want to take off your case?"

Mattie shook her head no and sat down while I dug out the last two sandwiches, handing her one.

"It's another smoked ham and cheese," I said, taking a bite. Then I remembered the bottle of water Jacob gave me, I found it in the pannier and handed it to her. She took a long drink.

"Um, yes," Mattie said, handing it back. "This was a good idea."

"Nothing like a little food to keep a body moving," I said, standing up and taking a drink then returning the bottle to the backpack. I looked over to the river, more and more people were showing up on the other side. A few had already crossed, they were standing on the bank on our side watching someone come across. I stood and held my hand out for Mattie, she grabbed hold and I gave a little pull, she smiled but then winced as she uneasily righted herself.

"Are you going to be okay? How's your ankle?" I asked.

"It's a little sore but I'll be alright," she replied.

"If you say so, but if it starts bothering you tell me and we'll take a break, okay?" Mattie looked at me and nodded.

I quickly folded up the tarp, shoved it in the pannier and we started out again, not waiting for Martin or the others. We made our way through the forest looking for the railroad tracks but found the tote road instead.

"How about if we walk the road for a change?" I asked. "We might bump into the stage coach or a homestead."

"Sure, that sounds good to me," Mattie replied.

Ten minutes later the light rain increased and a wave of water began to fall violently from the sky, a gust of wind blew a grey sheet of rain across the surface of the muddy road. Mattie quickly opened her umbrella and got it over her head just before another gust of wind hit us, pulling her umbrella backwards but she held on to it. The rain fell so hard we could hear it in the leafless trees and pounding against the ground in bursting droplets. It came down in a terror.

"The tarp!" I said, stopping. I leaned forward so the backpack was parallel to the ground.

"Take it out," I said. "Quick, take out the tarp!" Mattie hurried to open the backpack and dug it out. Once she did I stood back up, opened it up and flung it over both of us. Mattie closed the umbrella and we started out again. We fell into step, holding on to the edges of the canvas covering as we walked.

"That's better," I remarked.

"It's like having a roof over our heads."

It rained on every tree and every rock, the sky spat rain and it coughed rain. A monsoon poured down on us like a waterfall. It rained so hard and fast it felt like we'd certainly drown just from breathing, our feet were soaked through and through. I could feel the water squishing between my toes. I was so wet it felt like my insides were waterlogged and my brain was moldy. The damp cold air was making its way through my wool coat and invading my body, digging into my bones making me numb. All we could do was put one cold soggy foot in front of the other for what seemed like hours until Mattie lifted an arm from under the tarp and pointed.

"Look!" Mattie cried. "Up ahead!"

XIX
GOLD BASIN

I raised my eyes and squinted through the rainfall — the railroad tracks were back close to us on the tote road and through the sheets of rain and trees I could make out the squat outlines of a few cabins in the distance. A smattering of shanties and sheds were over closer to the river and a sturdy building with a sign that read, 'Post Office,' sat between the tracks and tote road. As we got closer I spied a shed of scrap-wood and tin near a cabin, we headed over to it and got out of the downpour.

"This rain is unbelievable," I said, letting go of the tarp and taking off my hat to shake it off.

"Should we try and wait it out?" Mattie asked.

"I don't know, maybe. My legs could sure use a break."

"Mine too."

"How's your ankle?"

"Better, it doesn't hurt as much."

We both sat down on a short stack of cord wood and looked towards the rushing river. Over on the riverbank were the workings of a mining operation, a sluice and rocker box, buckets and shovels, and a trail of black sand coming up from the bank and over to th cabins. One close-by cabin had smoke curling out of its chimne pipe. A second later a bushy grey head stuck itself out of the do and looked at us, then pulled back in and closed the door.

“Well that’s not very friendly,” Mattie observed.

“Apparently,” I said. “How about some peaches?”

“Yes! That sounds wonderful,” Mattie replied. I leaned ov and she dug through the back pack, finding the can.

“Oh, wait. I don’t have an opener,” I said, righting mysel Mattie stood there with her arms crossed, holding the can up wit her wrist bent.

“So what are we going to do, chew it open?” she asked.

“Maybe we can go and knock on that guy’s door and borro one,” I replied. Just then Martin showed up with a few of our grou most of them went over to the post office building. Martin saw u over in the shed but he went straight over to the cabin and bange on the door, then turned around and motioned for us to come ove We looked at each other and started to walk towards the place whe the door opened.

“Polecat! Yee old digger,” Martin said. “Let me in!”

“Duke!” the old miner replied, “get in here and out of the rain Martin turned to us.

“Come on,” Martin said, then looked back at his friend. “ storm for the ages wouldn’t ya’ say! And don’t tell me ya’ haven’t noticed there’s no train?” Martin said with a laugh as we went inside.

“Oh, Lordy yes, Katie Moffatt told me and everybody else a about it. It’s been kind-a quiet ‘round here lately,” the fellow said an looked at us. “Who ‘er these two wet pups ya’ got with ya’?”

“This is Oliver and Mattie, me friends from Monte,” Marti replied.

"Mighty fine ta' meet ya'!" Polecat said.

"Good to meet you too!" I said.

"Yes, thank you for sharing your roof," Mattie offered.

"Go ahead, sit down a spell," Polecat said, now sitting on his bed in the corner and pointing at the chairs.

The cabin was stuffy and small, there were picks and shovels piled in a corner, a table with mismatched chairs, and a cook stove with a cracked stove-pipe leaking acrid smelling wood smoke. The three of us sat down with steam coming off our clothes while Martin and Polecat talked.

"I've got a whole gang of Monte folks behind me," Martin said.

"Things still washed out upriver?"

"They are," Martin answered, "The railroad dumped an old growth tree farther up to cross the river and all the trestles in Monte got hit pretty hard. They got those passable by foot."

"Yep, well, that's to be expected seein' how it's been rainin' forever."

"It's been a storm for the history books," Martin replied.

"That book is getting' pretty big!" the old miner drawled. "So ya'll had to hike out?"

"Last two days. There's another hundred plus coming along shortly," Martin said.

"A-hundred people!" Polecat exclaimed.

While Martin and Polecat talked Mattie looked at me and held up the can of peaches still in her hand. I shrugged my shoulders and listened to the two continue.

"How's the diggin' been lately?" Martin asked the old timer.

"Oh, not too bad. Found a little color a few weeks ago and darn near filled my poke. The fever still holds me like the teeth of a lion," the miner said, his eyes glazing over like he'd momentarily lost himself in a dream.

"Ah," Martin said, "I can see that the gold still blinds yee."

The two friends kept bantering away with mining stories until Mattie finally slid the can of peaches across the table to me so I spoke up.

"Before we head out, would you happen to have a can opener I could use real quick, Polecat?"

"I do, son. It's right there next to the sink," he said, gesturing. I got up and took two steps over to his ill-fated kitchen where a pile of dirty dishes sat in a filthy sink and saw the opener on the counter. I quickly opened it with my back to them while they chatted. Next to the door was a metal bucket half-full of garbage. I dropped the can lid in it, stepped back to the table and handed the peaches to Mattie, whispering.

"Have some of the juice," I said. She lifted the can to her lips and took a slurp.

"That tastes good," she murmured, handing the can back to me. I took a sip and handed it back.

"Drink the rest of it." I turned and looked at Martin.

"How much farther to Robe?" I asked him while Mattie drank from the can. Martin turned around.

"Oh, I'd say about six 'er seven miles," he answered. Mattie pulled a peach out of the can with her fingers and put it in her mouth. She grinned and held the can out for me, I picked out a peach and devoured it.

"That's about right," Polecat added.

"Okay," I said. We finished the peaches and I dropped the can in the garbage pail.

"Thanks for the hospitality. See you out there, on the way," I said, turning towards the door.

"Thank you," Mattie said, standing up and stepping out of the cabin.

"You betcha," the old miner replied.

"I'll catch up to you in a bit," Martin said as we closed the door behind us.

The rain had let up and the sky was beginning to brighten as we made our way back over to the tote road. We fell back into a rhythm and had walked a-quarter mile when around a bend I stopped, Mattie did too, and she looked at me.

"Aw, son of a gun, would you look at that," I said, pointing ahead. About a hundred yards farther up the railroad tracks were swallowed completely by an enormous mudslide, sprinkled through with fallen trees, rocks and debris but the slide stopped short of the tote road.

"It must have slid just the other day, looks pretty fresh," I said, sighing.

"Gosh, it's gonna take a long time for them to get those tracks cleared," Mattie groaned.

Moments later the sound of a whip and the galloping of horses came through the air.

"Sounds like the stage coach," I said, motioning to the side of the tote road.

Mud flew from hooves and the coach swayed up and down while the driver snapped the reins as they rolled past us. A man in the coach saw us and tipped his hat as they stormed by, the wheels splashing dirty water and slop all around.

"Looked like that fellow was the only passenger," I commented.

"Not many folks headed to Monte right now," Mattie replied.

"Or to Silverton, I guess." We kept walking.

"What's the first thing you're going to do in Bellingham?" I asked.

"Take a hot bath and wash this dress," Mattie quickly answered, looking down at herself.

"And you?" she said.

"Get out of these wet clothes and get a good meal."

"Thanks for helping me during all of this," Mattie said, appreciatively.

"Oh, no need to say thanks. Happy to do so."

As we walked I began to think about what we'd been through and wondered what was still to come. Then I wondered about my aunt and hoped she was doing better. I thought about my mom. I was glad I'd sent her that telegram and knew I'd have to send another as soon as I could. Next, I thought about my father and the emptiness inside me returned with the thought of missing him but I figured he'd be pleased that I was helping Mattie, and all. I began to wonder how Charlie O'Connell was fairing and everyone else in Monte. Finally, my thoughts turned towards myself. I wondered if, with every step that I was taking: *Was I walking towards discovering myself? Was the true me somewhere up ahead or at the end of this adventure, and if, when I reached the end of this journey would I find who I really was, find true consciousness, find true north and become my true self?* When the sound of steels wheels rolling in the distance moved up the valley.

"Hear that?" I asked. We stopped and listened.

"I do," Mattie replied. "What is it?"

"It sounds like somethings coming up the tracks."

Up ahead a handcar rolled around a corner and up the tracks towards us, two men were standing on the car pulling and pushing the handle in a frenzy, tools were strewn on its deck. As they approached I waved at them but they kept rolling by.

"What's it like down below?" I hollered. One of them turned and looked at us but the other kept pumping the handle.

"Say what?" the man yelled back.

"We heard that the tunnels were filled with log jams," I shouted, pointing downhill.

"Oh, we got a good jump on them already, should be all cleared out soon!" he yelled.

"Okay, thank you!" I hollered back. We kept walking.

"That sounded good," Mattie said.

"It did. Maybe the train will be able to get to Robe in a few days," I added.

"Lord I hope so; my feet are killing me."

"How's your ankle doing?"

"Starting to hurt a little, again," Mattie replied.

"Should we stop and take a break?"

"No, I want to get out of these mountains. I'll be fine."

All we could do was keep walking, and as we did the constant movement of my body made me feel like I was no longer in control of myself and my mind started to play tricks with me again. I started to think that my existence was outside of me and everything was out of reach. The meaning of life darted in and out of my mind and living became dimensionless, everything was together but then apart, everything was all or nothing, and I felt like I was on the edge of existence and the ground began to blur. I took off my hat, shook my head then put it back on.

I looked behind us to check to see if Martin or anyone else was there, but no one was. I went back to thinking again, but this time about Mattie and me. I sure wanted to be with her and stay by her side. I thought about the life we could have together when my thoughts changed and I started to think about the adventure we'd been going through. Then I started telling myself that this adventure had actually been something I'd not soon forget. My facial expression must have been changing with each thought because Mattie spoke up.

"What are you thinking about?"

"Who, me?"

"Well who else is there?" she said.

"Oh, nothing."

"Nothing?"

"I was just, well . . . even though this hasn't been easy, it's been kind of an adventure. An interesting journey, sore feet and all," I said. Mattie looked at me.

"You know, the day the trestle went down I was overtaken with worry. It just felt like we were in all kinds of trouble, but now walking out of these mountains with you, it feels much better than before because it feels like everything's going to be okay, and that we'll make it," she said, grinning. "In fact, this might sound strange, but the last two days haven't really been that bad. I feel like I've, I mean we've, accomplished something. Like we made a right out of a wrong. Do you know what I'm trying to say?"

"I do," I replied. "I know exactly what you mean. We were faced with a situation that was not of our making and we accepted it and worked through it. All of us, together."

"We did, didn't we?" she replied.

"Oh, absolutely. It's been a challenge but a good one," I said as the pain in my back from the pannier shot down my legs. We kept walking but I was getting more tired and worn out with every step, my legs were beginning to feel like rubber.

The road began to level out and the forest became less dense. I saw two deer feeding on the side of a hill when the shrill cry of a hawk came through the air, so I took my hat off and looked up. Above us, a red-tailed hawk circled in the sky, it called out again with a hoarse, raspy scream, and made me feel like we were invading its territory. Hearing the hawk cry made me wonder why a beautiful bird that flew with such majesty could convey so much fury and rage in its voice. I kept walking with my hat off and watched the hawk land on the limb of a tree.

Then I remembered drawing the Hawk's Nest cabin that morning, instantly the hawk above became the living personification of my art work. A labyrinth of thoughts filled my mind like an overflowing river and everything came full-circle. My life and my art and the natural world with all of its many faceted dimensions coalesced and rushed through my body and mind as one.

The meaning of life combined with the earth and all its inhabitants and I realized that we were all connected and that everything was a circle. I instantly understood that we were dependent on each other, bonded in a delicate world that needed one another for balance and sustainability.

In a rush of consciousness, a sonorous sensation of pure existence welled up inside of me, one that was rich and full. But then my thoughts changed and I understood that for the last few months I'd been reproducing landscapes in two-dimensional paintings that I'd never really fully comprehended, all I'd been doing was replicating the natural world in a self-generated profit earning capacity without feeling or experiencing the true nature of my surroundings.

Self-doubt crept into my mind — *was everyone who gave me positive compliments about my paintings just being polite?* My mind raced back in time with the words people spoke, I could see their faces in my mind's eye. *Were the tourists buying my paintings because they loved Monte Cristo or because they loved my art?*

I gazed back up at the hawk, it was preening itself. It stopped and looked at me for a moment, then opened its wings and took to flight. I watched it circle the sky and for the first time in my life I found myself experiencing the wilderness in sharp relief with all its dimensions in a tangible sense and I felt a part of it; the wilderness showed me my true self and purpose. The self-doubting disappeared and my body buzzed with the drive to be the very best artist I could be.

In awe I watched the hawk as it circled again and then gracefully glide and land on the top of a dead snag. I smiled with the satisfaction that the world and all of its plants and animals were wonderful profound beings meant to be cherished. My quest of self-discovery had just revealed itself to me in a tapestry of the natural world combined with what I'd just realized was to be my life's work; my art. I felt replenished and invigorated with creative impulse, motivation and inspiration flowed through my veins.

I put my hat back on and a feeling of reincarnation fell over me. A few steps later the pain in my legs and back began to fade away.

XX

ROBE

Traveling on, we came to find ourselves overlooking a wide valley surrounded by foothills, above us the sky was overcast with clouds but on the horizon to the west we could see a wide ribbon of blue. The sun was just beginning to drop into the opening, casting a golden ray of light that grew into a bolt of sunshine that soon created an iridescent life-affirming sheen over both of us and the burgeoning timberland below.

"Beautiful," I said, looking to the sunset, the warmth of sunlight on my face.

"It is," Mattie replied, smiling wide and bright.

"I think the next town is down there."

"We're out of the mountains, aren't we?"

"I believe so."

As we descended into the valley, the green of the trees and plant-life glistened from moisture, the reflected light causing the landscape to glow a natural silver — it made me feel like we were walking through a heavenly wilderness garden. A half-mile later the tote road crossed the railroad tracks then angled away, we followed the road a short distance and found a bridge that crossed the river, a sign was on the ground next to it propped up against some rocks.

"Looks like this is the one that's been worked on," I said, slowing down.

"It does, doesn't it?"

"They've got it so it can be walked over, I think." We went over to the sign, it read, 'Ok to cross by foot. No horses no wagons.'

"Well this is a pleasant surprise," Mattie said.

"Yes, much better than that tree bridge," I replied. We walked out to where there was some planking nailed down to a few support timbers. The river crashed loud below and still ran brown with silt.

"It looks good," I said, starting to walk towards the repaired portion. "I'll go first."

"Fine with me," Mattie replied. Once I got over I turned around.

"No problem. Come on!" Mattie came across without a hitch and we continued.

Near the valley floor we came to a short bridge that crossed a creek that flowed down from the mountainside, shortly after it there was another bridge that crossed a bigger creek. Up ahead on the north side of the tote road was a rough, single room homestead cabin with a split rail fence, but there wasn't anyone about. A tiny bit of smoke was curling from the chimney and a few chickens were scratching and scurrying around in the yard.

"That looks like a great little place," I offered. Mattie nodded her head.

"Yes," she said, winded with a tired voice.

A half mile later we saw a trail pioneered up through the trees, and soon the road straightened out and the river angled closer to us. Up ahead was a dilapidated cedar shake cabin that looked like it was about to fall down, giving in to the laws of gravity. A crude picket fence encircled the shanty, along with dozens of stumps. Across the wagon road was a log home on the river, then we saw an unpainted frame home on the left with a good-sized building across from it.

"Gosh, look at that," Mattie observed. "It looks like a schoolhouse."

"It kind-a does, doesn't it," I replied, walking by.

We came upon a small log home with a shingle-sided addition. Two young girls and a boy were playing outside with a black dog next to a harvested garden area. A man wearing a white shirt, suspenders and felt hat was splitting cedar shakes by hand next to a shed attached to the side of the house. We waved at him. The man stopped what he was doing and looked at us.

"Where ya' comin' from?" he hollered, raising a hand to wave back.

"We're hiking down from Monte Cristo," I replied.

"Do you need a place to stay for the night?" the man asked as his children went over and stood next to him. Mattie and I stopped and looked at each other.

"Well, that's kind of you to ask," I said. "How much farther to the next town?"

"It's about two, three miles, give or take. My wife Julia has some venison stew on the stove," he offered, pointing over his shoulder with his thumb at their house.

"Great! Thank you," I answered, stepping towards the invitation. But Mattie grabbed me by the arm and whispered, "The Monte kids need it more than us." I stopped and nodded, quickly realizing that she was right.

“There’s over a hundred people behind us,” Mattie said, pointing back up the tote road. “With lots of children. I’m sure they’re more in need than us.”

“A hundred people? With children?” the man replied, a look of surprise swept over his face as his eyes grew large.

“Yes, the whole town is hiking out with over thirty kids,” Mattie replied.

“Oh Lord, I better tell the missus,” the man said.

“Okay! Thanks for the offer but we’ll keep going,” Mattie said.

“Is there a place to eat in town?” I quickly asked.

“You bet, at the hotel,” the man replied. We both waved while he and his children went inside their home.

“That was nice of him,” Mattie said.

“Uh yes, but some of that stew sure would have hit the spot,” I replied.

“I’m sorry, I could have easily had some, too. The kids are more important though, we’ll be fine.”

“Oh, I know. So, did you see the look on his face when you said a hundred people?” I asked.

“I did and I’m guessing that same look is on his wife’s face right about now.”

We continued walking through the dense forest, the terrain leveled out and the sun was beginning to fade. A half-mile later I saw a man in a horse drawn carriage coming up the road. It was a welcome sight to behold, it felt as if we’d made it back to civilization.

“Look Mattie!” I cried. “There’s someone up ahead.”

“Oh my lands, there is.” We stopped and watched as he got closer.

"Whoa, there Button," the fellow said, pulling back on his reins as he approached us. He sat with a straight back and had a leather satchel sitting next to him on the bench.

"Good evening," I offered, raising my hand. "Good to see someone."

"Where ya' comin' from?" he asked. He had on a black wool coat and a wide brimmed hat.

"Monte Cristo," I replied. "Had to hike out since the flood washed out the railroad, spent the night in Silverton."

"You too little lady?" he asked, glancing at Mattie.

"Yes, sir. At the Silverton Hotel," she answered.

"Did ya' now," he replied. "And you?" he inquired, looking at me with a sober face.

"At a cabin owned by a friend of Martin Comins," I answered.

"Martin Comins!" he exclaimed. "Where's Martin?"

"Back up the way," I said, pointing up the road the way we had come.

"You two walked down?"

"We did, the last two days."

"And Martin's behind ya' say?"

"That he is, with over a-hundred more people," I said. The look of worry came over his face and he bit his lip. He tilted his head as he looked us over and saw the condition of our situation. Then he stared into the distance for a moment, up the tote road.

"There's women and children hiking down too?"

"Yes, a good number of them," Mattie answered.

"I'll tell you what, let me turn around and you two climb on, hen I'll run ya' back to town where I'll hitch my wagon an' maybe ;et some more help an' come back for them. How's that sound?" he said. As he spoke he snapped his reins and wheeled the horse and buggy around.

"Fantastic!" we both said at the same time. I tossed the pannier on the back of the carriage while Mattie disentangled herself from her shoulder straps. I set her case next to the pannier and we climbed up and squeezed ourselves next to him onto the bench seat.

"Thank you, thank you so much, sir," I said.

"Aw, don't mention it. Name's Ike Davisson, you?" he said, snapping his reins again.

"Very good to meet you, Ike. This is Mattie de Graaf and I'm Oliver Cohen."

"So, the flooding left ya' stranded up in Monte did it?" he asked as we picked up speed, the wind in our faces.

"It did," I replied. "The river knocked out the main trestle bridge in town plus the other one just downriver, and the town is low on food. Telegraph is out too." He glanced over at us.

"Well, that's not good," he replied, making conversation. "You two sure don't look like a couple of miners."

"No, no. Mattie's the schoolteacher up there and I'm a pai — I'm an artist."

"Schoolteacher? And an artist?"

"I do landscapes and sketches," I replied. "What about you?"

"Oh, I homestead and run the mail up from Granite. I was about to do a couple of special deliveries, one for Wiley McPherson and another for Peter Edlin, but that can wait. You two look a might peeked and in need of a roof and some dry clothes."

Enormous hemlock and Douglas-fir trees lined the way as the muffled *clip-clop* of the horse's hooves sloshed and splashed through mud-puddles. We passed a few more homesteads and Ike made a left turn off the wagon road that came to another that went down a slight grade. The road turned again and flattened out, up ahead we could see the town. He pulled the carriage up in front of the post office with a flat façade painted white that was next to a two-story hotel built of unfinished lumber with a gable roof. Dusk was just beginning to come over the small town.

"Here ya' are," Ike said, pulling back on his reins. He looked at Mattie and said, "You should be able to get a room for the night here, young lady. And down the block there's a boardinghouse that serves the local workers, they might have something for you, son."

"Great! Thank you, Ike," I replied, hopping down and going to the back of the rig for the pannier and Mattie's piece of luggage.

"Yes, thank you so much for the ride, Mr. Davisson," Mattie said, taking hold of her overland case.

"My pleasure," Ike replied, then he looked at Mattie. "Let Mona in the hotel know I'll be bringing more Monte folks to town shortly."

"Okay, I will," Mattie answered. With a crack of his reins Ike turned the carriage around and headed back east.

"I'm starving," I said, setting my back pack down on the plank sidewalk. I looked up and down the thoroughfare — a few people were milling about, some were looking at us. Across the street the railroad tracks laid vacant and idle, behind us a huge pile of cord wood was stacked between the post office and hotel. A man came out of the hotel and grabbed an armload of wood.

"I'm starving, too, but I think I'd like to get a room first," Mattie said, glancing over at the man.

"Howdy, folks. Fresh in town?" he asked. He was heavy set and balding, a handlebar mustache nearly covering his plump cheeks.

"Yep," I replied. "Just came down the mountains, from Monte."

"We heard it's all washed out up there. The railroad crew's been working down below clearing out the tunnels. Would you be in need of a room?"

"Yes," Mattie quickly replied. "Do you have any bath facilities?"

"We do, Ma'am," he said, tipping his head. "Hot water and everything. Come on in outta the cold." Mattie about charged right after him and I followed.

Inside the hotel we found a tidy foyer with wood floors and whitewashed walls, a kerosene lamp sat on a table in the corner of the entry. The man dumped his load in a large box next to a potbellied stove and went behind the counter. He opened the register book and looked at Mattie just as a woman came down the staircase.

"Ah, we have guests," the lady remarked. She was wearing a brown dress and had long grey hair done in a braid. The three of us turned our heads towards her.

"Mona, these folks just got in from Monte," the man said.

"Yes," Mattie replied, "and there's more than a-hundred people behind us. Ike Davisson just gave us a ride in his buggy and is going to go back up with his wagon to help carry some of them down."

"A-hundred people!" the woman cried. She stepped over behind the counter while the man moved to the side as Mona picked up a pencil.

"What's this town gonna do with a-hundred people?" she said in the air. Then she turned to the fellow. "Bill, what are we gonna do with a-hundred people?"

"Well I guess we're gonna fill the hotel and make a pile of money!" he replied, laughing.

"Silverton was pretty crowded last night," Mattie remarked.

"I can imagine. So, what'll it be? One room if you're married or two if you're not?" she asked.

"Just one for me, we're not married," Mattie replied.

"I was going to try down at the boardinghouse," I put in.

"Oh, Betty's place is plum-full of railroad and timber workers. That I can tell you. You'll have to board here for the night, we've got plenty of rooms," Mona said.

"How much for a room?" Mattie asked.

"It's a dollar a night, per person," Mona replied.

"Any news on the railroad?" I asked. "A railroad guy said they were clearing out the tunnels."

"We heard earlier today that they'd be running soon, I believe they're clearing out the last tunnel," Bill answered.

"That's good to hear," Mattie replied. "I'll take a room, please."

"Yes, and could I get a room, too?"

"Sure, but, we might have to double you up in separate rooms with other people tonight. In fact, now that I think about all those people you say are coming down the mountain we'll be *tripling* everybody up. But it's still a dollar a piece," Mona surmised.

"What about meals?" I asked, pulling out my pouch.

"Supper and breakfast are fifty cents each. Supper will be ready shortly, but we better put some more soup on the stove," Bill answered. Mattie and I each placed two dollars on the counter and signed the register. Mona set two skeleton keys on the counter but then quickly snatched them back.

"Bill, how about if you run up and open their rooms," she said. "We're gonna have to keep the doors unlocked, folks," she said, her eyes darting back and forth between us. "People are going to be coming and going, you understand?"

“We understand,” I said, nodding slowly, more worn out and tired than I’d ever been.

“Do you have you any hot water for a bath?” Mattie asked.

“I’ll draw you some right now,” Mona replied. “Now then, all the men will be on the left side of the hall upstairs and the women and children on the right.”

“Okay, thank you,” I said, picking up my backpack by the strap.

“Yes, thank you so much,” Mattie replied. We headed up the stairs behind Mona. Bill was already coming back down after opening the doors to our respective rooms.

“The women’s bath is down at the end of the hall on the right, I’ll go and get everything ready for you,” she said, looking at Mattie.

“Okay, thanks,” Mattie said. She smiled at me and said, “See you in a bit,” then ducked into her room and closed the door. Mona headed down the hall.

I stepped into my small room, there were two single beds with night stands and a window that looked out to the street. I leaned my pannier up against the wall and started to pull some dry clothes out of the pannier when I heard voices outside and looked out the window.

“Whoa there Button,” I could hear Ike Davisson say. Under a darkening sky he was pulling up in a wagon loaded with Monte people, another wagon-load was behind him. Both wagons had torches mounted to their side boards, the light casting an eerie glow on the passengers, I saw Martin in the second one. People started jumping off and filing into the hotel, and in no time the whole building was alive with commotion. I quickly changed into some dry clothes, left my pannier up against the wall, then went downstairs and saw Martin in the foyer.

“Martin! Good to see you!” I said. He looked up and grinned

"Oliver, lad," Martin replied, smiling.

"Looks like everyone's gonna make it off the mountain tonight."

"It does, everyone should be safe and sound for the night," he said, stepping over to the front desk. "Canna' a man get a room for the night or should I just grab a piece of floor in the dining room?"

"Take your pick," Mona said, laughing from behind the counter.

The next morning I awoke in the middle of a dream. I could hear a *chug-a, chug-a* sound and steam blasts bursting through the air as I yawned and then glanced around me. The room was carpeted with men whose snoring luckily didn't interrupt my reverie; boys were covered in blankets. But then a quick *toot* of a whistle sounded. I tried to get upright but my body was so sore I could barely roll over and had to push myself up off the floor to my knees. I could see out a window what I hadn't seen in over a week, a train idling on a railroad track.

"Yeehaw!" I cried in the air. A couple of men raised their heads and a few others rustled around. One of them opened his eyes.

"What's yer' problem, bub?" he said, staring at me red-eyed.

"Sorry, fella," I whispered. "The train's outside," I softly said, pointing.

"That's good," he sniffed, rolling over and pulling his blanket over his shoulder.

I slowly stood up and a sharp pain shot up my back when I bent over and grabbed my boots. I achingly picked up my pannier and went out into the hall. I limped to the men's washroom and rinsed my face, pulled on my boots and went downstairs. Bill and Mona were already up, going back and forth from the empty dining room to the kitchen. On the table were mugs, dishes and silverware, plus a plate of pancakes and a little brown jug of syrup.

"Mornin'," Bill said, setting a plate of biscuits on the table. Mona was right behind him with a kettle of gravy.

"Good morning," Mona said, wiping her hands on her apron. "You're up bright and early. How'd you sleep last night? Get any rest?"

"Oh, yes. Slept pretty well in fact, but boy am I ever sore," I replied, sitting down. Bill came out of the kitchen with a coffee pot, he filled my mug. I put a biscuit on my plate and poured gravy over it.

"The train whistle woke me up," I said, cutting into the biscuit with my fork.

"Conductor Speer was just in," Mona said, standing in the kitchen doorway. "They're going to do a special run down to Everett and back this morning and another in the afternoon."

"We'll try to be on it," I answered, then took a bite. "Do you know if the telegraph is working?"

"It is, over at the depot," Mona replied.

"And the post office?"

"Oh yes, Myrtle's open. She's over there, she's probably pretty busy with a big new load of mail from Everett."

A few folks from the Monte group walked in to the room. I greeted them all with a nod as they sat down when Mattie came around the corner. She was moving slow but when she saw me she smiled ear to ear.

"Well good morning," I said, wiping my mouth with a cloth napkin. "How are you today?"

"Good morning to you, too, but my body sure hurts," she replied, taking a seat next to me.

"Mine too and thank God the train is here, I don't think I could have walked to the next town!"

"No kidding, we should get on board right away," she said. "Make sure we get a seat." Mona poured her a cup of coffee. Mattie saw the pancakes and put a couple on her plate.

"Mona said the telegraph is working again, or at least it is here," I told Mattie.

"That's good, I should send my sister a note," she said, pouring syrup on her cakes.

"Yeah, I need to send one to my mom. And I've got a letter to mail for Jacob."

More and more people came down the stairs and started to fill up the dining room. Martin walked in coughing with a hand up to his mouth, looking tired and pale.

"Good morning Martin!" I said. Others at the table greeted him.

"Aye, good morning, everyone," he replied between coughs. "Looks like they got the tunnels opened up," he remarked, filling his plate with biscuits and gravy.

"Yep, we'll be on our way soon," I offered. Martin took a bite and then looked at me.

"How'd yee sleep last night?" he asked.

"Good, thank you, and you?"

"Not bad," he replied, coughing again. "Some adventure, huh?"

"One I'll never forget," I replied.

After breakfast we went down the plank sidewalk and over to the post office, the sky held broken clouds and the sun was just beginning to break through. Mattie waited outside while I walked in to the small building. There was a long counter that went from wall to wall, a lady was standing behind it next to a table sorting an enormous pile of mail.

"Good morning, I've got a letter to mail," I said. The woman glanced up. She was wearing spectacles and had a red scarf on her head tied under her chin.

"You need to buy a stamp?" she asked, her hands moving quickly through the envelopes.

"Nope, it's already got one."

"Just set it in the basket on the counter then, please," she said. "I'll get it."

"Okay," I replied, placing the letter in the square wicker receptacle beside a Myrtle Starr Postmaster name plate.

At the depot a man wearing a blue suit and hat with a beard was sitting behind a desk jotting down words as his key machine sounded out *dits*. He looked over at us.

"Telegram?" he asked quickly.

"Yes, I'm sending out of state and Mattie here is sending in state," I said, nodding. "And we need tickets to Everett."

He pointed at the forms we had to fill out on the counter and said, "Standard rate and ten word minimum."

I thought about what I could say in ten words while Mattie worked on hers. In a minute I had it: *'Monte flooded – hiked out – train now to Bellingham – Love, Oliver.'*

A moment later the telegraph man was finished with his task, he got up, came over to the counter and looked at our forms.

"Ten words for a buck for you," he said, looking at me. "And fifty cents for yours Ma'am, one-way tickets to Everett are a buck each."

Mattie dug through her coin purse and I pulled out my pouch, we each placed our money on the counter with our forms. The man looked at them and reached under the counter for our tickets, he set two in front of us.

"Okay, I'll get these out right away," he said, going back over to his key machine.

Mattie and I climbed aboard the train and sat in the back of the middle car near the coal heater. The interior and benches were just like I remembered them, quarter sawn oak and the familiar finished fir floor. The raised curved veneer ceiling with small horizontal windows on each side running the length of the car was the same as before, even Conductor Speer was the same, coming down the aisle in the same suit and the same hat. The familiarity was comforting.

"Good to see you," I offered. We held out our tickets.

"Yes, it's good to be running again," he said, accepting them from both of us.

"How long before the trains can get back up to Monte?" I asked.

"We're hoping sometime in February, so about two months, maybe," Speer replied. He tipped his hat and continued down the aisle. We saw Martin come aboard, he sat up at the front of the car with some other folks and a married couple took the bench seat in front of us. Others climbed aboard and soon the car was filled.

"Are you nervous?" Mattie asked.

"About?"

"Going and staying in a town you've never been to," she said.

"Not really. If room and board is about a dollar a day I'll be okay." Just then the train whistle blew, the bell rang as the train lurched forward and began to pull away from the depot.

"Well how much money do you have?" she inquired.

"Oh, somewhere around sixty-five dollars, maybe more," I replied.

"Sixty-five dollars! You did pretty well this summer, but still, that will only pay for a couple of months." Slowly we pulled away from the town and rolled past the small saw mill operation I saw on the way up months before.

"I'll start painting right away, I've got my box easel with me and yesterday when we saw that hawk it inspired me to be a better painter. You might think I'm crazy but I had kind of an epiphany. Seeing and listening to that hawk cry put me more in touch with the natural world and I realized that I'd just been reproducing the landscapes and not really interpreting them. I think I need to find my own style, something that sets me apart from other painters. If that makes any sense," I said.

"It does, I noticed you were kind of lost in a trance when we saw it."

"You did?"

"Yes, I could tell it affected you. You're already a good artist, Oliver. I believe in you."

"Thanks," I replied. "I'm going to re-dedicate myself to my art." We sat and looked out the window and enjoyed the scenery as the train rolled past the river.

"Are you excited about seeing your sister?"

"Oh, yes. I'm pretty sure I'll be able to stay with Jocelynn, it'll be good to see her again. And I might be able to find some temporary work substitute teaching or waitressing, maybe."

The train followed the river bank and sunshine began to stream in through the windows, then we dropped down into the canyon. Granite cliffs were over on the far side and the river still flowed mightily, but now it wasn't the same emerald green like my first time on the train, instead it ran brown with silt and riddled with small bits of wood and tree limbs.

"We might have to find rooms in Everett and stay the night, depending if we can get a train north today or not," I said.

"I was thinking the same thing," Mattie replied. "But the train will stop at Fairhaven before it gets to Bellingham, I'll get off there because that's where Jocelynn lives and if she gets my telegram by then she might be at the depot. Maybe you'll be able to meet her."

"I'd like that."

"Bellingham has a very natural setting, it's right on Puget Sound near the San Juan Islands and to the east is Mount Baker. The vistas in every direction are fantastic with more than enough landscapes to paint," Mattie offered.

"Mount, what'd you call it?"

"Mount Baker," Mattie replied. "It's a dormant volcano and covered in snow all year long."

"Mount Baker, a volcano," I replied, thinking back in time. "Oh right! I remember seeing that one from Everett when I first came up here. It'd be a great subject for a painting. You know, I like the thought of being up in Bellingham, and not just to paint, but because I'll be near you," I said. I looked over at her, she was grinning at me.

Along the tracks dozens of railroad workers were cutting flood strewn timber with crosscut saws while others were throwing pieces of cut up wood off to the side. Then it went dark, we were in the first tunnel. When we came out the other side there was drift wood and tree debris all along the side of the tracks, more workers were cutting up-rooted trees as others were tossing and dumping bucked wood into the river. The river bank was covered with the leftover rubble of flooding. We rolled into another tunnel and up ahead were more tunnels.

Once we were rolling through the darkness of the last tunnel I could see the shadow of the couple in front of us, they were kissing. Mattie could see them too. I knew she could because I felt her hand squeeze my knee. I turned to face her and gave her a peck on the cheek when all of a sudden, she put her other hand on the side of my face and kissed me hard. I kissed her right back. In a flash, bright sunshine filled the car and we pulled away from each other. Mattie blushed as she fussed with her hair and straightened her dress.

"That was a pretty long tunnel," I said, turning and looking into her diamond blue eyes.

"Too bad it wasn't a little longer," Mattie whispered, smiling wonderfully.

XXI

GRANITE FALLS

The sun was shining brightly as the train slowly eased up to the depot. Right when we stopped the door to the car opened and Conductor Speer poked his head inside and said, “Granite Falls! fteen minutes!”

Gazing out the window there were people of all ages about — ildren with their parents, men in work clothes, and two fellows ood waiting on the platform in suits. The sheds beside the tracks ere full of cedar shingle bundles ready for shipping and railroad s were strewn all around. We’d rolled right past the saloon and is time I could see the sign, ‘Depot Bar’, painted across the top of e façade with a hand and finger pointed downward towards the or. On the windows gold letters spelled, ‘Sample Room’.

A few riders began to disembark to stretch their legs and take e air, including Martin. I saw him get off and walk up the board-alk towards the bar. I looked over at Mattie.

“I’m going to go and say goodbye to Martin,” I said.

“Yes, of course,” she said. “But don’t be long.”

“I’ll be right back.”

Walking up the boardwalk I noticed two ladies go in a side entrance to the saloon. I took a few more paces and stopped just before I went in. Above the door were the words *'no minors allowed'* and I laughed to myself thinking it was a good thing that they didn't spell it, no miners, since they probably wouldn't do much business.

Inside, two men in long white aprons scurried about serving customers, both wore suspenders and white shirts, one with a four-in-hand tie. Looking around people were sitting at tables having breakfast while others sat talking, Martin was standing at the bar. I went over and stood beside him, without his noticing me, just as the bartender brought over a shot glass and bottle.

"Ah! Thank yee, Mr. Difley," Martin replied.

"You betcha, Mr. Comins," the bartender said, filling the jigger. Then Martin said out over the room, "Anyone seen Charly Maul or Richard Roesiger today?"

"Yep," a man playing checkers said, "saw Charly earlier over at Swinnerton's."

"He have his wagon parked out front, Will?" Martin asked, turning around and seeing the man sitting at a table with three other gentlemen drinking coffee.

"That he did," Will replied. "Why?"

"Oh, I was looking for a ride home," Martin laughed. "I've done enough hiking in the last two days and me feet are a bit sore."

"So, Martin," I said, speaking up. "Mind if I join you for a drink?"

"Tiz a fine day when I hear an offer like that," Martin responded, turning around and seeing me. "Ah, Oliver! I thought I recognized that voice."

I put two quarters on the bar and nodded at the bartender. He set down another glass and poured the liquor.

"I just wanted to say thank you for helping us all down the mountain safely."

"No need to be thanking me, lad," he replied. "Ya' did it all on yer' own. Where ya' off to?" he asked.

"We're headed to Bellingham, Mattie has family there."

"And will ya' come back?"

"Oh, absolutely!" I proclaimed. "She's still planning on being the schoolteacher and things make sense to me in Monte Cristo, I love it up there. You?"

"Whenever I need to work out from the homestead I'm up there."

"You have a homestead?"

"I do, down on the lake. A hundred odd acres," Martin replied.

"That's a lot of ground, what do you do with it all?"

"Well I live on it, lad," he said, chuckling. "That's what a homesteader gets with a claim. As long as a place is built and the land is worked, that is. I've got a cabin right on the lake and a plot of potatoes and carrots that I need to go and dig up."

"Sounds like you've got a great place," I said.

"Tiz," he replied. "Maybe someday ya' can stop by and see it, with Mattie."

"Sure! I bet she'd love to see it, she's the best," I said. Martin nodded and grinned. He stroked his thick reddish mustache, paused for a moment and spoke again.

"I have no doubts about that, lad," he said. Then his eyes opened wide, they glassed over and he stared at me. The look on his face turned to divine benevolence.

"Go and grab that lass and never let go. Sweep that beautiful young gal off her feet and hold on. Love her and take care of her. She's good for ya' and yee is good for her. Carry her away and live a life full of joy and happiness. I know it. I can see it," Martin said, and the conviction in his voice rang deep down in my soul.

I knew he was right. My heart started to pound a life-changing everlasting drum beat. I knew right then and there in that moment that I would do everything I could to make her happy and do everything I could to hold her in my arms forever. I smiled and stuck out my hand.

"You're right, Martin. She's beautiful, and she means everything to me. Thank you," I said. Martin reached out and grabbed a hold of my hand with a firm grip and placed his other hand on my shoulder. When he did a bolt of inner divinity zinged through my body and struck my heart. My whole being buzzed and tingled with an inner tranquility that I'd never felt before. I instantly realized that I'd just taken the last step towards becoming myself, and in turn understood that Mattie was who I wanted to share the rest of my life with, as long as she felt the same way. Just then the train bell rang, we both turned our heads in the depot's direction.

"Fare thee well, lad. Now go, go and begin to fulfill yer' destiny," he said.

"It's been great knowing you," I said, raising my glass. "I'll see you again someday."

"Yes, indeed, we will see each other again. To Oliver and Mattie!" Martin said, lifting his whiskey. "May you be poor in misfortune and rich in blessings!"

"I'll drink to that," I laughed, downing the contents of the shot glass. "Fare thee well, Martin."

"Yes, lad. Fare thee well," Martin replied. I started to go but stopped and turned around when he had more to say.

"Just remember, lad," the Duke said, "Yee have got to do yer' own growing, no matter how tall yer' Father grew to be."

In a rush of understanding, the words he spoke soared deeper and farther into my being than any opera or painting ever did. He made me think of and miss my Father — and in a primordial quickening the blood inside of me rushed. It felt like Martin's presence and his words were filling the void that losing my Father had left behind. I gathered my senses and nodded, knowing that even if our conversation occupied just a small space in time his words and their meaning would last me an eternity. Because true words spoken by a great man never die.

I looked directly into his eyes and stuck out my hand, again. He grabbed it with another firm grip and squeezed hard, harder than before.

"Thank you for everything Martin. Meeting you has changed my life, and all for the better. I'm a better man knowing you, much more so than ever before. I'll see you in the spring. Thanks again and so long for now." I let go of his hand, turned and walked away, and as I did I looked over my shoulder at the Duke of Monte Cristo, then raised a hand and waved good-bye.

Martin Thomas James Comins

POSTSCRIPT

By mid-February of 1897 the Everett & Monte Cristo Railway was repaired and running again. Mining resumed, and those who chose to return picked up mostly where they had left off. By the spring of that year the mines were producing 1,000 tons of concentrated ore per week and the district was regarded as the most productive in Washington. However, the flooding was far worse the following fall of '97, portions of the tracks and most bridges washed away completely and one locomotive and its cars were stranded in Monte Cristo. Evaluating the damages against the expected incomes, Rockefeller at that time chose to not re-build the line.

The blame for the continued railroad washouts was laid on the initial decision to build the track line too close to the waters of the South Fork of the Stillaguamish River, over the choice of building the road on a higher route.

During the following three years the Rockefeller group bought out as many claims as they could, and in March of 1899

Rockefeller's agents ordered the railroad rebuilt from Granite Falls to Robe and work recommenced. Three months later, in June, John D. Rockefeller came to Everett and met with James J. Hill and sold Hill all of his interests in Everett. By the spring of 1900 Rockefeller announced that the railroad would be fully rebuilt from Robe to Monte Cristo and workers were hired.

Once the railway was running its full length again it created great optimism, people returned and miners were re-hired and put to work at Monte Cristo. During summer months tourists poured into the scenic town, filling the hotels sometimes with as many as five-hundred people per train ride. But by August of 1903 Rockefeller sold the bulk of his interests in Monte Cristo to the Federal Mining and Smelting Company located in Coeur d'Alene, Idaho, yet he did retain some ownership with the new holding company. Rockefeller then moved quickly and sold the railway to the Northern Pacific.

One month later Federal Mining sold the Everett Smelter to the American Smelting and Refining Company which was controlled by the Guggenheims, who were only interested in the smelter and not the mines. This sale, in turn, ended Rockefeller's involvement with Federal Mining.

Then, in December of 1903, the Guggenheims announced that they were closing the mines at Monte Cristo after they had already begun to sell off the machinery and other salvaged items. Without working mines, Monte Cristo drained of its citizenship and soon became a ghost town. Ownership of the mines changed hands again, but by 1907 most mining operations at Monte Cristo had ceased.

For years thereafter, Monte Cristo operated as a tourist destination until flooding ruined the approaches to the Sauk River

Bridge just downstream in 1980. The old Boston American mining cookhouse building that had been converted into a lodge and museum burned down under mysterious circumstances in 1983. Since then Monte Cristo has become a beloved hiking destination and a favorite of outdoor enthusiasts.

ACKNOWLEDGMENTS

A simple thank you can barely express my deep gratitude and heartfelt thanks to all of my family and friends who supported, encouraged and helped me complete this project. I could have never done it without all of you! At this time, I would like to thank the following who assisted in bringing this novel to fruition: Susan Harrell, David Cameron of the Monte Cristo Preservation Association, Fred Cruger and Tom Thorleifson of the Granite Falls Historical Society, Ted Cleveland, Miles Auckland, Monika Teuscher-Schramm, Skyler Cuthill, Cassidy Cuthill, Lisa Labovitch of the Northwest Room of the Everett Public Library, and Daryl Jacobson of Northwest Underground.

I would like to convey an enormous debt of gratitude to David Cameron and Fred Cruger for their patience, time and generosity in sharing their knowledge of all things Monte Cristo and the Upper South Fork of the Stillaguamish River Valley. David and Fred were the historical conscience of the project and for that I am eternally grateful to both of them. I could never have completed this story without their combined and much-appreciated contributions. Thank you, David and Fred!

I owe a great deal of thanks to my son and editor Skyler Cuthill, without his hard, diligent and tedious work I could not have done or finished this venture. Thank you, Skyler!

The Pride of Monte Cristo is a conception of the author's imagination. The bulk of the primary characters are historical persons who lived and/or worked at Monte Cristo with the exception of Oliver Cohen, Mattie de Graff and Eva Cohen who are fictional.

For the last one-hundred and thirty years much has been written and said about Monte Cristo, this author has attempted to bring voice to those who struggled to survive and thrive in a remote wilderness setting. May their lives never be forgotten.

ABOUT THE AUTHOR

Malstrom Award winning author J. D. Howard was born in Seattle and raised in Everett. He currently lives in the foothills of Snohomish County, Washington. For the last 50 years he has been an avid student of history and literature and is the proud father of two wonderful children. *The Pride of Monte Cristo* is his third novel, other works include: *Both Sides of the Wish* (2013) and *Sawdust Empire* (2016).

Snohomish County Tribune

OFFICIAL CITY PAPER

VOL. XXIV SEMI-WEEKLY SNOHOMISH, WASHINGTON, JANUARY 28, 1913 No. 41

January 28, 1913

"Duke of Monte Cristo" Dies

Martin T. J. Comins, "the Duke of Monte Cristo," died at Providence hospital in Everett Monday, of tuberculosis, aged 63 years. Mr. Comins was a pioneer of the county, and was well known as a student philosopher. He was educated for the priesthood and during his life spent much of his time in study, farming to earn a livelihood, and living alone in the solitude of the mountains. He has no known relatives and the body is at Jerread's undertaking parlors awaiting instructions from friends of the deceased.

Made in the USA
Middletown, DE
08 March 2019